FROM THE DEEP OF THE SEA

Map of Baffin Bay and Davis Strait
showing the course of the Whaler *Diana*, 1866-67.

FROM THE DEEP OF THE SEA

THE DIARY OF
CHARLES EDWARD SMITH

Surgeon of the Whale-ship *Diana*, of Hull.

EDITED BY HIS SON, CHARLES EDWARD SMITH HARRIS

NAVAL INSTITUTE PRESS

Published and distributed in the
United States of America
by the Naval Institute Press,
Annapolis, Md. 21402

ISBN 0–87021–932–4

Library of Congress Catalog No. 78–51909

Printed in Great Britain

PREFACE

My late father's diary of his terrible experiences in the whale-ship *Diana* in 1866–67 has been in my possession for a great number of years. It was not until a ship I was surgeon of happened to go to Hull in October, 1920, that I became aware of there being some relics of the *Diana* in existence still, and on exhibition in two of the Hull museums.

It was the sight of these relics that reawakened my interest in the story of the *Diana*, and which impelled me to take in hand at last my father's old manuscript with a view to editing it for publication. The curator of the Hull museums—Mr. Thomas Sheppard, F.G.S., F.R.G.S.—very kindly looked through the diary, and encouraged me in the project; I take this opportunity of thanking him for his ready assistance.

An account—evidently largely drawn from my father's diary—of the *Diana's* fatal voyage appeared first in the *Cornhill Magazine* in 1867. This article was written by the late Captain Allan Young, commanding the " discovery ship" *Pandora*. His preliminary remarks in that article will serve admirably to explain here the general scheme under which the British whale-ships worked some sixty, seventy and more years ago, a scheme which the *Diana* was following on this particular voyage.

Captain Young wrote:

" Owing to the high value of whale-oil and seal-skins, and the great demand for whale-bone (which had reached the value of nearly £700 a ton), quite a fine fleet of steam and sailing vessels used to leave various English and Scottish ports for the Greenland seas.

" The ships used to sail about the end of February, having engaged all their principal officers, harpooners, boat-steerers, and seamen, from their port of departure. They would then fill up their complement of boatmen from amongst the fishermen of the Shetland Islands.

" Then the ships used to sail to the East Greenland coast and the neighbourhood of Jan Mayen Island for the seal-fishing, which was conducted amongst the ice packs and floes on which the young seals are born. Incurring the greatest risks from collision with the ice-packs, the violent gales, and the loss of boats and men sent away searching in all directions for the seals, the ships would return to Lerwick after some weeks of this laborious work, and often without having found any seals at all. This is what happened on this particular voyage of the *Diana*.

" The sealing season having come to an end, the ships used to return homeward to recruit their crews and replenish their stores for the ensuing voyage to Davis Straits in search of whales.

" At one time the whalers used to be content with trying the seas on the West coast of Greenland, in Davis Straits, and in the vicinity of Discoe Island, beyond which it was considered impossible to pass. Owing to the expedition, which was sent in 1818 for the discovery of the North-West Passage, having given information of the great numbers of whales seen in the extreme northern limits of Davis Straits, more particularly on the western side, the whale-ships began to penetrate that inhospitable region, often with astonishing success.

" As the whales always seek the protection (from the attacks of the swordfish) of the land floes (the ice still attached to the land and bays after the main bodies of ice have broken away during the summer), the whale-ships used to time their arrival in the neighbourhood of Pond's Bay about the commencement of July. The ships' passage there and back was always attended with considerable difficulties of navigation amongst the drifting ice-floes, and with many dangers therefrom.

" Northern Davis Straits and Baffin Bay are full of a vast loose pack of floating ice and enormous icebergs, either driving on to the land or being driven off it according to the direction of the wind at the time.

" To arrive at the north-western limits of Baffin Bay, the whale-ships used to travel up the West coast of Greenland, pushing along between the land floes on the one side and the sea floes on the other, and often getting fatally crushed in the process."

The history of the old whaling industry teems with horrifying tales of disaster, some of which are related in this diary. Many a fine ship has gone north and never been heard of again. The *Diana* was more lucky, for she managed to return fourteen months later, but only after terrible hardship on the part of her unfortunate crew.

In the case of most of these old whale-ships, the story of the sufferings of their crews has merely been retailed orally by the survivors on their return to port. In the case of the *Diana* we have a record of each day's adventures, written as soon as they had occurred, or even while they were actually occurring.

Here we have an account straight from the pen, while the heart was still palpitating from some narrow escape or from what seemed at the time certain destruction.

To me, the diary is enthralling reading, and I marvel how it could have been written with such minuteness, calmness, and with such strikingly descriptive power amid so much danger and suffering.

As regards the editing of this diary, a very great deal of detail—meteorological notes, sailing directions, details of medical cases, etc., of no great interest to the general reader—has been omitted. Some of the technical words have been replaced by others more generally understood, while a few sentences here and there have been reconstructed or re-arranged. Otherwise the descriptions of scenery, adventures, escapes, and sufferings are given in this book precisely as they were written fifty-five years ago. Nothing whatever has been added to the diary, save that it has been divided into chapters with headlines, and a few foot-notes added, mostly to corroborate some of the statements and reminiscences which appear in the diary.

The sketches in this book are copied from those in my father's diary.

In conclusion, I might add that my father was a Quaker, which accounts for the somewhat quaint phraseology.

CHARLES E. S. HARRIS, MB., Ch.B.

CONTENTS

ix

LIST OF ILLUSTRATIONS

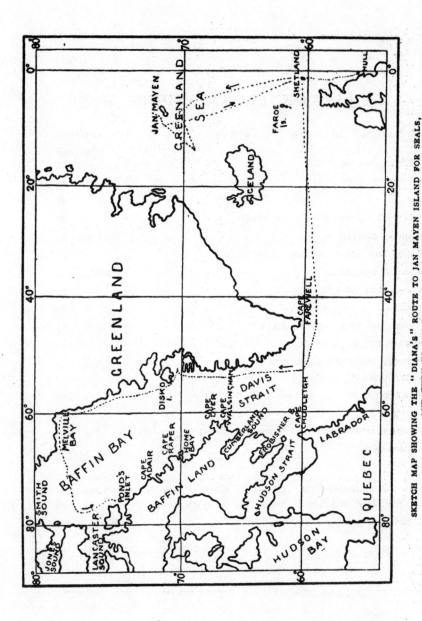

SKETCH MAP SHOWING THE "DIANA'S" ROUTE TO JAN MAYEN ISLAND FOR SEALS,
AND THEN TO BAFFIN BAY FOR WHALES.

FROM THE DEEP OF THE SEA

CHAPTER I

AN INTRODUCTION TO THE DIARY

" Nihil humani alienum est puto mihi."—TERENCE.

Thursday, March 22nd, 1866.—" Made the ice in latitude
69·45 North, longitude 8·40 West. Ship standing to the westward through patches and streams of young ice. The island of
Jan Mayen bore N.E. by N., about 70 miles distant."

Thus, by the above extract from the ship's log, I commence
my private account of the history and adventures of the screw
steamship *Diana* of Hull, bound on a sealing and whaling voyage
to the Greenland seas, and thence to Davis Straits.

Hitherto I have been too sick or too lazy to make the necessary effort at commencing a regular diary. Indeed, there has
not been much to chronicle, day succeeding day with no variety
save the shifting of sails to suit the variations of the wind; the
routines of breakfast, dinner, and tea; and the vicissitudes of
rain, snow, and sleet, fair weather and foul. Of this latter we
have had by far the greater proportion. Indeed, so rough and
boisterous a passage as we have had during the past fortnight
has totally precluded all attempts at reading, let alone the use
of a pen. However, having arrived at last in smooth water,
let me attempt to make up for past omissions by writing a
general description of the voyage we have had thus far.

In the first place, let me premise that I propose to make this
book, not a mere log only, but an *omnium gatherum* of all sorts
of miscellanies—whatever information I may gather from
others bearing upon the fisheries and maritime life generally;
whatever anecdotes of interest or " tales from the sea " that
may come to my ears; all that may interest or amuse. Earth,

sea, and sky; Nature and human nature; men and things—all will be faithfully recorded herein. It will be my endeavour to act up to Terence's noble sentiment, and feel with him that nothing that concerns humanity in any degree is foreign to my purpose.

I think it is in " Eyes and No Eyes " that we are told, whilst some men visit the greater part of the world and remember nothing of foreign countries but the signs of the various taverns and the prices and qualities of the liqueurs retailed therein, others, like Franklin, " cannot cross the Channel without making some observations useful to mankind." Without expecting to benefit humanity at large, at least I may hope to benefit myself by making the most of such opportunities as this voyage may present. If spared to return, these pages may recall to the mind's eye in after years scenes and incidents, persons and places, which in all probability I may never have the opportunity of seeing again. God grant that the retrospect of this voyage may be a pleasant one.

Nor must I forget that a journal or log, diary or common-place book, or whatever you may choose to call it, such as I propose keeping cannot fail to be of the greatest interest to one's friends and relatives, who will naturally expect much information and entertainment from such an adventurous and uncertain voyage. Debarred themselves from the possibility of visiting these remote regions, they will eagerly peruse any description of such by an actual observer, especially if the voyager be one of their own kinsmen. Therefore, it will be my object and duty, O reader, to bear thee in mind while entering in my log my daily budget of hearsay and observations. I will endeavour to record the events of this voyage, not only in as cheerful, lively, and intelligent a strain as I may be capable of at the time, but likewise in as good and clear penmanship as the movements of the vessel, the temperature of the fingers' ends, the quality of the ink, the temper of the pen, or (what is more probable than all these contingencies to make all my efforts unavailing) the uncertain light of this most miserable oil lamp, will permit. Bear in mind that the state of one's health and one's mental temperament at the time of writing may often produce much that may appear poor and prosy.

But "patience, and shuffle the cards," as Shakespeare has it. Let us hope that what the Romans would call blind fortune, but which we humbly believe to be the inscrutable workings of a beneficent and all-wise Providence, may conduct us through a varied, safe, and successful voyage, blessed with sound health, good spirits, and with peace and goodwill amongst all on board.

It may be that herein, O reader, thou mayest find recorded thoughts upon various subjects and reflections which may seem strangely out of place in such a book. Understand, therefore, that such are written not so much for thy perusal as for mine own satisfaction hereafter. I do not esteem it wisdom in a man to permit the suggestions and reflections of a nine months' voyage amongst strangers and amidst strange scenes to pass away from the mind unrecorded and unimproved.

Look not with scornful eye upon any attempt I may make at representing in pen or pencil any scenes or objects of interest. I am no artist, such as thou mayest be. My poor drawings, though rude and contemptible, will serve to remind me of my Arctic travels, and that more vividly and effectually than the descriptions of Richardson or Scoresby Jackson, or the admirable steel engravings in Kane's " Voyages." Some sketches will be drawn to refreshen my memory, but more will be attempted for the amusement of my friends and thee. If thou art contemptuous or ungrateful, I am sure my friends will not share thy feelings.

So I will betake me to my task, assuring thee that, like the poets as described by one of themselves, I heartily desire both to do thee good and to delight thee.

" Aut prodesse volunt, aut delectare poetæ."—OVID.

CHAPTER II

STORM AND DISAPPOINTMENT WITH THE SEALING

The particulars of a voyage to the Greenland seas and Davis Straits in the screw steamship "Diana" of Hull, commanded by Captain Gravill.

WE weighed anchor about 8.30 a.m. on Monday, February 19th, 1866, and were towed by a steam tug as far as the mouth of the Humber. Our departure seemed to create an immense sensation amongst the seafaring population, and also with the workmen in the dockyards, crews of other vessels, and, in short, amongst the inhabitants of Hull generally. Every pier, wharf, ship, and "coign of vantage" was covered by a multitude of well-wishers who cheered lustily. I am told this public interest attaches to all whale-ships, their arrival and departure causing the greatest excitement amongst the seafaring classes and attracting the attention of all classes in the town to which the ship belongs. I conclude this arises from the novel and precarious nature of the voyage, and the inevitable dangers and risk attending the whale fishery.

During the next two or three days we had fair weather, but the remainder of the passage to Lerwick was extremely tempestuous.

On Thursday, March 8th, at 8.30 a.m., we weighed anchor and steamed out of the harbour by the North entrance. Our full ship's company of fifty-one was now complete, half our hands having been engaged at Lerwick as line coilers, rowers, etc. From this date up to March 22nd we experienced such a miserable fortnight of storms, adverse winds, rain, sleet, snow, and cold, that one was tempted to think that the Spirit of the North was determined to do his utmost to dishearten us or delay our approach to his icy regions. The movements

4

of the vessel prevented all exercise on deck and all reading
or writing in the cabin. We had to eat our meals by a
succession of conjuring tricks. Literally we " drank tea by
stratagem."

Thursday, March 22nd.—At noon we made the ice in latitude 69° 45′ North, longitude 8° 40′ West, first meeting with
lumps of ice like pancakes and then entering a regular field
of young ice, swaying to and fro in unbroken curves with the
swell of the waves.

Saturday, March 24th.—A beautiful clear day. The island
of Jan Mayen, distant some 40 miles, presents a most magnificent appearance. Covered with snow to its summit, the
volcanic mountain at the northern extremity of the island
towers aloft 1⅓ miles high. Purple clouds float across and
around it, while its deep ravines and gorges stand out in beautiful relief. All day long has this majestic cone been in sight,
presenting new phases of beauty with every atmospheric
change or with the various positions of the ship. The sunlight caused its snowy sides to glitter and gleam against the
dark clouds behind it till one imagined oneself gazing upon
some terrestrial similitude of " the great white throne " in
the Revelation.

Yesterday the gunpowder, percussion caps, sealing knives,
sheaths, and steels for sharpening the knives, were served out.
The ship's rifles were distributed ten days ago, and the men
have been busy casting bullets. Unfortunately, I have no
mould for my rifle, and must content myself with bullets a
size too small.

Tuesday, March 27th.—" The shop " was open all yesterday
morning—*i.e.*, the " slop " bags were heaved up on deck and
the men supplied with jackets, trousers, shirts, sou'westers, skin
caps, tea, sugar, coffee, tobacco, etc., in readiness for the sealing.

Spoke the s.s. *Camperdown* of Dundee, Captain Taylor,
who reports having seen some thousands of seals near Jan
Mayen Island, all heading in a south-westerly direction.
Ship's course altered accordingly. Numerous seals seen, all
heading S.S.W. Weather cold and foggy. Towards the
afternoon got up steam, as the ship is surrounded by numerous
small icebergs. A gale which is threatening makes our posi-

tion not a little risky, as these icebergs are as hard and dangerous as so many rocks. We stood out to the East to get out of the ice-pack. Numerous seals seen, all heading South-West.

Wednesday, March 28th.—A very heavy swell on all last night and this morning. We are out of the pack and in the open sea.

In the afternoon we stood into the pack again, shaping for the South-West. At 5 p.m. we spoke the s.s. *Windward*. They had not fallen in with many seals.

At the present moment the *Windward* and *Diana* are " dodging " in a hole in the ice. A few seals seen, all heading South-West. We are now not far from the North end of Jan Mayen Island, but we are unable to determine our exact position, the sun having been obscured these last two days.

My little dog " Gyp," a rough-haired Scotch terrier, has had her feet affected by the frost during the last three days whenever she goes on deck.

Have hardly seen a single sea-fowl of any species since last Sunday.

Thursday, March 29th.—The *Windward, Polynia, Tay,* and three other steamers, were in sight at breakfast-time this morning.

We passed through a good deal of heavy ice to-day, and after tea a large " school " of some hundreds of male seals could be seen playing in our wake. This makes us conclude the females and young are not far off.

At the present moment we are lying close in the pack with all sails furled and ship motionless. We *may* get beset in the ice and be unable to extricate the ship from the ice closing in upon us. The wind is blowing very strong. We do not know where we are, but imagine ourselves to be North-West of Jan Mayen Island. The sun is obscured and we have made no observation now for three days.

Captain Gravill's Chat about Seals.

" The seal which we go after to Greenland is the ' Saddle Back ' (*Phoca Greenlandica*), which the Newfoundlanders call ' Harp Seals.'

" They are by far the most numerous seal there is. I've

seen them in Greenland extending on the pack for a distance of 20 to 30 miles, young ones and old, just a solid body of seals. They always like to lie in a line with each other, which makes them run out such a length, while the whole body of them would be only a few miles in breadth.

" The ' Ground Seal ' (*Phoca barbata*) is mostly met with inshore, in bays and bights. It looks in the face just like an old man with a white beard.

" The ' Blethernose ' or Hooded Seal (*Cystophora cristata*) has a regular hood which reaches to the back of his head, and which he blows up to form a regular helmet. When attacking them on the ice, we generally try and break the blether so as to get the chance of a fair stroke at the skull.

" They are very bold, fierce animals, and they give a terrible bite, I assure you. If you approach an old ' he-blether ' on the ice, he will come forward immediately to meet you and give you battle. I've seen one of them beat off a whole boat's crew after they had broken two or three oars over his head. They were obliged to fire a harpoon into him before they could take him. I have never noticed them fight much amongst themselves.

" I've no particular idea what they feed on, but I've seen them jump out of the water, trying to catch a mallie. I believe they eat a good deal of cod on the banks.

" Once, when in Greenland, I watched a school of ' Bottle-noses ' constantly going backwards and forwards beneath a piece of ice on which there was a seal laid. Every time they went under the ice they struck it with their tails, but whether it was to break the ice or to frighten the seal off I don't know, but the seal was frightened enough of 'em, I assure you.

" I sent a boat away to fetch the seal aboard, for, says I, ' There's no fear of his leaving the ice while them things is there ! You'll get him easy enough, I warrant.' And so they did. The seal never offered to leave the ice; the ' Bottle-noses ' would have worried it directly if it had."

Friday, *March* 30*th* (*Good Friday*).—This is a day which will never be forgotten by me.

After writing yesterday's diary I lay upon the sofa reading

the Life of the Rev. John Newton till about 10.30 p.m., when I fell asleep. Being very weary, I did not awaken till 2 a.m., when I found the ship in violent motion.

Upon going on deck, I discovered that the wind had increased to a strong gale, there was a fearfully heavy swell, and that the ice-pack we had been in was breaking up.

Not being aware of the danger we were in, I retired to my berth, but could not sleep, partly from the motion of the ship, but principally from a feeling of uneasiness. Rising, I found the captain dressed and looking very anxious. I went forward to smoke a pipe, and Bill Clarke, who had charge of the watch, came down to put on his sea-boots. He advised me to do the same, as we might have to take to the ice at any moment. I learnt then that the ship was in the greatest danger of being stove in by the immense masses of old ice which, in violent motion, surrounded us on all sides.

I returned to the cabin. The captain fully corroborated the alarming statements of the officers, and added that, from what he saw of our position and considering the size of the ice, the unprecedentedly heavy swell, the fearful gale, and the distance we were from the open sea, he had very little hope of saving the vessel, less still of our saving our lives in the event of our having to take to the ice.

I went to my berth and dressed myself carefully, pulling on three flannel shirts, two Shetland neck wrappers, three pairs of stockings, my sea-boots and hair-skin cap. I put four sticks of tobacco, two pipes, and two boxes of fusees in my pocket, and then returned to the cabin.

Having made these few preparations, I had nothing further to do but await my fate with such constancy and resignation as I was capable of.

3 *a.m.*—All hands ordered on deck. The night was not very dark. The gigantic swell, thickly covered with massive pieces of ice, rolled all around us as far as the eye could see. The gale roared through the bare rigging with a noise like thunder.

A glass of rum was served out to all hands on the quarter-deck. I declined to take any, believing that I should be better able to resist cold and exposure by refraining from taking stimulant.   Three bags of biscuit, with a few cheeses and preserved meat, were placed on the lee side of the wheel and covered with a sail, in readiness for lowering into the boats. The tackle for hoisting out the boats had been rove, oars handed up from below and lashed beside the boats, axes placed in readiness for cutting away the masts, fenders hung over the sides to protect the ship as much as possible from the effects of the numerous collisions.   The men were employed incessantly in working these fenders, bracing the fore and main yards to turn the ship's head when threatened by ice, working the pumps, etc.   I employed myself in assisting them as much as lay in my power, more particularly in working the fenders.

4 *a.m.*—Our chances of escape seem most desperate.   Mr. Clarke, first mate, told me that if we were saved 'twould be by a miracle.

As the day broke we obtained a clearer view of our danger, and truly no prospect could seem more hopeless.

The ship lay in the trough of the sea under bare poles (our mainstay sail having been blown in two by the force of the gale), lurching heavily to leeward, and thus coming in collision with the ice with double force.   All around us were terrible-looking masses of ice, hard as rocks, and just as dangerous; massive, jagged, cold, cruel monsters, rising, falling, and retreating on the crest of the swell, and then rushing down the slope towards us in lines and columns, abreast, in straggling groups, or dense companies, rushing with irresistible force full upon our starboard side, retreating with the next swell, and then returning to the charge.   All this in an interminable succession, the ship drifting slowly to the South-West, and only able to lessen the force of the collisions by manœuvring the yards, going ahead off and on with the engines, or interposing the fenders or coils of rope over the sides.

In this way we had to run the gauntlet through innumerable dangers, through interminable masses of ice stretching ahead as far as we could see, hour after hour, expecting every moment to be crushed, despairing of escape.   The excitement, the state of mind, was intense.   It was one long agony of danger, a protracted mental torture, almost more than I could bear.

8 *a.m.*—Breakfast in the cabin—coffee and biscuits. Very little eaten. Each of us absorbed in his own reflections, which, for my part, were gloomy enough. During the forenoon remained on deck assisting with the fenders. The crew worked well, doing their duty to a man, exerting themselves to the utmost, but 'twas little we could do for the ship beyond attending to the fenders and shifting the yards. But there was no skulking; no appearance of fear, faint-heartedness, or despair; no unmanly croaking or prophesying the worst (though all expected it) among them. Every man kept up his own spirits and cheered his fellows. Never in my life did I feel so proud of being an Englishman, so proud of the calm, self-possessed, resolute bearing of my fellow-countrymen, who, with sudden and inevitable death staring them in the face, yet did their duty as though nothing unusual were occurring.

1 *p.m.*—Dinner in the cabin. A poor meal, and eaten in silence. We fully expected it to be our last meal together on earth. Everything looking desperate; expecting the ship to be stove in and sink at any moment.

2 *p.m.*—All hands that could be spared were ordered aft to the cabin. The captain told us in a few words that we had done all that men could do, and that we must put our trust solely now in the mercy of God. He exhorted us to prepare for the eternal world, and proposed to sing a hymn, " and mind you sing it with all your hearts."

We then, with voices choking with emotion, sang those lines :

> " Commit thou all thy griefs
>   And ways into His hands;
> To His sure truth and tender care,
>   Who earth and heaven commands,
>
> " Who points the clouds their course,
>   Whom winds and seas obey.
> He shall direct thy wandering feet,
>   He shall prepare thy way."

The captain then, kneeling down, prayed very earnestly to God to have mercy upon us all, to spare us for the sake of our friends and families, or, should He see fit to take our lives, to watch over and comfort them when we were gone. This worthy man then urged us to offer up mental prayers when on the deck, at the wheel, aloft, wherever we might be.

It was a very fearful, solemn sight in that cabin. Men were there of all ages, youths, boys, with pale faces, expecting instant death, with the ice thundering against the ship, which even then, for aught we knew, might be filling and going down. May I never forget that scene and that prayer aboard the *Diana*.

The afternoon wore heavily away, the ice as thick and heavy as ever, and the ship lurching fearfully to leeward, making it extremely difficult to keep the deck. One's ears were filled with the roar of the wind tearing through the rigging, the scream of escaping steam, the monotonous clash of the pumps (with the men lashed to the decks to enable them to keep their feet while working them), and the cries of the officers in command. The sea rolled around us in gigantic billows crested, not with foam, but with masses of old ice, which bore down upon us in incessant streams as though determined upon our destruction. The black sky overhead hung over us like a funeral pall about to descend upon our closing scene. Through it all the ship staggered along, rising and falling and reeling to and fro like a living thing conscious of its danger and struggling for dear life. Add to this the terrible consciousness that, if the ship were crushed, *we must perish inevitably* from cold and exposure in open boats or upon the floating masses of ice. All these scenes (and feelings) made up a picture such as I heartily trust I may never see or feel again.

Though distressed enough in mind and fearfully uneasy at times, I felt remarkably free from that secret terror of the mysteries of eternity, especially after the service in the cabin. Nay, at times I felt cheerfully resigned and prepared for the worst. I contemplated death without the slightest fear— 'twas only a few minutes' struggle in the waves, one of the easiest deaths to die.

As the afternoon wore on the joyful news was spread that the barometer was rising, and hope began to spring up in our breasts.

At 6 p.m. I was sent for by the captain, who asked me cheerfully and in tones that I shall never forget if I would care for a glass of wine. In reply to my enquiries, he said he considered the ship was getting out of danger, and that we should be in the open sea before nightfall. We then sat down to tea and made a hearty meal, after which I felt so utterly and completely exhausted, so worn out by mental anxiety and the long, protracted torture of suspense during that dreadful day, that I lay down on the sofa and fell into a dead sleep.

Saturday, March 31st.—Rose at midnight and went on deck. The night was thick and foggy, with driving snow-showers, rendering it difficult to see the heavy ice-floes, which were still pretty numerous, though not so large as they were yesterday.

We are in the open sea, occasionally coming across streams of young ice and numerous pieces of heavy ice washed away from the pack and wandering across the heaving billows like uneasy and troubled spirits of the darkness, looming up suddenly upon our quarter and disappearing again in the darkness.

After breakfast I returned to the deck. The gale was higher than ever. The swell was fearful, and, being unrestrained by the young ice, broke over our windward quarter and swept our decks in heavy seas. The cold was intense; everything—spars, rigging, boats, oars, our faces and beards— was covered with ice. The decks were one sheet of ice, the seas freezing as they came aboard. Our clothes were frozen stiff upon us, while the ship's hull was covered with ice from stem to stern to a thickness of 2 feet.

At noon we contrived to set the main topsail. After dinner I retired to my berth, feeling indescribably grateful for our happy escape. I may add that I did not recover from the feeling of weariness for several days, and am, in fact, writing this account of the storm after the interval of a week (April 7th), not being able to bring my mind to dwell minutely upon its various particulars. 'Tis a subject I dreaded to think of at all, and so delayed my log day after day till compelled to apply myself to the unwelcome task.

Sunday, April 1st.—Morning beautifully clear. Sea calm and beautiful, in strange and delightful contrast to the recent storm. Our difficulties during that time were added very much to by our ignorance of our exact position. The sun having been obscured for many days, we had not been able to make an observation since the Monday preceding the storm. We only knew that we were driving between the island of Jan Mayen and the coast of Greenland, and suspected ourselves in imminent danger of being driven upon the tremendous cliffs of that desert island. It is supposed that we drifted 40 miles through the pack and another 40 miles before we were clear of the heavy ice.

Divine Service, attended by all who could. A very solemn and affecting meeting, bringing vividly into mind our last assembly on Good Friday. The captain gave out the 189th hymn:

> " God of my life, whose gracious power
> Through varied depths my soul has led,
> Or turned aside the fatal hour,
> Or lifted up my sinking head,

> " Oft hath the sea confessed Thy power
> And given me back at Thy command.
> It could not, Lord, my life devour,
> Safe in the hollow of Thy hand."

The captain then read a short sermon and offered up a prayer of gratitude to God for sparing our lives.

EDITORIAL NOTE.

Having survived the storm, the " Diana " was turned north-eastward again towards the ice-fields in the neighbourhood of Jan Mayen Island.

During the next eighteen days the ship was steadily forced through the ice searching in various directions for seals. Other ships were sighted from day to day, as many as ten sail being in view one morning, all engaged in looking for the seals which, in previous years, had always been found in great numbers in this locality. However, the search was fruitless. A few seals were seen from day to day and an occasional one killed, but the main herds remained undiscovered. Such entries in the diary as " Spoke the barque ' Kate ' of Peterhead, Captain Martin, but could get or give very little information on the all-important topic, the seals," show that other ships were equally as unsuccessful as the " Diana " in finding the seals.

The weather during this period was very variable, one day being beautifully clear and warm, the next day cold and foggy, while fierce squalls of wind would come down on the ship all of a sudden. One day's entry reads, " In evening a very sudden and dangerous gale sprang up, and we nearly lost our main topgallant mast and sail. I am told that the neighbourhood of Jan Mayen Island is always dangerous from the sudden squalls that blow off it."

There are frequent references to the gorgeous appearance of this island when seen from a distance on a fine, clear day. The note made on April 11th was, " The mountain of Jan Mayen beautifully distinct, like a magnificent purple cloud, at 82 miles distance. The captain says he has seen it distinctly with the naked eye from a ship's deck at the distance of 120 miles."

Another little observation of interest is the statement, " The ordinary rate at which an ice-pack travels or drifts is reckoned to be 10 miles in the twenty-four hours." Another little entry reads, " It is remarkable how soon seagulls of all species make their appearance immediately upon the death of a seal. The boat had not left the ice half-a-dozen lengths before these voracious scavengers of the ocean were alighting upon the ' cran,' or carcase, by dozens."

On April 12th the diary records, " The ' Kate ' and a brig seen steering due North, evidently having given up all hopes of falling in with seals, and are now off for whales in the North Greenland seas."

However, the " Diana " continued the search till April 19th, when the entry is made in the diary, " The captain of a Norwegian brig came on board. He had only got six seals. To-day we bore away for the Shetlands, it being too late now to hope to get any young seals until they take to the edge of the pack. By waiting for them we should materially delay our subsequent voyage to Davis Straits for whales."

And so the " Diana's " preliminary voyage to the North in search of seals was unsuccessful and nearly ended prematurely in disaster. The succeeding voyage to Davis Straits, as described in the remainder of this diary, was a long struggle against one misfortune after another. The diary is a remarkable and, in many places, a deeply stirring record of endurance amid death, disease, and disaster, on the part of a whale-ship's crew of York-shiremen and Shetlanders.

The island of Balta in the Shetlands was sighted in the evening of April 27th. That day the observation is made, "As we approached the land, the 'mallies' (fulmar petrels), our constant and inseparable companions in the open sea, disappeared, whilst an occasional sandpiper and the guillemot showed that we were nearing the land."

That the ill-success of the voyage thus far was a very personal matter to the crew is evidenced by the following remark, "Much of the pleasure of returning to one's native land was taken away by the melancholy fact of having a 'clean ship'—i.e., having been unsuccessful at the sealing."

On April 28th the ship anchored in Lerwick Harbour.

BLETHERNOSE SEAL

CHAPTER III

LERWICK AND A FRESH START

AND now for the next ten days my life ceased to be aquatic. Most of my time was spent ashore. I slept at the only hotel that Lerwick can boast of. My days passed happily in knocking about the adjacent country.

It is impossible to describe the exhilarated feelings of those who, having been battered about on the ocean, set their feet once more on land, and see again the old familiar country objects. The singing of the larks never seemed so sweet to me before, while the sight of some primroses in a sheltered nook among the rocks by Gulverwick brought back all manner of home recollections.

On several occasions we entered the houses of the country-people. Their dwellings are rudely built of stone, and have a thatched roof kept in place by bands of straw, with large stones dangling at each end. The houses consist of one room, with bed cabins ranged round the sides, a peat fire burning on the middle of the floor, while the smoke fills the place to suffocation and finds its way out at its leisure through a hole in the roof.

The country has the bleakest and most wretchedly barren aspect On all sides gaunt, grey hills covered with moors and mosses and with the everlasting little stacks of peat. There is nothing to be seen but droves of small, shaggy ponies; small, active, long-woolled sheep; and small, stunted cattle, listless men and boys followed by collie dogs attending to the stock, and little groups of women, girls, boys, or aged men, carrying the turf upon their backs in baskets along the winding roads, and all busy knitting and talking as they creep along.

On the farms the women, girls, and old men manure the ground with seaweed and plant the potatoes, which are

16

dibbled in and covered over by a light harrow, which invariably is drawn by a woman. I never saw a horse or pony put to work upon the land.

The hooded crows frequent the shore at low tide. 'Twas interesting to watch them pick up a shellfish, and then, flying up to some height, let it fall upon the stones, and then descend to pick the mussel out of its broken shell.

The linnets must have been hard up for bushes to build in, for I never saw a bush or tree, save where they had been planted in a garden.

We left Lerwick Harbour at 3 p.m. on Tuesday, May 8th, under steam and with all sail set, getting into the open sea at 8 p.m.

Since this date we have been favoured with the most magnificent weather. A splendid breeze from the South-East has been driving the ship along, generally with all sail set, studding sails and all, at the rate of from 7 to 10 knots per hour. Captain Gravill tells me that in all his experience he has never had such a quick and favourable passage. At the time of writing (May 17th) we have passed Cape Farewell, the southern point of Greenland, and are driving along before a steady breeze at the rate of 9½ knots. We expect to have the ship headed up the Straits some time to-morrow.

EDITORIAL NOTE.

The run from Lerwick up to the above-mentioned date was uneventful. The diary here is only interesting on account of the little natural history notes, such as, " The mallies made their appearance again when we had got some 50 miles from land" ; " When some 200 miles from land, a pair of curlews alighted upon the vessel" ; " When about half-way across the ocean, the captain noticed a shag upon the water" ; " Several ' pot-heads,' or Round-Headed Porpoises, made their appearance, rising slowly out of the water to breathe and lazily disappearing head first. Their breath as they swam to windward was horribly fœtid. It is this species of fish that is sometimes driven ashore in herds by the Shetlanders, and called by them the ' ca'ing whale' or ' driving whale.' "

Some information here about whales and whaling is of interest.

A very large "finny whale" seen blowing not far from the ship. This species is distinguished from the ordinary Greenland whale by the possession of a soft dorsal fin. It is known to measure over 100 feet in length, and probably is the largest of all known animals, according to Darwin's " Natural History."

Bill Clarke tells me that, when aloft, he has seen them pass under this ship's hull (and she measures more than 40 paces from the wheel to the forecastle), and far exceed the ship in length. They are never meddled with by the whalers, as they yield but a small quantity of blubber, and, besides, are very tenacious of life. Captain Gravill says they would run out all the lines in the ship, and that he never thought it worth his while to risk losing lines by trying to take a " finny " whale. Besides, the whalebone is remarkably short, not measuring twice as many inches as that of the Greenland whale does feet. The dorsal fin resembles a fleshy horn upon the back, and is situated very close to the rump of the fish. It feeds upon fish, and is very abundant, both in the Greenland and Straits' seas. An American vessel comes every year to the neighbourhood of Iceland in pursuit of these whales, which are killed by firing both harpoon and rocket into them simultaneously.

Thursday, May 18th.—We are now past Cape Farewell, having made the passage from Lerwick in nine days. This run usually takes three weeks, and only last year took the *Diana* eleven weeks to do. We have been remarkably favoured thus far, and trust to have a shift in the wind to-morrow night to enable us to run up the Straits. Before we alter the ship's course materially, we are compelled to run at least another 100 miles to the West to avoid collision with icebergs, which usually abound off the Cape and are a source of great danger and anxiety. Many vessels have been lost in these seas; we trust we may be mercifully preserved.

Friday, May 18th.—We have run 172 miles to-day. Ship's head laid N.E. by N. We are running now up and towards the middle of Davis Straits to avoid the icebergs on the Greenland coast. The ship has been, and is, pitching heavily, the sea being very rough and tumultuous from the meeting of the Greenland Sea's and Straits' currents.

Editorial Note.

The "Diana" continued to make good progress northward. In the fortnight from leaving Lerwick she covered 2,000 miles, "more than was ever known by any man on board." The members of the deck crew were kept busy reeving boat falls, the rifles were served out again, while the harpoons, harpoon guns, and rockets were overhauled. Next, the whaling-boats were swung outboard, the harpoon guns fixed in position, and long whaling-lines spliced.

Ice was encountered on May 20th, and the ship forced gradually through it.

On May 27th the ship was off Discoe Island, of which the diary states, "Formerly South-West Bay and the neighbourhood of this island were great fishing stations, the whalers seldom going much further North."*

On May 28th, by Hare Island, the "Diana" fell in with another whaling-ship, the "Polynia," who reported that the East Side fleet of whale-ships was close by; that the "Alexander" of Dundee had caught four "fish" (whales), the "Wildfire" three, and the "Intrepid," "Esquimaux," and the "Truelove" of Hull one fish apiece, all of which was cheering news. The following day the "Diana" joined up with a portion of the fleet ("Narwhale," "Windward," "Esquimax," "Wildfire," and "Alexander"), and that afternoon the "Diana" sighted her first whale of the season, but failed to get it.

The ship continued on her north-easterly course, "being anxious to get across 'The Bay'—i.e., Melville's Bay—as soon as possible, it being the most dangerous part of the voyage. In the year 1830 no fewer than twenty-one ships were lost in the ice in this bay."*

An unusual amount of ice was encountered all along the coast, and the "Diana's" progress was very slow. The coast scenery along here is described as consisting of "stupendous precipices, with a background of very lofty mountains whose snow-covered summits towered above the clouds into a purple sky. Noticed a small iceberg which seemed as red as blood, and which evidently had been formed upon and broken away from some ferruginous rock."

* See account of old whaling days, pp. 81-83.

*At the Fraw Islands (or Woman's Islands) further progress
North was stopped by an ice-field. Here the " Diana" again
fell in with the " Polynia," " Narwhale," " Esquimaux," " Wildfire," and " Intrepid." All the ships being fitted with engines,
they determined to try and force a passage in company through
this particular ice-field. A little sketch illustrates the scene, which
the diary describes thus : " The ships that lay moored behind the
islands now made their appearance, steaming along between the
islands and a floe, presenting a very pretty sight as they threaded
their way in a long line amongst the intricacies of the ice bergs,
rocks, shoals, and islands—uncommon dangerous navigation."*

*The first three ships got through, but the " Intrepid," " Wildfire,"
and " Diana," having inferior horse-power to the others, failed,
and had to make fast to an ice-floe near one of the islands.*

The diary continues, under date June 5th :

The surgeon of the *Intrepid*, Mr. Galloway of Dundee, a
student of Glasgow University, called upon me. Saw great
numbers of eider ducks on the floe edge. They are beautiful
birds, but extremely shy. The cry of this species of duck is
exactly like the bark of a dog.

Went with George Clarke to one of the islands near by. Had
a terrible climb up the sides of the rocks, which were covered
with snow, and then up the sides of the loftiest peak on the
island. I never had such a climb in my life, and I wonder how
we succeeded in scaling the precipice. We were frequently
up to the thighs in snow, or at times crawling along the brow of
a precipice with only a few inches of frozen snow between our
feet and the slippery rocks below.

After an hour's hard work we reached the summit, and there
found a cairn of stones which evidently had been raised there
many years ago by visitors such as ourselves. We repaired it,
and wrote the ship's name and port upon an adjacent snow-
drift for the information of anyone who might visit the cairn
before next winter.

We had a most magnificent view of the ocean and numerous
islands and icebergs, the sun shining brilliantly and the sky
without a cloud. By means of a very powerful telescope
which one of the Shetland men had carried up we could see

MEDUSÆ

LITTLE AUK (ROTCH)

EIDER DUCK

CAPE SHACKLETON OR "HORSES HEAD"

MELVILLE'S MONUMENT, AS SEEN FROM THE MASTHEAD THROUGH
A TELESCOPE AT A DISTANCE OF 20 MILES

PTARMIGAN

Sketches from the Doctor's Diary, referred to on pages 20, 21, 22 and 26.

WHITEY SEAL

THE FLEET STEAMING PAST FRAU ISLANDS

Sketches from the Doctor's Diary, referred to on page 20.

the three steamers ahead of us.   Utter silence and desolation on all sides.   Patches of dead heather and moss where the rocks were sheltered from the snow, and a peculiar straggling plant with bright purple blossoms.

Our return was much more expeditious than our outward journey.   The easiest method of descent was to squat on one's hams and slide from top to bottom of the hills.   Seeing a white object upon a large boulder, we looked at it with the telescope, and lo! 'twas a ptarmigan.   George Clarke crept near and shot it.   'Twas a beautiful bird, snow-white (except for a few black feathers in the tail), and with brilliant red wattles over its eyes.

Returned to the ship at midnight.   The sun shone brilliantly all night.   Noticed from the ship's side a great number of large medusæ, so large that the circulation of drops of water could be seen quite easily with the naked eye as they floated past.

June 6th.—Directly after breakfast the ship raised steam and followed the lead of the *Wildfire* and *Intrepid* in and out amongst the islands and bergs till brought up about eleven o'clock by a floe, through which we forced our way with some difficulty.

At twelve o'clock we were brought up again by another floe, through which the other ships passed readily enough, but which our inferior horse-power was not equal to.   Till seven o'clock at night did we struggle at it, some of the men fixing ice-anchors on the various pieces of ice, and the rest manning the capstans and either forcing the ship's stem through the floating masses or reversing the engines and straining with all our might, engines and men, to tow the pieces of ice out of our way   Others of the crew were busy with ice-poles pushing the ice aside.   The whole ship's company did their best to force the ship through the pack, which was only about 150 yards wide.   After getting her two-thirds of the way through we were compelled to desist, on account of the ice closing tightly upon us.

The day was very warm.   We were working at the capstan bars in our shirts.   There was clear water ahead of us as far as we could see.   Yet here we are, stuck in a paltry narrow floe, whilst our late companions are steaming merrily away to the North and will be across the Bay in no time if this magnifi-

cent weather continues.   Day ends with the ship fast in the
ice off Berrie's Island, the most northerly of the Fraw group.

Thursday, June 7th.—Was on deck this morning before six
o'clock, and found the ship steaming and sailing, the ice having
opened up at about eleven o'clock last night, liberating the
ship at 2.30 a.m.

This has been one of the hottest days we have had in this
country, the sky being without a cloud and the sea as smooth
as polished steel.   We have been running along the coast all
day.   Numerous tracks of bears visible on the floes.

Have passed Cape Shackleton, called " Horse's Head " by
the sailors, at the southern entrance of Ingstone Bay.   The
northern point of the bay is a noted " loonery."   Some years
ago the *Tay* made fast to an island in this harbour, and gathered
off it no fewer than a thousand dozen of ducks' eggs.   Returning the next morning, she gathered ninety dozen more before
breakfast.   Captain Gravill was in the harbour in the *Chase*
at the time.

Two ships in sight from the mast-head, supposed to be the
Intrepid and *Wildfire.*

Friday, June 8th.—This morning the wind shifted and the
ice closed us in.   We had the mortification of seeing the other
ships get clear and stand North under steam and canvas.

At about five o'clock a bear was seen at some distance.   I
went to the crow's-nest and watched it with a glass for some
time.   It was ranging about the ice in search of seals, incessantly stopping and snuffing the air or lying down behind the
hummocks.   It looked miserably gaunt, and as lean as a grey-
hound.

Old John, one of the men, tells me he remembers a bear
attacking a ship's company of forty men sealing on the ice.
Two years ago the *Constantia* fell in with a dead whale covered
with bears.   The ship's crew shot no fewer than sixty of these
bears, out of which number they got forty-five.

CAPTAIN GRAVILL'S CHAT ABOUT BEARS.

" A bear can dive a very long way.   I remember in 1827,
when I was mate of the *Bruce*, the master called me up one
morning to look at what he thought was a dead fish.   ' Yes,'

says I, ' 'tis a dead fish sure enough, and, what's more, I can see a bear on top of it.'" (The captain always has had, and still has, remarkably good eyesight. Though now more than sixty years of age, he can distinguish objects from the deck or mast-head better than any man aboard that I am aware of.—C. E. S.) "' Well, Mr. Gravill,' says he, ' I want you to go first and fetch me that 'ere bear, and I'll send a boat afterwards to tow the fish alongside.'

"Well, I went and struck a lance into the bear, but didn't kill it. It dived below a very large and broad piece of ice that happened to be near, and then came up the other side of the ice. That bear actually kept that boat's crew pulling round that ice for more than an hour. It kept on diving and coming up again at the opposite side before I could get another lance into it, and it was wounded and bleeding and weakening all the time from the first lance.

" I remember once watching a bear ranging along the floe edge when a seal popped up its head. The bear laid down flat on its belly, and directly the seal showed itself again the bear dived head first after it. However, it did not succeed in catching the seal, though I don't doubt they often do. They must be very quick and clever to catch a seal under water.

" If a bear sees a seal laid on a floe near its hole it will crawl and creep towards the seal like a cat after a mouse, hiding himself behind the hummocks and taking advantage of any rough ice to get within reach, when he springs upon the seal. Or the bear will lie in wait near a seal hole and take the seal when it comes out. When a bear sees a seal laid near its hole where there's no possibility of getting near it without being seen (for a seal is very watchful, always lifting its head and looking round him for danger), the bear has been known to dive down another seal hole and come up at the very hole where the seal is laid against, and so take the seal easy enough. If a seal's retreat to his hole is cut off, he doesn't know what to do or where to go.

" Every seal has its own hole, and lays on the ice with his head close against the hole, ready to dive at a moment's warning.

" When you are pulling after a bear in the water and are coming up to him fast, in nine cases out of ten he'll turn round and face you, though I have seen them dive and come up astern of the boat. They are nasty things, you know, for they'll get hold of your oars or anything with their tusks. Old Captain Hawkins, when he had the *William*, was pulled clean over his boat's bow by one of them bears.*

" Bears is very affectionate animals. I remember in 1860, when I had this ship, we saw a she-bear and her cub on a piece of ice. I sent George Clarke and Byers away after them, with orders to shoot the old bear and bring the young one on board alive. Byers shot the old bear dead. The young one laid itself down on the body of the mother, and never took the least notice of the men.

" Well, they made the old bear fast to a rope and rowed away, towing the body. The young bear came to the edge of the ice, and when it saw the mother, as it were, swimming away, it jumped into the water and followed close astern of her. When the boat was well clear of the ice, the men lay to and ' snickled ' the cub with a rope at the end of a boat-hook easy enough. They towed the dead bear alongside the ship, the young one swimming after her without requiring to be dragged along by the rope.

" We first hoisted up the young bear with a spike-fall. When on the deck it rove and tore and snarled as fierce as possible till the mother was sent up the ship's side, when the cub became perfectly quiet. Directly it lost sight of the mother, though, it snarled and snapped, and rove and tore about, and nearly bit its tongue in two with rage at finding itself fast. We was obliged to have the dead bear hoisted up again from between decks to quiet the cub. It laid down beside her and moaned and sobbed most pitiful, and licked

* In *Hull Museum Publications*, No. 31, the above incident is recorded as follows:

" In 1818 Captain Hawkins, of the *Everthorpe* of Hull, at Davis Straits, nearly lost his life whilst attacking a bear. The animal defended itself with fury, got partly into the boat, seized the captain by the thigh, dragged him overboard, and swam away with him to some distance before it let him go, the animal being closely pursued by the *Everthorpe's* boat."

the blood from her wounds and tried to lift her head up with its paws. 'Twas most distressing to look at.

" Yes, bears is very affectionate animals, I assure you. We took that young bear home and sold him for £12. I've known good ones fetch £20. I suppose they are bought for Zoological Gardens.

" When we want to catch bears alive, we ' snickle ' them with a rope round the neck when they are swimming in the water. We prefer to ' snickle ' young bears, as it is difficult to find a cask large enough to hold a full-grown one. We cover the head of the cask with a grating of iron hooping riveted together. We feed the bears with crang if we have any, but they'll eat almost anything; I've fed 'em with soup. Sometimes I've given them a little whale-oil, but that makes them dainty. We heave buckets of salt water over them daily, and play upon them with a hose to keep them clean. If the weather is calm we hoist them up, cask and all, with a tackle and drop them overboard, or else set the cask on end and half fill it with water.

" They soon get to know the person who feeds them, but they are not to be trusted, though I have rubbed their noses with my hand through the bars. I remember when the *Mercury* lay in Lerwick Harbour we had a bear aboard. The 'spectioneer's dog put his nose through the cage, and in an instant the bear had his paw upon the dog's head and tore his jaw off. We had to drown the poor dog."

EDITORIAL NOTE.

The ship got out of the ice-pack the next day and continued her progress northward along the coast, being constantly impeded by the unusually heavy ice-floes. An entry for Sunday, June 10th, states : " Several bears seen. One was nearly run down by the ship early this morning as it swam across our bows. Being Sunday, the captain would not allow a boat to be lowered in pursuit of it, or it would have been shot quite easily. We are now in the much-dreaded Melville Bay, the ' Breaking-Up Yard' of the sailors."

The diary continues :

Tuesday, June 12th.—We have steamed 10 miles through the ice during the night in the midst of dangers. Had the ice closed at any time, the captain tells me, we must have been crushed like an egg-shell. *Intrepid* and *Wildfire* in the ice some 3 miles distant.

'Tis a glorious, hot summer morning. The skin of my face is peeling off from the heat and the reflected glare off the snow. My eyes are aching with the dazzling light, and my complexion is as brown as that of a gipsy. This is first-rate weather. The excitement, the danger, the hard work at the capstan, the tugging and warping, the pushing of ice aside with ice-poles, the fixing of ice-anchors, the scrambling about on the floes and shooting at birds, etc., is all very enjoyable indeed.

We are well in sight of land, being off Melville's Monument, a peculiar pyramidal mass of rock. Beyond are high headlands and mountain ranges, with tremendous glaciers from which the icebergs are formed.

We are now in the throat of that much-dreaded bay at the head of Melville's Bay, where the ice is locked up, unaffected by currents or changes of the wind, and, consequently, where a ship may be frozen up for months without chance of escape.

We are at the edge of a tremendous land-floe, with enormous sea-floes around us. Should the wind set in from the South-West, probably all three ships would be lost. I have been packing up all my traps in a vast canvas bag in readiness for taking to the ice at a minute's warning. All the crew sleep prepared for the worst, with their spare clothes stowed away in bags and their everyday clothing strapped together and placed convenient to their hand.

Wednesday, June 13th.—All hands engaged this morning in getting up casks of provisions (biscuits, beef, pork, etc.) from the fore-hold, in readiness for lowering into the boats should the ship be lost.

Got up steam at breakfast-time and steamed along the edge of the land-floe. A good many rotches (Little Auks) seen heading to the westward, a sure sign there is open water there.

Steaming all day off Cape Walker, the other two ships being ahead of us. At tea-time all hands were called to warp the ship through a most dangerous-looking channel, there being only a few feet between the land-floe and the sea-floe. It was a very anxious time, but fortunately the ice did not close upon us, though the wind was actually from the South-West. We warped the ship through in triumph, and then all hands drank a glass of grog at the capstan with uncommon satisfaction. Made fast at 7 p.m. to the sea-floe in company with *Intrepid* and *Wildfire*.

Thursday, June 14th.—Tried to continue on our way through the bay ice, but failed.

George Clarke nearly harpooned a narwhale this morning. Their ivory, which formerly only fetched twenty to thirty shillings a horn, is now extremely valuable, fetching twenty-four to thirty shillings a pound weight. Captain Gravill has had horns weighing 20 to 22 pounds apiece. It is said that these horns are eagerly sought for by the Chinese as ornaments for their pagodas or temples. The horn is one of the incisor teeth prodigiously developed, Captain Gravill having seen horns 12 and 14 feet long.

At 7 p.m. there were seen upon the ice some dark objects which the ship's telescope showed to be Esquimaux. I went with a boat's crew to meet the party, which was in three sledges, driving at a great speed towards the ship. The party consisted of three men, who were delighted to see us, and who soon pulled up at the ship's side.

The first sledge was drawn by six dogs, remarkably fine animals, the size of a wolf, and covered with thick shaggy hair. Most of the dogs were of a yellowish-white, exactly the colour of a bear, while a few were marked with patches of black.

The sledges were very ingeniously made of bits of light firwood, with runners of walrus tusk cleverly pegged together, and fastened to the woodwork with strips of raw hide. The handles consisted of a small walrus tusk, and upon them were coiled their lines (made of strips of hide) and their small spearheads. These are made of narwhale's horn, and were all tipped with iron, very neatly fastened in and rubbed to a sharp edge with stones.

Upon the sledges were bits of skin, blubber, mittens, bags stuffed with grass to make a soft seat, and the skin of a rotch to serve as a pocket-handerkchief.   This was mainly for rubbing their eyes with, for these poor creatures seem to suffer a good deal from the irritating glare and refraction from the snow.

The dogs were harnessed to the sledges with long lines, and ran abreast with great regularity, guided by the cries of their master, and urged on by a whip with a lash 20 to 30 feet in length, and which the Equimaux used with unerring skill.

Two of the natives were very short men, being about 5 feet 2 inches in height.   Their faces were broad and swarthy, eyes dark, lips prominent, noses well developed, and cheek-bones very broad.   Their hair, jet black and as coarse as a horse's mane, hung in confusion about their heads and faces. They had no beard, but a slight moustache.

On coming aboard the ship they seemed lost in a world of wonders.   Evidently they had never seen a gun before, and they laughed with surprise at the noise of its report.

The captain obtained two walrus horns from the ends of their spears for a couple of large sealing knives, whilst some of the crew got the smaller spear-points in exchange for a couple of needles apiece.

Later in the evening the Esquimaux drove to the *Intrepid*, leaving their stores of needles, biscuits, knives, and other treasures, with us, in whose honesty they seemed to have implicit confidence.

Friday, June 15*th.*—Our aboriginal friends returned this morning looking decidedly seedy.   Captain Gravill gave them a breakfast of coffee and biscuit upon the skylight of the cabin, and then spread on the deck a couple of sails in which the Esquimaux rolled themselves and were soon in a heavy sleep.

The oldest of them, "Tatalata," had exchanged his bear-skin breeches for a pair of old trousers, of which he seemed very proud.   Here he is, taking his breakfast.   His jacket consisted of the skins of sea-fowls, with the feathers towards his body, and a hood of the same material.

The tallest of the trio, by name "Meuuk," was dressed in a jacket and hood made of the skin of the "ugdhu," or ground-seal, with trousers of bear-skin.   His boots were very neatly made of seal-skin from which the fur had been scraped.   The third man's jacket was made of wolf-skin.

All day did these poor creatures remain aboard, showing the greatest confidence in us. They were ignorant of the use of tobacco, and would not taste rum, signifying by signs that it made their heads ache.

The crew were busy to-day getting snow aboard, to melt for drinking water. The " Yaks " (Esquimaux) readily assisted in passing along the buckets, in heaving at ropes, etc., showing the greatest desire to assist or oblige us.

Saturday, June 16th.—The Esquimaux, who had been aboard the *Wildfire*, returned to us last night about midnight, and retired to their slumbers amongst the ashes and dirt of the blacksmith's smithy.

" Tatalata," the old man, is completely transmogrified. He has obtained a jacket, waistcoat, cap, comforter, mittens, and a paper collar from some of the crew of the *Wildfire*. Also he has actually had his face washed and hair cut, so that he is not recognisable. He is extremely proud of his new toggery (which, by the by, is really old and ragged enough to disgrace a scarecrow), but has not the remotest idea as to how to put on his clothes when once he removes them. His difficulties in getting into his waistcoat would have made the most solemn undertaker's assistant die of laughter.

The Esquimaux left us this evening, their sledges being loaded with all sorts of odds and ends (though invaluable treasures in their eyes) which they picked up about the ship. They tell us their journey home will take two days.

Sunday, June 17th.—A dull, heavy, foggy day.

At about 5 p.m. the ice suddenly began to slacken. Boats were sent ahead by all three ships to ascertain if a passage were practicable, for the fog prevented us from seeing any distance. By 6 p.m. we were steaming through the narrow channel between the land and sea floes with a wind from the North-West dead ahead of us.

Our captain is extremely relieved in mind at our escaping uninjured from this dreaded bay. He assures me that a strong South wind would have driven the ice upon us and crushed the ships. With his accustomed piety he distinctly traces the finger of God in this unexpected and fortunate movement of the ice, which is the more remarkable as the wind was blowing

from a quarter unfavourable to such a change in the ice
to-day.

We passed between some heavy ice on the edge of the floes
where there had evidently been great pressure. Here the ice
was piled up in heaps and distorted, and there the ship would
have been nipped flat as in a monstrous and irresistible vice.

We were clear of the floes by 8 p.m. There is nothing but
clear water ahead of us now, so hurrah for Lancaster Sound
and Pond's Bay! Let's hope we get plenty of fish, a full ship,
and a safe voyage home again. We ought to feel thankful
for our preservation from innumerable perils during the past
week. We have been beleaguered between two heavy floes
of ice, only moving slowly and painfully along when it opened,
and depending upon a change in the wind for our safety and
perhaps for our lives. Providentially, the weather has been
beautifully calm and tranquil, with very light winds from the
S.S.W., which is unusual at this time of the year. The captain
tells us he has seldom known such weather in this country
during the month of June.

Editorial Note.

*The following day the " Diana " was progressing westward
with all sails set, " running at 5 knots an hour, safe and sound
in the long-looked-for North Water. The crew has just given
three hearty cheers for the North Water (a custom amongst whalers),
and an extra ' tot' of grog is being served out at the capstan head"
(another very laudable custom amongst the whaling community).*

*Preparations were started now for dealing with the whales
they anticipated catching. Up to the present the " Diana's "
decks had been littered with " shakes "—i.e., bundles of staves
shaped ready for making into oil casks. The crew were put on to
the job now of assembling these staves, hooping them, and then
stowing the casks so constructed away in the holds until required
for whale-oil, " as we heartily hope they may be.".*

*On June 20th the " Diana " was off Wolstenholme Island.
The cliffs on the mainland opposite this island, the diary states,
" are in places of a bright scarlet colour. This, I believe, is
peculiar to these rocks, and does not arise from the discoloration of
the snow by the fungus ' Protococcus nivalis,' or Red Snow Plant."*

Great quantities of ice were encountered in the North Water, and the diary for June 21st has the following note: "We are sanguine in our hopes of making the West Water to-morrow. Many of the men tell me they have never been so far North as we have been compelled to come this year on account of the great body of ice still remaining in the North Water."

On this fact, the sinister significance of which was borne in on them later, resulted all the subsequent trials and sufferings the crew of the "Diana" had to go through before they finally got clear of the immense ice-fields to the south of them.

There are frequent references during this time to the great heat they experienced on cloudless days. The diary for June 14th, for example, says: "To give you some idea of the weather in these regions during summer, I may mention that for the last three days we have had no appetite for meat at all, the joint leaving the dinner-table untasted." Again, on June 21st, in the diary is the entry: "Another magnificently clear, hot, and summery day, reminding me of a tranquil harvest day in England. The sky is cloudless, the water without a ripple and glistening like steel, the icebergs on the horizon elevated by the refraction into a thousand grotesque shapes. The heat is so great as to make all on board feel lazy and indisposed for the necessary exertion at the windlasses when warping the ship through the ice."

The next day the "Diana" was in the West Water—"plenty of open water, with streams of loose ice now and again." The weather had changed completely overnight, being "dull and gloomy, with slight showers of snow, very cold and chilly. Men busy stowing barrels in readiness for receiving whale-blubber."

The diary continues:

Saturday, June 23rd.—This morning I found the ship off the entrance to Jones Sound and Leopold Island.

We have been running all day before a fine breeze to the South and West, and within 7 or 8 miles of the shore. The coast is high and rocky in some parts, low and level in others, and is backed with lofty ranges of hills covered with snow. We passed several valleys opening upon the coast and filled with ice, which slowly and surely advances towards the sea, and breaking by its own weight, or being severed by the violence of the waves, forms those tremendous icebergs with which we are so familiar.

We passed an immense " loonery " upon a large and rocky island opposite to the entrance to Jones Sound. We arrived off Cape Horsburgh and the entrance to Lancaster Sound at about tea-time. We are now (11 p.m.) running past the entrance to the Sound before a pleasant breeze. The sea is covered with loose land-floe ice very much broken up—more so than any ice we have yet gone through.

To-day has been uncommonly bright, brisk, cold, sunny, and genial, with the ship running at 7 or 8 knots before a sharp breeze. All hands are cheerful and exhilarated at the prospect of being in Pond's Bay, possibly, to-morrow night and securing a good voyage.

The decks are clear of all lumber, casks have been set up and stowed, lances and boat axes sharpened, tackle hoisted for getting the whales up by their heads and tails, and everything arranged in complete readiness for " taking," " flinching," and " making off " at any moment.

Now at last we are on the West side and in whaling waters, with all hands in good health and everybody on board anxious to do his best to forward the object of this long and dangerous voyage.

So ends this week.

STEAMING THROUGH THE ICE-FLOES

CHAPTER IV

DISAPPOINTMENT WITH THE WHALING

Sunday, June 24th.—Was called this morning by the captain to see a whale which had risen near the ship at about seven o'clock. The officers on watch had lowered two boats in pursuit, contrary to the known wishes of the captain, who always has been a strict observer of the Sabbath, and never allowed the business of the voyage to be carried on upon a Sunday if he could help or prevent it.

Unfortunately, he is alone in his views and opinions upon this point. Everyone else on board considers that a whale rising near the ship is to be killed if possible, piously arguing that it is directed to them by a kind and considerate Providence for their benefit, and should be accepted more as a mark of Divine favour than anything else.

When we reflect upon the dangers and uncertainties of the voyage; the risks run in the pursuit of fish; that the crew's pay almost entirely depends upon the success of the voyage; that most of the men are married and have families to support; that the capture even of a single fish puts a considerable sum into their pockets in the shape of oil, bone, and " striking money "; that fish are few in number and often difficult to approach; that there are other ships owned, commanded, and manned by men to whom no trick, no artifice, is too mean to resort to in order to deprive us and each other of a fish at every opportunity, one cannot wonder at our crew objecting to lose the chance of getting a fish because it happens to make its appearance near us upon a Sunday.

I do not blame them myself. Nay, rather I am disposed to entertain their views upon the Sunday fishing question. However, their efforts were unavailing to-day, much to their own chagrin and the satisfaction of the captain.

33

Five ships to be seen from the mast-head fast to the land floe and close inshore. We expect to find all the seven ships that have preceded us made fast in company, as these Scotch skippers are very averse to allowing any of their number to move about much lest by any chance he should get a fish without giving them an opportunity of " doing " him out of it, if possible. Some of them have been successful off the Sound,* for we saw some " mallies " to-day feeding upon a piece of fresh blubber and washing themselves in the water, as is their custom after gorging upon a " crang."

EDITORIAL NOTE.

The " Diana " sighted nine other whale-ships all more or less together. However, she continued to cruise round on her own, the movements of the ship being restricted a good deal at times by great fields of drifting ice.

Whales were sighted occasionally and pursued without success. " We are all very blue at our ill-luck. The captain piously ascribes it to our having gone in pursuit of that whale last Sunday. He affirms that he never saw whales play about so fearlessly and give the harpooners so many chances of striking them and yet escape uninjured."

However, their ill-success did not last very long.

Saturday, June 30th.—This day ought to be marked on our calendar " with a white stone," as the Romans phrased it.

At 2 a.m. a whale was seen, and three boats sent away in pursuit. At four o'clock the ship resounded with the cry, " A fall! a fall!" All hands rushed on deck in their shirts and pants and crowded into the other boats, which were instantly lowered and put off in a state of the greatest excitement. Bill Reynolds was fast to a fish at the floe edge some 200 yards from the stern of the ship.

I ran along the floe and stood in the bows of the boat. The line was running out very fast, the fish having gone under the floe. The boat's jack† was hoisted at her stern, while the ship's jack flew triumphantly from the mizen mast-head. The other six boats lay on their oars at different points along the floe

* Lancaster Sound.   † Flag.

edge, awaiting the reappearance of the whale to strike her again.

She soon came up off the ship's starboard quarter, and was fired into again. At six o'clock she was floating dead alongside the ship, and all hands set to work to flinch her (*i.e.*, to remove the blubber in immense strips), cut out the whalebone, etc.

At nine o'clock another fish was seen and pursued. Suddenly the captain sang out, "A fall! a fall!" and again ensued the same scene of excitement and confusion. Byers was fast to a fish very near the spot where we secured the first one. But something went wrong. Suddenly his boat was dragged nearly under the water, the boat's crew leaped out on to the ice, the line flew up, the jack was lowered. Alas! the whale was free. The line had got entangled, and had it not broken we would have lost the boat and all its gear, and had it not been close to the floe, might have lost her crew as well. All the boats but two returned to the ship, and we resumed flinching with saddened hearts.

Again the cry was raised, "A fall! a fall!" Strange to say, the same fish had risen again, and George Clarke had buried his harpoon in her side. By 11.30 a.m. she was dead, and brought alongside the ship at twelve o'clock, just as we had finished flinching the first one.

After dinner we set to work upon whale No. 2, and finished flinching her by six o'clock.

We consider we have got 20 tuns of oil from the two fish. The value of the two fish may be reckoned thus: 20 tuns of oil at £50 a tun is £1,000; 1½ tons of whalebone at £700 per ton makes £1,050. Total value of this day's fishing, £2,050.

All hands turned in early, very greasy, wet, and weary. Our decks and everything about the ship were slippery with oil and grease. An immense number of mallies surrounded the ship, feeding greedily upon the oil and scraps of blubber, fighting and chattering and making a prodigious uproar.

Sunday, July 1st.—Many thousands of narwhales have been passing the ship to-day, all heading up the Sound in little companies. The captain tells me they always make their appearance here at this time, and are sure indicators of the presence of whales, the whales appearing immediately after the narwhales.

Two Esquimaux came aboard this afternoon. Their object was to secure a load of " muck tuck," or whale's skin, which is to them a great delicacy. Some of our men boil and then fry it, and find it an agreeable article of diet. I ate some myself, and found it had the exact flavour of periwinkles.

Captain Gravill's Chat about Whales.

" We always can tell a likely spot to look for whales by the colour of the water. Whales feeds upon small insects which swarm in good whale water in myriads, making the water look quite thick and dark brown. When we see the water have this appearance we keep a good lookout for fish. If there is no food in the water you may be sure you won't see no fish, unless they happen to be passing on their way up or down the country, or are on the search for good feeding ground.

" It's my opinion a whale can go a long time without meat, but when they *do* feed they swallow a tremendous quantity. We often take bucketsful of whales' food out of their throats and mouths when cutting out the whalebone.

" Whales' food consists of small red insects or animalcules, or whatever you may choose to call them, of a regular, uniform reddish colour, and spindle-shaped, tapering away to the tail. They are found principally in the Arctic and Antarctic Seas, where they exist in enormous numbers. They don't exceed an inch in length, yet they are the principal food of these great fish.

" Whales is sportive and playful enough. You often see them spring clean out of the water, which they does by doubling their tails under their bellies like a bow. It is quite common to see a fish amusing herself by standing on end with her body out of the water as far as her fins, and she threshing the water with her tail and making the seas fly again. In still weather you can hear them several miles off threshing the water. You often see fish rolling themselves over and over on the surface of the water, but whether they do so for an amusement, or because they've been wounded by harpoons or by sharks, or because they are annoyed by their lice, I don't know.

" If you kill a whale you are pretty sure to have plenty of sharks swimming about you as you are flinching your fish. They are very bold; don't take the least notice of you, not even if you wound 'em. They scoop great pieces of blubber as big as a plate out of the fish at every bite. They'll soon spoil a fish for you, I assure you. Sometimes you fall in with a dead fish adrift, but what with bears and birds above and sharks below water, they ain't long before the blubber is all away.

" I never knew these Greenland sharks to bite a man when in these waters, though their mouths is full of rows of teeth. They are very tenacious of life. We generally try to cut off their heads with a knife. I've seen us cut up a shark into pieces and bury them in the snow. On going to look at them twenty-four hours afterwards the bits were alive and moving about.

" I think your book's wrong about sharks attacking whales. I've been fifty years amongst them, and never knew and never heard of their doing such a thing.

" I fancy the fish they have put down as a shark that attacks the whales is what we call a ' swordfish,' though 'tisn't really a swordfish. I never could find a description of this fish or what name they call it in any book on Natural History.*

" They are always ranging and searching about for whales, and swim under a whale and ' job' this sword into it's belly. They go about in schools, old ones and young ones together, as old-fashioned as can be, ranging every bight and crack in the ice in search of whales.

" One year when we was to the southward of Pond's Bay we saw several whales up a crack in the ice. A school of these swordfish came ranging along the floe edge, but stopped directly they got to the crack, as if they knew the fish was there. The old ones went up the crack, whilst the young ones lay to and dodged outside.

* Probably Captain Gravill referred to the Grampus (*Orca gladiator*) This is described as a marine cetaceous mammal, about 25 feet in length. It is carnivorous and remarkably voracious, attacking whales with great determination.—C. E. S. H.

" I sent off the men across the ice with guns to put a ball into 'em, for, says I, ' Confound them ugly things! they'll frighten every fish out of the crack.' And so they did, but we got one of the whales that same day away down to leeward of where these swordfish was.

" If we see swordfish about we never think of looking for whales, for if any have been in that neighbourhood them swordfish are sure to drive them away. Whales is frightened to death of them. My son John, when he had this ship, saw a lot of swordfish a good way to the eastward of Cape Fare-well. When he come to take notice, he found they had surrounded a whale and had nearly tormented her to death. She was very far spent; nearly done for. He told me if he'd had his boats and lines ready he could have got her easy enough.

" When I had the *Chase* I saw a number of fish one Sunday off Agnes's Monument. They kept on the top of the water nearly all the time. One fish lay for three and three-quarter hours like a stone—may have been asleep for aught I know.

" If I was full I would not kill a fish for the sake of her whalebone unless there was another ship in sight to take her blubber, though it would be a great temptation to kill her for the sake of the owners now that whalebone is such a price.*

" I believe the whalebone is mostly made up into ostrich feathers. You don't see one umbrella in a hundred that has bone ribs nowadays. There's one particular family in France that buys up the bone to make ostrich feathers.

" When I was in St. Johns in the *Polynia*, and was in a shop buying trinkets to barter with the Yaks, a lady came into the shop and bought an ostrich feather. Says I to the man, ' Isn't that feather made of whalebone?' He stared at me and confessed that it was, and was going to show me a real ostrich feather. ' No occasion,' says I; ' I've seen plenty of 'em. Fetched lots of 'em home from Cape Colony when I was there.'

" A real ostrich feather is a very expensive affair, I can tell you, but these whalebone ones are cheap and looks just like the real feather. Put whalebone into water and heat it, and you can make it into any shape or any thing you like."

* See Appendix I.

EDITORIAL NOTE.

July 1st *and the next two days are noted in the diary as being " miserably wet and foggy; deplorable weather for whaling, as we cannot see* 100 *yards from the ship. Such thick, foggy weather is very unusual in this country at this time of the year, and is very annoying."*

On June 3rd the ship was off the entrance to Pond's Bay, the favourite locality for catching whales. The bay, though, was full of ice, and there was no getting into it. Captain Gravill was much astonished at the unusual quantity of ice in this place and " at the amazing way the hummocks of ice have been piled upon each other." However, the diary optimistically remarks: " We are in good time. The whales seldom make their appearance in Pond's Bay before the 7th or 10th of this month."

A strong south-westerly wind cleared the bay of ice, and on July 7th the " Diana" entered this Mecca of the whalers in the wake of nine other whaling-ships (" Polynia," " Tay," " Ravenscraig," " Narwhale," " Wildfire," " Alexander," " Victor," " Retriever," and " Intrepid"), and followed by the " Windward." As the diary remarked, " Everything looking bright and cheery, with first-rate prospects for the whaling."

Alas! the very next morning the scene changed absolutely. An easterly wind sprang up, drove the ice back into the bay, and completely hemmed in the eleven whaling-ships there, severely nipping the " Narwhale" and " Alexander."

The following days were ones of disappointment and apprehension. On July 20th the diary reads: " The past fortnight has been a very dull and, at the same time, a very anxious one. Here we are, unable to stir, with a tremendous land-floe on one side of us and, on the other side, a body of ice extending as far as we can see from the mast-head; the wind blowing steadily from the East, bringing all the ice in the country down on us. All this at the height of the whaling season, when this bay is usually alive with fish, which, of course, cannot enter the bay at all now on account of the ice. Captain Gravill is utterly confounded at this unprecedented state of matters here. All on board are idle and depressed, and despair of ' getting a voyage' after all our labour to arrive at this ' promised land' of the whalers. What is *worse than all, should a strong South-East wind set in, the whole fleet would inevitably be crushed and 600 or more men turned adrift upon the ice with very poor prospects of relief from other ships, and no chance of saving their lives but by travelling over the ice and in their boats some hundreds of miles to the settlements in Exeter Sound and Cumberland Gulf. Truly our prospects of late have been bad enough, and, what is more, continue to be bad—so bad that I scarcely have heart to sit down to record such gloomy intelligence in my journal."*

Visits to other ships did not serve to lessen the feeling of gloom and apprehension. *"Took tea aboard the 'Polynia' (Mr. Van Wahershuit, surgeon). Captain Nicholl completely nonplussed by the present state of affairs. He never saw or heard of the like."* Again, *"Went aboard the 'Wildfire,' where Mr. Traill, student of Aberdeen University, kindly gave me some medicines I was out of. Captain Souter confesses that the present state of the bay is unprecedented, and that the fish must have gone past the bay in search of open water. He regards this season as a hopeless one for whaling and a most dangerous one for the ships."* These opinions evoke in the diary the prayer: *"God grant that the 'Diana,' an old ship of very small horse-power and with only some 30 tons of coal left in her bunkers, may be mercifully guided through these accumulating dangers and reach home again at last."*

A northerly wind started to blow on the evening of the 23rd. Slight movements of the ice between the 24th and the 27th led to the formation of various lanes and pools of water in the bay, and to the appearance of a few whales, with an occasional kill by some of the other ships. The diary for July 27th contains the curious statement, *"Multitudes of unicorns, the sea agitated by them as though a gale were blowing."* On the following day is an entry which sounds like a veritable *"tale of the sea."* It runs thus: *"One of the men from the 'Wildfire' tells us that the unicorns were so numerous round that ship that they were compelled to thrust their heads and horns vertically out of the water, so closely were they crowded together by the ice enclosing them. The men actually seized them by their horns and dragged them upon the ice. They lanced some sixty of them."*

The northerly wind continued to blow steadily, and on July 29th *the ice had been driven away from outside the bay, for the diary for that day states laconically, " No ice in sight in the offing."*

Monday, July 30th.—Commenced steaming directly after breakfast. Put the ship's head South and steamed across the bay, followed at intervals by the entire fleet. About 7 p.m. we were beyond the South point of Pond's Bay, to which we have now bid adieu after three weeks' inactivity and bitter disappointment. Such a disastrous and melancholy Pond's Bay fishing has not occurred within the memory of the oldest whaler.

In the evening the fleet made fast in a long line to the land-floe, the *Diana* being the most southerly ship in the line. All on board are glad to get away from Pond's Bay, and eager to try our fortunes in " fresh fields and pastures new."

The *Alexander* was hove down this morning to enable them to inspect the state of her port side, she having been badly nipped on July 10th. She is very much distorted, her port side being bent like the letter S, several of her beams broken, and one of her tanks burst.

Tuesday, July 31st.—Was up at 2.30 a.m. Three whales made their appearance close astern of us. Lowered two boats, but could not get near them on account of the great quantity of loose ice, which extends as far as the horizon.

At about 10 a.m. three fish were seen ahead of the ship. We sent two boats, and followed with the ship under canvas. George Clarke nearly got fast to a large fish, but the loose ice prevented him approaching near enough to her in time.

EDITORIAL NOTE.

The following day the captains of the whaling fleet evidently agreed it was useless, with the great quantity of ice about, to attempt to prosecute the whale-fishing any further. The season was nearly over, and the time was coming for the ships to get started on their homeward voyage. Practically the whole fleet returned to Pond's Bay on August 1st.

CHAPTER V

SEARCHING FOR A WAY OUT

EDITORIAL NOTE.

DURING the next fortnight or so the " Diana " and all the other ships of the whaling fleet, while keeping a lookout for whales, sought diligently for a way out amongst the ice-fields along the West coast of Baffin Bay. A few whales were seen now and again in the lanes of water, but the " Diana " failed to catch any.

During this period the diary is depressing reading :

August 2nd.—Everybody aboard down-hearted. There is such an immense quantity of ice in the country* that it is extremely probable we shall be unable to get South on this side. We may have to go back by our old route round by Melville Bay and the East side.

Sunday, August 5th.—There was no service to-day, as Captain Gravill is far from well.

Tuesday, August 7th.—Stood under canvas to the southward with all the fleet. Unable to get far South on account of the ice, which is jammed hard down on the land by the prevailing North-East wind.

Wednesday, August 8th.—All the ships in sight, standing off and on, ratching to and fro, killing time, unable to get to the South on account of the ice, or to get inshore after whales. The wind from the North-East is jamming the ice down on the coast. There is nothing to do, and no prospect of doing anything till the wind shifts and drives the ice down the country.

In the evening we spoke the *Intrepid*, and Captain Deuchars afterwards came on board. He reports that scurvy has broken out on board his ship, owing to the spoiling of their potatoes and the inferior quality of their meat.

* Whalers' term for the waters of Baffin Bay and Davis Straits.

The sun sets now at about 10 p.m., and the evenings are rapidly becoming darker and darker. A little snow fell to-day.

Thursday, August 9th.—Still dodging off and on. Weary work. The best part of the whaling season already over, and our precious time wasted inactively, with no chance of getting to the South until this detestable North-East wind has shifted. Such a season as this in Davis Straits has never been known.

The *Wildfire* has stood off to the East, intending to try and get South through the " middle ice " or along the East coast if possible.

We have nothing to do all day but watch the manœuvres of our fellow-whalers in distress as they ratch up and down. We rather think we are now off the opening of Pond's Bay.

Friday, August 10th.—Still standing on and off.

About midday a heavy fall of snow came on, with strong wind from the North-East, increasing during the afternoon to half a gale with a nasty sea   Rest of fleet dodging or laid to. Twelve ships in sight.

Such a sea is seldom seen in this country. Altogether, this season has been a very remarkable one.

Saturday, August 11th.—This morning cold, snowy, and cheerless; hardly any wind; a listless swell on the sea. The ships are idly standing off and on. Precious time is wasting slowly and heavily away, and there is no prospect of our getting further South or prosecuting the object of our voyage. The past week has been indescribably dull, gloomy, and cheerless. Everybody is in the blues. The men are talking of nothing else but the return home, despairing of doing any good during the remainder of our stay in this wretched country. Such a deplorable whaling season has never been known by any man on board. We are longing for the signal to bear up for home. Eleven ships in company.

Monday, August 13th.—Wind blowing very strongly from the South-West, driving masses of heavy ice upon us. With no further chance of getting to the southward along the West land we have stood out to the North-East, and have been driving in that direction all day. The weather is hazy, with showers of sleet and snow.

Tuesday, August 14th.—To-day has been deplorably wet and

miserable. There have been showers of hail and snow, with very thick weather all day, strong gales from the South, and the sea running very high.

Such weather at this time of the year in Davis Straits is altogether unprecedented. The captain and officers tell me they never experienced such gales and heavy seas here. Altogether the whaling season of 1866 has been one of the most remarkable for the complete subversion of wind, weather, seas, ice, climate, and bad fishing, that ever was heard of.

Thursday, August 16th.—Ship running before stiff breezes amongst a vast number of bergs and streams of heavy ice. The captain never remembers meeting with so many bergs in this part of Baffin Bay.

We are in company with three other ships, running North-East, rushing along at a racing speed, smashing through streams of ice, and shaving past an immense number of bergs. The weather is clear and exhilarating, and thoroughly enjoyed by myself and all on board.

But, this sort of work is not whale-fishing !

We trust to get across to the East coast somewhere about Duck Islands, then run South and get round the South end of the ice to Exeter Bay, where we trust to fall in with some fish.

EDITORIAL NOTE.

The following day the " Diana" sighted Cape York, and was " once more in the much-dreaded Melville Bay." To their extreme consternation, they found the whole area choked with icebergs and heavy floe ice—" and this in the middle of August !"

Here the " Diana" was joined by all the rest of the fleet, including the " Wildfire," whose lone attempt to get through the " middle ice" had been unsuccessful.

On August 18th the ships found that it was impossible to get any further East or South, so they turned wearily to the westward again, evidently not liking to remain any longer than was absolutely necessary in such a sinister and dangerous neighbourhood as Melville Bay.

Owing to the rough weather the " Diana" had pumped 30 tons of water into her tanks to act as ballast. The ship was now very short of coal, and so did not make use of her engine power for this return trip to Pond's Bay. The wind having dropped, the rest of the fleet left the " Diana " rolling like a log on the water with all possible sail set, yet making little or no progress. "We are some 45 miles to the South of Cape York, and are shaping our course, such as it is, direct across to Pond's Bay."

On August 22nd the " Diana " was in sight of Pond's Bay once again. There was no sign anywhere of the rest of the whaling fleet.

It was on this date that their position really began to look a serious one to them, and that the chances of their forcing a way through the ice were getting decidedly less. The diary for August 22nd put the position succinctly thus : " Altogether our position, alone, almost without coal, and with only some two months' provisions on board, the country full of heavy ice beyond the experience of any man in the fleet, is far from enviable. We are at the mercy of the winds entirely. A few stiff gales from the North-West would open up a passage. Should we not be so favoured, there is nothing for us but to meet our inevitable fate, a lingering death from cold and starvation, like men. All on board are beginning to look and talk seriously. Let us trust that a way of escape will be found for us. At present we have but two or three days' coal on board, so that the " Diana " is little better than a sailing vessel, and, as such, her chance of getting through some six or seven hundred miles of ice is very poor indeed."

Friday, *August 24th.*—Still dodging about, praying for a stiff breeze from the North-West to carry us and the ice down the country.

The mate thinks our chances of getting down this West side are very small, the country being as full of ice as it can hold. He offers to bet 2 pounds of tobacco against 1 pound that we have to make our way across to the East side again before we have the ghost of a chance of getting away home. This bet is a very heavy one, considering we have only 1 pound of tobacco apiece remaining on board.

The mate is a very experienced hand, having been eighteen years in this country, so his unfavourable opinion of the state of affairs sounds very ominous. We are afraid that when this thick foggy weather clears off the frost may set in keenly. Bay ice would form and freeze together all the loose ice, and thus settle all our doubts and anxieties very definitely indeed. Let's hope for the best, whatever befalls us.

Saturday, August 25th.—Dull, foggy, thick, miserable ! These words describe to-day most faithfully. Wind from the South-West. Ship ratching to the North-West and South-East, amongst streams of light ice, driving we hardly know whither. The compasses are out of order, fog and mist surround us, while snow and sleet continue to fall. All on board are dull and wretched, and are longing for a change in the wind and for clearer weather.

This is the last day of the most miserable fortnight I have experienced since we left Hull. No pleasure, no satisfaction; nothing but crosses and disappointments; everything dark and gloomy. Let's trust that the new week has better winds and weather in store for us.

Sunday, August 26th.—Early this morning the wind blew gently from the West, then veered round till at 4 a.m. it was blowing fresh from the North.

When we assembled at breakfast the ship was running South at some 8 or 9 knots speed amongst the loose floes. At tea-time we were brought up by a neck of very heavy ice which extended between a most tremendous land-floe and a large, loose floe.   This the ship failed to force her way through.

At 7 p.m., whilst smoking a pipe in the galley, the ominous cry was heard, " All hands on deck to get up provisions !"

The ship was fast in the nips, with heavy ice drifting down upon us with amazing speed, and the floes and loose pieces crushing and forcing each other upwards all around us. The ship was creaking, groaning, and straining under the fearful pressure, with a very thick and heavy mass of ice at her bows and several large bergs pressing upon the loose floe and jamming us as in a vice.

Four casks of beef, several casks of pork, two barrels of biscuits, twenty-seven tins of bouilli soup, and some cheeses, were got up, the boats cast loose ready for instant lowering, and the men then employed in stowing away their clothing in their bags.

The pressure upon the ship continued to increase, the ice being forced tightly against us by a very strong North wind. The captain and officers in the greatest anxiety; all on board gloomy and depressed, everybody expecting the ship to give way any moment.

I must confess it was with the greatest anxiety I watched these doleful preparations for leaving the ship, and noticed the disheartened bearing of the crew. I went below and dressed myself carefully in my warmest clothing, the gloomiest presentiments of my probable fate weighing upon my mind. " It's not much use taking such care of your crang, doctor," said the mate. " This sort of weather will soon finish us all !"

The captain also assured me that if the ship went, our chances of saving our lives at such a distance from other ships or settlements were not worth a rush. Truly the old man seemed utterly disheartened at our prospects.

However, I packed my bag, made up a small selection of medicines in a handkerchief, put some tobacco in my pocket, and returned to the deck.

You may depend upon it there was many a prayer put up to God for mercy as we paced slowly and silently to and fro, watching the dog-vanes to detect the slightest change or lull in the wind.

Most marvellous to relate, the wind *did* abate ! It chopped round to the westward, and blew directly off the land from the very quarter we so earnestly desired. The ice slacked off, the ship was relieved from the fearful pressure, and by midnight we considered ourselves out of danger. We went to our beds indescribably thankful for our deliverance and wondering at our narrow escape from such imminent peril. I am assured that a very little more pressure must have stove in the ship.

Monday, August 27th.—This morning the ice had slacked away, leaving us made fast to the land-floe. We are in a pool of water, but the bergs and loose ice outside us prevent us from getting out.

All day the wind has blown half a gale from the North-East, driving the loose ice and bergs South at great speed. There is a very strong current to the South along this coast.

The gale increased towards night, and two watches had to be called to warp the ship further into the land-floe and tow aside the masses of ice that kept coming down upon our starboard side and threatening to nip us a second time.

Tuesday, August 28th.—This morning all on board very much surprised to see a ship to the northward of us. We cannot make her out, and wonder who she can be, as we were the last ship to leave the North Water, the rest of the fleet having got away to the South-West before us.

There is nothing to be seen to the southward of us but a solid sheet of ice, without a perceptible hole or break in it. How we are to get down this West side, a distance of more than 500 miles, is more than we can tell. Our provisions are very scanty, and the captain already talks of putting all hands upon short commons. The mate and other officers tell me they see little or no chance of getting out of the country at all, either by the West side or East side, unless matters take a very speedy and wonderful change for the better. The country, as we have discovered, is full of ice. We have attempted to get through on the East side and failed. We are now trying the West side for the second time, and have failed to get further than Scott's Bay (where we are now made fast). All on board anxious and fearing the worst, which means having to winter here with only some two months' provisions on board, with no chance of subsisting upon the land or receiving assistance from other ships. It will take the most powerful steamers in the fleet all their time to get clear.

The ship to the North of us turns out to be the *Intrepid*. She has made two unsuccessful attempts to get into the hole of water in which we are made fast. We are having strong gales from the North-East, with very thick weather. The ship is driving along very fast with the pack to the southward.

Wednesday, August 29th.—Captain Deuchars of the *Intrepid* joined company with us in the afternoon, and came aboard after tea. He reports he has just come down from Melville Bay, where he was jammed for some days amongst very heavy ice 15 miles off Cape Melville. The country there is in a fearful state; nothing but solid floes of very heavy ice.

He found it impossible to get further to the East side, and so called all his ship's company aft and gave them their choice whether to remain in Melville Bay awaiting the chance of getting down the East side, or to return to the West side and attempt to get South in that direction. They decided to attempt the West side once more. From the reports of Captain Deuchars and his boat's crew, the state of the country is frightful and our chances of escape very small indeed. All on board dull and wretched, including myself.

Thursday, August 30th.—Ship dodging and ratching up a hole of water in company with the *Intrepid*.

All on board indescribably dull and wretched. We have been reckoning up our provisions to-day, and find we have about 2½ tons of biscuits, four casks of beef, some casks of pork, a little rice, oatmeal, and peas, and some two dozen tins of bouilli soup, which *may* have to last us till next July! In short, if we fail to make our escape from the country—and that very speedily—we have the sure and certain prospect of a lingering death from scurvy, cold, and hunger. Nor have we any chance of getting seals, bears, or other animals, as they all move off to the South during the winter months.

Both captains are extremely anxious and uneasy at our critical situation, whilst tales of horrible sufferings and deaths from starvation on board unfortunate whalers that have been beleaguered amongst the ice in these dreadful solitudes form the staple conversation amongst our crew.

Friday, August 31st.—After breakfast Captain Deuchars and Mr. Galloway came on board.

Captain Deuchars intends trying to get South as soon as the fog clears up, but the two ships will remain in company for mutual assistance and, if necessary, for mutual preservation as long as possible.

At two o'clock this afternoon we cast off from the floe and steamed after the *Intrepid*, but were unable to force our way through the first loose ice we encountered. After attempting for a couple of hours to make a passage, we steamed back to the land-floe and made fast to it in a small bight. Here we are lying now, waiting with no small anxiety for a strong

West wind to carry off the ice and open up a passage for us down the country.

To-night is calm, cloudy, and still. Aurora Borealis just visible, glaring like a blood-red streak beneath a dark bank of clouds.

The *Intrepid* made fast amongst the loose floe about a mile to the South of us, unable to get any further. Captain Deuchars has assured Captain Gravill that he will not leave us alone in this dangerous position, but will stand by us as long as possible.

Saturday, September 1st.—At 11.30 a.m. the *Intrepid* got up steam.

Whilst the *Diana's* boilers were heating, all hands were employed warping the ship along the edge of the floe towards the opening where we were foiled yesterday and where the ice is beginning now to slack off.

We got up steam soon after 1 p.m., but the ice began to run together again, so we returned to our old quarters. In a short time the ice slacked once more, and again we attempted to force a passage, but without success. A third time we returned to the charge, but were compelled to desist on account of the ice closing rapidly. We returned to the edge of the land-floe, afterwards shifting to our old berth in the small bight.

The gallant and generous captain of the *Intrepid* was more fortunate. He managed to force his way through the loose floes, and evidently got into clear water, for he was seen from the mast-head to steam away to the South with great rapidity. By tea-time only his topsail yards could be distinguished with the long glass.

The curses of our crew, as they saw the ship which had promised faithfully to stand by us basely deserting us at the first chance, were not loud but deep.

Our last chance of succour or of safety has gone now, and we have nothing left to depend upon but the merciful providence of God. This day's steaming has nearly exhausted our coals, and the carpenter has been busy cutting up a spare topmast spar for fuel for the engines. The " shakes " also are condemned to be burnt. This shows the extremity to which we are reduced now for firing.

The heartless conduct of the captain of the *Intrepid*, with his 60 h.p. engines and 90 tons of coal on board, is only to be explained by . . .

Editorial Note.

I think it best not to reproduce any more of the intensely bitter remarks recorded in the diary concerning Captain Deuchars. To the unfortunate and despairing men in the " Diana," the " Intrepid's " action must have appeared the acme of human callousness.

I have some recollection of having been told, or of having read, many years ago, that Captain Deuchars asserted he was fully convinced of the " Diana's " ability to get out of the ice without any assistance from him, and that he was under the impression that she had successfully got through the only portion of the pack that was at all likely to hold her up.—C. E. S. H.

To-night the wind has chopped round to the North-East, the most unfavourable quarter, as it will bring down the ice upon us and jam us up tight.

There are only some 6 or 7 miles of loose and broken-up floe between us and the clear water to the southward. This stretch of ice had slacked off into lanes and channels, with a few necks of ice here and there, but just enough to baffle our miserable 30 h.p. Through this, to him, trifling obstacle Captain Deuchars easily could have lent us a friendly tow, but his promises of assistance and solemn assertions that he would not run away from us were all forgotten. . . .

(Here follows another bitter outburst.)

This is the first of September. Every day that passes over our heads only serves to increase our anxiety by hastening the approach of winter, and diminishing by one day our chances of escape.

I have just been down into the half-deck, and found the harpooners and men in very low spirits, bitterly reviling the inhuman conduct of Captain Deuchars, who " wasn't going to see us stuck behind a point of ice without giving us a pull out."

The officers assure me that if he had only steamed a little

nearer towards us, and broken the small point of ice that stopped us, the rest of the floe was so loose and so broken up into lanes and channels that they believe we could have made our way through it without any further assistance from the *Intrepid*.

To-night the wind is blowing from the North-East, and the ice has closed all around us, leaving us in a small hole of water.

Sunday, September 2nd.—Went to bed last night at eleven o'clock, and woke at, or soon after, midnight—very contrary to my usual habits—with a strange presentiment of danger upon my mind. A few minutes afterwards Mr. Clarke, the mate, came below and told the captain that the point of the floe to which we trusted for shelter had broken off, and that the ice was coming down upon us very fast, before a strong gale from the North-East.

In a very few minutes the ship was jammed tight and in the nips, or, in other words, exposed to the full force and pressure of miles and miles of heavy floes driving before the wind.

I rose instantly and dressed myself carefully, as all hands were called to get out the boats.

A scene of terrible earnestness then ensued—men working against time for the chance of saving their lives. The heavy boats were lowered and dragged convulsively along the floe to which we were made fast. Other men endeavoured, without success, to unship the rudder, which was jammed by the ice, and threatened to tear away the stern post or spring some of the planks attached to the post.

At the first signal of the point of the floe giving way the watch on deck had endeavoured to get the ship unmoored, intending to lay her behind another point of ice. This they were prevented from doing by the sudden descent of the broken floe upon the ship.

Meanwhile the ship lay groaning and straining under the frightful pressure, which was principally upon her bows and stern. We attempted to turn her stern into a crack in the floe, but the warps broke.

The massive fragments of ice were forced one upon the other, and piled up in heaps around us. The wind roared through the rigging, and the blinding snow flew into our faces as we struggled at the windlasses or at the tackles of the boats.

Men worked with the energy of despair, with their hearts in their mouths, and a horrible death from suffering and cold and starvation before their eyes.

Having done what little we could for the ship, we proceeded to pack our clothing in our bags and stow away guns, ammunition, kettles, firewood, sails, etc., into the boats as they lay on the ice. We got the remainder of our provisions on deck in readiness for lowering on the floe if the ship was stove in. Then, having done all that was in our power, we walked the decks, watching the movements of the heavy masses of ice as they drove one over the other, " heaps upon heaps, heaps upon heaps," or eyed the dog-vanes with intense anxiety to detect the slightest lull in the wind.

You may depend upon it, many an earnest prayer ascended from that helpless and despairing ship's company. Basely forsaken by our fellow-men, our sole dependence was upon God. Bitterly did we reflect upon the cruelty of Captain Deuchars in leaving us alone to perish.

But a greater than he watched over and guarded us during this gloomy and dreadful night. The gale gradually died down, the ice slacked off us a little, the ship was relieved from the pressure, and at 3 a.m. the watch was set, and the rest of the crew sent below.

I lay down in my bunk at 4 a.m. with my clothes and boots on, but you may be sure I did not sleep much. The continual grinding of the ice against the ship's side made me start from my uneasy slumbers in the greatest apprehension.

Rose at 6 a.m., and found the gale had nearly died away. The atmosphere was charged with fog and mist, which, clearing partially away as the day advanced, revealed the extent of our danger.

All around us, as far as the eye could see, the floes were lying piled one upon the other. The ice was broken up into huge masses 6 or 7 feet in thickness, which were forced one upon the other in tremendous ridges. This was so more especially at the very point to which we had attempted to move the ship when the floe gave way ahead of us. Had we succeeded in warping the ship to this spot, she would inevitably have been crushed flat, so fearfully had the ice been driven up just there.

We had the usual Divine Service in the cabin in the morning; a very affecting time. We met together as men may be supposed to meet who have been snatched from the jaws of death. The captain gave out this hymn:

> " Give to the winds thy fears;
>   Hope and be undismayed.
> God hears thy sighs and counts thy tears;
>   God shall lift up thy head.
>
> " Through waves and clouds and storms
>   He gently clears thy way.
> Wait thou His time, so shall this night
>   Soon end in joyous day."

Then the captain read a sermon from the text, " What I say unto you I say unto all, Watch." In conclusion he offered up a most affecting prayer of gratitude to the Almighty for our wonderful deliverance, and implored His protection and guidance during the coming week.

I retired to bed at 1 a.m., feeling thankful to God for preserving one so unworthy as myself amidst such perils. I have thought a great deal about home of late, and am very glad that my relatives and friends know nothing of the dangers to which I and all on board are exposed. The thought often crosses my mind: " I wonder if our people in England are thinking of us poor fellows." I doubt not we are often borne in mind. You may depend upon it that thoughts of wives and children, parents and relatives, are seldom absent from the minds of all on board the *Diana*. I tell you that many a man aboard the *Diana* of Hull has an aching and anxious heart in his bosom.

Monday, September 3rd.—This morning at four o'clock the ominous cry of " All hands !" resounded through the ship. However, this time it was for the purpose of taking in the boats, as the ice had begun to slack off, and a lane of water towards the southward was opening out directly in front of the ship's bows.

It took some time to get the boats, full of the heavy lines, etc., dragged back over the ice and hoisted again into their old places on the davits. However, the ice began to close again very rapidly, so we did not attempt to move the ship.

The morning was very cold and frosty. It had frozen so keenly during the night that all holes and lanes of water were covered with bay ice (young ice) nearly an inch thick. This was a very serious matter, as the loose ice might freeze up altogether and compel us to winter just where we are lying, exposed to every gale and liable to be crushed by any movements of the tremendous floe pieces which surround us on all sides.

The captain called the harpooners aft, and had a short consultation with them as to the gloomy state of our prospects. He then summoned all hands, and told us that we must go at once upon short allowance. He said it was extremely uncertain whether we could get out of the country or not this year, and very probably we should be compelled to winter in this frightful region. He calculated our two months' stock of provisions might be made to hold out until next May. He asked any men who had saved any biscuits or other food to bring these supplies aft for the general stock, the men to receive it back again in the event of our getting clear. He said that all the ship's provisions and stores would be locked up, and the keys given to the inspectioneer (the principal harpooner), who would weigh and distribute the stores to the ship's company. The captain added that he and his officers in the cabin would fare the same as the men and boys.

To this arrangement all hands agreed, and proceeded to bring aft their spare food, which amounted altogether to over 13 hundredweights.

Provisions are to be dealt out at the rate of 3 pounds of biscuits per week to all on board, with ¾ pound of salt meat daily. Potatoes, rice, flour, oatmeal, peas—in short, everything aboard ship—to be doled out with strict impartiality amongst the ship's company. The key of the spirit room was to be given to the inspectioneer.

All this ominous and discouraging (yet very necessary) business passed off satisfactorily. We consider ourselves particularly fortunate in having an abundance of tea, coffee, and sugar on board, but our tobacco is now nearly exhausted.

We next sank the deep sea lead line, with hooks attached and baited with pork, hoping to catch some cod-fish, but were unsuccessful. The depth of water was 95 fathoms.

Immediately after breakfast one of the boats was lowered and a party of nineteen men with three rifles, some flinching knives, and other instruments, made up to go upon an expedition across the ice to where there was a dead whale. The intention was to load the boat with the whale-skin (" muck tuck ") as an addition to our small stock of provisions.

We set off in cheerful and happy mood.

It was a gloriously clear and frosty morning, with a burning sun glaring down upon us from a cloudless sky. The lofty range of mountains which fringe the coast of this dismal region were glittering and flashing in the blue heavens, whilst the ranks of icebergs aground on the shallows all around us seemed transformed into dazzling rocks and thrones of transparent crystals.

We had to drag the boat for some distance, launching her across cracks and holes in the ice, and scrambling over her pell-mell till we came to a large hole of water, across which we pulled. It was difficult to force the boat through the bay ice, which was extraordinarily thick and tenacious, considering it was the result of only one night's frost.

Leaving our boat drawn up upon the ice at the further end of the hole, we proceeded on foot towards the bergs near which the whale lay. We had some difficult, not to say dangerous, leaps across the cracks and holes in the ice, which consisted of broken-up fragments piled up in heaps and masses and lofty ridges by the tremendous pressure of yesterday.

We got to the largest of the bergs at last and climbed to the top, which was much higher than our mast-head. From this elevation we could see the whale by means of a telescope, and found the carcase to be at a very much greater distance from the big berg than we had expected.

On we went. But now we came to broad lanes of water, which we had to ferry across upon flat pieces of ice, standing as close together and as still as possible whilst two or three of the hands pushed and paddled us over with the boathook and whaling spades. Sometimes we had to cross in two or three parties. On one occasion the fragment of ice sank under our weight until the water was half-way up to our knees. Such passages could only be effected by the greatest nicety, steadiness, and tact, and were in the highest degree dangerous and ticklish experiments.

After crossing three or four lanes of water in this manner, and finding ourselves still at a great distance from the whale and our advance opposed by a very broad lane of water, and finding, moreover, that the ice was opening in all directions, we called a council and resolved to return to the ship immediately.

We did not come to this decision a moment too soon. The ice continued to open up, and the lanes and streams of water became broader and broader and more and more perilous. We crossed two or three in safety, but found one stream had widened out so considerably as to form a formidable passage. The only available piece of ice for crossing upon was the heavy floe fragment that had sunk so much under us on our outward journey.

However, a party of seven crossed upon it in safety, and one of their number piloted the raft back to our side of the stream. Just then we saw that the ship's fore-topgallant sail had been loosened as a signal for our immediate return. So we embarked upon our dubious piece of ice without stopping to search further for any other.

Standing close together, motionless as statues, we pushed off, and had reached the middle of the stream when the cry was raised that the ice we stood upon was sinking. Two or three of the lads rushed to one side of the bit of ice, which lurched over and started to sink rapidly under our weight. "Swim for your lives!" cried the mate as he leaped into the water.

This seemed unwise advice, for we were so crowded together as to impede each other's movements, whilst those who could not swim would certainly cling to the swimmers and drag half of us down with them.

However, the men remained very cool and collected. One

after another they left the ice as it gradually sank. I remained till the water rose to my middle, not having been able before to get clear of the wreck without embarrassing the movements of the other men swimming for their lives.

At last I saw a chance and struck out for the floe, heavily encumbered as I 'was with pea-jacket, sea-boots, guernsey, bullets, powder, etc. Fortunately, all the other men had left their jackets in the boat or aboard the ship, as the sun was so hot.

I reached the edge of the floe and tried to drag myself up the steep, slippery wall of ice, the floe being several feet thick. The strong current, though, drew my legs under the ice, and I should never have extricated myself had not the second mate, more fortunate, succeeded in getting on to the floe. He drew another man on to the ice, and then a third, to whom I sang out, and was pulled on to the floe in my turn. Last of all we dragged out the cooper.

Meanwhile, we had left five men behind us upon the raft, which, lightened of its load, righted itself and fortunately did not turn over with these poor fellows on it. They ferried themselves across and joined the first detachment, who had stood watching us without having it in their power to render us the slightest assistance.

Two out of the seven men who took to the water swam to the further side of the stream, leaving only five of us still to cross. And oh ! how bitterly cold it was as we shivered on the floe, emptying the water from our boots and wringing out our clothing, whilst two lads slowly and cautiously paddled the same heavy fragment of ice across to our rescue.

Upon this uncertain and dangerous vehicle we were mercifully favoured to cross in two detachments. Had the ice again sunk under us, we were too cold, stiff, and weak, and too heavily encumbered with our soaked clothes, to have made our escape a second time by swimming.

Most marvellous to relate, three out of the five who had remained upon the ice when it was going down and had kept their balance as the ice righted (a most difficult thing to do) were totally unable to swim, whilst the fourth was a little lad and but an indifferent swimmer. Had these poor fellows left their frail support they must inevitably have been drowned. So close together were we upon the raft when the catastrophe occurred that some of us certainly would have been clutched hold of and gone to the bottom with them. My heart was filled with wonder and amazement and, let me hope, fervent gratitude for my preservation from such great danger.

The cooper got into the water a second time whilst attempting to hold the raft steady, and it was with great difficulty we dragged him up the edge of the floe, the current ran so strong.

We had no time for congratulations, but had to hurry on towards the great berg. Here again we had the greatest difficulty in crossing another lane of water. The ice was opening and the lane widening very rapidly, and the raft of ice was a very small one. Only one man could use it at once, but " Cross, cross for your lives," was the cry, and, thanks be to God, we got safely over.

From the iceberg to the boat was also a dangerous journey, especially to us poor shivering, dripping, freezing fellows. We were very weak and very far gone, weighed down with our heavy wet clothes, and only enabled by the energy of despair and love of life to leap across the chasms and holes. In places we actually had to run over bay ice only formed a few hours previously, and yet were supported and preserved by the same Providence that had rescued us from the water.

At last, nearly exhausted, we reached the boat, broached the biscuits and rum, and had a dram each. We launched the boat and pulled as hard as we could for the ship, those who had got wet bending at the oars to keep warmth and life in them.

The ship had her fore and aft canvas set, and was standing away to the southward. So inconceivably rapidly had the ice opened that we found a broad expanse of water all the way to the ship, except at one point where two floes were closing, and where we narrowly escaped getting the boat crushed. We forced her through the crack only just in time.

We got alongside the ship at 2 p.m., changed, dined, and then for the first time had time to discuss our wonderful escape and ponder upon the perils of our return journey. All the ship's company are astonished at our escape.

The remainder of the day was bright and clear and freezing

very hard. There is a light wind off the land, and the ice is opening both North and South of us. Towards midnight a swell set in, and we are earnestly hoping that the ice will be so much loosened and broken up as to admit of our departure to-morrow. Ship made fast to a floe for the night.

Tuesday, September 4th.—At breakfast-time the weather was thick and foggy, with the barometer falling rapidly. The captain tells me this presages a gale of wind. God grant it may not come from the North-East, for it would place us again in the greatest peril.

This anxiety is very hard to bear. We are praying for a breeze off the land to liberate us.

This morning we attempted to warp the ship through one of the floes, but the weather is so thick we cannot see where we are going, so returned to our old berth at the floe edge.

The wind is very light, and flies about the East and North-East. It has been snowing slightly, and the weather is very thick and gloomy, but not so gloomy as our hearts are at this moment. We feel ourselves so helpless and know ourselves to be in the greatest jeopardy. We cannot tell what an hour may bring forth, the movements of the winds and ice in this country are so rapid and so uncertain.

The men keep tolerably cheerful, and are busily discussing to-night the practicability of passing the winter in Pond's Bay, if spared to escape from this dreadful bight and unable to find our way South. The mate, a sensible, experienced man, tells me he hardly dares hope to get the ship home this year, nor can he see how we can get through the long winter upon such a small stock of provisions.

To-day we have caught a few mallies (Fulmar Petrels) with hooks, and are carefully preserving them as food. Ere long, though, every bird and beast and living thing in the country will go South before the winter overtakes them.

11.30 *p.m.*—The wind is blowing strongly *from the North-East.* O God! be merciful to us and enable us to live through this night. The ship is made fast to a light floe. Snow falling heavily, the night dark, wild, and gloomy. We cannot measure our lives just now by weeks and days, but by *hours and minutes.*

Wednesday, September 5th.—The gale blew very hard all last night, so hard that we had to have three warps out to hold the ship to the floe. Fortunately for us, the ice around us is comparatively light and rotten, so that, ordinarily speaking, we are pretty safe so long as the ice does not drive down upon us in too great a body.

We are trusting that this gale may drive the ice further down the country, and that the swell may break up the heavy floes amongst which we are laid; then that a wind may blow off the land and carry us out into the North Water in safety. Such are our hopes and plans, but we are in the hands of One who knows better what is for our advantage than we do ourselves. We can safely cast all our cares upon Him.

This morning I was busy serving out stores to the crew, this afternoon casting bullets, cleaning my rifle, and repacking my clothes, medicines, etc., " setting my house in order," in instant readiness for any emergency.

11.30 *p.m.*—Wind much abated, but still blowing very fresh from the North-East. We all feel much easier in our minds at the prospect of getting out of this bight when the gale dies out and the swell breaks up the floes.

ALONG THE EDGE OF THE LAND FLOE

CHAPTER VI

LAST DESPERATE EFFORTS TO ESCAPE

Thursday, September 6th.—The gale has now died out, and there is a considerable swell which, alas ! does not affect these ice-floes, so tightly are they held together by the bergs.

At dinner-time the wind moved round to the South-West, the very quarter from which we have so long and anxiously awaited a breeze. This should carry the loose ice out to sea and liberate us.

Worked all the afternoon at the capstan bars, assisting in turning the ship round so that we could set canvas directly we had wind enough from the land. We had a great deal of difficulty in shifting the ship's position, as the ice was closing upon us. After some hours of hauling, pulling, heaving, and cutting away projecting points of ice, we got her slewed round with her head to the North-East.

Nearly all the mallies have departed to the southward.

Friday, September 7th.—The wind continued from the South-West, but very light—" No heart in it," as the men say. We have every stitch of canvas set, trusting that this light wind may increase into a breeze and carry us out of this dangerous place. But patience, patience; we shall make our escape, let's hope, in good time, and find our way to the East side, where, if matters are as we expect, we hope to find plenty of open water and a clear way down the country.

Only three mallies flew round us to-day. I shot at and wounded one. Also wounded a large burgie, which got away, much to our chagrin, for in our present half-famished condition even a seagull is a great acquisition to our dinner.

10 *p.m.*—There is hardly a breath of air stirring. What little wind there is is from the *North-East!* God grant we may be spared another gale from that quarter. We are living

on from day to day, hoping and fearing and desponding, at times well-nigh despairing, so closely are we hemmed in with heavy floes and chains of bergs. This has been the longest and most anxious week I think I have ever lived.

Saturday, September 8th.—This morning was calm and still.

I have been talking about our prospects to the captain. He is afraid that when we do get into the North Water (which is the body of water that keeps clear between the East and West ice-fields) we shall meet with our greatest difficulties. As we all know, the country is full of ice, and he fears we shall never be able to struggle through it into the East Water unless the weather continues mild with strong South-West winds. The frost has set in; bay ice forms rapidly and soon binds all the loose ice together into an impenetrable floe unless kept from forming by a swell or breeze of wind. He hopes we may be able to find some crack or opening through the East ice into the East Water. If unsuccessful, our only alternatives are either to winter in the country or *take the middle ice and drift South in the pack*—i.e., ramming the ship amongst the heavy floating ice and drift with it down the Straits into the Atlantic.

This is a most hazardous and perilous adventure during this season of the year, when strong gales are liable to set in. These would drive the ice down upon the ship and crush her, without giving her the slightest chance of avoiding her fate as she lay frozen and entangled in the midst of hundreds of miles of ice. Neither she nor a soul on board would ever be heard of again. Several ships that have been compelled to risk this dreadful hazard have been lost with all on board.

The captain tells me that the climate and the state of this country has altered entirely. For the last three years the most powerful steamers have had the greatest difficulty in making their escape from the ice with which the country has been blocked up, whilst the bay ice has begun to form much earlier than usual.

10 *p.m.*—A strong breeze from the South-West. The ice moving about a good deal. Night clear and frosty. Spars and rigging glittering in the starlight and coated with frost,

which shines like silver. We all entertain the most sanguine hopes of being in open water to-morrow.

Sunday, September 9th.—Shortly before 5 a.m. the startling cry of " All hands !"—a cry that brings every man's heart into his mouth and makes him spring from his berth in apprehension—resounded through the ship. However, this time it was for the purpose of attempting to warp the ship into open water, as the ice was opening ahead of us. For a short time we got her along cheerily enough, but the ice closed again and we were brought to a standstill.

In a short time the ice rallied a little, and then commenced a scene of hard unflagging exertion. The capstan bars were doubly and trebly manned, the men tugging and straining as if for dear life to drag heavy floe pieces on one side or force the ship through narrow openings in the ice. Others were busy backing and filling the sails, hauling the yards to and fro, running the jib and fore-topmast staysail up and down as required, and filling and brailing up the mizen spenser. Other hands on the ice were fixing ice anchors or cutting away the ice from before the ship's bows, and in other ways aiding her slow and painful progress. Every soul on board was working thus with might and main except the cook, half-deck boy, and the steward, who were busy preparing our breakfasts.

Thus inch by inch we fought our way, materially assisted by a stiff breeze from the South-West. The ice, though, was so closely jammed together and held fast by a chain of bergs outside the pack that we only advanced by the most strenuous and unremitting efforts. At 8 a.m. we were finally brought up by a barrier of broad floe pieces, to which we made fast, sending all hands except the watch to breakfast.

To-day we consider ourselves particularly fortunate in receiving, each of us, ½ pound of flour, which is made up into two cakes apiece. One of these cakes and a wretched little scrap of very inferior Irish salt beef formed what I consider an unusually sumptuous breakfast.

After breakfast the ice slacked again, and we succeeded in warping the ship considerably nearer a lane of water which we think will lead us into the open sea without much further trouble. We had uncommonly hard work, as the ice closed

IN BAFFIN BAY

LOON SHOOTING

CAPE SEARLE FROM THE S.E AS SEEN FROM 12 MILES DISTANCE

Sketches from the Doctor's Diary, referred to on pages 26, 42 and 83.

NARWHAL, WITH HORN.

TATALATA

MEDUK.

WHALES' FOOD
(CLIO AUSTRALIS)

ON THE ICE FLOE

NARWHAL OR UNICORN
WITHOUT HORN

Sketches from the Doctor's Diary, referred to on pages 27, 28, 36 and 39.

again rapidly, so that at 11 a.m. we were compelled to knock off and make fast, to await the slacking of the ice.

3 *p.m.*—After another desperate struggle we forced our way into a lane of clear water, and are now running at 8 or 9 knots before a stiff breeze, passing a number of gigantic icebergs aground on those treacherous " Hecla and Griper Banks." We have had a very severe fight this afternoon to work the ship out of the floes. Thanks be to God, we have succeeded at last.

I cannot describe what an anxious time it has been to all of us whilst fighting our way through the ice. The ship is spinning along now at a great speed, laid over on her broadside by the force of the breeze. We only have to weather the bergs and force our way through a lot of loose ice and then we shall be in open water. I feel indescribably thankful and, I trust, grateful for this merciful escape from such a dangerous bight, which nearly proved fatal to the ship on two occasions.

4 *p.m.*—We had the usual afternoon service in the cabin. The captain commenced by giving out the 287th hymn. This he prefaced by saying that when on the wreck of the *William Ward* with his ship's company, after being six days exposed without shelter and with no probability of saving their lives, he had retired to his stateroom and had just read the first two lines of this hymn when the cry was raised that a ship was in sight. He therefore selected this hymn as suitable to our providential deliverance from the ice this afternoon.

> " Omnipresent God, whose aid
> No one ever asked in vain,
> Be Thou this night about my bed,
> Every evil thought restrain.
> Lay Thy hand upon my soul,
> God of my unguarded hours;
> All my enemies control—
> Hell and earth and Nature's powers."

The captain then read a sermon on the text, " O that thou hadst hearkened to My commandments! then had thy peace been as a river, and thy righteousness as the waves of the sea." He concluded with a fervent prayer of thanksgiving to God for delivering us from our besetments in the bight of Scott's

Bay, and implored His guidance and protection during our perilous passage through the middle ice to the East side.

All this evening we have been close hauled upon a stiff breeze from the South-West, with a considerable swell on the sea. We have passed streams and detached fragments of heavy ice, whilst directly ahead of us on the horizon is the ominous blink which indicates the position of the body of ice through which we must pass to gain the East water.

The captain shakes his head and says he doesn't like the look of the blink, and evidently thinks we shall have great difficulty in getting through.

We are about to attempt this dangerous adventure, being abreast of Black Hook, with 270 miles to run from land to land, some hundred of which, more or less, will be covered with heavy ice. Fortunately, this South-West wind is greatly in our favour, as it will open up the ice and possibly enable us to find or force a passage. But woe be unto us if a North-East gale overtakes us whilst entangled amidst the pack !

Whoever reads this can have no idea of the wonderful relief of mind we all experience at having effected our escape from Scott's Bay. For the last fortnight we have been face to face with death, never knowing for six hours at a time whether or not we should lose our ship; retiring at night hoping, fearing, and doubting, uncertain whether the morrow's sun might or might not find us homeless and helpless among the floes, exposed to the fury of the gale and the terrible severity of an Arctic climate. " I shall sleep to-night, doctor," said one of the officers to me this afternoon, " and it will be my first sleep worth mentioning for a fortnight. I never dared close my eyes whilst we were amongst that ice." And this man had spent his whole life from boyhood in the whale-fishing.

Another officer assures me that had we succeeded in warping the ship's stern *only three or four yards* during the gale last Sunday she would certainly have gone. The edges of the two floes met just clear of her rudder, and had her quarters been caught between them they would have been crushed flat. What wondrous goodness and mercy and compassion of our heavenly Father thus to thwart our poor schemes of safety, and turn what we considered at the time a great misfortune into the only means of saving our ship! It was, indeed, a practical illustration of the text, " *Be still*, and know that I am God."

10 *p.m.*—A dark, cloudy night. Ship driving before a gale of wind, and the seas breaking over her bows. We are rushing along through the darkness towards the middle ice, with masses of heavy washed ice, bergs, etc., looming occasionally through the gloom. We must trust implicitly in the guiding and protecting care of the Almighty for our safety through the long starless Arctic night, which to Him " shineth as the day."

Monday, September 10th.—Strong breezes all day from the South-West and hazy weather.

In the morning we attempted to get to the South-East, but were compelled to turn back by reason of the prodigious quantity of heavy floes and sheets of ice which we encountered.

We next tried to get down to the South-West, but were baffled again by the ice. The country is full of it, and the captain entertains the gravest doubts as to our being able to get away this year.

In the afternoon we stood away to the North-East, ratching in and out amongst streams and floes of heavy ice. Probably we shall have to go a long way North before we get a chance of crossing into the East Water. Wind still blowing strong from the South-West, which is a great mercy, as it will loosen and open the ice for us.

Tuesday, September 11th.—All this morning the ship has been winding in and out, and doubling amongst streams and patches of broken ice, most of it very heavy. We have been mercifully favoured with a continuance of strong breezes from the South-West, without which we should not have been able to get so far along as we are now. This breeze has separated and scattered the ice, and opened up a passage for us in a most marvellous manner. All the same, we have been embarrassed with so much ice that we have made comparatively little Easting and a good deal of Northing. The blink in the sky shows that the great body of ice is to the South-East of us, whilst the dark appearance of the horizon indicates water to the North-East, which is the course we are attempting to follow as well as the packs and patches of ice will permit.

We are raising steam in our anxiety to do everything we can to get across to the East Water as soon as possible, whilst the ice is slacked off. We are all excited, anxious, and full of hopes and fears. God grant that we may get safely through. We have had to head so much to the northward that we expect to make the land somewhere about Duck Island in Melville Bay, instead of coming out at Black Hook as we were expecting to do.

7 *p.m.*—Just now we are coming to a barrier of ice which separates us from open water beyond. The captain has sung out from the crow's-nest, "Fire up! *We must get through!* Give her all the steam you can." The second mate is issuing his orders to the two men at the wheel in loud, excited tones, " Steady!" " Hard up!" " Steady!" while the men grouped on the forecastle are eyeing the broad body of ice ahead of us with anxious, troubled countenances. We all feel that *now* is the critical time.

The ship is now thumping and battering amongst the ice as though she would smash her bows in.

8.30 *p.m.*—Happily we succeeded in forcing our way through the opposing ice, and also through a second barrier of loose, heavy floe ice. We drove the ship along at full speed till half-past eight, when darkness fell upon us, so that we could not see our way amongst the floes. We have made fast for the night to a floe that lay right across our course. Both engine fires are banked up and steam at hand.

The captain has been at the mast-head nearly all day, and, as may be supposed, is very anxious and uneasy. He is doing the best he can with his ship, putting all his trust in Him to whom he has been accustomed to look for strength and succour during fifty years at sea, mostly spent in the whale-fishing.

Wednesday, September 12th.—We cast off from the floe at half-past three this morning, and commenced steaming to the South-East under all possible steam and canvas. As our coals are as nearly as possible exhausted, we are feeding the engine fires with the " shakes " (staves for casks). This will show the extremity to which we are reduced for fuel. Mixed with a little coal these staves answer very well, but, as may be supposed, are a very expensive kind of firewood.

12.30 *p.m.*—Have been running and steaming along broad lanes of water formed by the breaking across of what probably was a solid mass of heavy ice before the late gales and swell. We are approaching what the captain and mate consider to be an impenetrable barrier of heavy ice extending between the floes and right across our course. If we cannot find or force a way through it, we must bear up for the northward and go round it if possible.

2 *p.m.*—We were unable to get through the heavy ice, and are now standing dead to the northward, intending to get round the end of the pack if possible.

We find by observation at midday that we are 150 miles from Scott's Bay, and are, therefore, about half-way across Baffin Bay. We were compelled to run so far to the North yesterday, and have gone over so much extra ground in manœuvring amongst the floes, that we have not made nearly so much Easting as we hoped and expected.

9.30 *p.m.*—Hardly can I find heart to sit down to this journal.

At five o'clock this evening we were brought up by a tremendous floe of very heavy ice, which extends as far as the glass can range from the mast-head, completely baffling all our attempts to get to the East side. We dare not attempt to go North into Melville Bay. We tried to get South before this attempt of ours to cross to the East Water. The only alternative left us is *to return to the West side,* again running the gauntlet through the dangers and embarrassments which we have risked to-day and yesterday.

To attempt to describe the misery and despair that now well-nigh overwhelms us is impossible. Our poor old captain is quite done up. He fairly melted to tears when he came down from the crow's-nest. The mate, as stout-hearted and sensible a man as I ever met with, and who has spent eighteen years in the whale-fishing, was completely overcome, and wept tears of anguish at the tea-table. I have noticed several of our most experienced men and officers wiping the tears from their cheeks, whilst the Shetland lads are completely down-hearted.

Truly our situation is most desperate. We are 150 miles from the nearest land, expecting North-East gales, and with not the remotest hopes of saving our lives if the ship is lost. If ever we felt the need of the care, guidance, and merciful compassion of God, it is at this moment. O God, have pity upon us; spare us in Thine infinite mercy. Thou art able to deliver us out of these perils.

Our coals are nearly all gone, and we have burnt a good many of our shakes and the remainder of the topmast spar. We are laid now amongst heavy ice at the edge of the pack, with engine fires banked up and orders given to have steam ready for the return passage at two o'clock to-morrow morning.

Some unicorns rose near us at 8 p.m. A boat was sent away after them, not for the sake of their horns, valuable as they are, nor their blubber, but for their flesh as food for ourselves. The young men and lads are looking weak and thin already upon their short allowance. How some of them will get through the winter, if we are spared to get the ship back in safety to the West land and have to winter there, I cannot tell. I dare not think of the misery we should be compelled to endure from want of food and firing.

Death seems close at hand; stares us in the face on all sides. We know not how soon we may be overwhelmed by the ice, and called upon to meet our fate from cold and exposure upon the floes. We may none of us be living by this time next week. O God, have mercy upon us all!

Thursday, September 13th.—Cast off the ship at 2 a.m. So intensely hard was the frost last night that the young ice formed a serious obstacle, and delayed us for an hour before we could get away from the floe to which we were made fast. Had we not had steam power to assist us, I am assured we should have been frozen up just where we lay.

Rose from my berth at 3 a.m. and went on deck. The cold was very severe. The rising sun cast a glow and flush of amber, green, gold, and crimson over the entire heavens long before he made his appearance above the horizon.

Whilst on deck soon after three o'clock, we were all very much astonished to see a whale rise several times not far from the ship. Dejection and despair now gave way to excitement and hope, so instantaneously did the prospect of getting a fish drive away all thoughts of our own unhappy position. However, the whale disappeared.

The ship is steaming to the northward amongst heavy rank ice, the captain having determined to run as far up the North Water as he judged safe and expedient, and again attempt a passage round or through the floes to the East side. He has been in much better spirits to-day than could have been expected after our bitter disappointment of last night. The men are more cheerful. Hope is reviving again in our breasts. We *may* possibly succeed in getting to the East side. If not, we must do our best to brave out the horrors and severities of an Arctic winter with such resignation as we are capable of. Time flies very quickly. In three weeks' time or a month the whale country will be frozen up solid.

Friday, September 14th.—We have been steaming all the morning through open water along the pack edge. We hope to find open water leading East when we come to the end of this pack.

Hope is reviving again in our breasts. I fervently trust we may not be disappointed.

We are 80 miles from Cape York, and within 30 miles of where we were on the 19th of August, when attempting then to get round to the East Water.

We have burnt both spars and most of the shakes, and have been cutting up our spare oars to-day for fuel.

Saturday, September 15th.—We commenced steaming directly after breakfast, and have been reduced now to burning our warps (stout ropes for making fast the ship, towing, etc.) for fuel.

9.15 *a.m.*—The pleasant news has just flown through the ship that the captain can see the land from the crow's-nest, with " an ocean of water " leading to the North-East.

We are steering North-West to get round the end of the pack, when we hope to haul the ship round to the North-East. Hope is again reviving in our breasts

9.45 *a.m.*—The mate has just come down from the crow's-nest, and reports that packs of ice extend to the North-West, beyond the point we are approaching, as far as the glass can range, most effectually preventing all access to the water beyond them. This intelligence has plunged us all in the depths of despondency.

At ten o'clock the captain held a consultation with the officers and harpooners. They decided it was no use wasting time and fuel in further attempts to get round these apparently interminable floes into the East Water. We are only 30 miles from where we were on the 19th of August, when we found it impossible to get through the ice. No alternative remains but to bear up for the West land again, and make a third forlorn attempt to get down that side of the country.

The chances of success are very slight. The ice always drives to the West side and moves along that coast, down the Labrador coast to Newfoundland, and is finally dissolved and broken up in the Atlantic. Our sole hope of finding a passage depends entirely upon the wind. Should West or North-West winds prevail, the ice may be blown away from the land and leave us room to get along. If we are jammed amongst those heavy floes by gales from the North-East, away goes the ship from under our feet, and there is nothing for us but certain death.

We hope and expect to get a whale or two off the West land as we move down South, not so much for the oil and bone, but for a supply of fresh meat for ourselves. I understand whale's flesh is very tolerable eating. Captain Gravill has eaten it frequently, and speaks favourably of it. At any rate, in our present circumstances we shall be only too glad to get hold of any fresh animal food—whales, seals, unicorns, sea-horses, mallies, burgies, sea-fowl. All will be " fish that comes to our net."

10.30 *a.m.*—Bore up for the West land, set all possible canvas, and let steam run down. All on board very much disheartened at our failure to get to the East Water. We estimate we have sailed and steamed between four and five hundred miles since last Sunday in our attempt to get through the ice into the East Water.

In the afternoon the men became more cheerful, though

I observed that several of them had been in tears as they discussed the melancholy prospect before us. I find it is the thoughts of the women and little children at home that so completely unmans our crew, most of whom are married men. You see, no intelligence of our fate, whether we are living or dead, can possibly reach home, so that their friends and families will be kept in suspense, which is not a pleasant reflection. Besides, the poor fellows have decidedly strong prejudices in favour of seeing their wives and children next month instead of next winter, and are anxious to get home in preference to perishing of cold, starvation, and scurvy out here. It is the thoughts, though, of wives and children, not the prospect of personal sufferings, that cause the stoutest-hearted men on board " to play the woman," as Shakespeare phrases it.

Sunday, September 16th.—At tea-time a pleasant breeze sprang up from the North-East, and increased to a pretty stiff blow. Ship rolling and lurching over with heavy seas thumping down on her. We are driving now (10.30 p.m.) to the South-West at a great speed through the darkness. A collision with a berg or a mass of heavy ice may send us to the bottom before the morning. We have need for all our skill, foresight, and seamanship just now, but far more need for God's guidance and protection, without which all our efforts are in vain.

Monday, September 17th.—Running all last night.

This morning the usual weekly allowance of 3 pounds of biscuits per man was served out, with tea, coffee, and sugar.

I felt very faint and queer this morning for the first time since we were put on short rations. Many of us, myself amongst the number, made too free with our miserable stock of biscuits on Wednesday last, when we were so confident about getting through the ice into the East Water. Consequently we found ourselves in very reduced circumstances indeed during the remainder of the week.

The ship is running to-day at 5 and 6 knots to the South-West before a stiff breeze from the North-East. This wind is helping us down the country pleasantly enough, but, at the same time, will be jamming the ice upon the West land.

Tuesday, September 18th.—Soon after dinner we could make

out the land indistinctly. At two o'clock we came in sight of the fleet of bergs aground upon the "Hecla and Griper Bank." We recognised our old acquaintance, the "pinnacle berg," to which we walked over the floes when attempting to get to the dead whale. We also passed a low flat berg of tremendous length, towards which we had slowly and painfully warped the ship when we made our escape from Scott's Bay last Sunday week. That was only nine days ago, and yet it seems an age since we got clear of that dreaded bight.

To-morrow we begin our third attempt to get down the West side. All alone, with 500 miles of heavy ice to get through, our coals exhausted, our men weakened for want of food, winds prevailing from the North-East, our chance of success seems poor enough.

We are all anxious, restless, excited, hoping for the best, yet fearing the worst. We intend doing our best, and must leave the results in the hands of God.

10 *p.m.*—A very dirty night. A good deal of heavy ice knocking the ship about. Night dark with blinding snow-showers.

Ship just now received a heavy blow. Great commotion on the deck. My heart palpitating at a great rate, in spite of all my philosophy. Another crash ! We know not how near death may be to every one of us. God grant us a safe and speedy deliverance from these accumulating perils.

Wednesday, September 19th.—Last night was a most horrible night, dark as pitch—so dark that you could hardly see the men on deck when close to them. The wind was blowing half a gale, the snow and sleet blinding your eyes. The ship was driving heavily, with main yards aback, rolling and pitching in the heavy swell, and ever and anon coming in contact with masses of heavy ice, which the pitchy darkness hid from our view till they came down upon us.

To add to our apprehensions, we knew that in our immediate neighbourhood there were numerous large and small icebergs which might come in collision with us at any moment.

The captain was very uneasy and sat up all night, going on deck repeatedly. I did not retire till 2 a.m., and even then was unable to sleep. The swell beat against the ship's sides with a noise like thunder, whilst the crash of heavy ice against the bows and quarters kept one in a state of constant alarm. However, we were preserved from all accidents through the long, dark night.

During the morning the gale subsided, but the swell was worse than ever. All the breakfast furniture rushed off the cabin table, and was demolished at one fell swoop. This was a serious loss, as we have very little crockery left, and the steward is the most careless, clumsy brute of a fellow I think I ever met. He has contrived already to break nearly every bit of earthenware under his charge.

Thursday, September 20th.—The swell continued very heavy, but the day was beautifully clear and sunny. There appeared to be plenty of water ahead of us, so that we all began to hope and believe that our prospects of getting to the southward along the West land were not so hopeless after all.

Alas! as we got off the mouth of the River Clyde Inlet our joy was turned into sadness. The captain, descending from the mast-head, announced that a pack of very heavy ice extended to the edge of the land-floe as far as the telescope could range, effectually preventing all further progress to the southward unless the wind should start to blow strongly from the South-West and open up a passage along the land-floe.

This was most disheartening intelligence. The next alternative is to take to the pack and drift down the country in the ice. We would rather run even this dreadful hazard than return to Pond's Bay to die of scurvy and starvation.

Friday, September 21st.—This morning the ship is pyling along the edge of the pack towards the eastward, the captain having determined to *drift down the country in the pack !*"

SUGAR LOAF HILL

CHAPTER VII

BESET IN THE ICE

EDITORIAL NOTE.

September 22nd to October 21st.

As tersely stated at the end of the last chapter, Captain Gravill determined to boldly run the " Diana " into the ice-pack and drift with it into the Atlantic, where they would expect to be liberated about April.

This course was taken in preference to the only other alternative—namely, wintering in Pond's Bay, which meant not getting home for about a year.

On September 23rd the " Diana " was firmly held in the ice, and so started on her long voyage as a prisoner, a voyage which was to last for six dark winter months, and of which a good many members of the ship's company were destined never to see the end. As the diary for that date states : " We have commenced a most desperate and hazardous enterprise—in fact, we are playing our last card for dear life. To force his ship amongst the heavy ice, and take his chance of driving down in the pack into open water, exposed to gales, nips, collisions with bergs and heavy ice, is the whaler's LAST *resource. Alone and helpless during the short twilight days and long, dark nights, with every probability of getting stove in, our sole reliance must be, and I trust is, in the merciful pity and protection of God."*

The following day's entry in the diary has the plaintive note that the sun has crossed the Equator, " and now the days will shorten with great rapidity until we find ourselves bewildered for seven or eight weeks in total darkness. A pleasant prospect, truly."

Dr. Smith was appointed " fowler " and caterer for the cabin mess, and used to spend practically all day on deck " with a loaded gun, a rickety concern of fabulous age belonging to the carpenter,"

*keeping a keen lookout for birds or beasts of any description.
" We are not disposed to be fastidious. Everything is eatable.
Hunger is truly the best sauce." This arrangement seems to have
suited him. " I get abundance of exercise, while the necessity
of being constantly on the ' qui vive ' prevents me from dwelling
upon our critical position."*

As the ship was expected to remain fast in the ice for many
months, and so would not require to use her sails, the crew were
set to work on September 25th to dismantle her upper masts
and yards and to cut these up, as well as the seal clubs, for firewood.

In his keenness to add to the cabin larder, Dr. Smith used to
make expeditions over the ice in various directions. While out
thus, clambering over the masses of ice " as hard as granite and
as slippery as glass," he found " the silence and desolation
around him was positively horrible." However, these expeditions
were not altogether fruitless as a rule, for he speaks of one
" glorious tea—viz., a soup consisting of four fulmar petrels and
a burgie with a few potatoes."

The entry for September 30th is mainly devoted to a summary
of the month's doings and of the prospects before them. " It
has been a month of the greatest dangers, anxieties, preservations,
and mercies. We have made every effort to find or force a passage
out of the country, and been foiled in all our attempts. Unable
to do anything further, we have thrust the ship into the pack, and
are frozen up now in the ice, drifting to and fro, entirely
dependent upon the mercy and protection of the Almighty, who
alone can preserve our frail shelter from sudden destruction.
The days are getting shorter and shorter, the nights dark, long,
and intensely cold, while our fuel is rapidly consuming. We are
beginning to feel weak and incapable of any unusual exertion
from deficiency in food. All our water has to be obtained by
melting ice, which we shall be unable to do when our firing is gone.
We cannot direct our course or accelerate our progress down the
country. The ship is beset amongst light ice, and safe enough
at present, but ahead and astern and on all sides are heavy
masses of ice and a number of bergs. We are ' in for it,' and
must drive down the country in the ice. Let us humbly trust
that He who has guided and guarded us through such a month of*

perils will watch over us during the month that commences to-morrow, and will finally make for us a way of escape and restore us to our homes and friends."

And so the ship drifted on, the men's time being mostly employed in searching for and, if possible, killing any birds they came across. The diary now is filled largely with entries of such events, and the diarist apologetically remarks : " I mention these trivial incidents to show how eager our men are to get anything eatable just now. They roam about in bitter, freezing weather, well contented if they obtain a few little birds hardly any larger than sparrows. There are always several loaded guns on deck, in readiness for whatever may chance to come within shot."

In these pursuits various artifices were employed. Pieces of blubber would be put upon the ice near the ship to attract the birds within shooting distance. Occasionally bears would be sighted on the ice. Instantly a lump of blubber would be put on the cook's fire, and though the animals might notice " the putrid stench" and could be seen " snuffing the tainted gale," yet they never ventured within range of the " Diana's " rickety artillery.

For a while, with changes in the wind, the ice kept working about a good deal, and holes and lanes of water would form now and again near the ship. Occasionally a seal would appear and create some excitement among the half-famished men. On one occasion three unicorns were observed blowing and playing in the water. The appearance of unicorns occasioned some surprise, the captain remarking that he had never seen these animals so much scattered or straggling about the country sc much as they were this year. Evidently this was due to the unusual amount of ice, and the consequent interference with the whales' usual habits.

Careful observations of the ship's position were made whenever the weather allowed, and a record kept of the amount of drift. This varied, 16 miles being recorded for one day ; 45 miles for one week. On October 4th the ship was some 50 miles off the West land at Home Bay.

With nothing to do in the long evenings after darkness had settled over the ship, and with their dangerous position ever in their minds, it is natural that many reminiscences of previous

misfortunes in the Arctic seas should be retailed in the " Diana's "
cabin.   The diary for October 10th contains the following very
interesting details of old whale-ship history :

During the many years Captain Gravill has been to this
country he was beset in the ice and compelled to drive down
in the pack only once before our present embarrassment.
This occurred in the year 1835, when he was mate of the
Harmony (Captain Thompson) of Hull.

On that occasion, when there was hardly a particle of ice
to be seen from the mast-head, the weather became a dead
calm, with intense frost.   The ships *Harmony, Abram, Norfolk,
Lady Jane, Grenville Bay*, and *Dordon*, were beset in the bay
ice in company on October 9th, 1835, being somewhere in the
69th degree of North latitude.   They had on board them
the crews of several other ships that had been lost, in addition
to their own complements of men.

The *Harmony* had sixty-four men on board, and the rations
were reduced to 3 pounds of biscuit per man per week,
with a very small quantity of salt meat.   The cold was intense,
every rope being as hard and solid as a bar of iron.   Having
very little fuel, they suffered severely from frost-bites and
exposure, never having less than fifteen men disabled at
a time, principally in their feet and legs.   This the captain
accounts for as arising from the poor fellows persisting in
sitting in the galley with their feet in the oven to warm them.
They were so short of fuel that they were only able to cook
the meat once every three or four days, whilst they were compelled to thaw the ice for water and boil their kettles over
lamps.   The coals were all exhausted.   Every chip and scrap
of wood was gleaned up and put under lock and key, whilst the
smallest conceivable fire in one corner of the cook's furnace
was the only means they had for obtaining warmth.

By dint of great exertions, incessantly warping and tracking
and taking advantage of the least opening of the ice, they
succeeded fortunately in getting out into latitude 62° on
November 28th.

The other ships did not get out for two months or more,
and reached Hull (he believes) in February or March, some of

them in a terrible plight, having lost thirty men or more out of the crew from intense cold, starvation, and exposure.   When they *did* break out of the ice, the poor survivors had not strength enough to stow away their boats, but let them drop from the davits into the scuppers, where they lay during the passage home.

Many of the ships had only two or three men able to steer, and these were so weak that they had to be supported at the wheel or lashed in a chair.   They were so fearfully reduced in strength and numbers that the men lay for days alongside their dead companions, being unable to drag the bodies out of the berths* or lift them over the ship's side.

The crews being completely disabled (in some ships reduced to only twenty men), the ships crossed the Atlantic under double-reefed topsails, as the men were utterly unable to work the ship or set canvas.

The *Abram* of Hull had ninety men on board when they were beset, and, being short of provisions, had to live (or, rather, die) on six biscuits per man per week!

The *Dordon* was lost on October 28th, and her crew distributed amongst the other five ships, to add to their privations.   The ships *Mary Frances* and *Lee* were lost also, but their crews saved.

The *William Torr* of Hull was beset in the pack and never heard of afterwards—lost with all hands, with the crew of another wrecked ship aboard, numbering altogether one hundred souls.   From the fact of one of her casks being washed ashore at Shetland, it is supposed that she was stove in amongst the heavy ice when she broke out of the pack. The heavy ice always hangs at the edge and on the outside of the pack, and there is generally a tremendous swell on, especially if the wind is blowing from the South-West.

The ship *Viewforth* arrived at the Orkneys with her crew fearfully reduced in numbers, whilst the survivors were in a most deplorable condition.†   The *Jane* of Hull was beset, too, and did not arrive home till very late.   Many other

* A precisely similar incident occurred aboard the *Diana* as recorded on p. 260 of this diary.

† Fourteen men died aboard the *Viewforth*.

ships were beset that year, and all suffered the greatest miseries and privations.

From conversation to-night with some of the men over the galley fire I learn that the ill-fated ship *William Torr* was last seen in Home Bay (where we are now). Two of her casks were picked up at Shetland, which suggests the idea of her having made her escape from the ice and foundered, or run upon a berg, or in some other way been lost during her passage across the Atlantic. The Esquimaux reported that they saw a ship strike upon an island and break up at the mouth of Cumberland Gulf during the winter of 1835. This might have been the *William Torr*, though it is improbable that any of her casks would have drifted from that locality to Shetland, as they would have been carried westward down the Labrador coast by the prevailing current.

The Captain's Yarn after Dinner.

" The year 1830 was very fatal to the whalers. There was very little ice in the country, so little that some of the ships made 100 tuns of whale-oil in the month of October on their way home down the Straits. Melville Bay, though, was full of ice, and no fewer than twenty-one ships were lost in the bay.

" It was a common occurrence to lose four or five ships every year in getting through the bay when the ships had to be ' tracked ' along through the ice by the crews before steam power was introduced.

" This tracking was very hard work, all hands turning out and towing, perhaps, for twelve or sixteen hours at a stretch. When, maybe, they had come to a block and the crew had been allowed to lie down to snatch a short rest, the ice would open and all hands be called upon again to renew their exertions.

" This passage of the much-dreaded bay must have been an anxious time. The ships used to follow each other closely with jib-boom projecting over the taffrail of the preceding ship, the crews tracking along in full chorus or to the enlivening notes of fiddles, bagpipes, fifes, and drums. Thus you might see fifteen or twenty ships following each other as in a string. If calm weather, the ships had to be tracked 150, 180, or 200 miles by main strength.

" The ships were so numerous that they formed three fleets when in the bay—the North, Middle, and South Fleet.

" In 1830 Captain Gravill was mate of the *Eagle* of Hull, which ship belonged to the South Fleet (or fleet at the entrance of the bay). The ice closed upon them, and five ships of this fleet were lost—the *William, Gilder*, and the *North Briton*, all belonging to Hull; and the *Three Brothers* and another ship, both belonging to Dundee. The *Gilder* and *North Briton* were together in the same ice-dock, which was forced in. The ice closed so firmly upon the two wrecks as to hold them up for days after they were burnt to the water's edge. It is the custom among whalers, when a ship is stove in and irrecoverably disabled, to set her on fire. From the *Eagle* they could see the flames and smoke of the burning ships lost in the Middle and North Fleets, for all the fleets lost numerous ships that year.

" In 1829, whilst tracking the *Eagle* through the bay, the ice closed and crushed the *Horncastle*, which was so close astern of them that her jib-boom projected over the *Eagle's* rail.

" It is only from the year 1819 that the whalers commenced coming to Davis Straits in any considerable numbers, being attracted there by the newly discovered Pond's Bay and West side fishing. Previous to this the bulk of the whalers went to Greenland. Those that came to the Straits seldom went further North than North-East Bay or South-West Bay in Discoe Island. They used to bear up for home, whether full or not, on the 10th of July, to secure the Government bounty of £50 per boat, which bounty was granted to encourage the fisheries as a nursery for seamen for the Royal Navy. Each ship carried six boats (not including the jolly-boat), and thus drew £300 for the owners.

" In those days there was generally an abundance of fish in the neighbourhood of Discoe Island. Hence arose the old whaling distich, ' Dusky dipping,* whale fish skipping.' "

* Discoe appearing just on the horizon.

EDITORIAL NOTE.

Reference is made in the diary on other days to very many other whaling-ships which had been lost from time to time in the memory of Dr. Smith's particular informant.

To anyone conversant with the history of the old whale-ship days, the names of these ships may be familiar, but to the vast majority of us these names are but empty words. Those old whaling days must have been crowded with adventure and peril, and were frequently accompanied, if not ended for many a man, by terrible privations. Hardly any of the men who went whaling in the early days of the nineteenth century troubled to write any account of their adventures and escapes, so the stories of most of the old whaling-ships are lost for ever. The recital of the names of the following old whaling-ships, " Abram," " Swan," " Lady Searle," " Annie" (all of Hull), " Alexander," " Thomas" (both of Dundee), " Dee" (of Aberdeen), " Chieftain," " Gambier" (both of Kirkcaldy), " Commerce" (of Peterhead), and a host of others—" Lady Jane," " Grenville Bay," " Union," " Norfolk," " Viewforth," " Advice," " Arctic," etc.— will not convey a thrill to anyone nowadays. They were either smashed up in the ice in various years or else managed to return home with more or less loss of life among their crews and suffering to the survivors.*

As the " Diana" approached the narrow part of Davis Straits her rate of drift was accelerated, much to the satisfaction of all aboard the ship. Land became visible on either side of the ship, and the diary names from time to time the various headlands as they came into view—Cape Broughton on October 16th, Cape Searle (or Mallemouk Head, so called from the

---

* In 1835 the *Lady Jane* of Newcastle had 22 deaths.

In 1835 the *Viewforth* of Kirkcaldy had 14 deaths.

In 1836 the *Swan* of Hull had 25 deaths out of 46 crew.

In 1836 the *Dee* of Aberdeen had 46 deaths out of 58 crew.

In 1836 the *Norfolk* of Berwick had 16 deaths.

In 1836 the *Grenville Bay* of Shields had 20 deaths.

In 1836 the *Advice*, a Scottish ship, drifted into Sligo Bay, Ireland, in June, with only 7 men alive out of 69, while 3 of these survivors were in an almost hopeless condition.—*Extracted from " Hull Museum Publication," No.* 31.

*immense number of fulmar petrels or mallies that breed there)
on the 17th, Cape Dyer on the 18th, and so on.*

*When in the neighbourhood of Cape Searle, the captain re-
marked that when he was in the " Abram" some years previously
he came out of Merchant's Bay near Cape Searle on October 14th
and found Davis Straits absolutely clear of ice—not a particle
to be seen anywhere—and plenty of whales about. So do the
seasons vary from time to time.*

*The appearance of a large body of water to the South-East
of the " Diana" excited for awhile the greatest hopes of it being
the long-sought East Water. However, it turned out to be only
an unusually wide lane of water in the ice-pack.*

*For some time after the " Diana" was beset the ice-pack
continued to move about, opening and closing and working
about in an extraordinary way. This led Captain Gravill to
make the following observations : " The ice in this country and
in Greenland is perpetually moving and slewing about in a most
remarkable manner. I believe there is a regular ebb and flow,
the ice opening and closing in the pack regularly twice in the
twenty-four hours. That there are strong currents is evident
from the erratic courses of the drifting bergs and from the perpetual movement of all the ice down the country."*

*Reference is made in another portion of the diary to the erratic
movements of icebergs in a pack. " A berg got under weigh
about tea-time and moved rapidly across our bows against the
wind, being carried about by the strong currents. These monstrous
masses of ice often take the most erratic courses, tearing through
the young ice in all directions, and are most dangerous neighbours
to a ship that is fast in the ice and unable to get out of their way."
Again, on October 16th there is the note : " This afternoon I
have been watching the movements of three icebergs which have
been in sight for several days. During that period they have
moved from our starboard side right across our bows, and are now
off our port side."*

*The " Diana" was beset originally in rather young ice, which
by the middle of October had not thickened to any great extent,
and so did not afford the ship any protection against these wandering icebergs or against any pressure on the part of the pack.
So the crew were set to work to cut a proper dock for the ship*

in a large mass of thick ice near by. Her rudder was unshipped to save it from damage by any subsequent nip, and her water ballast was pumped out to enable her to rise more readily in the case of there being much pressure from the ice at any time. Evidently everything was done to give the ship the best chance of surviving the ordeal they all knew was before her.

As time went on the frost became more intense. In the third week of October the diary states : " A keen frost. Though the sun shone brilliantly, its beams had no perceptible warmth, the smallest particles of snow exposed to its influence remaining unmelted. If you stood still for a few minutes on deck the cold would seize upon your feet and hands like a vice. The cold searched you through and through, and seemed, as Dickens phrases it in his ' Christmas Carol,' ' to freeze the very marrow in your bones.' One really dreads going at nights to one's berth, where one shivers under a load of blankets, top-coat, and other clothing, with feet as cold as ice, and the bolt-heads frosted with rime."

On October 20th, after an attempt to shoot some sea-horses which had appeared in a hole of water near by, Captain Gravill provided some information about these animals, thus : " The walrus is very numerous on the coasts of Nova Zembla and Spitzbergen. The Norwegians send thirty or forty sail (sloops, schooners, and other small craft) annually to those regions for the sea-horse fishing. They get fast to the walrus with small hand harpoons not more than 2 feet long. Each boat carries half a dozen of these weapons, which fit into a socket in a long pole, the pole being withdrawn when fast to a sea-horse and another harpoon attached to it in instant readiness for a second throw. In this way they sometimes get fast to four or five sea-horses at once.

" The animals are killed for the sake of their skins, which are amazingly thick and tough, and valuable for making leather straps for machinery. The skins used to fetch 6d. a pound, and I have known a single skin weigh more than 28 stones. The flesh is very good eating, especially the tongues. One of the Norwegian ships was lost, and the crew wintered on Spitzbergen and lived entirely on sea-horse meat."

One of the other reminiscences of adventure among the ice

*is that given by Joe Mitchell, the " Diana's " cook. The tale
is given in the diary as follows :*

" The loss of the *Sarah and Elizabeth*, of Hull. This ship,
commanded by young Captain Gravill, was lost at the sealing
in Greenland on the night of Easter Sunday, 1857.*

" She was laid in the pack when a strong gale sprang up and
forced the ice upon her, stoving in her quarters. The *Diana*
was some 8 miles off. The ensign, with the Union downwards
as a signal of distress, was run up, but it was not observed. The
first intimation Captain Gravill, senior, received of the loss of
his son's ship was the sudden appearance of two of her crew
alongside of the *Diana*. The crew of the *Sarah and Elizabeth*
travelled over the pack to the *Diana*, leaving their bags on the
ice by their wrecked ship.

" The three following days were thick, with heavy falls of
snow. When the weather cleared up, the crew of the *Sarah
and Elizabeth*, together with a number of the *Diana's* men,
travelled to the wreck to get their clothes, etc., the ice being
horribly soft and rotten, and a strong gale blowing at the time.

" They found that the hull of the ship had filled and sunk,
but was held up by the main yard catching upon the ice.

" Whilst busy securing their bags, etc., which were alongside
the ship, a heavy swell set in and the pack started to break up.

" A terrible scene ensued, seventy or eighty men springing
from one fragment of ice to another, struggling for dear life to
get to the *Diana*, the pack breaking up and spreading more and
more every minute. My informant (Joe Mitchell) tells me he
was in the water repeatedly, having to jump and run and swim,
and so on, for 8 miles. The weather was very severe at the
time, there being an intense frost and a strong gale blowing.

" A number of the men were saved by being dragged and
forced along by their companions. Here you might see a man
kneeling on the ice and commending his soul to God; there men
sending farewell messages to their friends at home; others
staggering along, weak, exhausted, and benumbed by the
terrible cold and exposure to intense frost whilst wet through.

" The *Diana* was to leeward of the pack, and would have

* After forty-three years' service as a whale-ship.

been blown clean away from them by the gale had she not had steam power put into her that very year. As it was, she was able barely to hold her own and keep near the edge of the pack whilst her boats picked up the men off the fragments of ice.

"The two ship's companies were called over, and it was found that all had succeeded in reaching the ship, an astonishing thing considering the distance they had to travel after the pack began to break up and the intense cold and exposure whilst wet through."

WALRUS

"SNUFFING THE TAINTED GALE"

CHAPTER VIII

DRIFTING

EDITORIAL NOTE.

October 22nd to November 5th.

DURING the fourth week of October the "Diana" steadily continued her southerly drift, the extent of which was eagerly noted by solar observation or by recognition of the various prominent headlands of the West Land (Baffin Land).

On the evening of October 22nd the ship was nearing the entrance to Exeter Harbour. That night a kettleful of blazing tar and other combustibles was hoisted to the foreyard arm as a signal to the natives or settlers that a ship was in the pack.

The flare was hoisted again the following night in the hopes that the blazing signal might be seen and answered by our fellow-countrymen upon the land. Yes; even here, upon the edge of the Arctic Circle, in this howling wilderness, exposed to the greatest extremes of frost and cold, is an English settlement. I assure you that we all have long looked forward to being abreast of Exeter as betokening our return to the civilised world. All day long we were levelling telescopes in the direction of Exeter, hoping to see some signal or some indication that they were aware of our being in their neighbourhood, but without success. We are afraid we have drifted past the harbour without being observed. This is hardly to be wondered at when we consider the distance we are off the land and the improbability of any of the settlers being upon the hills or high land at this season of the year.

The British colony of Exeter was founded only last year by a Mr. Taylor, who had been twelve years engaged under the Danish Government superintending one of their colonies in Greenland. In recognition of his services, the Danish

Government granted him permission to found a British colony on the east side of Greenland.

Mr. Taylor went to London, and a company was organised for that purpose. I imagine their main object was the development of the trade in cryolite, a mineral which is found abundantly in Greenland, and which is rapidly becoming a very profitable article of commerce. The metal aluminium is prepared from it.

At one time the company was under treaty to purchase the *Diana*, but ended by building the powerful steamer *Eric*, which came out loaded with all the necessary materials for forming a settlement. After several attempts to get through the ice to the coast of Greenland, the ship was compelled to abandon that enterprise. Rather than give up the attempt to found a colony altogether, Mr. Taylor resolved to see what could be done on the West side of Davis Straits, and disembarked his stores, houses, live-stock, etc., at Exeter Bay.

The colony is established upon a low point of land 10 miles up the bay. A number of the intending settlers, mostly foreigners, refused to remain with Mr. Taylor, and Captain Gravill left three or four of his Shetland men there last year in place of the disheartened Germans.

How the colony has been getting on during the past twelve months we cannot tell, but the *Eric* was to convey a large quantity of ready-built houses, a small iron steamer, whaling-boats, stores, and materials of all kinds, and a number of Shetland and English men with wives and families to the settlement this season. Also Mr. Joel, who was surgeon to the *Diana* last year, and whom I met when at Lerwick, was to go out in the *Eric* as surgeon to the settlement.

The company must have been put to enormous expense already in founding and victualling this settlement. In what manner they expect to obtain a return for their capital is hard to say. Captain Gravill supposes that they entertain the lively but chimerical hope of catching an abundance of whales and seals, and, possibly, of discovering mineral treasures at present unheard of or unsought for in these desolate and inaccessible regions.*

* See Appendix I. (A).

EDITORIAL NOTE.

On October 24th Cape Walsingham was visible to the south-ward, and the ship was abreast of this "long-desired" Cape on the 26th. " For how many days (aye, several weeks) have I been longing to reach this point of land, looking at it upon the chart daily, and even several times a day, and thinking that if we were only 'there' we could begin to entertain hopes of breaking out of the ice this year. And here we are this day abreast of the said Cape, at a distance of 15 miles from the land."

On the following morning the ice around the ship had opened out into various lanes of water in all directions. Captain Gravill regarded this as a sign that the ice was slacking and spreading out after having passed through the narrow part of Davis Strait. It was remarked of the captain that he was in great good spirits that day, and told his officers that " if " the ice behaved so and so, " if " the wind did this, " if " the currents did that, and " if " the rate of drift remained so much a day, he had good hopes of the ship breaking out of the pack before Christmas. Alas for Captain Gravill when Christmas Day came round !

During this fourth week of October the cold was more intense than ever. Concerning this the diary for October 23rd states : " Bitterly cold again last night ; one of the—if not ' the '— coldest nights we have experienced as yet. It was almost im-possible to get to sleep, though covered with every available article of clothing. Your feet frozen as dead and cold as masses of ice, your backbone feeling like one long icicle, your hands tingling with cold, your nose pinched blue, your breath congealing upon the blankets. The keen cold air renders every inspiration as difficult and disagreeable an act as cutting your own throat might be supposed to be. Everything in your berth is frozen hard— towels, sponges, the stockings you took from your feet the previous night. The various oils and fluid medicines in the medicine chest are frozen masses of ice. How one escapes being frozen to death in one's berth is a matter of daily wonder and astonishment to me, and also, I trust, of daily gratitude."

Again, the following day is the entry : " Whilst engaged nailing up a bear-skin by the light of a small lamp (for my berth is a species of cupboard as dark as a wolf's mouth) I was astonished to observe every bolt-head, nail, and piece of ironwork was coated thickly with glittering spicules—not merely hoar frost, but respectable little icicles. The woodwork, too, was varnished over with a thin sheet of ice. This will give the reader some idea of the severity of the cold we have already experienced thus early in the winter season. What we may have to endure later makes me shudder to reflect upon."

A little flash of humour is extracted even from out of all this discomfort. A large bear ventured close to the ship one morning, and was shot at twice without success. It then lay down upon the ice, and W. Reynolds, the harpooner, walked up to it and fired at it when only a dozen yards off. " His hands were so benumbed by the intense cold (though only a few minutes upon the ice) that he could hardly get his gun off. However, it went off at last, and so did the bear, uninjured."

October 24th.—I have not forgotten that to-day is the anniversary of my birth. Doubtless my sisters have borne it in mind. Probably they are expecting to hear from me by every post, as I told them we should be home by the end of this month. I am thankful to think that none of them will have received as yet the dismal intelligence of our position when last seen by the *Intrepid* in Scott's Bay, and the poor prospect of seeing us for many months, if indeed they ever see us again. To be told that the *Diana*, when last seen, was tightly beset in the ice, her coals nearly exhausted, and her crew on short allowance, will strike dismay into the hearts of our relatives and friends at home. Many a poor woman will consider herself as good as widowed when she hears the ill news, so fearful are the odds against any ship's company surviving through the protracted winter on such hard terms. However, here we are, driving down in the pack, and already more than abreast of Exeter, and humbly trusting that the Divine mercy and pity will continue to guide and guard us, as it has done hitherto in the most remarkable manner.

October 29th.—The usual weekly allowance of 3 pounds of biscuit per man was served out. It is just two months to-day since we were put upon short allowance. As for myself, I feel remarkably light and not very strong on my pins (to use a pugilistic phrase). I notice a great falling off in the appearance of the boys and growing lads aboard this ship. These poor fellows feel the effects of deficiency in food much more severely than do those of our company who have arrived at full growth. The Shetland men, taken as a body, look much more emaciated than the English crew.

EDITORIAL NOTE.

The doctor being a keen naturalist, the diary heretofore has contained copious notes regarding the bird and animal life of these northern regions. At this period, though, is the dismal entry nearly every day: " Not a single living creature seen to-day." The " Diana's " company, deserted by their fellow-men, was deserted also now for days at a time by the bird life of that inclement neighbourhood.

There are the usual meteorological notes, the hours of sunrise, sunset, and the rapidly diminishing amount of daylight being sadly recorded from time to time. On October 30th the diary reads :

The appearance of the sky at 8 a.m., immediately before the sun rises, is remarkably beautiful. The entire horizon is one brilliant purple, blue and crimson flush, not confined to the eastern quarter, but extending with almost equal intensity over the whole horizon and gradually fading away into the zenith. The most glaring specimen of what is known as " tinted cardboard," for drawing " sunsets " and " winter views " upon, will convey a by no means exaggerated idea of the magnificent appearance of the sky, both at sunrise and at sunset, in the Arctic regions as we see it now every day and night. The last few nights have been beautifully clear, the moon " walking in brightness " amidst countless myriads of stars. The Aurora Borealis has been flitting and flashing about, and just now (8 p.m.) is extended in a magnificent arch like a rainbow exactly over the mast-head, crossing the zenith and resting upon the opposite points of the horizon. It is not an irregular outline of light, but one unbroken arch of equal breadth throughout, the edges clearly defined and altogether presenting a wondrous and imposing appearance.

Editorial Note.

With very little to do during this period but await whatever Fate had in store for him, Dr. Smith spent more time than ever at his diary. He assiduously wrote down the various yarns, accounts of adventure, and whaling lore and history heard by him in the " Diana's " tiny cabin or in the men's mess deck. The captain provided much interesting information on the habits of whales, seals, walruses, etc., and flatly contradicted many of the statements made in the Natural History books. He had a poor opinion of the " discovery men " (as the Arctic exploration expeditions were dubbed by the whaling fraternity), and made sundry acid comments on the ways of ship-owners—a favourite subject of conversation amongst sailors.

Some painful tales of adventure and hardship amongst the ice have been told already in these pages, but in this part of the diary are other yarns even more horrifying than those already recorded.

One such narrative is as follows :

The Year 1854 in Greenland (A Yarn by Bill Reynolds, Harpooner).

" I went to sea for the first time in '54 as half-deck boy aboard the *Violet*, belonging to Hull. It was the severest weather, perhaps, that was ever known in that country. One day we noticed something black on a piece of ice, and thought it was seals, so lowered a boat away. What do you think it was ? Why, five poor fellows laid side by side all froze to death, and another one by hisself on another bit of ice, kneeling on his hands and knees with a piggin hoisted up on a boat-hook as a signal. He couldn't speak at first, but we took him aboard, as well as the poor fellows that was frosted to death, and buried 'em next day. They looked as natural as life. The one that was still alive told us they belonged to a Danish ship, and had been away on the ice sealing when a gale came on. Their boat was stove in amongst the ice, and their ship driven clean away from them by the gale. He lived six weeks, and had to have both his legs took off, but he died after it.

" A good many ships was lost that year, specially foreigners. Dick Skelton, who was 'spectioneer of the *Orion*, told me they came across an awful sight—*seventy men frozen to death on a piece of ice!* They was the two companies of a foreign barque and brig. The barque was lost first, and her men went aboard the brig. This was lost too, with no other ships in company. They was all upon one piece of ice and, as they dropped off with the cold, them as was alive piled up the dead bodies like a breakwater on the weather side of the ice to keep the sea from breaking over 'em. Dick said there was only two or three of 'em left alive when they came across 'em. The dead men was frozen together solid like a wall.

" Three Hull ships were lost that year—the brigs *Germania* and *Hebe*, and the *Violet*, which I was aboard of. We drove into the pack in a gale of wind, and was stove in. We was eight days on the wreck, the empty casks in her holding her up, when the Scotch Fleet hove in sight. We had our ensign flying with the Union downwards in distress, but them unfeeling brutes actually sailed past us and never took the least notice, though we was well in sight and in clear water at the time. However, the Dutch Fleet was not far astern of them Scotch skippers. Directly they see'd us in distress they lowered away their boats, and was fairly wrangling among themselves as to which ship we was to go aboard, and when we was aboard they was quarrelling as to whose berth we was to turn into. I shall never forget them Dutchmen, they was that kind !

" After this we went aboard a Norwegian, but they was just as selfish and unfeeling as the Dutchmen was good to us.

" There was a deal of ships lost that year. Some of our men was wrecked three times over before they got home. It was fearfully cold, too. You'd see ships dodging in holes and lanes of water with their ensigns flying for doctors. They was cutting off feet and legs. You see, there was a great many wrecked men as had got frost-bit, and as none of these foreigners carried doctors, it took the doctors of our ships all their time, they was that busy cutting off feet and legs and attending to 'em afterwards."

EDITORIAL NOTE.

It is a relief to turn from such terribly tragic tales to some of Captain Gravill's quiet chats about whales and whaling. He had some remarks to make about American whalers.

" The Americans used to send a good many ships to Cumberland Gulf at one time, but there's not so many of them comes now.   Formerly, American whalers was very numerous. I have known no less than 400 sail out of the port of Nantucket alone, but they were mostly engaged in the sperm whale fishing in the South Seas.   They make a three years' voyage of it, wintering in some of the Pacific Islands, and they boils down their oil aboard.

" The Americans also sends a good many ships to the Behring Straits, where whales used to be very numerous indeed.

" The United States Government, whenever they sends out expeditions, always gives particular directions about noticing where whales is to be found.   'Tis the first thing they look out for, and report on when they goes home.   You see, them Americans are a much more enterprising people than we are. They're always wide awake, and looking out for the main chance and seeing where they can make trade.   *Our* ' discovery ships ' never thinks of noticing anything so low as whales. They think it beneath their dignity.   If you look into their books about their discoveries, you never hardly see a whale mentioned from beginning to end.

" Our Government ought to encourage the fisheries, and give these ' discovery men ' (whom *we* have to pay and keep up) orders to report and particularly observe where it is the whales goes to.   But the fact is these ' discovery men ' are jealous of the whalers, and are afraid we will discover more than they do.

" There never was a ' discovery ship ' on this West side. 'Tis all discovered and laid down as you see it on the charts by the whalers.   You'll see many of the bights and headlands is named on the charts by the whalers.   There's ' Dring Bay,' after old Captain Dring of Hull; ' Bon Accord Harbour,' after the old *Bon Accord*. Here's 'Cape Truelove,' after the old *Truelove* that you saw in Hull Docks. There's 'Abraham Bay,' after the old *Abram* I was master of. Here's 'Cape Durban,' after the *Durban*, which was lost in the pack when we was beset in company in 1836, when I was mate of the old *Harmony*; and lots of other places besides, all along this West land."

Editorial Note.

In another place the diary remarks: "The Captain tells me that some of these 'discovery men' (a class for whom he has considerable contempt) affirm that there is no perceptible current in Davis Straits. That they are incorrect we have daily proof before our eyes. During the last twenty-four hours the pack has most certainly shifted 10 miles further southward during a total calm, and without a perceptible breath of wind from any quarter to assist or retard its progress."

So much for the practical old whaler's opinion of the Government scientific expeditions to the Arctic !

With regard to whales and whale-fishing the captain is quoted, as follows :

" I went to Greenland for eleven years before I came out to Davis Straits. The bulk of the whalers used to go to Greenland before they found out this Pond's Bay and West side fishing. Formerly the fish were very numerous. When the ice has been coming in, I have seen a bay so full of fish that you daren't for your life lower a boat down, as it would be sure to be capsized. There wasn't room for a boat to swim amongst them.

" I remember in the year 1818 being in the *Cherub* of Hull. We were up in North Greenland, and the cold was terrible. Our two lower tiers of casks, which were filled with salt water to serve as ballast, were frozen solid. What was worse, we couldn't thaw them, either. Our half-decks, 'tween-decks, and everywhere were filled with blubber, and there we was with fourteen dead whales alongside the ship and couldn't do nothing with 'em. We hadn't nowhere to put the oil if we flinched the whales, our two bottom tiers of casks being frozen solid, as I told you. We lost nearly all these fish. They commenced to swell and burst alongside us before we could flinch 'em. We just had to let 'em adrift, for when they burst we can do nothing with 'em.*

" Not long afterwards our skipper went away in a boat, and got fast to a young whale which went away under the ice. So he made the end of the line fast to a hummock on the ice, and left the boat-steerer, with the boat's flag on the end of a boat-hook, to stay by the hummock and prevent any other ship from claiming the fish, though to be sure there was only the old *Perseverance* in company at the time. Well, the boat pulled back to the ship, leaving the boat-steerer on the pack. It came on a dense fog, deadly thick. When it cleared up, what should we see but the poor boat-steerer perched on top of the hummock, and three large bears at the bottom looking up at him. Of course, we pulled off immediate, and found him in a terrible fright and crying like a child. He was sure the bears were going to worry him. Bless you! there was no occasion to be afraid in the least. The bears had their bellies full of the crang of the whales that had burst and been turned adrift, and which had all floated off to the edge of the ice. Them bears was full enough, I warrant! I never did see a field of ice swarm so with bears; it was perfectly alive with them. They was attracted no doubt by the scent of the dead fish, of which there was a great many on both sides of the pack. I assure you, them fields was beaten by the bears' footmarks into broad tracks as hard and smooth as a highway, specially along the edge of the ice.

" Your book says that a whale has been known to stay an hour and a half below the water. I believe they can stay as long as they like. I've struck a fish, and had her remain two hours and twenty minutes under water before she showed herself again. This was in clear water, with no ice or bergs about, so that we should have seen her immediately if she had come up to breathe. We like 'em to remain below a good while after they get the harpoon, as they lays longer blowing . on the surface, and so gives us more time to come up to 'em and give 'em a second harpoon or the lance.

" Sometimes, when a fish is struck with the harpoon, she'll

* See Appendix II.

dive right down to the bottom and bury herself in the mud if the bottom is soft, and die there. I've got several fish in this way; hauled 'em up dead. Whether they suffocate theirselves in the mud or what, I don't know. I expect they are regularly stagnated at being struck, coming altogether quite unexpected, and so lose their heads altogether, and never stop running till they are brought up at the bottom. They often break their jaws and crown bones if the bottom is rocky, they go down with such a speed and force. At other times a fish will roll about at the bottom and cover herself with mud, besides winding the lines about her in the most extraordinary manner.

" You may get a fish very simple sometimes, with wonderful little trouble, but others is just the opposite. I've had one fish in Greenland take out no less than nineteen lines, each line being 120 fathom (240 yards) long, and weighing a hundred-weight and a half. Let's see, that's within 200 fathom of 4 miles of line on one harpoon, and would reach from Hull to Cottingham. As each line weighs a hundred and a half, there would be a strain of a ton and eight hundredweight and a half, or very near a ton and a half, on that harpoon. After we'd killed her and come to look at the harpoon, we found it was drawn out as fine as a pipe shank—not a bit thicker, I assure you— with the weight of the lines it had had to bear. When we got home the owners took that harpoon to their office, and kept it there as a curiosity.

" Another fish, which we lost, got away with two harpoons in her—nineteen lines on one harpoon and seven on the other. Yes, sir; that 'ere fish actually went off with better than *five miles* of line trailing behind her. This would be a dead weight of *two tons*, within a hundredweight, not to mention the extra work of dragging it through the water or along the bottom. The master of the ship, old Jackson, nearly went out of his mind at losing so many lines.*

" Some fish, as I said before, is killed easy in a very short time; others takes a deal of killing. I remember seeing the *Zephyr* of Hull four-and-twenty hours killing one fish. I should say there was at least twenty boats after her—boats from every

* See Appendix III.

ship—but she kept flying about so that it was almost impossible to get a second harpoon into her; but they killed her at last.

" When we see a she-whale with a calf (or sucker, as we call it), we always endeavours to strike the calf without killing it, and then the mother is generally sure to be got as well. You see, she'll not leave the spot, but will keep constantly rising, coming up close to the boats, and not seeming to take the least notice of them, she is so anxious about her calf. They do say the she-whale takes the calf under her fin if you get fast to it, but I can't say. I never saw them do it myself.

" The largest whale I ever heard of was got in Greenland by the old *Molly* of Hull. It yielded no less than 40 tuns (the old-fashioned tun), and I believe it was the largest fish that ever was known to be got. It was before *my* time, and we have a public-house in Hull, in Dock Street, with the sign of the *Molly* to this day.*

" The old-fashioned tun was one-sixth less than the imperial tun. The way the owners gets the better of us is that they engage and pay us at so much per imperial tun of 252 gallons, and they sell the oil at so much per ton weight of 20 hundredweights. You'll find if you reckon up that there's a difference of exactly a quarter of a hundredweight, or 9 gallons of oil, in the owners' favour."

Editorial Note.

Thus did old Captain Gravill chatter on, drawing from his deep knowledge of all that pertained to those northern waters. Many pages of the diary are filled with transcriptions of his remarks, which ranged over such subjects as currents and winds, the drift of the ice-fields, bears' power of diving, unexplored portions of Greenland, making whalebone into ostrich feathers, whales' food, salt in the ocean, and many more topics. The full recital of Captain Gravill's chats would be deeply entertaining, and possibly instructive, to those who take an interest in the physical geography and natural history of the Arctic, but might prove wearisome to the general reader.

The other great raconteur in the " Diana" appears to have been

* The *Molly* made this catch in 1787.

William Reynolds, one of the harpooners. One reminiscence of his is interesting on account of a little sidelight anent the Scotch whalers. After describing the loss of his ship (the "Emma" of Dundee), of which he said the surgeon was Fred Skey, son of the superintendent of Morningside Asylum near Edinburgh, he went on to remark :

"The rest of that day we was pulling in the boats. A good many of the men was very drunk. 'Twas a Scotch ship, you see, and they had got at the rum casks and filled themselves beastly drunk. I was the only Englishman aboard her besides the master. If some of us hadn't kept sober, I know several of 'em would have gone down in the ship, they was that helpless. When we fell in with the fleet I went aboard the 'Xanthus' of Peterhead, where I was very well treated. Them Peterhead men don't seem half bad sort of fellows. The ship was very well victualled, and they had plenty of grog served out. The Peterhead men was very kind to us, they was. They seem very different men to them Dundee men. There's a great coolness between the Dundee and Peterhead whalers. They hate one another like poison; jealous, I reckon. Peterhead ships has generally been the best ones at sealing, but them Dundee skippers is more for whaling."

During this period the "Diana" had been lying quietly in the drifting ice-pack. However, shortly after midnight on October 1st the ship's company was rudely aroused by a " sudden convulsive movement " of the ship and an immediate battering of the ice against the ship's side. The ice remained in movement for a few hours, but was quiet again by daylight, leaving the captain and officers undecided as to whence came the swell which had caused the sudden alarm. It proved to be a warning of much worse times ahead of them, when the ship's safety was despaired of.

November 1st.—I have been reading over my log for the past month, and find we have much to be thankful for. During this time we have drifted no less than 275 miles. The captain and officers admit they are surprised when they reflect upon the distance we have driven. Let us trust that before the month just commenced has come to a termination we may have made our escape into open water. We are in His hands who controls these mighty forces of Nature, and who is as able to extricate us from this fearful ice as He was to still the tempest upon the Sea of Gennesaret, when the men marvelled greatly and said amongst themselves: " Behold, what manner of man is this, for even the winds and the sea obey Him?" So I read this morning, and I assure you it gave a poor fellow a good deal of comfort to reflect upon it.

November 3rd.—Cape Fry in sight. We must be very near the spot where the American whalers picked up, in September, 1855, Her Majesty's ship *Resolute*, which had been beset in the ice somewhere up Lancaster Sound, and abandoned by her crew. She had driven down in the ice, and was picked up uninjured by the Yankees and presented by the United States Government to Great Britain.*

EDITORIAL NOTE.

On November 5th the ship was off Cape Mercy, and was only some 15 miles from the land. The diary records the serving out that day of the weekly allowance of 3 pounds of biscuit per man, and the monthly dole of ½ pound of tea, ½ pound of coffee, and 3 pounds of sugar. The dismal note is made : " Tobacco we have practically none, a loss which the men feel acutely, so necessary is this article to the comfort and consolation of the seafaring portion of mankind."

To the accounts given already of various wrecks and tragedies in the Arctic regions may be added this final one, told by Captain Gravill one afternoon :

" In the year 1832 the *Shannon*, belonging to Hull, was lost on the East side of Cape Farewell, when on her way out to Davis Straits on a whaling voyage. You see, they were

---

* H.M.S. *Resolute* (a " discovery ship," as the whaling men would term her) was abandoned at Melville Island in May, 1854. She drifted " down the country " in the ice, and was found in September, 1855, off Cape Mercy by Captain Buddington of the American whaler *George Henry* of New London.

The *Resolute* was in good condition, there being only about 4 feet of water in her holds. She must have drifted in the pack from Melville Island, through Barrow's Strait, Lancaster Sound, and down Baffin Bay to where she was found, a distance of about 1,150 miles.

a good deal too near the land. They didn't give the cape a wide enough sweep, as there is always a vast amount of heavy ice and bergs hanging about off that coast.

"The misfortune that caused the loss of the ship occurred on a dark night, in thick weather, with squalls and showers of snow, wind blowing half a gale, and the ship driving along at 9 knots.

"The watch had just been reefing the topsails, and a dram of grog was being served out to them when the ship struck a piece of heavy berg ice. Her bows were smashed in and the galley driven no one knows where, as not one of the poor fellows who were sitting in there at the time was ever seen again. The sea that broke over her when she struck swept away seventeen men off her decks.

"The remainder clung to the wreck, which was held up by her empty casks. The sea broke over them constantly, washing them away one after the other as they became weak and exhausted.

"The survivors held on for several days, when, providentially, two Danish victualling ships that were making their way to the Danish settlements on the West coast of Greenland noticed pieces of wreck floating about, and, following these up, came to the hull of the *Shannon*.

"The few survivors that were picked up by the Danes were in a fearful state, and many of them suffered greatly for a long time afterwards from frost-bite, some of them losing both legs, others both their feet.

"Aboard Danish ships they have a custom of sending a man to the mast-head first thing in the morning and last thing at night, to see if there is anything in sight. If it hadn't been for the man noticing the bits of broken wreck, not a soul of the *Shannon's* crew would have been saved. They were completely out of the regular track of the whalers, and so were the Danish vessels. In fact, one of them had just signalled to the other to alter their course several points when the wreckage was observed."

CHAPTER IX

THE PERILS OF THE ICE-PACK

Tuesday, November 6th.—A dull, gloomy, foggy day, with a strong south-westerly wind, which forced the ice down upon us and jammed the pack hard upon the land.

At 4 p.m. the ship began to move about. Upon looking over the port bow, it was evident that the ice-dock which had sheltered us so long had given way, the ice having been screwed up and forced upon us by a large iceberg which is directly ahead of the ship. We are afraid this berg is moving towards us, the wind being dead upon it and driving it in our direction.

These monstrous masses of ice force up the pack around them for a great distance, and move about with irresistible force. They often pursue the most devious courses, according to how they are affected by the strong currents and winds.

We are a little uneasy about our safety. The captain declines to retire to his berth, and is just now attempting to get some sleep upon the sofa. It is difficult to convey any idea of the anxiety, apprehension, and dread which we all feel more or less at the least movement of the ship. We know and feel that our lives absolutely depend upon her safety, and that, should anything happen to the ship, we are all doomed men.

So long as we are in the pack, especially when laid as we are now amongst heavy ice with the wind blowing half a gale dead upon the land, and with numerous bergs around us, so long will we feel our lives to be in hourly peril. It is a most anxious, harassing, miserable feeling. We hope and trust that God in His great mercy will preserve us, and finally in His own good time deliver us from our anxieties and dangers.

Wednesday, November 7th.—Last night was what I may well term a *horrible* night. The ship was groaning and straining under the heavy pressure of the ice, our ice-dock was broken in, the wind was blowing strong gales from the South-West and was forcing the pack hard down upon the land, the night dark, wild and gloomy. We were unable to see the extent of our danger, uncertain whether or not the ship would hold out till day dawned. With a long night of sixteen hours, darkness passes wearily and anxiously away. One is unable to sleep in one's berth and is totally unable to do anything whatever to relieve the ship. Such nights as last night are never to be forgotten.

The morning dawned at last, thick, foggy and miserable. Its light revealed to our eyes a strange scene of confusion. There was the pack, torn and rent and forced together in piles and jagged heaps, the massive fragments of heavy ice forced one upon the other in the most extraordinary manner, showing the tremendous pressure to which it had been subjected. The bay ice, which had formed the starboard side of our dock, was driven up in heaps against the ship's side, whilst, strange to say, the fragment of bay ice on our port side was almost uninjured, though the heavy ice outside it was forced up into high ridges.

The ice continued to move about a good deal and press heavily upon our starboard quarter, so much so that at about 11 a.m. we were compelled to blast the ice on our port quarter to relieve the opposite side of the ship from the pressure.

This operation of blasting is performed by attaching canisters of gunpowder to the ends of boat-hooks, and thrusting them through holes made for that purpose in the ice which it is desired to break up. A gutta-percha fuse is ignited and the pole is thrust as far as possible immediately beneath the surface of the ice. A dull thud is all that betokens the explosion of the powder, whilst the ice is forced up and cracked and thoroughly broken by the force of the discharge.

We fired five blasts, which effectually smashed up the ice in the neighbourhood of our port quarter, so that the ship's starboard side was relieved from the heavy pressure. This permitted the ship to shift a little and she finally settled down in a bed of broken-up ice.

Meanwhile the wind had shifted round to the South-East, and it blew a heavy gale from that quarter during the day, increasing in fury towards sunset.

In the afternoon the sky cleared a little and showed us the dim outlines of several bold headlands and a lofty, iron-bound coast. It was evident that the large iceberg ahead of us had approached much nearer and was forcing up the ice for a great distance around it.

Add to these ominous appearances a thick, murky day, with constant showers of snow, and you will confess that we had good cause to be miserable and anxious, especially as the approaching night threatened to be as stormy and wild as the preceding one.

However, at about 9 p.m. the wind gradually died away, the mists dispersed and the blessed stars once more shone down peacefully and serenely upon us. I retired to my berth, happy in the prospect of a quiet and undisturbed repose.

Unfortunately, *the captain was taken ill* about 2 a.m. (he, poor man, having persisted in sleeping upon the cabin sofa in readiness for any catastrophe), so I was called up and had very little rest afterwards.

The captain suffers from a great weakness, fainting, and giddiness, which I attribute to nothing else but deficiency in food, want of rest, and constant anxiety of mind—three evils from which all of us are suffering more or less.

EDITORIAL NOTE.

The following afternoon there was another sudden convulsive movement of the ice and for a while such intense pressure on the ship that preparations were made for abandoning her. The pressure eased off again in the evening, leaving them all mystified as to the cause of it, for there was not a breath of wind or anything else to explain the sudden disturbance.

On November 9th the ship was only some 5 miles from the land in the neighbourhood of Cape Victoria, the North-East point at the entrance to Cumberland Gulf. " We could now contemplate the barren wilderness of a land to which we should have to flee for refuge in the event of losing the ship."

That afternoon the ice got into motion again, and as the scene seems to have been such an extraordinary one, the account of it is given here in full :

About 3 p.m. the ice again got in motion and for two hours continued to run about in the most extraordinary and alarming manner.

Our ship seemed to be the centre of a whirling pack of ice, the masses of ice on our starboard side moving with great rapidity towards the stern of the ship, then crossing her stern, advancing at great speed along our port side, then driving across our bows, and keeping up this movement for at least two hours.

From the mast-head, as far as the eye could range, the ice was seen to be in motion, running about hither and thither, now this way, now that, now taking sudden shoots towards the land, whilst other pieces were running in the opposite direction. Every separate fragment of ice seemed to be following the bent of its own inclination, whilst the bergs were pursuing their usual erratic courses in all directions. One of them came unpleasantly near the ship. The crashing, rending, grinding, groaning of the ice, the speed at which the berg moved (it certainly shot past us at a good walking pace of $3\frac{1}{2}$ to 4 miles an hour), and our total inability to do anything whatever for the ship, caused us the greatest anxiety. We could do nothing but look on and marvel as we watched the rushing streams of ice, and implore God's protection as we were borne along amongst the whirling, crashing masses.

We did attempt to warp one heavy piece away from our port quarter, but our efforts were ineffectual to control even a single fragment.

We had some pressure on us two or three times, but it is wonderful in what a marvellous manner we were preserved amongst these dangers. Positively the ice seemed to be guided and directed so as to avoid striking us, the ship being surrounded, as I have remarked before, by a whirlpool of heavy pieces of ice revolving around her.

At times the ice on one side of the ship would remain motionless, whilst the pack on the other side was driving furiously along. Then this ice would become quiet and suddenly some other portion of the pack would get under weigh. Thus we were kept in constant agitation till tea-time, when the ice became quiet.

We can only account for this phenomenon by supposing that the strong current from Davis Straits sets along this land and is checked by another current coming down Cumberland Gulf, whilst the high tides which prevail with the new moon aid in producing this extraordinary convulsion among the ice.

To attempt to describe the miserable state of anxiety, dread, apprehension, even positive terror, which seizes upon a ship's company in our critical position is impossible. We are entangled amongst a very heavy pack, driving daily nearer and nearer towards the land, with bodies of ice coming down upon us from Cumberland Gulf and from Davis Straits.

Once stove in, a steam vessel soon goes down. They have been known to be under the ice within two and a half minutes after being stove.

This is a dreadful life. 'Tis wearing us out far more rapidly than cold or want of food, or any other privations which we are enduring now. The slightest movement of the ice, any unusual noise or bustle upon deck, rouses us up in a moment. We cannot sleep, we cannot even eat what little food we have, we cannot rest below deck, in the cabin, upon deck, anywhere. Restless, uneasy, anxious, we will not have a moment's peace of mind or body so long as we are in this awful ice.

Saturday, November 10th (3 *p.m.*).—An awful day of dread, anxiety, and horror. The ship has driven close inshore during the night. The tremendous precipices are close to us. We are surrounded by the heaviest pieces of ice we have seen as yet in the pack. All the morning these masses of ice have been in constant motion, subjecting the ship to very heavy pressure about her quarters, which are her weakest part. The ice continues to run and crash around us in the most frightful manner.

Just now (3.15 p.m.) the sun has set, a great globe of fire amidst purple, crimson and gold. The darkness is falling fast, and the fog is hiding everything from our sight. We are drifting towards the shore and the ship may go from under us at any moment. Just now we are expecting a return of the same violent motion in the ice which we have observed every afternoon during the last two or three days. This state of suspense is awful, terrible!

7 *p.m.*—Soon after four o'clock I was requested to attend a prayer meeting about to be held amongst the men. I found nearly all the ship's company assembled. The carpenter gave out the hymn:

> "God moves in a mysterious way
> His wonders to perform."

He then read a Psalm, and finally offered up a prayer to God for His protection and mercy.

At five o'clock, strange and extraordinary as it may seem (but, as we are disposed to believe, most providentially and in answer to our prayers), the ice ahead of us slackened and opened, the ship was relieved from the pressure and commenced to go on towards the land.

At 6.30 the ship's head was so near the tremendous cliffs that the captain affirmed the land was within reach of a shot fired from the ship.

The ice continued to slacken and from that time to the present the ship has been driving along the land at great speed, moving at a rate that astonishes us.

Just now (7.30 p.m.) we seem to be driving broadside on and straight towards a large rock that lies off Cape Victoria. The night is starry and clear, with the Aurora Borealis flickering in the heavens like another bow of promise.

Later.—After drifting as though she would inevitably drive upon the large rock (Coburg Rock), the ship was carried away by the extraordinary currents to the southward and eastward, and was soon at a considerable distance again from the land.

I retired to my berth at 9 p.m., but was unable to sleep from the noise of the ice, which was running about in great commotion and pressing heavily upon the ship. So I rose and sat by the cabin fire for a bit. Retired to bed again, but soon sprang out in the greatest agitation. The ice was moving violently about and the ship was being heavily pressed upon by it.

You can hear the ice in motion some short while before the movement arrives at the ship. The shrieking, screaming and groaning of the immense masses as they are forced and ground together is truly horrible, especially when heard at the dead of night.

The ship is bending, writhing, and straining as though she were some living creature struggling in the agonies of dissolution. Meanwhile you lie quaking in your berth, expecting every moment to hear the dreaded cry: "All hands ahoy! Prepare to leave the ship." This simply means, prepare to perish on the pack from cold, hunger and privations, a speedy death being the greatest mercy. So you cannot wonder at my not being able to sleep, though nearly worn out with the agonising anxieties of the day. I resumed my vigil in the cabin, while the captain, poor man, slept upon the sofa, too exhausted to be aroused even by the violent straining of the ship. Went to bed again at midnight and actually slept soundly till 7 a.m.

Thus ended another day and another week of great mercies and deliverances from imminent peril.

Sunday, November 11th.—I have been reading over this journal for the week. When I reflect upon the marvellous and unexpected manner in which we have been preserved from destruction, our narrow escapes from drifting on to the cliffs and then on to Coburg Rock, our preservation from a collision with two immense icebergs aground to the South-East of Coburg Rock, and our danger amongst the ice when in motion, I am constrained to confess that in all these preservations the hand of the Almighty is plainly visible. In no *human* way can we account for the ship being safe and uninjured at this moment.

Monday, November 12th.—This morning the rudder was raised higher up the ship's stern, as the heavy masses of ice caught against it in its former position.

The sun does not show itself now till about half-past eight in the morning, and it sets at 3 p.m. So we only have six and a half hours of daylight. The long, dark, anxious nights are miserable, terribly trying, indescribably frightful, especially when laid as we are now amongst very heavy ice and liable to lose the ship should a strong gale set in from the South.

All day the ship was drifting up and down with the varying

currents, with the South side of Cumberland Gulf well in sight from the deck.

Tuesday, November 13th.—At 4.30 p.m. I attended a prayer meeting held in the half-deck. I understand these meetings are to be continued daily throughout the remainder of the voyage. I am very glad that the men have decided upon such a proceeding. We have great need to call upon God for His protection and guidance.

I saw a snowy owl flying past the ship during the afternoon.

EDITORIAL NOTE.

During the next eight days the ship continued to drift slowly to the South-West, towards the South side of the entrance to Cumberland Gulf. In general, the weather was misty and gloomy, with occasional falls of snow. The ice, though, remained fairly quiet, much to the diarist's satisfaction. " Meanwhile, every day is shorter than the preceding one. We are looking forward with feelings of dread to the time, which is fast approaching, when the sun will not be visible at all above the horizon. This prospect of total darkness, to men in our situation, is horrible."

In addition to the daily prayer meeting amongst the men, a Bible class was started on November 18th.

Although the ice had remained quiet for so long, the " Diana's " officers and men still remained vividly conscious of their ever-present daily and hourly peril from the ice. The surgeon records on November 18th that the captain complained of a pain in his side, to which the doctor proposed to apply a blister. " No," exclaimed Captain Gravill. " No blisters for me! I don't want to be tormented with them NOW. There's no telling what may happen to us almost at any time. We may have lost the ship within the next five minutes !"

That day's entry concluded with the remark, " It is a matter of astonishment to the captain and his officers that we have been kept in safety for so long."

Early in the morning of November 20th there was heavy pressure again on the ship for about two hours. After sunrise the heavy mists of the night rolled away and the ship was found

*to be some 25 miles from Hall Island, off the South side of the
entrance to Cumberland Gulf.*

*On November 21st the day's entry concludes with the remarks :
" The sun set behind the lofty hills and islands shortly before
three o'clock. Seldom have I seen such a beautiful sunset even
in this country. The light clouds were tinged with the most
brilliant carmine and lake, fading away into crimson, yellow,
and saffron, while the sky continued to glow with light and glory
for some time after the sun had disappeared. At twenty-five
minutes to four the moon rose solemnly in the East, reflecting
the deep rosy sunlight instead of her usual ' pale watery beams.'
The ship's decks and the glistening ice-fields all around us are
illuminated by her rays until you could almost persuade yourself
that it was daylight."*

Thursday, November 22nd.—The moon shone with the most
uncommon brilliancy all last night, the land being distinctly
visible during the whole night, though some 25 miles distant.

There has been a very heavy gale blowing all day from the
North-East, and the ice closed upon us during the afternoon.

We are laid in a most perilous position between two large
and heavy masses of ice. We attempted to warp the ship
from between them, trebly manning the capstan bars, but
the warp broke and the ship slid back into her old position.

Conversing with the captain as to our situation, he remarked
(speaking most impressively) : " It will be a miracle of miracles,
doctor, if we are spared to get out. In the words of the hymn,
' I every moment in jeopardy stand.' " These are his identical
words, for I made a memorandum of them at the time of our
conversation.

The usual prayer meeting between decks at 4.30 p.m. The
captain prayed most earnestly for our poor souls, dwelling
upon the almost inevitable certainty of our losing the ship,
averring that, *humanly* speaking, there is scarcely a hope of
her living much longer amongst such heavy ice and exposed
to such gales as the one that is now raging.

There is now a general impression amongst the ship's
company *that we have not long to live.* I have this conviction
pressing heavily upon my mind all to-day and cannot shake

it off. My mind is in an awful and troubled state. God be merciful to me.

At tea-time the captain remarked that we ought all to be prepared to die, as the ship might go at any moment. He said he had been in many dangerous and critical positions, but there had always been some hope of saving life, some chance of falling in with other ships, but *now* we had nothing but inevitable death if the ship were stove in.

Just now (6.15 p.m.) the gale is raging with great fury and the night has fallen thick, foggy, and intensely cold.

This is a fearful life. I sit down to this journal evening after evening with a heavy heart, for in all probability it will never be seen by any of my friends.

Friday, November 23rd.—The gale raged with great fury all night.

I was aroused by the movement of the ice soon after 5 a.m. At six o'clock I rose, dressed and went on deck. I found the ship undergoing a very heavy pressure, there being two immense masses of ice on the port side.

Whilst standing by the captain's side, looking over the ship's rail at the fearful prospect, two sudden loud cracking reports were heard. The captain exclaimed in a voice of the deepest despair: " She's gone ! She's gone ! Call all hands !"

That fearful cry rang down the hatchway: " All hands ahoy to leave the ship ! Ship's stove in !" The second mate ran up, exclaiming: " She's stove in ! I can hear the water running in below our 'tween-decks !"

My sensations were awful. Now for it ! Death on the ice ! No hope ! Nothing can save a man of us ! WE MUST DIE ! I thought of home and friends and their agony of anxiety on my account. A possibility of the ship even being never heard of again. Lost ! Lost ! Farewell all hopes, anxieties, and cherished thoughts of returning home.

I asked the captain how long it would be before the ship went down. He told me he couldn't possibly say, but he was certain she was stove in. I put on a little extra clothing and returned on deck.

The men were swarming about the decks in the greatest anxiety, their faces blanched with terror. We tried the pumps, but found they would not work, being frozen up. With some difficulty we thawed them, and then the indescribable anxiety of those first few strokes to see how much water there was.

Oh, great and unmerited mercy! *She was as sound as ever!*

Something had given way for a certainty, but the ship was not leaking. The revulsion of feelings was indescribable, I went to my berth, and am not ashamed to confess before all who may read this that I was enabled to pour forth such a prayer of gratitude as I think I never before prayed in my life.

Just now (10 a.m.) the ice is pretty quiet and the men are engaged in making holes in it to blast it. As seen from the mast-head, the pack is one solid body of ice.

We are all in an awful state, our minds troubled, perplexed, despairing. Spare us, O God! Cut us not off in our sins!

After dinner a special prayer meeting was held and the usual prayer meeting at 4.30 p.m.

So the day has passed over our heads, a day of the most extraordinary deliverance, the most awful day of anxiety and terror I have ever lived through.

Just now (8 p.m.) the ice is quiet, but the same two massive pieces of ice are jammed hard down upon the ship. O most merciful God, that delightest in mercy, that seest our despairing and hopeless position, spare us during another night. Give us a quiet night. Preserve our poor ship, I pray Thee. We are nearly worn out with anxiety and fatigue of mind and body. We are humbled in the very dust before Thee. Oh, deliver us from this ice and restore us to our friends. But if Thou in Thine infinite wisdom shouldst see fit to take our lives, oh, save our terrified, miserable souls. Snatch us from eternal misery as brands from the burning. Lord, have mercy upon us!

Editorial Note.

There is a complete break of four days in the diary here. Possibly the terrible sensations experienced on November 22nd and the subsequent revulsion of feelings brought on such a condition of bodily and mental exhaustion that the pen could not be put to paper for the time being.

What happened to the ship during those four days can be inferred in a small way from the subsequent entries in the diary.

Evidently the ship was severely nipped again on the 23rd, and preparations made for abandoning her. The entry for November 27th refers to the hoisting aboard that day of the boats, provisions, and other gear, which had been removed from the ship on the 23rd.

Evidently the weather had continued thick and they were in ignorance as to the ship's position. An observation of the sun on November 27th led them, by some error in calculation, to believe that the ship was actually off Resolution Island. Their " high spirits " of that day were changed to bitter disappointment on the 28th, when another observation revealed to them their real position. The ship had drifted up Frobisher Inlet. The rocky islets visible to them, and which they had thought were those off Resolution Island, were only too surely off the South side of Hall Island, 50 miles further North.

November 27th.—The ice astern of us opened, and all hands were called to attempt to warp the ship into a hole of water which was forming astern of us.

For more than an hour we were tugging and straining at the capstan bars, " overing " the ship (crew running in a body across the decks to give the ship a rolling movement), and exerting all our efforts to get her through some very heavy masses of ice into a place of safety. The moon shone brightly, and the heavens blazed with the coruscations of the Aurora Borealis. The stars glittered and sparkled in the thin, frosty air. Numbers of brilliant meteors were rushing perpetually across and adown the black arch of the heavens. Meanwhile we, with faces and beards hung with icicles, struggled with the frozen ropes, strained at the capstans, and put forth all the efforts that despairing men in our critical circumstances might be supposed to make to warp the ship through the heavy ice. Gradually, inch by inch, inch by inch, we tugged her through. Then the strain became less. Then was heard the cheering cry: "Now, lads, give her another pound! She's getting through! Go it, my bonny lads! She's nearly through!" Then the ship slid along more easily. Then we got into bay ice. "Now, lads, nothing but bay ice! Give her way! ' Over ' her! ' over ' her!"

So we got her into the hole and, finally, at about 2.30 a.m., made her fast to the ice on one side of the hole and then sent all hands below.

I had just gone to the cabin when two of the men came aft, as a deputation from the ship's company, to ask the captain to give all hands an extra biscuit, as they were faint and spent for want of food. This and a glass of grog was given to all on board, and I assure you I never felt so grateful for a biscuit in my life. I retired to bed at 3.30 a.m., feeling almost worn out with fatigue, bodily weakness and mental reaction.

Wednesday, November 28th.—Had a couple of hours' sleep last night. I would have slept longer had it not been so frightfully cold. My berth is glazed with ice; every nail and bolt-head is studded with icicles. Several of the men have their noses frost-bitten. I have lost the skin from the side of my nose simply from contact with the intensely cold brass eyepiece of the telescope. It is the opinion of our most experienced men that a single night upon the ice, during such terrible weather as we are now enduring, would finish every man of us. O God, what do we not owe to Thee for all Thy mercies!

Soon after 10 a.m. the bay ice around us and the edges of the pack began to slacken and open out into large holes and lanes of water. It was resolved to attempt to warp the ship into a larger hole of water, and then towards the South-East and clear of the rocky islands near us. So during the rest of the morning, till 1 p.m., all hands were toiling and working at the capstans or running backwards and forwards across the decks ("overing") to give the ship a rolling motion, and so break up the bay ice around her. A boat's crew was employed fixing ice anchors and removing them further ahead as we tracked the ship up to each spot where the anchor and warp had been made fast.

The captain is at a loss to account for the mistake he made in his observation yesterday. He can only suppose that he had been deceived by a parhelion or mock sun glimpsing through the clouds.

To-day has been the anniversary of the day (November 28th, 1835) on which Captain Gravill made his escape from the pack when beset in the old *Harmony* of Hull.

Thursday, November 29th.—The ship was tracked this morning still further away from the neighbourhood of the islands and the icebergs which lie off them. We lowered one of our oldest boats, which was placed ahead of the ship and perpetually raised and dropped by means of a rope passed over the end of the jib-boom, so as to smash up the bay ice by its weight and thus help to clear a passage for the ship. A boy in the boat swayed it from side to side, so as to give the boat a rolling motion to more effectually break up and disturb the thick bay ice ahead of the ship.

I occupied myself all the morning assisting the men in heaving at the capstans, " overing " the ship, and in heaving on the lines with a " row raddie." This is a belt made of canvas and attached by a button to the frozen, slippery ropes. It is passed over one's shoulder, and enables you to lean with all your *weight* upon the line. In fact, it is a species of " horse-collar."

I may remark here that never, since we went on short allowance, have I felt so weak and utterly incapable of any exertion as I did this morning. It really required an effort to move about at all. I am certain I was of no real use at the capstan, as it required all my energy to drag myself wearily along and keep up with the capstan bar. Several of the men are in the same state of exhaustion. Alec Robertson, one of our best hands amongst the Shetland men, was completely knocked up and obliged to go below.*

Went to bed at 10.30 with a most blessed sense of peace, and slept soundly in spite of the intense cold.

Friday, November 30th.—Ship safe and quiet amongst the bay ice. I feel much stronger and better this morning. This sound sleep, this freedom from immediate danger, this sense of peace and quietness, is indescribably welcome. Rest, perfect rest of body and mind, is what we all stand in need of. Thank God for His great mercy and compassion in allowing us this blessed season of quiet and repose.

This morning the cooper broached a cask of beef, which turns out to be " Christmas beef," killed last year, of excellent quality, very fat, and uncommonly free from bone. This is

* This man died of scurvy on April 6th.

indeed a great blessing. The reader can have no idea what real *happiness* this news has diffused throughout the ship's company. The quality of our little stock of beef may seem a very paltry matter, but if you, my boy, were actually starving and suffering for want of food and were exposed to such terrible cold as we are, you would consider it of no small importance to get a mouthful or two of good meat extra daily. With us it is a matter of life or death, more especially as we are about to knock off two " beef days " and live on oatmeal and cheese two days in the week, so as to make our meat hold out as long as possible.

A burgie flew past the ship to-day, while I was much cheered at the sight of a raven which flew round us and then departed, croaking hoarsely, to the land. " Surely," I thought, " if God cares and provides for this poor creature in this horrible wilderness, He will not forsake us in our extremity."

PINTAIL DUCK

CHAPTER X

THE "DIANA" ABANDONED FOR A TIME

Saturday, December 1st.—I was awakened soon after midnight by the ice getting on the move again, and during the remainder of the night sleep forsook every eye.

We listened to the roaring, rushing, rasping noise of the ice as it was crushed and piled up against both sides of the ship, now rattling exactly like a mill hopper, now roaring for all the world like an express train through a tunnel, now hammering with regular blows, as it broke up, with all the regularity of the clang of a blacksmith's forge. We felt the perpetual jump, jump, jump of the ship, resembling to my fancy the pulsations of the heart of some huge creature in the extremity of torture. Now a shuddering vibration would run through her whole frame, as though she felt herself trembling on the brink of dissolution.

All the while fifty poor souls were quaking with terror, knowing that their fate was sure and certain should a single timber give way.

I didn't go on deck, but commended my soul to God, and lay trembling with apprehension in my berth. You, my dear sir, may think me a poor, cowardly fellow, but I assure you there is not a man on board—and most of them have been accustomed to this country for a great part of their lifetime, and have previously gone through the most frightful dangers and hardships amongst the ice—I say, there is not a man on board whose heart does not jump at the slightest movement of the ship. Any unusual sound, the movements of the ice at a distance, the creaking of the ship's timbers, a hurried footstep on the deck, the clashing of a door, the fall of a handspike—in short, any sudden noise—sends a pang of apprehension through us.

After breakfast I went on deck and found the ship very near

the edge of the pack ice, with a large heavy mass of ice bearing down upon our port bow and forcing the bay ice into heaps as it moved slowly towards us.

During the whole morning the pack continued to approach us, the bay ice breaking up against the ship's sides and piling in heaps all around us.

The morning was clear and bright, but intensely cold—colder than we have yet experienced, and that is saying a great deal.

We dined upon oatmeal porridge and felt very thankful to God for providing such a plentiful and abundant meal. I assure you a full stomach is a very novel sensation.

Half a pound of oatmeal and half a pound of cook's fat was served out to-day to all on board instead of beef. This will continue to be served out once a week so long as the oatmeal lasts, so as to economise our stock of meat as much as possible.

You would have viewed the scene in the cabin with wonder and pity, our captain thanking God for His goodness in providing such a meal. There it was; the porridge smoked in a sooty saucepan, which had been placed upon the lid of a tea-chest to avoid burning the table. This dish was flanked by a plate piled up with rancid fat which the cook had boiled down from the scraps saved during the voyage, and which stunk like carrion. I think I never enjoyed such a meal with so thankful a heart in my life.

2 *p.m.*—The edge of the pack is now close to us. The sheets of broken bay ice are piled along our port side, in one place *coming up as high as the ship's rail*. The men of the watch on deck are employed in pushing the fragments of ice away as they climb, one over the other, over the bulwarks. Were we not to take this trouble, the bulwarks would be stove in and the ice would certainly come over the decks.

There is a very heavy pressure upon the ship. The captain has been over the side on to the ice and tells me that the ship's seams are all forced open by the tremendous strain she has to bear. A heavy mass of ice forward is now on a level with the ship's bows.

O most merciful Father in Heaven, we implore Thee, enable our poor old ship to hold out. Take not our anxious, miserable lives. Slack off this ice and liberate us, O God! Thou hast all power in heaven, on earth, and on the sea, whilst *we* can do nothing whatever for our safety.

Evening.—During the remainder of the afternoon the ice remained quiet, and we fervently hope it will continue undisturbed during the night. The masses of bay ice crowding and forcing each other up the ship's side had a most remarkable appearance. We were obliged to raise the boats higher on the davits, or they would have been lifted up and unhooked by the ice. The watch on deck were constantly engaged in pushing down the sheets of ice as they climbed up the bulwarks, or they would have forced themselves bodily over the rail and fallen upon the ship's decks.

The usual prayer meeting was held in the half-deck at 4.30 p.m. It was a very earnest and affecting time. One of the Hull men, Charlie Cobb, prayed very earnestly and with a simplicity of language that was quite touching.

And thus we are laid for the night, with the ship tightly nipped on both sides. God, in mercy grant us Thy protection during the long, anxious night. Spare us from being harassed and alarmed by the ice getting in motion again, and in Thy good time bring us out of this dangerous and uncertain situation.

Sunday, December 2nd.—This has been another day of wondrous mercies and most unexpected deliverances.

I was aroused at about 1 a.m. by the renewed movement of the ice. I composed my mind as well as possible to rest again, but at 1.30 was startled by a tremendous crashing of the ship's timbers apparently close to my berth.

I sprang out of bed and rushed in the greatest apprehension into the cabin, where I found the captain hurriedly dressing. The mate ran forward and shouted down the hatchway those appalling words, " All hands ahoy ! The ship's going !"

It was very certain that the tremendous pressure of the ice had wrenched away the ship's stern post. I dressed myself quickly, went on deck, and found all hands busy lowering away the boats and dragging them with all possible expedition on to the solid floe pieces that were gripping the ship like a vice.

It was a scene of the greatest confusion—hands employed

filling bags with biscuits, others filling bags with coal, others dragging spars on to the ice; the hatches open and casks of beef, pork, etc., being passed up from below; the whole ship's company engaged in making preparations for instantly quitting the ship.

I stowed away a few medicines, splints, bandages and a few articles of clothing, in a bag, put my Bible and a case of instruments in my pocket, and then had time to look around me.

The night was dark, foggy, and uncomfortable. The heavy ice was forcing the ship hard upon a thick, solid sheet of ice on our starboard side. It was a contest of endurance between wood and iron and heavy ice and strong currents.

For hour after hour the old ship continued quivering and groaning in every timber. At 3 a.m. the pressure was fearful. We expected to hear her give way every moment. How any ship *could* stand such a strain is astonishing !

After sending stores, sails, spars, coals, etc., upon the ice, the men were sent below to stow their own bags.

Thus the night wore wearily on. I ate a biscuit and a half, drank some tea, and awaited with a trembling heart the issue of events. Death, certain death upon the ice, if the ship went down ! I cannot describe the feelings of one's mind under such circumstances.

At about 6 a.m. the ice became quieter, while the eastern horizon became streaked with red and yellow, betokening the approach of day.

The ship was perpetually harassed by the ice, which continued to press heavily upon her till one or two o'clock in the afternoon. The captain had prayers in the cabin, but the poor old man was too agitated to read a sermon or even give out a hymn. We sang, " Praise God from whom all blessings flow," with bursting hearts, and then the captain offered up a very fervent prayer of gratitude for preserving the ship amidst such fearful ice during the night.

In the afternoon the ice again began to press very heavily upon us, so much so that all hands were called to drag the boats further away from the ship, lest they should be engulfed with her if she went down. A prayer meeting was held in the galley at 2 p.m. Two of the Shetland men prayed very earnestly.   These poor fellows seem to have lost all heart and have given way to utter despair.

As to my feelings, I can only assure you that I experienced this afternoon the most bitter, dreadful, agonising, and despairing state of mind that I think I have ever felt.   I felt utterly cast down, utterly undone, utterly lost, with no hope for this world and but a very faint hope of happiness in the world to come.   The crew seemed equally desponding, every man equally dejected, which is not to be wondered at when you consider our awful position.

There was another prayer meeting in the half-deck at 4.30 p.m., when three or four of the men prayed with great earnestness to God for mercy.   The ice remained quiet till 9 p.m.

So ends another day in which we have been spared again, when hope had fled from the hearts of all on board.   The captain is astonished at the marvellous manner in which our ship has borne the pressure of the ice.   Our carpenter, who is a Dundee man and has assisted in building nearly all the famous fleet of Dundee whalers, assures me that he could not have expected any of those powerful ships to bear such a pressure as was put on the old *Diana* last night and to-day.

We all acknowledge the hand of God in our preservation. It was the Lord's doing, and it was marvellous in our eyes.

I am about to lie down in my berth, fully dressed, with sea-boots on and all, in readiness for any emergency.   The writing of this journal is to me a most painful duty, as I hardly dare expect it will ever meet the eyes of any of my friends. Humanly speaking, we are lost.   Nothing can save our ship but the power and protection of Almighty God.

Later.—I attempted to sleep, but it was impossible, so rose and returned to the deck.   The night was still, dark, and dim, while the moon occasionally gleamed through the misty atmosphere.   The ship was tolerably quiet, but was gripped tightly by the remorseless ice as in a gigantic vice, from which there was no escape.   We all knew that with a very slight movement more, a little more pressure upon her, *go she must !*

I paced the decks in the greatest misery and agitation of mind.

Shortly after midnight the ice again closed upon us. The mate ran down into the cabin to arouse the others. There was no occasion to do that, for the horrid crashing of the ship's timbers caused the other officers to spring up instantly. The mate then ran forward and shouted down the hatchway: " All hands ahoy ! SHE'S GONE THIS TIME !"

Our poor fellows rushed on deck. The scene was indescribable. The ship rattled and crashed as though every timber in her was being split into firewood, writhing, jerking, starting suddenly, quivering through her whole frame, as though she *felt* the tortures to which she was being subjected. The decks were working up and down under the awful pressure until it was dangerous to stand upon them; we expected them to fly open and trap our feet.

The men were ordered first to get their clothes' bags and bedding upon the ice. Up they came—chests, bags, mattresses, bedding—pell-mell over the bows, whilst other men dragged and carried them further upon the pack. The harpooners were busy sending the provisions over the gangway, the casks being pitched upon the ice, from which they rebounded heavily, whilst groups of men seized them and rolled them away to the neighbourhood of a large sail. This had been spread upon the snow, and on it were laid our beds and other personal effects.

This exciting work was carried on by the lurid light of two lanterns at the gangway, with the ship crashing so loudly that 'twas difficult to hear the voices on deck or the shouting of the officers. The imminent peril to which those who remained on board to assist in saving provisions were exposed, the dark outlines of the men struggling with the heavy casks as they rolled them over the rugged and snowy surface of the pack, the terrible energy displayed by the officers, some of them deep down in the hold snatching casks of provisions from the wreck before the ice came clean through her—all these, contrasted with the deep stillness of the night, made a very striking scene.

The boats were dragged further away from the dangerous neighbourhood of the ship, and were filled with bags, fuel, rifles, ammunition, kettles and all sorts of articles, and then covered over with tarpaulins frozen hard and stiff.

The cook was busy looking after his pots and pans. Then, having seen that his galley was cleared out, Joe stood by with an axe in his hand, ready to cut the rigging so as to let the masts fall over the ship's side directly she showed signs of going down, the masts being intended for fuel.

Our small stock of coal was hastily put into bags, and the iron cressets or fireplaces were sent upon the ice. The ship, in fact, was thoroughly cleared out forward.

The cabin took longer, the captain's books and other effects, chronometer, charts, telescopes, clock, barometer, etc., were removed after the bread-locker, store and line rooms were cleared.

As you may suppose, it was dangerous work, and trying to a fellow's nerves, to be working in the hold, engine-room, or anywhere below deck, and expecting the old ship's sides to give way every moment.

When the ship was well cleared out, the poor old captain walked along the quivering decks and over the gangway. He went to one of the boats and sat down in her stern sheets, covering himself well up in his rugs. I stayed beside him for awhile, for he seemed very much cast down. He kept looking earnestly at the dark outline of the ship, distinct against the sky, and kept repeating: " There goes the poor old *Diana !* Good-bye to the *Diana !*"

I left him and returned aboard for my books, which had been carefully collected by Byers and Reynolds and placed upon the ship's rail. Made them up into a big bundle, and returned to the boats, where I found the captain walking up and down some flinching boards which had been laid upon the snow for his accommodation.

The ship continued to rattle and crash dismally. From the astonishing noise she made, not a man of us doubted that her sides were stove in bodily. However, the captain ordered us to try the pumps and see how much water she was making. With some difficulty the pumps were thawed, and to our astonishment we found there was *only some foot and a half of water in the hold !*

Upon this discovery being made, most of the crew returned to the ship, and very desolate she looked. All the chests, beds,

bedding, everything, had been cleared out of her, leaving
nothing but bare timbers and bulkheads.   We lay down anywhere—on the floor of the half-deck, in the empty bunks, on the
galley seat—tired, exhausted, mentally and bodily.   It was a
strange and melancholy sight to see the men, stretched out
in all positions, attempting to snatch a little repose, though
in the very jaws of death.   I noticed the kind and careful way
in which the harpooners covered up little Willie Shewen,
the half-deck boy, with their jackets, whilst the poor little
fellow slept heavily, though shivering with the cold.

The captain remained in his boat during the night.   So we
wore through the hours until daybreak.

Monday, December 3rd.—Last night wore through somehow
or other.   The captain remained in the boat under a pile of
rugs until between three and four o'clock, when he came on
board and spent the rest of the night in his easy chair.   It
was a miserable, anxious night with all of us.

The morning was cold and hazy.   After breakfast we began
to make arrangements, firstly for saving the ship if possible,
secondly for providing a refuge in the event of her being
seriously damaged or lost altogether.

The principal injury is somewhere about her fore-foot or
" ice-knees," for she makes a deal of water forward.   We
cannot discover the exact seat of injury or do much to remedy
it, as it is so low down.   The injury is only to be got at from
the outside, and this is impossible with the ship so deeply
buried in the ice.

The officers were engaged in preparing a thrummed sail and
in pushing it under her bows as far as possible.   They were also
making swabs and pushing them under her bows through a
hole cut in the ice, in the hopes that the swabs will be drawn into
the leak by the inrushing current.   They also foddered her
with ashes, sawdust, and all the refuse of the blacksmith's
shop.

Mr. George Clarke has been busy directing a lot of our men
in making a tent of spars, stunsail booms, ice-poles, etc., over
which the spare sails have been spread.   He has pitched this
frail—and, if the ship goes, only—refuge upon the most level
and solid fragment of ice he can find.   In addition to these

necessary precautions the ship's company are obliged to stick steadily at the pumps, as the ship leaks badly.

During the morning there was a very heavy pressure upon the ship, with a repetition of the awful crashings and other dread symptoms of the ship giving way.

Of course, our meals to-day have been very irregular and spasmodic. I have been engaged in rolling the provision casks to the tent, hauling and pulling at boats, working at the pumps, etc., and feel worn out by the protracted excitement and loss of sleep. The pack is very heavy and the snow upon it deep.

At 4 p.m. the ice again closing on the ship caused very heavy pressure upon her. Before nightfall we had got matters arranged as comfortably as practicable in a very respectable tent. The men's beds, bags, and sea-chests were arranged round the sides; at the further end were the biscuit bags and casks; whilst near the entrance was a blazing coal fire in a cresset. A lamp or two hung in the tent, and made it look far more cheerful than it really was. The floor was swept clear of snow, and there, upon this crystal foundation, stood our only refuge if the ship failed us. The captain had his bed and bedding arranged ready for sleeping. Even the canary and linnet were removed into the tent, and some lumps of crang were cut adrift as food for the dogs.

Evening.—The captain retired early to his cheerless couch in the tent. His bed had been surrounded by the ensign and ship's Jack, and thus made private. I saw him into bed and remained with him a little while. Mr. George Clarke and I had tried to dissuade him from sleeping upon the ice. The ship rattles and cracks so frightfully from the pressure put upon her, and he has had no sleep or rest for so long a time, that the captain was determined to try and obtain one night's undisturbed repose if possible. As for myself, I have brought my bedding back to the ship, as have all the officers, but a number of the Shetland men have turned in for the night in the tent.

There was a good deal of stealing during the confusion last night—sugar, raw pork, biscuits, etc.—as these various articles were passed up from the hold or sent over the side. In the darkness this could not be prevented, nor, considering the famished state of the men, could it be wondered at.

The ship is leaking badly, very badly. The pumps are continually getting out of order, freezing up, the valves breaking, etc., and it is very hard work this pumping, I assure you.

Tuesday, December 4th.—I was up all last night. It was not possible to sleep. The cracking of the ship's timbers, the noise of the pumps, the constant movement and bustle on deck, our deplorable and desperate position, all sufficed to keep slumber from my eyes, though I was tired to death and worn out with long-protracted anxiety and loss of rest.

It was *very* hard work at the pumps. They were constantly getting out of order, breaking, or becoming clogged with ice forming in them. It required all our exertions, with these frequent interruptions, to keep the water under. For the first time in my life I found out what pumping a leaking ship meant. I assure you it is very hard, monotonous, exhausting work.

The captain came on board between four and five o'clock. He had not slept much in the tent, and complained of feeling " chilled through and through." As he expressed it, his body felt " frozen solid," while he said, strangely enough, that his feet felt warm. I had visited him twice or thrice in the tent after he had retired, and given him some medicine for his asthma. He spent the rest of the night until breakfast sitting in his easy chair in the cabin by the stove. He said he felt very cold, as though he would never thaw again, and remarked that another night like that on the ice would kill him.

After breakfast the carpenter was engaged down in the " coal hole " in the ship's bows, attempting to get at the leak. The water was pouring into the ship in a steady stream, showing that she had received a severe injury somewhere about her fore-foot, an injury which could be remedied only from the outside.

The mate, engineer, and cooper were busy foddering the ship's bows, hoping that the current would suck the dirt and refuse, etc., into the leak and choke it.

I was engaged all the morning serving out stores, so that

the men might have a supply of tea, sugar, etc., at hand if the ship goes. The captain has humanely ordered an extra pound of biscuit and ¾ pound of flour apiece weekly for the remainder of the month. I had represented to him last night the utter impossibility of the men, and especially the Shetland lads, bearing up under such incessant and exhausting work at the pumps, especially as we all are weak enough already for want of food. Also, he ordered that a glass of grog should be given daily at the capstan head.

I should have mentioned that the ship made so much water last night, and it seemed to be gaining upon us in spite of our incessant exertions, that all hands were called at 8 a.m., as we could hardly hope to keep her afloat. However, the carpenter discovered the principal leak, and we hope to make it secure by caulking.

In the afternoon I felt very queer. The hard work of the whole of last night (not only I, but all of us, worked at those pumps until I, for one, was fit to drop from sheer exhaustion; one of the Shetland lads, Magna Nicholson, was actually groaning with physical debility, and yet continued hanging on to the rope beside me, straining away in an agony of exhaustion)—I say, the hard work of last night, the long-continued loss of sleep, the *intense* anxieties of the last week, the danger and the excitement, made my brain in a perfect whirl. I lay down on the sofa to get a nap, but no! I could not sleep. I went to my berth, but my brain felt all in a fever. I was unable to think rationally, could not remember the second lines of the commonest hymns or verses with which I had been familiar for years.

I rose and went upon the ice-pack. I remember stumbling about amongst the rugged masses of ice, scarcely conscious of what I was doing. I went to the tent and, taking out the opium bottle from my bag, I weighed out 2 grains of opium powder. I returned to the ship, swallowed the opium, and lay down in my berth again. Could not sleep. My brain was wandering. I was becoming delirious.

Returning to the cabin, I told the captain I believed I was in for brain fever. I requested him to get my hair cut off and to apply ice to my head when I became incapable, but on no account to give me any medicines. I then lay down on the sofa and, thank God! fell asleep for half an hour. This saved me.

I have recorded this incident so that the reader may judge of the terrible and exhausting strain upon our nervous systems induced by the events of the last few days. I recall the strange sensation in the brain, when reason is tottering, with the deepest horror. God preserve me from experiencing the like of it ever again!

The weather is thick and snow is falling. As there is no probability of stopping the leak, a watch was set and the other men sent below.

So ends the day, with the ship tightly nipped, the heavy ice piled in masses all around her, and the incessant "clank, clank, clank" of the pumps resounding fore and aft.

Wednesday, December 5th.—The same hard, exhausting toil at the pumps all night. I was on deck and at work and up and down for the greater part of the night.

Early in the morning the ship underwent some very heavy pressure which kept us on the alert and in misery for awhile. At 9 a.m. the ice began to move about and break up into lanes of water in the neighbourhood of the ship. All hands were called to get the provisions on board again.

We had a precious hard morning's work, rolling huge barrels of beef over the irregular snow-covered pack. The barrels kept sinking deep in the snow, and required great exertions on our part to get them along at all.

The ship continues to make a great deal of water, but we manage to keep it under.

Thursday, December 6th.—The same hard toil at the pumps throughout last night, rendered more trying by a gale of wind and the whirling snow. The men are weary and worn to death.

After breakfast some of the hands were engaged in taking down the tent and bringing on board the sails, spars, etc., of which it was composed. The ice is cracking and breaking, and is not a safe foundation for the tent any longer.

The tent was a great resort of the Shetland men, who lived and slept there. Many of them heartily wished the ship were at the bottom of the sea, that they might live in the tent free from the toil of pumping. They made no secret of their sentiments. They are rapidly becoming exhausted and indifferent, and only wanted to live a few days on the ice in peace, with nothing to do but eat—as long as the provisions lasted—and *die*.

Evening.—We have everything aboard the ship now except the boats, which are drawn up on the ice alongside. As you may suppose, the ship is in a strange muddle, with most of her provisions and stores lumbering the decks. I have all my property crowded into a sea-bag, which serves me as a pillow.

The captain is very far from well; in fact, he is very ill.

Friday, December 7th.—The same hard toil again last night. The keen frost fills the pumps with ice, so that they are perpetually getting choked or out of gear, or some part gives way, or the valves get out of order. They cause constant annoyance, and wear and tear of mind as well as body. The officers lose all temper over these wretched pumps, which, choking with ice, lift very little water at a stroke, and entail such hard work upon the men that I am sure the poor fellows will not be able to stand many more days of it. The blacksmith is perpetually employed in repairing the ironwork of the pumps (for iron breaks like glass in this cold climate), whilst the carpenter's services are in constant requisition to " sort " the valves, both day and night.

The day wore through with the same hard toil, the same gloomy weather, and the same far gloomier prospects of saving our ship and our lives. The Shetland men are getting thoroughly disheartened, and all of us are fairly worn out with work.

Saturday, December 8th.—The same despairing toil at the pumps all night. We are wearing out fast.

Though far from well, the captain continues to get about the ship, directing and encouraging the men, and cheering them on by example as well as precept, pulling away at the pumps when he sees the poor fellows flagging, and inspiring new life and energy into their wearied arms. But he is far from well. He remarked to the carpenter the other day that though he believed some of us would live to reach home again, after all, yet he never would.

Sunday, December 9th.—Another miserable night of work, followed by a dull, miserable, foggy day, with snow and sleet.

[The past week or so, beginning at midnight of December 2nd, was written in England from pencil notes taken at the time and from a most vivid recollection of that imminently perilous part of the voyage.

The log now continuing was written daily, as it meets your eyes.]

Monday, December 10th.—A quiet night last night. I would have slept soundly had not the captain been so extremely distressed with paroxysms of asthma that I was called up twice to relieve him. He consented to take a little hot brandy and water, which was the first spirits he has tasted for seven years.

I am not a little concerned about him. The anxieties and horrors of the last two weeks have been too much for him. Constant and hourly peril, loss of sleep, loss of appetite, and anxiety of mind, have pulled him down so much that he has scarcely strength at times to "stand on end," as he terms it. He is so weak and exhausted that I sometimes fear he will succumb to one of his attacks of bronchitis.

The pumps continued to work all day with great ease. There was no choking, no difficulty, no annoying accidents, and no breakages.

I have enjoyed most thoroughly the peace and quietness of to-day. Both body and mind crave for *rest, perfect rest.* One has a sense of weariness, extreme lassitude, and unwillingness to make the least exertion. One drops down upon a chest and craves to be left undisturbed. Peace and quiet! Such has been my feeling to-day and yesterday.

Now that the ship is firmly jammed up in the ice and we have no immediate prospect of being disturbed; now that the horrible excitement, dangers, terrors, and loss of rest, and, I might add, the constant *fever* of mind, are over, comes the period of reaction. I think I never felt so thoroughly done up, worn out, so weary, listless, incapable of any exertion, so much like an *old man*, in my life.

Withal, I have felt so amazingly hungry. Now that one has a little peace and quiet, the system puts in its claims for more nourishment. The stomach, so much neglected of late, makes most imperative demands for food. What a mercy it is that our stock of biscuit permits us to serve out the extra pound per man per week. I counted my allowance ('twas served out this morning), and found it amounted to seventeen biscuits. These, with the extra ½ pound of flour and the usual ½ pound of flour served out on Sundays, will enable us to eat *a whole biscuit to each of our three meals a day*.

The reader may think it very absurd of me to dwell at such length on so apparently trifling a circumstance; but if he were in our place, half-starved, half-dead with anxiety and fatigue, and living in hourly peril of his life, I am disposed to think that he, too, would thank God, the Giver of all, with a heart filled with the liveliest emotions of gratitude, for enabling us to eat a few extra morsels of bread. I am sure I never eat a meal without a grateful heart, 'tis such a new sensation to rise from the table with your appetite perfectly satisfied.

And what is it makes us poor fellows so supremely happy and grateful ? What's the bill of fare for to-day ? Let's see.

Breakfast.—A mug of coffee sweetened with a single teaspoonful of the coarsest sugar. A scrap of cold beef, perhaps weighing 1½ ounces. A biscuit.

Dinner.—A single ladleful of the thinnest possible pea soup—mere greasy water, upon my honour. A morsel of salt pork. A mug of tea and a biscuit.

Tea.—We had a saucepan of " burgoo "—*i.e.*, thin oatmeal porridge—but this occurs once a week. The ordinary tea consists of a mug of tea, a scrap of meat (one-third of our daily dole of meat, which is brought to table and divided into six portions every day at dinner-time), and a biscuit.

The only luxuries we allow ourselves are pickled onions and melted fat, which serves us instead of butter, and is very acceptable.

But enough of this ! We have something more serious to think of just now than eating and drinking. Our lives are in peril. No one can tell what a day—nay, an *hour*—may bring forth. Our ship is laid amongst the heaviest ice, with a leak sprung, and with pumps at work day and night. There is a large berg astern of us towards which we are driving. Ahead of us are two large bergs, which are shifting about perpetually and coming very near us at times. There are bergs on our port side, all adrift and ever on the move. There is a large island on our lee, and another on our weather side. We are exposed to strong currents—the ship is now driving up the gulf*—exposed to gales of wind, to a thousand dangers from ice, icebergs, and from rocks. Nothing but the mercy and compassion of God can save us from destruction. If the ship is lost, nothing remains for us but to lie down and die upon the ice. To attempt to reach these islands, dragging boats, provisions, materials for tents, etc., would be out of the question. We couldn't possibly do it. The ice is so heavy, so deeply covered with snow, and we are so weak and incapable of much exertion, that any attempt of this nature would be hopeless.

O God! almighty, all-powerful, full of compassion, whose mercies fail not, look down in pity upon us poor, helpless, despairing men. Our only hope is in Thee. We are prostrate at Thy feet. We can do nothing but implore Thy protection. Save us from the dreadful fate that threatens us. Let us not perish miserably in this awful wilderness. Hear our cries and prayers, and hear the prayers of our friends and relations In mercy spare our lives, and bring us back to our native land in Thine own time and way.

Editorial Note.

During the next nine days the ship continued to drift in the ice-pack up and down Frobisher Inlet with the ebb and flow of the tide and the changes in the direction of the wind.

There were numerous narrow escapes from charging icebergs, and the ship had to sustain some more heavy pressure at times from the ice. Life aboard continued full of alarms, and the diarist records that he would awake instantly should the men on

* Frobisher Bay.

watch on deck at night suddenly cease their regular tramp on the deck over his head. Also, "Should the monotonous thump, thump, thump of the pumps cease for a moment, men start up in their berths, and anxiously enquire what is the matter with the pumps."

Bitterly cold weather set in again on December 13th. The men working at the pumps in spells of half an hour each had their noses, fingers, and toes frost-bitten. The deck by the pumps was covered thickly with sawdust, a canvas screen erected on the windward side, and the spells at pumping reduced to a quarter of an hour for each man. Despite this, the men got frost-bitten during the strenuous labour of pumping.

The pumps HAD to be kept going day and night, because only five minutes' cessation of movement would result in the pumps getting frozen up and damaged.

On December 15th the surgeon wrote: "It may read like a yarn, but I assure you it is impossible to smoke a pipe on deck. However short the pipe may be, the moisture in the bottom of the bowl freezes and blocks up the hole in the stem. I tried repeatedly to smoke a short clay pipe, but it always went out, and refused to 'draw' until the bowl had been held over the cabin fire and thawed." He also records that the intense frost caused the ship's woodwork to crack at frequent intervals with quite startling violence and suddenness. Also, "the rigging is frozen, and clashes and rattles in the light winds. We seem to be dwelling in some haunted house, filled with unearthly and mysterious noises. We sit like hares, startled and alarmed at the slightest sound, dreading and fearing we know not what."

Regret is expressed that there was no thermometer in the ship capable of recording any temperature lower than 20° below zero, which was recorded soon after this spell of frost set in.

During this time daylight did not set in properly till nearly ten o'clock in the forenoon. Breakfast would be partaken of in the cabin, "brilliantly lighted by a single candle. Our banqueting hall (i.e., cabin) is so cold and full of draughts as to warrant its being mistaken for the old Greek Temple of the Winds."

The entry for December 19th concludes with the melancholy remark : "I feel there is little prospect of this journal ever meeting the eyes of my relatives and friends. Often I am inclined to give up the task of writing it."

Considering the awful straits to which the ship's company was reduced in January and February, it is a matter of astonishment that the diary was persevered with steadily until the ship was liberated at last from the ice.

DOVEKIE OR LESSER GUILLEMOT.

CHAPTER XI

DEATH OF CAPTAIN GRAVILL

Thursday, December 20th.—Last night was magnificently clear and bright. The brilliant light of the moon, reflected from the unsullied snow-covered pack, revealed the jagged heaps and torn masses of ice with startling distinctness. The islands and icebergs around us stood out in bold relief against the sky, a sky glittering with myriads of stars, and anon flashing and flickering with the ever-changeful coruscations of the Aurora Borealis. The ice and ship were quiet, and we were mercifully favoured with a night of undisturbed repose. This morning the sun rose in a sky gorgeous with purple and crimson, his lower rim clearing the horizon at a quarter to ten.

During the morning the ship was driving rapidly towards our old enemy, the grounded berg. The ice around us was frequently in great commotion, nipping up and crashing and grinding. We trust that the heavy masses of ice in which the ship is frozen fast will protect us from the frequent and alarming pressure of the fresh ice and bergs which are constantly coming down from Cumberland Gulf, and which loom heavily on our northern horizon.

The captain is confined to his cabin with asthma and bronchitis. He is very weak, and suffers mostly from sleeplessness induced by nervous excitement resulting from mental anxiety.

Friday, December 21st.—To-day has been the shortest day in the year, the earth having travelled its extreme distance from the sun. All of us have been looking forward to this day with no little anxiety, dreading that the sun might totally disappear for some days and involve us in darkness. Most providentially we have been spared this additional trial.

The captain was much worse this morning, but as the day advanced he became quieter and more easy.

Saturday, December 22nd.—At breakfast-time Bill Reynolds, who had been sitting up with the captain, told me he had been very restless and uneasy.

The captain lay upon the sofa during breakfast. He complained of no pain—nothing but mental anxiety and want of sleep, his constant cry being: " Oh, doctor, if you can, *do* give me something to make me sleep !"

In the evening he was in a very alarming condition. The harpooners took turns in sitting up with me, and in helping me to move the captain as required, for he is totally unable to move without assistance. He felt himself to be a dying man, for he said two or three times, " This is death !"

Sunday, December 23rd.—Busy with the captain. It is extremely difficult to move the poor old gentleman, with whom I spent pretty nearly the whole day.

Monday, December 24th.—Was up all night with the captain, who continues very ill. The different officers took it in turns to sit up with me; most melancholy work. This morning he slept, his breathing being easy and regular. There seemed to be such a change for the better that I began to entertain some hopes of his recovery, and so I felt remarkably cheered up and buoyant indeed.

Unfortunately, at about 2 p.m. there was some very heavy pressure upon the ship, and all hands were called to prepare for the worst. The pressure principally was in the immediate neighbourhood of the cabin.

On going into the cabin, it was evident the poor old captain had heard the groaning of the ship's timbers and understood the position, for a great change had taken place for the worse.

George Clarke, the mate, told him we were about to dress him, as the ship was " in the nips," and might give way at any minute, and that he must be dressed in readiness for going upon the ice should things come to the worst.

All this the captain understood perfectly well. It was piteous to see the great alteration that came over him— respirations hurried and difficult, pulse quick, face flushed, and so on. After he was fully dressed, with his boots, cap, and mittens on, he kept grasping my hand convulsively, as though wishful for human society and sympathy in his extremity. I assure you it was a very trying thing to sit beside this poor old dying man whilst the ship was groaning, quaking, and writhing under the heavy pressure, and the boards of the cabin deck jumping up under your feet.

However, at about 4 p.m. the ice became quiet and we were relieved of our anxiety, though the ship continued to make a great deal of water. The captain continued restless, and in a very much worse state than he was during the morning.

As you may suppose, I have been on deck very little of late. The weather continues most miserably thick, cold, and uncomfortable.

Tuesday, December 25th (Christmas Day).—I spent the entire night with the captain, who was extremely restless and uneasy. The weather during the night was horribly cold in the cabin.

At 8 a.m. I went on deck, and found the ship driving with great rapidity towards a large iceberg. We passed within three or four ship's lengths of the berg. We were most wonderfully preserved from driving upon it or being crushed by the whirling, crashing ice, which was in commotion far and wide around the berg, which is aground.

This morning the men held a prayer meeting in the half-deck, and, it being Christmas Day, they commenced with singing the chaunt, " How beautiful upon the mountains."

Flour and plums having been served out yesterday, Joe, the cook, was up at three o'clock this morning, busy as a bee making plum puddings for the different messes. Every man and boy on board had a large slice of very good plum pudding served out to him at twelve o'clock in honour of Christmas Day. As most of the men have been saving up meat, biscuits, etc., you may be sure every one of our ship's company enjoyed a good dinner. In the cabin we dined at one o'clock, and had a large plum pudding, which was equally divided, our usual ¾ pound of boiled salt beef, and a dish of *tripe.* George Clarke, the mate, had brought this, pickled in a jar, from home, and it turned out to be fearfully salt.

We ate our Christmas dinner almost in silence, each man's mind being occupied with gloomy thoughts of home, families, and friends. The poor old dying captain lay upon the sofa, occasionally turning over or dozing uneasily in a half-unconscious slumber.

What a Christmas dinner! What thoughts of the many merry ones at Sandon, and at home, and of last year's Christmas at Mr. Moffat's.* What a change! Thoughts of father, brothers, and sisters, at home on Christmas Day, and thinking of *me*, as I am thinking of them.

To these thoughts add my anxieties and apprehensions on the captain's account, and the gloomy prospect before every one of us. You will readily believe that a more miserable Christmas dinner would be difficult to imagine even. The dinner, such as it was, was soon despatched, and I was glad when 'twas over, it seemed such a horrible mockery of the spirit of an English Christmas.

At about 3 p.m. the ice was in motion again, and pressing heavily upon the ship. I happened to be on deck at the time, but instantly ran down to the cabin. Here I found the captain, whom I had left calm and tranquil and breathing regularly, changed for the worse in a sudden and alarming manner.

He had heard or felt the ship move under the pressure of the ice, and *knew very well what it meant*. He knew that the ship was in danger. He knew, whatever poor chance his ship's company had of saving their lives, *he* had none if the ship were stove in and we had to take to the ice.

Happily the pressure moderated and the ice became quieter. At 6 p.m. the captain was calmer, but evidently very much weaker, and more incoherent and difficult to understand.

Wednesday, December 26th (Morning).—This morning the captain is much worse, and is sinking rapidly. We continue our mournful watch by his couch. It is very affecting to see the good old man, his lips moving incessantly, as though in prayer, and conscious that his end is approaching.

Later.—The harpooners continued to relieve each other in the cabin every two hours. Bill Reynolds invariably knelt down upon entering the cabin, and prayed for the poor soul then passing away.

At 6.30 a.m. I felt quite worn out, so went forward into

* The late Dr. Paul Moffatt, of Dalston, Cumberland.

the half-deck and sat for a while with Bill Reynolds, feeling unutterably miserable, wretched, and cast down in my mind.

Twenty minutes later I returned to the cabin. Mr. Byers, who was there, said a great change had come over the captain. I ran to his side, and put my hand upon his wrist. He drew himself up twice; then his head dropped, and all was over.

Thus died Captain John Gravill.

The officers were aroused instantly; in fact, the ship's company in general was called, and such as desired went aft to see our dear old captain's face for the last time on earth. Alec Robertson and another knelt down in the cabin and offered up prayer, thanking God for having taken the captain away from so much suffering and misery, and rejoicing in the " sure and certain hope of his resurrection to eternal life " through the atonement of the Saviour, whom he loved so well, and believed in with such humble, child-like faith and confidence.

Afterwards Bill Clarke carried the body, sewn in canvas, up the cabin's narrow stairway and laid it down on the quarter-deck, where it was reverently covered from sight.

We then sat down together to a most melancholy meal, perhaps the most melancholy meal I have ever had.

After the past four days and nights of incessant watching and intense anxiety as to the issue of the captain's illness, in some sense it does seem a relief to have the question decided at last. Would to God, though, that our prayers and exertions had had a different answer ! I have the satisfaction of feeling that I did my utmost for him, nor did I spare myself in any way to save his life. This must remain now a consolation to my mind.

Thursday, December 27th.—Most miserably thick and foggy weather, with snow and a keen frost.

The ship's company is much depressed and low-spirited, each man brooding and unhappy, which is not to be wondered at. The death of the captain has cast a gloom like a funeral pall over us all. We are in miserable circumstances, too, with regard to means for warmth and cooking. The cook has been reduced to four buckets of coal per day for the galley fire. He endeavours to eke out the coal by burning " crang," or rotten whale's flesh, fished up from the tanks. Certainly it burns with a great heat, but at the same time fills the ship with an almost intolerable stench. Poor Joe is in despair, and does not see how he can possibly cook for all hands with such a pitiful allowance of fuel. We cannot afford more, though, for there is now *not a fortnight's supply of coal left* in the bunkers at this reduced rate of consumption. God help us ! How we are to get through the remaining months of an Arctic winter without firing I cannot tell. The men, poor fellows, suffer a good deal from want of their accustomed hot tea, and vainly attempt to boil their kettles over the lamps in the 'tween and half decks, a proceeding which causes the lamps to emit volumes of thick, horrible smoke, greatly adding to our discomfort and covering everything and everybody with a thick layer of soot. I noticed one man to-day trying to boil his kettle over a bottle full of oil with a tow wick.

Friday, December 28th.—The same wretched, thick, and gloomy weather, with constant snow and sleet; the same deep wretchedness and misery with all on board; the same dismal cookery over lamps; the same monotonous pump, pump, pump, day and night; the same wretched meals.

Our poor captain's body, frozen stiff and solid, has been removed to the bridge, where it lies protected from sight and from the weather by a tarpaulin.

Saturday, December 29th.—Whilst walking the deck with the engineer we were very much cheered at the sight of a large flight of rotches. They flew close past the ship, going to the North-East. The reader can hardly credit what an invigorating influence the sight of these little birds inspired. We know that their appearance indicates water. The direction of their course leads us to hope that spring-time, which these birds indicate, will come upon us early.

To-day there has been a very heavy gale blowing from the North-East—by far the heaviest gale we have experienced since coming into the country last May. The strength of the wind was something astonishing. The men could not stand at the pumps, and once, when passing the gangway, I was very nearly lifted off the decks and carried bodily away. At the same time it snowed heavily, and no moon was visible. An anxious, anxious night. I hardly closed my eyes, but lay in my berth listening to the roar of the gale as it tore through the rigging and amongst the piled-up, jagged ice, dreading to hear something give way or feel the ice get into motion.

Sunday, December 30th.—After our usual midday dinner the cook's fire went out, for the best of reasons—he had consumed his day's supply of coal in cooking.

I went below in the afternoon, and find it difficult to convey to you any idea of the cheerless appearance of the men's quarters. *Not a spark of fire*, mind you, but here and there a dull glow of light from a wretched oil lamp which scarcely emitted any light at all, and merely sufficed to make " darkness visible." The men, poor fellows, seem utterly miserable and dejected. They sorely miss, not only the warmth, but the *cheerfulness* inspired by the sight of a fire. As an American poet says:

> " A fire's a good companionable friend;
> He warms you, cheers you," etc.

It seems impossible to rouse our men's drooping spirits. This want of firing is indeed " the most unkindest cut of all," and is most keenly felt. Our tobacco, too, is almost done, and with it will be gone another great source of consolation to the sailor.

Monday, December 31st.—Busy this morning serving out the monthly stores to the men. Our allowance of biscuit is reduced to-day to 3 pounds per week per man.

We were much cheered at the sight of a " burgomaster " gull, who showed himself for a moment and then vanished in the fog.

So ends this year, with stiff breezes and thick, hazy weather; ship laid at the entrance of Frobisher Inlet, with her captain dead on the bridge, and the ship's company on short allowance from September 3rd.

If you have taken the trouble to read through this poor log thus far, it will be superfluous in me, O reader, to make any remarks or reflections upon the year that is fast passing away. Thou canst moralise for thyself.

CHAPTER XII

FIRST APPEARANCE OF SCURVY

January 1st, 1867.—I was roused at midnight by cheers and congratulations on the part of the watch in the half-deck. The men were welcoming in the New Year, congratulating each other upon its advent, and wishing that it may prove a happier one than the year just expired. I was dragged out of my bed to drink a " tot " from Harry Smith's bottle, whilst the good fellow forced half a biscuit upon me to eat along with it.

We presented a curious sight, half of us in our underclothes, drinking each other's health and happiness by the dim light of a couple of oil lamps, making merry over the New Year, whilst we ourselves are in the very jaws of death, with little or no prospect of saving our lives, in constant uncertainty and very often in despair.

To tell the truth, our lives just now, humanly speaking, are not worth a rush. We know it and feel it. Yet with the advent of the New Year hope springs up anew, and bony hands are shaken, smiles once more break forth on haggard faces, and " God bless you's " are exchanged as heartily as though we were in safety and at home.

After this pleasant little episode I crawled back to my bunk and slept away the remainder of the night, dreaming of home and friends I may never see again.

Daylight showed us that the ship had driven a long way to the eastward, the land to the South side of Frobisher Inlet being well in sight. In the afternoon a bear was seen upon the pack. The sun also showed himself, the weather was much milder to-day, whilst the amount of daylight is increasing perceptibly.

Thursday, January 3rd.—A ter-falcon visited the ship both

143

morning and afternoon. My poor little dog "Gyp" being out on the pack, the bird swooped down at her, evidently intending to kill her, but the dog facing the hawk like the brave little animal she is, it flew sullenly away to a hummock of ice, but did not remain long enough there for us to get a shot at it.

Alec Robertson washed some of my frightfully dirty underclothing this morning. In the afternoon I turned to and washed some stockings myself in the cabin, and hung them upon lines near the little cabin stove to dry. And very anxious I was indeed to get them dried, for in the cold, icy cabin 'twill take days to evaporate the moisture from thick flannel shirts and Shetland stockings. Should any accident occur to the ship now, I would find myself adrift upon the floes without any additional underclothing, for to put on wet clothes in this climate is out of the question. You would find them soon frozen solid, and yourself encased in icy armour and perishing miserably.

You can have little idea how anxious I was to get said articles of raiment dried as soon as possible. Could my medical friends have seen the quondam " Edinboro' swell " crouching over a wretched little stove, shivering with cold, and presenting the various features of a ragged woollen shirt to the feeble glimmer of a fire, and turning stockings round upon the line overhead to facilitate the drying operation with face expressive of the most absorbing interest, they would have gazed upon me with wonder and pity.

Happy is the man on board who has an abundant supply of underclothing. In this particular respect I am woefully deficient, having made provision only for a short *summer* voyage, and consequently am about the worst off in the ship's company for articles of dress. I am really very ill provided for struggling through an Arctic winter, especially upon such hard terms as ours, with barely sufficient food to support life and no fuel hardly to afford artificial heat.

Saturday, January 5th.—To-day has been observed as Old Christmas Day by the Shetland men, most of whom have been saving up meat and biscuit of late in order to do honour to the anniversary as kept in the Shetland Islands.

Monday, January 7th.—Laurence Stewart, harpooner, belonging to Lerwick, was very queer and out of sorts to-day in consequence of overeating on Saturday in honour of Old Christmas Day. The poor rogue had been saving up during the previous week for this event, and this is the result !

Tuesday, January 8th.—The ship leaks less daily, and only requires pumping dry every now and then, which is a great relief to us. At the same time I consider the fact of the ship having sprung a leak has been in reality one of our real blessings, as it has compelled the men to work, and so obtain the active exercise so necessary to their health.

Up to now our poor fellows have been remarkably free from illness, but to-day my worst fears are realised. The dread which has weighed for long upon my mind has become an alarming reality. Fred Lockham, the fireman, and Magna Grey (senior) show *unmistakable signs of scurvy !*

They complain of pain in and tenderness of the gums, which are swollen, livid, and spongy, and bleed to the touch, whilst the hard and soft palates are inflamed and the teeth loosening.

There is no mistaking this peculiar disease, and, in our situation, *there is no curing it !* We have some 3 gallons of very inferior lime-juice, which, with twenty-seven tins of bouilli soup, are our only fresh provisions. Medicine is of no use, and, if it were, there is very little left now in the medicine chest.

I am very much cast down when I reflect upon the *inevitable fate of our poor fellows*, and also of myself, should scurvy become general, as in all probability it will, before we can expect to escape from the pack.

I told Mr. George Clarke that scurvy was on board. We agreed to keep the dreadful news to ourselves, dreading the depressing effect it would have upon the spirit of the men. My only wonder is that this disease has not shown itself before now, as we are living on very low diet, salt meat, crowded together for warmth, dirty, unwashed, unclean, with no ventilation, exposed to intense cold, and with everything around us to depress and lower not only the vital, but also the mental powers. All these are circumstances extremely favourable to the development of scurvy, and *it has come amongst us at last.*

Fred Lockham, the first to complain, is of decidedly strumous constitution. He is one of our firemen, and, in fact, is one of the very men whom I had set down in my own mind as the most likely subjects for this disease. Magna Grey is a Shetland man, more than fifty years of age, and has been a hale, hearty man all along.

The temperature to-day has been remarkably mild and open.

Wednesday, January 9*th.*—I awoke this morning half-poisoned by the thick, suffocating smoke of a lamp which hangs abreast of our berth, and over which the officers in the half-deck are in the habit of boiling their kettles.

Everything in the berth—blankets, coverlets, top, sides, everywhere—covered with a thick layer of *soot.* It cannot but be very injurious to inhale such an impure atmosphere into our lungs. As the lamp hangs on a level with our berth, we get the full benefit of it, but every beam and bulkhead in the half-deck is covered thick and deep with soot from the lamps. Everything and everybody is as dirty as constant residence amongst lamp smoke, without the use of soap and water or necessary changes of raiment, can induce. 'Tis wonderful, really, how accustomed we are now to this life of dirt and misery, and how little it seems to inconvenience us.

Going on deck, I found the morning thick and foggy, with constant showers of soft snow, and the temperature most remarkably mild and open. This in the depth of an Arctic winter! Now that we are accustomed to severe cold, this mild temperature is very far from pleasant, as it seems to relax and unfit us for any exertion.

The ship makes very little water, only requiring to be pumped out once or twice every half-hour.

We have driven much further to the southward than we have been before, Resolution Island and Gabriel's Straits being well in sight.

Thursday, January 10*th.*—*Some more of our men are complaining of their gums.*

Luckily for my purpose, most of the men—and more especially Fred Lockham—have been smoking tea-leaves for

want of tobacco. This innocent leaf provides an excellent
" scapegoat," getting the blame for causing sore mouths, and
thus diverting the men's minds from the real nature of their
complaint. *Anything to keep from the crew the awful fact that
scurvy is on board !* 'Tis a disease all sailors have an instinctive
dread and horror of. They know how hopeless and how fatal
it is, and the intimation of its presence amongst us would
sound in their ears like the knell of doom.

The carpenter drew my attention to-day to his legs. I
found them thickly covered with the spots so characteristic
of incipient scurvy.

Upon looking at my own legs I find myself similarly affected.
So is Bill Reynolds, and, indeed, most of the officers and
probably most of the men.

I do not want to excite alarm by appearing to attach
importance to these little red spots, though I know full well
their fatal meaning. I endeavour to laugh and chaff and
cheer up the men, and appear cheerful and, like Mark Tapley
in " Martin Chuzzlewit," jolly under trying circumstances.
At the same time, my mind is wellnigh depressed to the utter-
most when I reflect upon the probable fate of our poor scurvy-
stricken fellows. *And I am the doctor of the ship*, the one to
whom they will look for life and health, but will look, alas!
in vain. God help me! What can I do but trust in His
mercy and pity and power to save ?

Friday, January 11th.—This day is memorable for the
melancholy fact that I have had *my last pipe of tobacco*, and
have put away the well-worn clay till brighter and better days.

This tobacco is really a serious loss. Wanting their accustomed solace, the men find time to brood over their misfortunes,
and become quarrelsome and ill-natured towards one another.
I assure you I would rather see a couple of pounds of tobacco
apiece come on board than 10 pounds of bread, though,
mind you, 10 pounds of bread more than represents three
weeks of our present allowance of biscuit. The men's tobacco
was finished some time ago, but what I have just finished
to-day was the last of my share of some 3 pounds of cavendish
which belonged to our poor captain, and which was divided
amongst the officers after his decease.

It has been my custom, ever since we went on short allowance, to smoke a pipe of strong cavendish before breakfast. I found it an admirable adjunct to my poor apology for a breakfast. It deadened the sense of hunger and, in fact, formed by far the most important item of the morning meal. Now that the tobacco is done, depend upon it, I shall feel hungrier than ever.

Saturday, January 12th.—At 3 p.m. the ice began to open into lanes and holes of water, and we were very much pleased at seeing five or six dovekies or rotches in a hole not far from our port bow. You can understand the joy with which we gazed upon these harbingers of spring. They seemed to tell us that the time was coming when the ice *must* break up and free us from our miserable thraldom and restore us, please God, to home and friends.

With solemn thoughts of scurvy, disease and death ever uppermost in my mind, you may imagine my feelings as I gazed upon these little messengers of hope. What the dove and the raven were to Noah, prisoner in his ark, so are these poor little sea-fowl to us. Their presence seems to say, " Be of good cheer! You are not alone in this awful ice. Let not your hearts be troubled; trust in God, and all will be well with you yet." Thank God for the birds! As Hayes says, when some dovekies made their appearance near his ship when wintered: " I would not for the world have hurt a feather of their trembling little heads."

To-day has been celebrated amongst the Shetlandmen as " Old New Year's Day," and there has been much talk amongst these poor fellows of their homes and friends.

The Shetlanders are singularly attached to their islands, and are ever disposed to yearning and home-sickness. With scurvy on board, and quite enough in our present circumstances and prospects to depress us, *this will not do*, and must be actively combated and dispelled if possible. I have hard work to keep up heart in the Shetlandmen, but it won't do to let them get " down in the mouth."

Sunday, January 13th.—This morning I found in my berth the fag end of a cigar, the last remnant of a few cigars which belonged to the captain, and which were divided amongst the cabin company after his decease. This, cut up and crammed into my pipe, was smoked slowly, and with every effort to protract the enjoyment as long as possible.

I have knocked the ashes out of my pipe, and now—farewell to tobacco for the remainder of this voyage.

I have been thinking of Sir Walter Raleigh and how, half an hour before his execution, he " smoked a small pipe of tobacco." For aught I know, like him I may have smoked my last pipe on earth. Situated as we are, a sure and certain death is ever very near to each and all of us. Laid amongst this frightfully heavy ice, no man can assert that the ship is safe for the next five minutes.

Monday, January 14th.—Our carpenter is busily engaged on the melancholy task of making a coffin for our poor captain out of the flinching boards. Andrew complains that the unwonted exertion of cutting up and smoothing these rough planks makes him feel very weak and faint. The coffin is to be kept in readiness to receive the captain's body, should we be mercifully spared to make our escape from the pack.

Our cook is in great despair. He does not know how he can possibly manage to cook food for all hands upon the still further reduced allowance of two buckets of coal and a " shake " daily. So, you see, the doctor is not the only man on board who has to contend with difficulties and anxieties in the performance of his duty towards the ship.

Tuesday, December 15th.—Daybreak calm, with little or no wind. Several flocks of rotches flying to and fro, evidently in search of water; also a flock of loons, two snow-birds (ivory gulls), and an owl. Three poor kittiwake gulls approached the ship and were shot instantly, skinned, and made into a " pan slash " almost before the heat was out of their bodies. They were in miserably poor condition (something like ourselves!).

8 p.m.—A breeze sprang up from the South-East in the afternoon, and now there is a fearfully heavy gale raging.

I regret very much to find symptoms of scurvy very prevalent amongst the men. Poor old John Thomson and Alec Robertson, both Shetland men, show unmistakable scurvy in their gums, with bleeding upon pressure, toothache, and other ominous signs of this dreaded disease. I have rated old

John soundly for smoking tea-leaves and given Alec an astringent gargle, and have left them both in ignorance as to the real nature of their complaint.*

The gale blew itself out towards midnight.

Wednesday, January 16th.—At nine o'clock this morning the sun broke through the gloom. It was a curious and interesting sight to see nearly all hands on deck gazing at this novel spectacle. It is almost the first time we have seen the sun since the New Year, and we hail his appearance with all the enthusiasm of the ancient Persians. " Truly the light is good, and a pleasant thing it is for the eyes to behold the sun." So says Solomon, and so we thought and felt. Upon my word, it cheered us up like a message from home.

At noon the land was seen running all round the starboard quarter. We must have driven a very long way up Frobisher Straits, as nothing but ice is to be seen from the mast-head, whilst the South Island, to which we have been so near, is on the far horizon.

The officers consider we are now in for a very long spell of wintering. We are so far up the straits that in all probability the pack will freeze up solid from land to land, and detain us here till May or June. When we hear these experienced Arctic seamen express such unfavourable opinions, it makes us all feel miserable enough, I can assure you. The men and, indeed, all on board, are very much cast down at finding the ship such a long distance up the straits.

I am sorry to have to say that signs of scurvy are pretty general amongst us now. I extracted a tooth to-day, a good sound tooth, but completely loosened by scurvy, and only remaining in the swollen gum as a foreign body, causing irritation, pain, and annoyance when the man attempted to eat.

Thursday, January 17th.—Spent the morning on deck. The ship has driven still further to the North-West, and is now in a deep bight, the North shore extending round the ship's stern to almost opposite her port quarter, whilst the South shore is off our port bow. Nothing but strong North-West winds can possibly drive us out of this land-locked position. There is hardly a breath of wind stirring to-day.

* Both these men died.

Friday, January 18*th.*—There has been rather an unpleasant commotion on board, consequent upon the discovery that one of the bread casks has been robbed systematically. These casks have been kept in the 'tween-decks ever since they were sent below on the 3rd inst. to preserve them from exposure to wet and moisture during the recent mild weather. Some of our poor starving fellows have managed to get out the bung from a cask, and help themselves *ad libitum* to the broken biscuits.

The officers have determined to knock off ½ pound of biscuit per week per man for all on board until the thieves are reported.

Two biscuits a week less is a serious loss, and, as you may suppose, there has been a good deal of unpleasantness amongst the men, who are suspecting and accusing one another.

Monday, January 21*st.*—The wind still prevails from the East, and the ship has drifted further inshore during the night.

Monday is the usual day for serving out the weekly allowance of biscuit. As we all are to go upon ½ pound less than usual, to make up for the biscuits abstracted from the cask, the men are in a state of considerable wrath towards the suspected plunderers.

Early this morning I was aroused by an angry discussion on this subject in the galley, where the cook had just lighted his fire for the morning. (There is no fire after midday for sheer want of fuel.) However, through one impeaching another, it is pretty clear that Bonsall Miller, Fred Lockham, Philip Pickard, and Robbie Hewson are the principal causes of this " bread riot."

It seems that poor " Bonse " first discovered the practicability of invading the cask. Assisted by Fred Lockham, he extracted the bung on the night of Sunday, 13th, yesterday week. They imparted the news to their bed-mate, Philip Pickard, who joined them in plundering the cask. Robbie Hewson—and, in fact, all four of them—confessed their guilt, and accused several others, including Purvis Smith, who made a very able defence when brought before the mate, and was acquitted for want of evidence.*

---

* All these men except Hewson died before the ship got back to Lerwick.

I do not doubt that a good many others are as culpable as the four first named, as a considerable quantity of biscuit had been taken away.

On board most ships under our circumstances the culprits would have been exposed over the windlass, and would have received a blow over the " starn " with a rope's end or, what is more severe, the blade of a saw, from every man on board. It was necessary to do something to punish these poor fellows, so as to prevent a repetition of this offence, which is a grave one, considering our position. Their allowance of biscuit has been reduced to $2\frac{1}{2}$ pounds until the deficiency is supposed to be made up, the rest of the ship's company receiving the usual allowance of 3 pounds.

I am sorry for these poor lads. Three of them are young, growing fellows, who require more nourishment than do bearded men who have arrived at their full stature and development. They will find it very hard to subsist upon such a pitiful allowance. Indeed, they generally contrived to finish their 3 pounds of biscuit by the Friday night, when their hunger would be so ungovernable that they were unable to resist the impulse to make such a heavy inroad upon their biscuits as to leave them destitute of food again till the return of " bread-day." How they will get on now upon their very reduced quantum I know not. The men have very little pity for them, regarding them as men who would live in plenty when their ship-mates were starving—" live upon our blood, sir !" as one of the men termed it.

This is the first unpleasant piece of business that has occurred to disturb the peace of the ship since we were first beset, or, indeed, since the voyage began, a fact which speaks volumes for the character of our poor ship's company.

As we have only one cask of beef and five casks of pork remaining, the ship's company has been reduced to an allowance of $\frac{1}{2}$ pound of meat daily.

Our coals, " crang," and sawdust are all burned, so that poor patient Joe, the cook, is reduced to using " shakes " for fuel.

Joe is one of the best fellows I ever met. The amount of bother, trouble, and worry he puts up with in the execution of his office is something tremendous. He tells me it is hard to keep the poor fellows away from his fire, or to prevent them putting scraps of his scanty daily supply of wood on to it to boil their kettles. So he leads the life of a martyr, his good nature and good heart revolting against even the appearance of unkindness in word or deed. You hear him scolding and fuming and fretting away over his rapidly wasting firewood, or over his furnace hampered up with tea-kettles, wondering "How the dickens do you expect me ever to get that 'ere beef biled with you poking the fire so, and burning everything up like that?" Then, when the "messes" of meat have been whacked out, or the "burgoo" duly measured, and Joe has time to retire to the half-deck and consume his little portion with his mess-mate, Mr. Byers, his day's work is done. He wipes his heated brow, forgets his troubles with the dinner he has swallowed, and, if the weather be not too cold, betakes himself to a little bench beneath the porthole in the galley, where he busies himself with converting bouilli soup tins into kettles or into strange funnel-shaped pots in which to heat water, or some such work of general usefulness.

You must know that Joe is quite a mechanical genius: nothing comes amiss to him, and he is ever ready and willing to do anything to oblige anybody. So, as you may suppose, the cook is a general favourite with all on board, as, indeed, he deserves to be; and no man has a greater regard for or admiration of his generous, self-denying character than myself.

WHITE GULL.

CHAPTER XIII

SUFFERING FROM THE INTENSE COLD

Tuesday, January 22nd.—During to-day we had light, variable airs and clear, bright weather, with very severe frost. This is the coldest day we have had this year, and is a great change from the open, mild, sloppy, foggy weather which has prevailed of late.

I am sorry to have to say that the scurvy cases are increasing amongst the men, and those who first showed symptoms of the disease are becoming worse.

Wednesday, January 23rd.—Very cold, *bitterly cold* last night, with little or no wind.

Was on deck at 7 a.m. 'Twas a gloriously clear, frosty morning, with a most magnificent sunrise. The weather was extremely cold throughout the day—even colder than yesterday. At midday the sun's rays had some perceptible warmth in them. The sun is coming northward at the rate of 14 miles daily !

There was a great amount of refraction to-day, the land and the numerous icebergs and islands around us being elevated and distorted in the most remarkable manner. There were light, variable airs from all quarters of the compass, while the ship was drifting very fast with the tide to the North and East.

Afternoon.—The sea-edge (though 'tis probably only a stream or hole of water) was visible from the main-top, and later from the deck, the horizon being lifted up by the unusually strong refraction. We seem to be in the middle of a large pack of heavy ice, adrift, with water all around it. We think that strong westerly winds would speedily carry the pack out to sea and, of course, our vessel along with it.

Evening.—There was very severe frost all day. When the

sun had set in a magnificent glory of purple and crimson, blazing up to the zenith, and converting the whole arch of the heavens into one brilliant and wondrous canopy of colourings unseen and undreamed of by any save the Arctic voyager —I say, when the sun had set and the intense cold had all its own way, the ship began to resound fore and aft with strange and startling crashings and explosions caused by the unequal contraction of the wood and iron work.

The night fell dark, but starry, reminding me of those beautiful lines by the poet Moore:

> " When night with wings of starry gloom
> O'ershadows all the earth and skies
> Like some dark, beauteous bird whose plume
> Is sparkling with unnumber'd eyes,
> That living gloom, those fires divine,
> So grand, so countless, Lord, are Thine !"

The moon does not rise till late on in the night. All of us were kept on the *qui vive* by the ship's continual and alarming crackings and crashings, which effectually banished sleep. Situated as we are, and have been for so many weeks, not knowing what an hour—nay, five minutes—may bring forth, accustomed to hear the frequent summons to face danger and death, the least unusual noise at night rouses us instantly. So the freaks of the intense frost with our ship's wood and iron work are anything but pleasant.

Our cabin clock struck work to-day, the machinery being affected by the low temperature. My watch stopped long ago, and is perfectly useless. The rigging is covered with ice, which makes my daily visit to the " crow's-nest " rather a ticklish piece of business.

Thursday, January 24th.—I was on deck at daybreak. The morning was clear and frosty, the clouds tinged with the most lovely crimson and purple, whilst the eastern horizon was one magnificent blush of roseate hues. Before the sun rose the lofty mountain-tops and islands and the pinnacles of the numerous bergs assume the most imposing tints and colourings, incessantly varying in intensity and character. Then, when the golden orb ascended above the horizon, every object around us glowed in the gorgeous blaze of light, as though steeped in some effulgent and unearthly flood, ever changing, evanescent, and most wondrous to look upon.

No written description can possibly convey to the mind of the reader the marvellous magnificence of an Arctic sunrise. I think the usual transformation scene in a Christmas panto-mime, when the fairy scenery is illuminated with intense lights of different colours, approaches most nearly to the beauteous display which excites our astonishment and admiration daily.

As the morning advances and the sun climbs higher in the heavens, we are entertained by the most curious and wonderful refraction. Icebergs, islands, the lofty hummocks in the pack, are elevated, transmogrified, are perpetually assuming fresh shapes and undergoing the most fantastic distortions. This applies especially to the icebergs, each individual one seeming to possess in itself the properties of a Proteus. Further away the distant lanes and holes of water, with bits of ice floating in them, are reflected in the sky above them with the utmost fidelity. These phenomena are confined to the eastern horizon principally, and generally continue with varying distinctness throughout the day until sunset.

The ship is driving to the North-East, carried by currents, for there is little or no wind. Outside us the icebergs, which, of course, draw a great depth of water, and doubtless are acted upon by the counter-currents, have been moving regularly to the South-East.

Afternoon.—Extremely cold; if anything, colder than yesterday.

At four o'clock the water at the pack-edge was to be seen very plainly, being lifted up by the refraction already referred to. There is water inshore of us and all around us, from the surface of which after sunset dense columns of thick, dark vapour rise steaming up like the smoke of a sacrifice. The lofty mountains, bergs, and pinnacles, are bathed in deepest radiance some little time after the sun has disappeared. The whole scene reminds me of those lines:

> " The Andes hills of trackless snow,
>   Where mortal foot has never trod,
>   At sunrise and at sunset glow
>   Like altar fires to God."

The intense and painful stillness that reigns around impresses the mind with a feeling of awe and reverence as you gaze and wonder and silently adore:

> " For these emit a solemn sound
>   As if they murmur'd praise and prayer.
> On every side is holy ground:
>   All Nature worships there."

Evening.—Mr. George Clarke, the mate and now the master of the ship, has slung his hammock in the cabin. How he contrives to sleep in that icy apartment, without fire or extra clothing, is a mystery and a miracle to me. However, it is necessary that someone should sleep aft. There might be a very heavy pressure upon the ship's quarters without its attracting the attention of the watch on deck, so insidiously and silently does the ice, influenced by currents, etc., close upon and compress the vessel without any external indication that it is in motion.

I rather think, though, that George's real motive in taking his bed aft is to escape from the smoky, suffocating atmosphere of the half-deck, where the rest of the officers and the English crew sleep. Here everything and everybody is covered with soot from the oil lamps, lives in an atmosphere of soot, sleeps amongst soot, breathes soot, is begrimed and smothered with soot. Chimney-sweeps would look respectable beside some of us!

The most wonderful thing is that the captain's canary and a linnet belonging to the engineer continue to live through such intense cold. Certainly, they are not very lively, but there they hang in their cages, with solid ice upon the skylight and ice on the beams and bulkheads of the cabin. Every morning we expect to find them dead. The steward is very careful about attending to the canary and, indeed, we all take a great interest in the poor bird.

Our oatmeal is getting very low, so we have knocked off the allowance for this particular day of the week, to make the meal spin out as long as possible.

Friday, January 25th.—Last night was calm and still, but intensely, *terribly* cold—by far the coldest night we have had this year.

There has been a very clear refraction all day, especially at midday, when the lanes of water and the ice towards the edge of the pack were lifted up to an uncommon height. For aught we know, this water may be 40 or 50 miles distant. When in the *Fame*, Scoresby saw and recognised his father's ship, refracted, at 30 miles distance.

Saturday, January 26th.—Up to this time Captain Gravill's order that all on board should have a glass of grog daily at the capstan head has been carried out. As our stock of rum has been diminishing rapidly under this generous liberality of our dear captain, we have been compelled to knock off giving grog daily. After this date it will be served out three times a week. For my part I seldom meddle with it, knowing that in such a climate alcohol is worse than useless, but 'tis waste of breath—in fact, not worth my while—to attempt preaching such a doctrine to the men. As they almost invariably carry their little quantity of grog below (a wineglassful of rum and water), and take it in small doses, like medicine, in their tea, I cannot see that it will do them any harm. If it comforts and cheers them up a bit, why, so much the better!

Sunday, January 27th.—Our ½ pound of flour was made into a dumpling apiece to-day, as the miserable quantity of fuel served out daily will not heat the oven sufficiently to bake the little cakes with which poor Joe has regaled us every Sunday up to now. There was half a dumpling for dinner, the other half being reserved till tea-time and then eaten, fried in rancid fat. Nothing like twenty weeks on short allowance and an Arctic climate to give a fellow an appetite!

Very hard frost all to-day; keen, cutting weather. All hands were ordered on deck to knock about and keep themselves warm by as vigorous exercise as possible.

Monday, January 28th.—Intensely, horribly cold last night. Without doubt it must have been the very coldest night we have experienced since the New Year, if not since we were beset. All night the ship's upper works cracked and rattled, keeping us uneasy and awake by the constant series of short, sharp explosions, now here, now there, perhaps close to your head, perhaps above or below you, as you lay in your bunk vainly wishing to sleep.

The day breaks now soon after 5 a.m., whilst at 5.30 this morning the outlines of the islands were discernible. At seven o'clock it is broad daylight, whilst the sun rises soon after eight. Of course, all depends upon the state of the atmosphere, but during this keen, clear, frosty condition the rays of light which are reflected from the hundreds of square miles of dazzling snow materially tend to shorten the hours of darkness.

At 9.30 a.m. I was serving out stores for the ensuing month. I regard the return of these store days every four weeks with great interest, as it shows that another month of our weary imprisonment has passed away, that we are preserved still, that we are so much nearer to our liberation.

It was most awfully cold in the cabin to-day. I could hardly hold a pen in my benumbed fingers, whilst some water accidentally spilt upon the floor close to the little stove was frozen solid immediately. The bulkheads and cabin door are covered with an icy hoar-frost, though a small fire is kept burning all day and sometimes to ten o'clock at night.

I served out ½ pound of tea and 1 pound of sugar per man. *This is the last of our sugar.* The little that remains will be divided amongst the officers, as 'tis impossible to divide so small a quantity amongst the ship's company generally. *We have no groceries left now but tea,* the rest of our stores of this kind being exhausted.

Afternoon.—It has been most frightfully cold on deck. As proof of this, I may record that my nose was frost-bitten for the first time since the voyage commenced. There was hardly a breath of air stirring—nothing but *solid frost !* The pumps were frozen up, and had to be lifted and cleaned out this morning. It may serve to show you in how terribly low a temperature we are making shift to live when I tell you that Mr. George Clarke's boots, when he pulled them off this evening, *were sheeted inside with glittering ice,* the moisture of his feet having frozen upon the leather.

Not a living creature seen to-day, excepting an owl.

Tuesday, January 29th.—Horribly cold again last night.

Doubtless yesterday and last night were the coldest day and night we have experienced as yet. It was very cold again this morning—so cold that it was almost impossible to keep the men upon the deck. No sooner had they pumped the ship out than they would slip below for shelter until called again to " suck her out." The weather is thick and foggy, with no wind, but with this intense frost.

We opened two cases of port and sherry which have been lying on the quarter-deck since the night of December 3rd. We found the wine frozen solid, one or two of the bottles broken by the expansion of the freezing liquid, and the corks of all of them more or less forced out by the same cause. It is a curious and novel sight to see a bottle of wine cut up and eaten. I am to use this wine amongst the sick men. Half a dozen of the worst scurvy cases come aft daily and get a glass of port, which wine, of course, requires breaking up and thawing over the cabin stove.

Afternoon.—The watch employed in cutting a pathway in the deep snow on the pack along the port side of the ship. The object of this work is to exercise and employ the men— firstly, in constructing the pathway; and, secondly, in walking and running round it.

Upon overhauling the lime-juice cask it was found that the small quantity that yet remains is frozen solid.

The cooper has been engaged opening *our last cask of beef* to-day. Happily for us, it turns out to be prime Christmas beef. Of course, the contents of the cask were frozen together in one solid mass, and the iron hoops had to be taken off, in addition to unheading the cask, before we could get at the meat.

Evening.—Still, quiet weather, with intensely hard frost.

Our poor fellows are very apt to skulk into the 'tween-decks when wanted upon deck; they can hardly face such terrible cold. It was horribly cold in the cabin. The small fire in the stove was very little use; had to keep myself warm by constantly walking up and down the confined apartment. The very oil in the cabin lamp freezes, and causes us a world of trouble to keep alight.

An owl flew over the ship to-day.

Wednesday, January 30th.—Cold, cold, bitter cold again last night. At 4 a.m. the pumps were choked with ice, and two watches were kept busy from then till seven o'clock in clearing them out, a fact which will show the amount of ice which had formed in them.

Now that our men are becoming exhausted, there is great difficulty in lifting these pumps, even with the aid of tackles. The frequency with which this operation requires to be done during this severe weather makes it very trying both to temper and body. It is cold, exposed work and, what is bad, consumes a great deal of our small stock of fuel. This morning half a " shake " (a whole day's fuel) was required to heat water over the half-deck stove for the purpose of thawing out the pumps. During this forenoon the mate's watch were employed thawing out the pumps thoroughly by unshipping them and placing them longitudinally over cressets full of fire on deck. Thus away goes more of our precious fuel.

I spent most of the morning upon the ice cutting away at the projected pathway. It was uncommonly cold.

Afternoon.—Terribly cold. *There is not a spark of fire forward.* Mark that, sir ! The day's allowance of fuel is consumed in cooking the day's dinner, and then there is no more fire for our poor fellows till six o'clock to-morrow morning, when the cook kindles to-morrow's fire for the purpose of cooking to-morrow's dinner. With no artificial source of heat, it is just a *plain, downright contest of endurance* between every man's constitution, enfeebled and diseased as we are, and the most terrible cold of an Arctic winter. We are bearing up under it with grim fortitude, but the contest can't last much longer with some of us. I expect every day to find men dead, frozen in their berths. May it please God to mitigate the severity of the weather, and that speedily, or we shall be forced to succumb. We can't endure much more of this.

The watch employed upon the ice for exercise, shovelling away a path through the snow, and cutting deep channels in the mass of ice formed on the deck by the rapid freezing of the water as it is pumped over the starboard side of the ship. This ice is level already with the gangway, and requires cutting through to allow the water to escape after it has been raised by the pumps.

Evening.—Most dreadfully cold. The cabin walls are encrusted with ice, which sparkles in the dim lamplight as though one were sitting in a veritable cave of Golconda. Your boots, damp mittens, etc., freeze solid, though placed close to the stove and almost in contact with it.

It is utterly impossible to keep warm. I thought we had met with cold weather before, but I never knew what cold really was until the last two or three days. Our poor fellows are suffering very much. God help them ! God help us all ! This is awfully trying work !

The sun has been shining brilliantly all day, but there has been no wind except light airs, no movement in the ice, and not a living thing seen besides ourselves.

Thursday, January 31st.—Intensely cold again last night.

This is dreadful work; it is murdering us ! We cannot endure it much longer in our starving, exhausted condition. The mate, who sleeps in the cabin, tells me it was the very coldest night we have experienced yet. The pumps were frozen up solid again, and our breakfast was delayed for two hours whilst the mate, Bill Lofley, and the engineer were engaged assisting the men to unship the pumps, clear them out, and replace them in working order. The iron barrels of the pumps are swathed in felting torn from the boilers, and a fire is kept burning in the pump well, but it is impossible to keep them from becoming columns of solid ice with only a small orifice left where the pump spears work up and down.

The forenoon was terribly cold, though the sun shone brightly as if in mockery of our miseries. I spent the morning on deck, employing myself in shovelling away the snow and in attempting to keep warmth in my benumbed and stiffened limbs by active exertion.

It is difficult to persuade the men to keep on deck; the poor fellows' faces are purple with the intense and terrible cold.

A raven flew over the ship this morning. The bird's neck was encircled by a glittering ring of ice formed by the freezing of the moisture in its breath upon the feathers. As the bird approached us, this ring of ice sparkled in the sunlight like a diamond bracelet. It is wonderful how these hardy birds contrive to find a living in this awful place.

Afternoon.—Cold, cold, cold! Upon going down to dinner, I found the thermometer stood at −22° in the cabin, where a small fire has been burning since 7 a.m. It is impossible for me to take off my cap at meal-times. I have to sit patiently until the cap-strings melt out of the mass of solid ice which encumbers my beard before I can eat a mouthful.

We have had a good deal of trouble to get the Shetland men to go over the side and walk about in the sheltered pathway we have cut in the snow. One man, Gideon Frazer,* doggedly refused to remain on deck, and was brought up from below several times. As he complained that his feet were frost-bitten, I was sent for to give a decisive opinion. I found that he was not suffering from frost-bite, but was thoroughly disheartened and disposed to give in. I remonstrated with him, pointed out to him the imperative necessity of moving about to keep up warmth and circulation, and finally persuaded him to return to the deck. He refused to go upon the ice, where the rest of the watch were walking about, sheltered under the lee of the ship.

It is necessary to be firm with these disheartened men, so I ordered him to be sent over the side in a rope's end. Actually, this huge fellow, 6 feet 2 inches high, lay down upon the icy decks, rolling about, moaning piteously, the blood running from his swollen and ulcerated gums, crying out to be left alone to die in peace and quietness.

I assured him he should do nothing of the sort; that I, as surgeon of the ship, was responsible for his life; and that I was determined he should go home alive, whether he wished to or not. " You want to die, do you ? No, by Jove ! You *shan't* die !"

At this he seemed rather astonished, and continued to walk up and down the deck with me till two o'clock, when I told him to go below. I shall never forget his remark as he disappeared down the hatchway, over which I had kept watch and ward till then: " I hope, sir, next time I come up this ladder it will be as a corpse !"

* Died on April 2nd, the day the *Diana* got to Ronas Voe, in Shetland.

Our Shetland men are very much disheartened, and quite ready to give up in despair and let the ship go to the bottom. Of course, we are determined to keep her afloat as long as we can. We can depend upon our English crew " hanging on to her " as long as they can stand, but these Shetland men cause us a world of trouble. It is the most difficult part, not only of my duties, but of every officer in the ship, to keep heart and life in these poor wretches. We cannot dispense with their services, nor are we going to see them desert their duty whilst the rest of our crew work themselves to death. The way in which the officers of the different watches bear with them, without striking or maltreating them, is incredible. I am often struck with the patient forbearance exercised towards the Shetlanders. Truly, we are officered by men of whom Hull may well be proud, and all of poor Captain Gravill's training.

Evening.—Awfully cold. Impossible to keep your feet warm. Your sea-boots freeze and are lined with ice though placed close alongside the little stove, whilst your feet are numb and insensible though so close to the fire that your trousers are scorching. After many vain attempts to keep warm in the cabin I gave up in despair, and went forward to my berth before 7 p.m.

So ends a month of strange extremes of temperature. Thank God, we all have lived through the last most trying week's exposure to intense cold that we have experienced since the winter set in.

CHAPTER XIV

COLD, STARVATION, DISEASE, AND DEATH

Friday, February 1st.—Thank God, the first of February has arrived at last! How wearily and anxiously we have watched for and counted upon its coming! What new hopes and heart and life the advent of a fresh month gives to us. Last month was remarkably quiet as regards the ice, freedom from pressure, etc., but to me it was a month of the greatest anxiety, seeing that the long-dreaded scurvy had made its appearance amongst us.

The following men of our crew show unmistakable signs of this awful malady:—*English :* David Cobb, George Blanchard, Fred Lockham. *Shetlanders :* Alec Robertson, Mitchell Abernethy, Gideon Frazer, Peter Acrow, and Magna Grey, senior. Of these, Blanchard is the worst case.

I am doing my utmost to keep these poor fellows in ignorance of the real nature of their disorder, and am giving them lime-juice disguised in other medicines, with gargles of alum, tannin, and other astringents. This is about all I can do for them besides urging upon them the paramount necessity of taking as much exercise as possible in the open air and keeping themselves as warmly clothed as they can, especially at night

Fortunately for the success of my well-intended dissimulation, many of the men have taken to smoking tea-leaves since their tobacco has come to an end, which said tea-leaves are saddled by me with the blame of producing so many sore mouths! You must understand that were these poor fellows to be told plainly that they had the *scurvy*, it would have such a depressing influence, not only upon themselves, but upon the ship's company in general, as would tend seriously to aggravate their disorder and induce it in others. If a single man knocks off his work and takes to his bed, you may depend upon it half a dozen others soon will follow his example.

O God, that has brought us through so many trials and dangers, forsake us not now, though indeed most of us seem to have utterly forsaken Thee and gone back to our old ways and wickedness, even as a dog returns to his vomit. Thou hast kept our ship for several weeks in quiet and safety, and we have basely stiffened our necks, hardened our hearts, shut our eyes, and done despite to the Spirit of Grace. By our words and actions we have shown that we have accounted the Blood of the Covenant an unholy thing.

Our daily prayer meetings have been discontinued. Those that once took the leading part in these simple services have disgusted the men by their perpetual squabbles and want of concord amongst themselves. Some of those whose voices once were raised in prayer now blaspheme openly. The Bible is a closed book. We are a miserable company of most miserable men, wretched, perishing with cold, half-famished, with no prospect of breaking out of the ice till late on in the season, with scurvy aboard, and every man wretched in himself. To sum up all in the words of the Apostle, we are " hateful and hating one another."

O God, have mercy upon us. Let us not perish miserably in this awful wilderness. Look down with renewed pity upon fifty poor sinful souls for whom Christ died. Oh, cut us not off! Spare us, O God! Bring us out of this ice. Give us, we implore Thee, milder weather, for Thou knowest this fearful cold is killing us. We are too weak to endure much more of it. Oh, send such winds as shall bring us out of this ice. Restore us *all*, *every one*, to homes and friends. Let us have no more deaths on board. Grant that the new month that commences to-day may be a month of hope and happiness.

This morning the weather is fearfully cold. The thermometer in the cabin was standing at 9° below freezing-point during breakfast, though as large a fire was kept up as the little stove would admit of. Your coffee, taken boiling hot off the fire, and poured direct from the copper kettle into your mug, is nearly cold before you have finished your scanty meal of half a biscuit and a scrap of meat I need hardly add that the said scrap of meat is frozen as solid as a stone, and requires to be warmed in a little tin pie-dish with some cook's fat before it is eatable. The lamp will hardly burn at all, in consequence of the oil freezing solid and requiring to be held repeatedly to the fire and melted. The cabin clock stopped work days ago, having been brought to a standstill by the intense cold. The water in the fountains in the bird-cages requires to be thawed frequently during the day.

It is wonderful how the canary and linnet endure such a terribly low temperature. One thing is in their favour. Their natural temperature is 108° or 110° (some 10° or 12° higher than the ordinary temperature of the human body), and also they are not reduced yet to short allowance of food, as we are. The cabin skylight is one thick crust of ice—thicker, the mate tells me, than he ever saw before—whilst the doors and walls of the cabin are glazed with ice, which glitters and sparkles in the dim lamplight as we crouch round the little stove.

We in the cabin are badly enough off and suffer quite enough from cold, with only our wretched little handful of fire to keep us from positively *perishing*, but how the rest of the crew live through it is hard to say. There is no fire in the galley after the midday dinner, excepting a handful to boil kettles at four and eight o'clock when the watches are relieved, so that all the poor fellows can do to keep warmth in their bodies is to turn into their cheerless beds or keep walking about between decks.

Could you look into one of their bed cabins you would swear a dog would die in it: sides and top one solid crust of thick, sparkling, pure white ice, the congealed moisture from the breath of the three or four poor fellows who sleep in this frosted sepulchre. No wonder they complain! No wonder they dread " turning in "! No wonder they give way to despondency!

I never saw the men so fearfully depressed during the whole of this disastrous and trying voyage as they are just now. We have the greatest difficulty in keeping them on deck and on the move at all. They *will* skulk below, if possible. But take exercise they must, or else make up their minds to die.

Lately, I have felt most fearfully depressed myself. This awful cold, this very short allowance of provisions and the want of firing, is killing us slowly but surely. A good many of us will not be able to hold out much longer if this severe weather continues.

Soon after breakfast I was sent for to look at the cooper's toes. Two of them are severely frost-bitten. I fancy he has brought it on himself by putting his feet into warm water, though he assures me 'twas barely tepid. I dressed his toes and hope to be able to save them.

Spent the morning knocking about the decks. Fearfully cold weather. Watch employed in getting up the pumps and thawing them.

Evening.—Sat shivering over the fire till about 7 p.m., when I despairingly gave up the attempt to get warm and so went to my bunk in the half-deck.

I have been *most unutterably miserable* during the past three days. Unfortunately, I was too extravagant with my 3 pounds of biscuit during the fore part of the week, and am reduced now to live upon a single biscuit per day, with a scrap of meat of a size such as you may imagine would remain out of $\frac{1}{2}$ pound of salt meat boiled, with no allowance for bone ! What with this positive starvation and the awful cold, I can say with Cain, " My punishment is greater than I can bear "

My heart is full of murmurings and repinings, questioning the justice and goodness of God in bringing us into this awful place to perish slowly of cold, hunger, and scurvy. I forget my own wickedness and the wonderful instances we have had of God's mercy and goodness towards us since we were beset. O God, bring us out of this fearful place ! Spare our wretched, miserable lives !

The men with scurvy are getting worse and worse. Magna Grey's gums present a horrible appearance.

The lime-juice was to have been served out to all hands last Monday, but *we cannot get it thawed !* It has stood close to the cabin stove all the week, but still remains a solid mass of ice. My medicines freeze solid, whilst the bottles I give out to the men are frequently broken by the action of the cold upon their contents. To lose medicine bottles *now* is rather a serious matter, for I much fear I shall have only too much use for all the bottles I possess.

Saturday, February 2nd.—Very cold again last night. Before breakfast the thermometer in the cabin was standing at 22° below freezing-point.

As I have said before, we are obliged to warm our little scraps of meat over the cabin stove to melt them before we can make a meal.

This week I have really suffered from " lack of bread." You see, our weekly allowance of biscuit has been reduced from 4 pounds per man to 3 pounds, our meat reduced from ¾ pound to ½ pound, and this we get only on six days in the week. The Thursday's ½ pound of flour has been discontinued. The Saturday's ½ pound of oatmeal has been reduced to 6 ounces. We are compelled to make our poor 3 pounds of biscuits spin out more and more and supply a fabulous number of meals. So what with the sudden reduction of food and the most dreadful, intense frost and want of firing, we all suffer most miserably.

The men, poor fellows, are almost entirely without firing, a single " shake " having to serve the galley stove *for two days*—to cook the food, boil the kettles, and keep warmth and life in forty-four men for two days !

O God, who dost not *willingly* afflict nor grieve the children of men, have mercy and pity upon us. Liberate us speedily, for, as Thou knowest, very many of us cannot hold out much longer. The cold and want of food is slowly but certainly killing us. Send us more moderate weather, O Father of Mercies ! Give us strength to bear up under these almost unbearable privations. Hear the cries and prayers of our friends at home, and oh ! in Thine infinite mercy, restore us to them.

This morning the cooper was engaged in opening a cask of biscuits and *our last cask of flour*. The eager, hungry looks of the watch as they gathered round and eyed the biscuits being handed out and sent below in bags to the bread locker would have made a very effective and touching picture of want and despair. The officers of the watch kept a sharp lookout to see that no biscuits were stolen, whilst two ravenous starved dogs picked up the mouldy scraps with all the voracity of famine.

The cooper also was employed in emptying *our last cask of beef* (broached a few days ago) into a more secure cask, to prevent the possibility of its being stolen by the men, some of whom, poor fellows, are becoming desperate and reckless with hunger.

Some of the men continue to eat the greater part (in some cases *all*) of their biscuits by the middle of the week. Consequently they have nothing to live upon till Monday evening but the pea soup, "burgoo," and the little scraps of meat served out at dinner-time. Many of the men are utterly weak and exhausted, and are failing very fast. I can observe an almost daily alteration for the worse in two or three of them.

At midday I went up to the "crow's-nest." This is very ticklish work, the rigging and "Jacob's ladders" being one mass of ice and requiring the utmost caution to ascend and descend without slipping. In our weakened state a single slip upon these icy ladders would probably be fatal. We could never "bring ourselves up" or, in ordinary words, retain our hold and support ourselves by our hands. I found myself so weak that my legs fairly trembled and shook under me as I went up the rigging. Did not see much aloft.

We had our usual pot of "burgoo" (oatmeal porridge) for dinner, no meat being allowed on Saturdays. I could not afford myself any bread. The plateful of porridge, seasoned with a lump of cook's fat (stuff at which your stomach, my dear sir, would revolt, and which your best judgment and opinion might lead you to suppose it cart-grease), and a mug of tea, formed my dinner. For breakfast I had half a biscuit, smeared with the before-mentioned cart-grease, with a mug of coffee. The remaining half of the biscuit, plus cook's fat, washed down with a mug of tea, will complete the sum total of solid and fluid nourishment that must sustain me for four-and-twenty hours. Every man aboard has had the same fare, though such as have been frugal with their biscuits will enjoy more or less of that article, according to their several fancies, appetites, or inclinations.

There is a wonderful deal of "character" to be observed in the way each man manages his biscuits. As before stated, some cannot make it last half the week; others run through it by Friday morning. Some parcel it out in separate handker-chiefs, one package for each day; others divide their supply still further into "meals." Some stick steadily and resolutely to a regular meal-time, while others are nibbling perpetually at their biscuit between meals. Some swap their bread for rum, others their rum for bread. Some are so dubious as to their strength of mind in resisting the temptation to eat that they are compelled to employ others to keep their biscuits for them under lock and key, and dole out only a certain quantity to them per day or even per meal. Some men are per-petually trying to borrow a biscuit; others contrive to have two or three biscuits in hand.

However, the fact is this is fearful work! The cold is intense. There is no prospect of getting out of the ice. If this severe weather continues, death from hunger and cold stares a good many of us in the face. I am certain that several of our crew cannot possibly bear up much longer.

Evening.—No fires forward, and the weather intensely cold; freezing horribly keenly. The cook has used up all the day's allowance of wood in boiling to-day's porridge, so the men in the 'spectioneer's and captain's watches are unable to get their tea-kettles boiled.

There is considerable ill-feeling and irritation amongst the people in the half-deck, who complain, and justly too, that they are perishing for want of firing. The mate consented at last to allow the stove in the half-deck to be kept alight after four o'clock and through the night to warm the half-deck and heat the men's kettles. This arrangement has given every satisfaction, though 'tis hard to say where the fuel will come from. God grant us milder weather as the year advances.

Sunday, February 3rd.—I hardly slept at all last night. The men who slept in the bunk above us left for other quarters at our request, for, if the truth must be told, we blame them for introducing amongst us one of the plagues of Egypt. But we find we have jumped from the frying-pan into the fire. All the heat of our bodies ascends now through the loose boards into the bunk above, and we found ourselves most miserably cold. I dozed off and on through the night, and in the morning found myself as stiff and nearly as cold as a corpse, all my bones and joints aching and completely chilled through and through. This is really dangerous work. No constitution can stand it long. Such a miserable night I have not had since I moved my quarters forward.

On going on deck, I was glad to find that the wind had moved round to the East. The weather was thick and foggy and milder, though still severe enough for me to get my nose frost-bitten during the course of the morning. In winter-time North-West winds, which blow off the frozen land, are always the coldest, while Easterly winds, which blow off the water, are the warmest. In the summer-time it is just the reverse.

To-day the men have their ½ pound of flour made up into a dumpling apiece. I assure you, the sensation caused by the advent of these wretched little dumplings from the cook's coppers is not easily to be described. Some of the men have been saving portions of their meat and biscuits to add to their dumplings, and so convert them into a small species of meat pudding. Anyhow, the Sunday's dumpling is the great event of the week now. It is the only really decent and satisfactory meal the poor fellows have in seven days and, naturally enough, they look forward to it with fond anticipation, and look back upon it with regret. *Half* my dumpling, with a spoonful of currant jam, a little raspberry vinegar, and a mug of tea, formed *my* Sunday's dinner. Half a biscuit smeared with fat, with a mug of coffee (no meat, my dear sir), formed my Sunday's breakfast.

Soon after dinner, whilst crouching over the cabin stove busily engaged in scribbling this journal in pencil (for it was far too cold for one's numbed fingers to hold a pen and, besides, the ink was frozen solid in the bottle), my poor little dog Gyp, who was sitting beside me, suddenly began to bark wildly. She ran under the sofa, and thence out of the cabin into my berth, where she continued to bark in a strange, shrill, yelping key. I remarked to the mate, who was lying in a hammock suspended immediately above my head, " I must shoot that dog, George. I believe she's going mad."

I pulled on my boots immediately (but, oh, with what a heavy heart !), took a loaded rifle from my berth, called her up on deck and shot her, as I dreaded the possibility of her strange conduct being the first symptom of hydrophobia.

Poor little Gyp! How many weary miles hast thou trudged behind my heels! Through what fearful scenes of danger hast thou stood by my side! What hunger, cold, and misery we have endured together! And this is what thou hast come to at last! God only knows but that my fate may be impending, as sudden and as unexpected.

Spent the rest of the afternoon on deck, or walking about on the ice on the lee side of the ship.

Evening.—Crouched over the stove, or walked up and down the cabin to keep warm, till I went to bed at 8.30 p.m.

Monday, February 4th.—Had another miserably cold, uncomfortable night. It is impossible for any constitution, enfeebled by five months' short allowance and exposed to the rigours of an Arctic climate, to bear up long against such a low temperature. Sleep is impossible.

Thank God, another bread day has come round. I never suffered so much for actual want of bare bread as I have done during the latter half of the past week. It has been the most miserable, trying, suffering week for all on board that we have experienced since we have been beset. You see, the mild, open weather which we had during the first two or three weeks of the New Year unseasoned us, as it were, and made us very unfit to endure this low temperature, especially on a reduced allowance of food. All on board admit that last week was *the* most trying week we have had yet. In our weakened and exhausted state we all have felt the cold *most bitterly*. It is killing us off rapidly.

There is a new moon to-day, and the highest tides may be expected during this week. God in His mercy keep the ship quiet amongst this awful, heavy ice, and preserve us from all danger. In mercy, O God, moderate this bitter weather!

'Tis a gloriously clear, cold, frosty morning. Biscuits were served out in the cabin at ten o'clock as usual. It is exactly *five calendar months* to-day since we were put upon short allowance on that Monday morning in September when beset in Scott's Bay. Also, it is two months to-day since the ship received her heaviest nip and sprang a leak, when we took to the ice with all our boats and provisions, and stood looking on, expecting to see the last of the old *Diana*.

The afternoon was clear and cold, but, thank God, much milder. This change is a wonderful relief.

Evening.—Actually the cabin felt agreeably warm for the first time for I dare not say how long. Comparatively speaking, the air is quite nice on deck to-night.

Tuesday, February 5th.—I was quite warm last night, and slept very well, the carpenter and Reynolds having covered the top of the berth with a bear-skin, a linen sheet, a mat, and some bread bags.

Upon going on deck at eight o'clock it was evident that the ship had driven with the ice to the northward and off the land. The morning was most beautifully fine and mild, a wonderful and blessed change for which we all feel indescribably thankful. The late cold weather was murdering us.

The cooper was employed unheading the lime-juice cask. What little lime-juice remained was frozen into a solid cake of ice. We melted it over the galley fire and distributed it amongst the ship's company. It barely ran to $\frac{1}{2}$ pint per man, and proves to be miserably poor stuff. It is nearly all water, and appears to have been prepared from fusty lemons instead of limes.

Evening.—Was called forward to look at Philip Pickard's fingers. The second and third finger of each hand to all appearances seem *dead*—killed by frost-bite. The unfortunate lad tells me he has been in the habit of thrusting his numbed and frozen fingers into the lamp flames, there being no fire lately at night at which he could have warmed them. The consequence is his finger-ends are totally dead and insensible. I pushed a needle deep into the flesh without his feeling the least pain. However, I have wrapped them up in cotton-wool for the night, though I have little hope of saving them; two of them certainly will have to come off.

I dread having to use a knife, for in the present weakened and exhausted condition of the men the most trivial wounds make very slow recoveries. How this poor anæmic lad would fare were I to cut off four of his fingers I dare only guess at. I am very doubtful if he would recover from the operation

The blood is so impoverished as to be unfit, almost, to perform its office in the healing process.

Wednesday, February 6th.—During the night the weather was mild and open, but this morning the air is cold, with a keen frost. The pumps were frozen up again, and required to be unshipped and thawed.

Soon after breakfast we saw on the pack a large bear, completely worn away to a skeleton with hunger. He was lying down, and seemed utterly exhausted and scarce able to raise his head. His shoulder-blades almost protruded through his hide, like the hump of a camel. Altogether he was a most miserable-looking object.

The mate tells me he would go after the bear, with every prospect of shooting it, only the snow is so deep as to make travelling over the pack both difficult and dangerous. The mate states that, in his opinion, a great many bears must perish of hunger every winter; that they are said to be able to live without food for months—in fact, so long as there is " a bit of grease " remaining upon them.

Many years ago Captain Gravill took home some seven or eight young seals. During the voyage they seemed lively and active enough. They were supplied with food, but did not seem to eat much of anything. They were sent to the Zoological Gardens at Hull, where they lived in a pond until all the fat on their bodies was absorbed, and then died. Thousands of people went to look at these seals.

Evening.—The weather is variable, mild, and then frosty. Nothing but light airs all day. As seen from the mast-head, the pack is all broken and split up into lanes and channels by the action of the high spring tides which prevail just now.

It is the opinion of the mate and officers that if we were favoured with strong North-West winds during the prevalence of these high tides, there is every probability of our being blown out to sea; in fact, there is nothing to stop us. However, though we have the tides, there is hardly a breath of wind from any quarter.

Looking at George Blanchard's legs to-night, I found them covered with the deep purple patches of effused blood so characteristic of scurvy. The poor fellow, too, has the greatest difficulty in moving about at all, owing to stiffness of the muscles of the thighs. Alec Robertson, Mitchell Abernethy, and David Cobb, all complain of more or less stiffness and inability to move their limbs, whilst three or four more of the men have begun to complain of soreness of the mouth and gums. Unless God, whose compassions fail not, sees fit to deliver us speedily from this ice, we shall inevitably lose a number of our crew from scurvy. I am the surgeon of the ship, but, God help me! what can *I* do for these poor fellows ? They are utterly beyond the aid of medicine; altogether out of my hands. Medicine is of little or no use in controlling, checking, or averting this fearful malady. It is a disease of the blood which can be cured only by the timely administration of fresh vegetables, fruit, and fresh animal food. These we are almost altogether without. We have a few tins of soup and bouilli, which are my only hope.

Lord, have mercy upon these poor suffering men; have mercy upon us all. We know not whose turn it may be to die next. This is a fearful, awful life.

Thursday, February 7th.—Weather dull, thick, and much colder to-day. The lanes and holes of water are covered with bay ice, and the pumps once more frozen up. The sun broke through the clouds at about eleven o'clock, and really shone with some perceptible warmth. Just now he is coming North at the rate of 19 miles daily.

A Thursday is what the men call " banyan day." We get no broth or soup, our " burgoo " has been knocked off, and ditto our Thursday's ½ pound of flour, so we only get for dinner our scrap of meat and about half a biscuit.

Here is our bill of fare for the week, or, I should say, for week after week. We all fare exactly alike fore and aft, the youngest boy on board receiving as much (or, rather, as little) as the master or officers of the ship.

Breakfasts and teas are exactly alike. They consist of as much of your whack of biscuit as you can afford, with a third of your miserable ½ pound of meat if you have contrived to save any of it from your dinner. On Saturdays, when no meat is served out, you have to go without that luxury for that Saturday's dinner and tea and Sunday's breakfast.

The dinners for the week are as follows:

Sunday.—Half-pound flour dumpling. Half-pound salt boiled beef.

Monday.—Ladleful of weak pea soup, thickened with biscuit crumbs. Half-pound salt pork.

Tuesday.—Ladleful of " burgoo " (porridge). Half-pound salt beef.

Wednesday.—Ladleful of barley broth. Half-pound salt pork.

Thursday.—" Banyan day." No extras. Half-pound salt beef.

Friday.—Ladleful pea soup. Half-pound salt pork.

Saturday.—Ladleful of " burgoo." No meat.

The meat is weighed with the bone, and runs up a great deal in the boiling. When our ½ pound of meat comes to the plate, I assure you solemnly it is reduced frequently to *less than three ounces of meat.* The pea soup is made for forty-nine of us out of 5 pints of peas, to which some 3 pounds of biscuit crumbs are added to thicken the precious decoction. I assure you this strange " hodge-podge " makes one of the best and most satisfying dinners of the week. Each man and boy gets a single ladleful of this and of all other broths, such as barley soup (made out of 5 pints of pearl barley) and oatmeal porridge (3 ounces of oatmeal apiece).

As I have stated before, the Sunday's dumpling is the great event of the week.

The only *luxuries* we can afford ourselves (and, mind you, they *are* felt to be great godsends, I assure you) are ½ pound of cook's fat per week per man (serving us as butter for our biscuits) and a wineglassful of weak rum and water. This is served out at the capstan head at 11 a.m. every Monday, Thursday, and Saturday. There is a fair amount of tea, and we in the cabin have a little coffee and the remains of the sugar. The men forward have no coffee, as it is nearly all consumed.

Add to the above bill of fare the liberal allowance of 3 pounds of biscuit per week (which averages from twelve to twelve and a half biscuits, or less than two ship's biscuits per day), and you have the full, true, and particular account of our manner and mode of living on board the s.s. *Diana*, whaler, of Hull, at present beset in the pack in Frobisher's Inlet.

Afternoon.—Engaged in the cabin making up the leeway of this log. In other words, I was copying on to the pages that now meet your eye the contents of a " pocket-book and cedar pencil " log which I have kept when fingers were too numbed, ink frozen solid, the fireside too near and dear, and perhaps the heart too sick and heavy, to make the necessary effort with pen and ink.

This log has been the great bore of the voyage. It has been abandoned again and again, yet resumed again from a sense of duty to myself and more so to my friends. Ah! there's where the shoe pinches. Thoughts of home and anxious, sorrowing friends, and the great improbability of these pages ever reaching them; the heart-sickening feeling of mistrust, despondency, and despair of ever seeing home or friends, father, brothers, sisters, or old college chums, uncles and aunts, relations, acquaintances, and neighbours any more; the reluctance to sit down to record one's miseries and privations in black and white, to chronicle the poor events of each miserable day as it slowly drags itself along after its equally miserable predecessors; the deadening, numbing influence of cold, privations, discontent, and despondency falling like a deadly blight upon one's mental faculties; the weary, weary life one leads—all these tend to make log-keeping and journalling (to coin a word) fearfully uphill and distasteful work. Then, if the ship is in trouble, in the nips, and expected to be stove in any minute, how can I sit down to this log with my heart in my mouth and a horrible death staring us in the face ?

You, my good sir, might be able to write as coolly as did old Kempenfeldt when he went down in the *Royal George*, or as Napoleon did when the cannon-ball dashed the sand over the paper upon which he was penning a despatch. But I confess I can't do it, and so this log has been neglected, returned to, and neglected again and again, till now I have a very heavy leeway of pencil notes to copy out and make up for your interest and instruction.

Now that the afternoons are lengthening and the cabin is tolerably warm I have essayed myself to my task for your sake much more than my own.   It is getting so light of an afternoon that I can see to write up to 4 p.m., even with the cabin sky-light coated thickly with frost.

I went on deck at five o'clock and saw the new moon (some three days old) shining brightly and sweetly, the horizon still tinged with the radiance of the recent sunset, and the evening quite light and cheery.   At 8.30 it was a beautiful starry night, with a flickering Aurora Borealis, cold, clear, and frosty. The weather during to-day has been curiously changeable, alternatively mild and freezing keenly.   The ice was moving about a little during the evening, causing the old *Diana* to rattle and crack occasionally.

Friday, February 8th.—Was aroused at four o'clock this morning to look at a Shetland man, Purvis Forbes Smith, who had fallen on deck and was reported to me to be in a dying or, at least, in an alarming condition.

I found the man's extremities extremely cold, his pulse feeble, his mental faculties confused, his senses of sight and hearing very much impaired, evidently the whole economy sinking under the influence of cold. . . .

This cold is playing havock* with our men.   All of us are suffering more or less from it, but Purvis is the first man to succumb to the recent hardships, exposure, and want of firing.

There was a warm discussion amongst the officers in the half-deck as to the propriety of allowing the men, more especially the Shetland men, to suffer so severely for want of a fire.   The result was a conversation with George Clarke, the mate and present commander of the ship, and he gave orders for the manufacture of another stove, which is to be placed in the alleyway so as to heat the berths of the Shetland men.

Emanuel Webster, the engineer, was busily employed during the morning converting an iron coal bucket into a stove, which was completed, erected, and in full operation by three o'clock in the afternoon.

The great difficulty, of course, will be to provide fuel for these stoves—viz., the one in the half-deck and this new one in the alleyway.   They are to be lighted after twelve o'clock noon (when the galley fire goes out after cooking our dinners) for the

* *Havock* was the old spelling of *havoc*.

double purpose of heating the men's kettles and also heating their berths and the ship forward. Truly, the men are in such a lamentably enfeebled condition now, and their blood is so impoverished, that a comparatively moderate degree of cold takes a severe hold of them. This morning the air was not particularly keen, but Ned Hoodlas's nose was fearfully frost-bitten whilst its owner was actively walking the deck. It was the severest case of frost-bite of the nose I have seen during the voyage.

So, fuel shortage or not, we *must* have these fires kept up, despite any expense or damage to the ship, or else make up our minds to lose a number of our crew. The men now cannot stand the cold that they endured previously with impunity.

Afternoon.—Purvis very weak still, pulse hardly perceptible. I saw that he got his dinner (pea soup), into which I poured some 2 ounces of port wine. He is warmer, but very feeble and incoherent—" daft," as the Shetland men term it.

I am glad to be able to say that I have arranged with the mate that half a dozen of the scurvy cases shall have bouilli soup for dinner four times per week. This fresh meat and vegetables is their only chance of life unless God in His mercy sees fit to bring us speedily out of the pack.

The carpenter was employed during the afternoon in sawing up chocks, etc., for firewood. During the last two or three days the engineer and steward have been busy pulling down and then cutting up the woodwork between the coal bunkers.

Yesterday the men in the 'spectioneer's watch were employed in removing the frozen moisture from the beams and deck forming the roof of the 'tween-decks (the special habitation and resort of the Shetland men). They scraped off and carried away no less than *thirty-five bucketfuls of solid ice!* Other men were engaged in removing the ice from the sides and top of their sleeping berths. No wonder the ship is dreadfully cold when sheeted and glazed inside and out with ice and, until to-day, with no fire forward for the poor fellows to get to after midday or before six o'clock in the morning.

To-night there is a stiffish breeze from the North-West, and a very cold breeze it is, too. Pray God it may continue, but I am afraid the frost will stop it.

Saturday, February 9th.—During the mate's and 'spectioneer's watches last night the wind blew very strongly from the North-West, with singularly variable weather, alternately mild and freezing keenly. This morning is very cold indeed.

The new stove in the alleyway gives great satisfaction. Jamie Williamson, a Shetland lad, remarked as he sat and eyed the unwonted blaze and enjoyed the unaccustomed warmth, " Ah ! 'Tis many a day since I saw such a sight as that, sir !"

Purvis Smith, the Shetland man, is not much better this morning. With great difficulty I have obtained for him three extra biscuits out of the bread locker to carry him on till Monday next.

George Clarke put the question to the officers in the half-deck whether or no this man was to have these extra biscuits on the doctor's recommendation. There was considerable difference of opinion as to the propriety of allowing one man more bread than the rest when all fare alike, and when, by prudence and economy, the poor wretch might have made his 3 pounds of biscuit spin out as well as the other men did. It was argued that if once the example were set of giving sick men extra bread, we should have abundance of invalids in no time, that the Shetland men especially would hail this precedent as the signal for taking to their beds immediately in the sure and certain hope of getting extra grub and immunity from work.

It was resolved that, in the case of Purvis Smith, the three extra biscuits requested by the surgeon should be allowed, but thereafter no more extra biscuits or other provisions would be given to any of the ship's company that may be disabled or indisposed.

So the matter was settled, greatly to my satisfaction, though it gave very little satisfaction, I can assure you, to the ship's company generally. The man Smith is not a favourite with them. Still, he has a human life to save or lose, and I am bound to do my utmost for him.

The morning was extremely cold; hardly able to face the

cold on deck. The wind continued pretty strong from the North-West, and the ship has driven a good way to the northward and eastward since yesterday. At dinner-time the thermometer in the cabin stood at 7° below freezing-point, and that with a fire burning in the place for the previous five hours. Upon taking off his boots after dinner the mate found not only the hair soles, but his socks even, were positively frozen to the soles and sides of his boots, the natural moisture of his feet having frozen everything together. It is a wonder and a mercy how our toes and feet escape. God grant we may weather safely through this month, for February is reported by those who have wintered in Cumberland Straits to be a very cold month generally, with high winds.

In the afternoon there was a good refraction, which showed water to the North and East of us, but how far off or how near none of us can tell or even guess at. The pack is broken up into lanes and holes here and there, but, as the mate says, " we needn't care about seeing any water until different weather sets in, for as fast as water appears ice forms over it."

At five o'clock the moon shone brightly, whilst the horizon was yet one flush of purple and crimson from the radiance of the recent sunset.

Evening.—Sat in the cabin, which was fearfully cold—so cold, indeed, that I could not find courage enough to leave the closest neighbourhood of the little stove for the table. So this log for this day was scribbled in pencil and is now (Monday, 11th) faithfully copied out in black and white.

Sunday, February 10th.—Upon going on deck at 8 a.m. I found the wind blowing very strongly from the North-East, with thick, foggy weather. The weather was so cold that the pumps were frozen up again last night, and again frozen and required to be unshipped and thawed during the mate's watch this morning. The wind was horribly cold. Indeed, it was almost impossible for me to bear it at times, though I had three pairs of mittens on my hands, while my nose, now very tender from a recent frost-bite, was swathed carefully in a silk handkerchief.

I spent the greater part of the afternoon on the ice, walking

up and down the pathway cleared in the snow on the lee side
of the ship.

Monday, February 11th.—We had breakfast in the cabin
without the aid of a lamp for the first time for many weeks.

The morning was very cold and sharp, and the pumps
again required unshipping and thawing. A wind sprang up
again from the North-West, and blew pretty heavily at times.
Thus the poor old ship is bandied about, first by North-East
and then by North-West winds, and driven a few miles to the
South-West one day and to the eastward the next day. However, these winds are doing us good by keeping the great body
of ice in which we are laid in constant motion, and thus preventing it forming into a land-floe, in which we might be beset
hard and fast until far on in the season.

Biscuits were served out at 10 a.m., an extra ½ pound being
allowed per man on account of the extreme severity of the
weather and the weakened, exhausted state of many of our
crew.

The following men—Alec Robertson, Mitchell Abernethy,
Magna Grey, George Blanchard, David Cobb, and Fred
Lockham—being the six worst cases of scurvy on board, have
this day received ½ pound of bouilli soup apiece instead of the
usual ½ pound of salt pork. I hope and trust the poor fellows
may derive great benefit from the little fresh meat and
vegetables we are able to give them. I entertain hopes of
seeing a change for the better in all or most of them now that
they are getting fresh provisions in the place of salt meat.

Two other men, Peter Acrow and Gideon Frazer, are bad
with scurvy too, especially the latter, while others are beginning to complain of sore and tender mouths. The man Purvis
Smith continues in a very critical and alarming state.

Lord, have mercy upon us, and bring us out of this ice
speedily, or many of us will perish miserably. I can do very
little for these poor fellows beyond giving them astringent
gargles for their mouths and urging upon them the necessity
of constant exercise and keeping their hearts buoyed up and
hopeful.

Tuesday, February 12th.—Weather keen, hard, and frosty.
Was on deck all the morning and the greater part of the

afternoon. Light airs from various quarters. Ship moving to the northward.

The main topsail mast and gaff were sent down this afternoon and cut up for fuel. The pumps required to be lifted again and thawed during the mate's watch this evening.

Purvis Smith worse, unable to eat at midday, and sinking very fast. Sat in the half-deck all the evening in attendance on the poor fellow, who continues to sink rapidly till now (10.30 p.m.) he is very near his end.

Wednesday, February 13th.—I sat up all last night, until five o'clock this morning, in attendance upon the unfortunate man Purvis Smith, who continued to sink gradually throughout the night. I hardly expected to find him alive when I awakened at 7.30.

I went forward at intervals during the morning, each time expecting to find poor Purvis had breathed his last. I went forward again immediately after dinner (at 12.30 p.m. or before) and found he had expired.

The body was removed to the quarter-deck, where it will remain until an opportunity offers of burying it ashore or on some rock or island. Failing this, it will be sent overboard, as we have no wood suitable for making a coffin.

I find sailors have a not unnatural horror of a watery grave. I trust we may have an opportunity of giving these poor remains a Christian burial.

In the afternoon I made up the cash accounts of the poor man, and assisted at making an inventory of his clothes and effects—a most miserable collection of rags. I wrote out a statement of the causes of death for the official log, and so ends the tale.

The awful question frequently recurs to my mind, " Which of us will be the next to die ?" If we do not make our escape from this land-locked bight very speedily I see nothing else but death in prospect for many of our poor fellows. As before stated, eight of them are more or less disabled by scurvy and must die unless we can get them fresh meat, etc., whilst a number of others are beginning to complain of soreness of the mouth, ulceration of the gums, etc. We are now consuming our last cask of beef. We had *our last dinner of barley soup to-day*, and must fall back upon rice, of which we have one bag.

O God! have mercy upon us.   Have mercy upon us *all* and bring us safe out of this awful ice.

To-night the moon enters her first quarter.   We are looking forward to the full moon, and trust that the high spring tides that accompany it may be accompanied themselves with such winds as will bring about our deliverance.   There has been hardly a breath of air to-day and the ship has been drifting with the ice to the northward.   Bill Lofley tells me she drifts for a range of some 7 miles backwards and forwards from South-West to North-East, being carried in the ice by winds and currents.

Thursday, February 14th.—A beautifully fine sunny morning, most decidedly the finest day we have had since the new year commenced.   Positively the sun is acquiring such power as to thaw the flakes and patches of ice upon the side of the ship exposed to the influence of its beams.   This is most noticeable where the thin patches of ice are situated upon the black painted portion of her hull and upon the boats, which also are black.

I was knocking about on the ice and upon the decks during the morning, enjoying the sunbeams, though, mind you, it was freezing pretty hard at the same time.   I noticed Bill Reynolds rubbing out a very ugly frost-bite from the end of his nose immediately before breakfast.

It is curious how men who have gone through much severer weather without being in the least affected by frost-bites find themselves constantly bitten now, especially in the nose.   The cooper, whose nose was never frost-bitten before, was bitten severely there the day before yesterday.   I conclude that our systems have become so much exhausted and our blood is in such a thin and impoverished condition that we are now in the worst possible condition to resist cold, even though it be nothing like so low as that which we have successfully contended against.

There are a good many slacks and lanes of water visible from the mast-head, but as quickly as the water appears the bay ice forms over it.   We must rest contented to wait, probably until much warmer weather sets in, when the water will remain open and the ice, once parted and broken up, ceases to freeze together again.

After dinner the officers of the ship came to the cabin in a body to consult with George Clarke as to what was best to be done to supply the cook's furnace and the two stoves with fuel. The main topsail mast and gaff, the thwart davit, chocks, etc., have been burnt recently, while our " shakes " and empty casks are going very fast. The question now arises, and a very serious question it is, too, " What's to be burnt next ?"

The discussion, perhaps, was much more animated than polite, sentiments and opinions being exchanged in the simplest possible form of words and Quaker-like directness and freedom from base flattery or dissimulation. Before this question was decided another one still more important arose in the course of the discussion. This was, " Who is now the master and commander of the ship ?"

All hands were called aft, the ship's articles read (by myself), and the question put, " Whom do you elect for commander in the room of the late Captain Gravill ?"

You see, our mate, Mr. George Clarke, unfortunately is without a mate's certificate. Tom Hornsby signed on as mate to clear the ship at Hull, while George Clarke signed on as ice-master, though in reality acting as first mate and having charge of a watch as such.

The men unanimously elected George Clarke master of the ship, and agreed to stand by him and obey his lawful commands during the remainder of the voyage. The officers also tendered their allegiance.

The men were told then that any man knocking off his watch without being ordered to do so by the doctor would have his bread stopped; that any man stealing provisions, either from the ship's stores or from his ship-mates, might rely on getting a sound rope's-ending; also that any man complaining of having been robbed by others, and so causing a disturbance, without such can be proved by him to have been the case, would receive a sound rope's-ending.

George Clarke having consented to take command of the

ship and William Lofley to navigate her home, the men were dismissed and the discussion returned to the original topic— viz., *firewood*.

It was resolved that, so long as this severe weather lasted, the fires are to be kept up at any expense to ship and cargo; that we were engaged now in a struggle for life or death, and that warmth was indispensable in the present weakened and exhausted condition of the men. Therefore everything that possibly can be burnt, without endangering the safety or sea-worthiness of the ship, shall be burnt if necessary. The officers then retired, the matter having been settled to the satisfaction of themselves and also of all on board.

To-night the weather is clear, cold, and freezing keenly.

It is exactly a year ago to-day since we signed this ship's articles in Hull.

Friday, February 15*th.*—To-day the sun rose at about 7.45 a.m. in a blaze of deepest crimson, his red fiery orb glowing over the edge of the pack and tingeing the dazzling snow-plains with a purple hue. At the same time the opposite horizon was tinted with the most beautiful shades of carmine, purple, and green. The lofty headlands, the mountain-tops, the cliffs, the islands, and more especially the glittering pin-nacles of the numerous icebergs in the offing, were all bathed in the same flood of deep purple light, and assumed the most lovely tints and colourings. Such sunrises and sunsets as we have beheld lately require to be *seen*, for no language can describe adequately their wondrous, ever-changing, and evanescent beauties.

Every day after dinner a jampot is passed round the cabin table, and each of us takes a teaspoonful of jam as an anti-scorbutic. 'Tis the only fresh vegetable acid we have left, our lime-juice having lasted some three days at the rate of a wineglassful apiece daily. We have some four small jars of jam which belonged to the late captain. I trust that taking a little jam daily may tend in some small measure to ward off the insidious approaches of the much-dreaded and dreadful scurvy.

I regret that three or four of our men are in a very poor way. They are getting weaker and stiffer in their limbs, and in other ways are losing ground daily. I think the bouilli soup they are getting, small though the quantity is, is exhibiting beneficial results already upon two others of my worst cases.

Our tobacco, of course, has been finished long ago, and tea-leaves have been condemned as a very unsafe substitute, irritating the mouth and gums. Now some of the officers have hit upon the novel and ingenious device of smoking coffee-grounds dried over the stove. They find great comfort and consolation therein. Bits of " fore-goer " (rope), cotton waste, etc., all have their advocates as substitutes for tobacco.

Ye who smoke not, who turn up your noses with pious horror at the puff of a passing pipe or cigar, who regard smoking as a " nasty, filthy, pot-house habit " (as poor father used to phrase it), ye little know what an immense loss this want of tobacco is felt to be. It was our only solace, our only luxury, our only consolation. Often did I use to apply those lines of Propertius to my pipe: " Tu mihi curarum requies, in nocte vel atra lumen, et in solis tu mihi turba locis " (" Thou art a rest to me in my cares, a light in the night and darkness, and in solitary places thou art as much company as a crowd "); or that beautiful passage in Cicero's " Pro Archia Poeta ": " Adversis perfugium ac solatium prœbent: pernoctant nobis-cum: perigrinantur rusticantur " (" Afford a refuge and a solace in adversity; pass away the night with us; are with us when we go abroad and when we travel in the country "). In short, a pipe of tobacco is a never-failing friend, always most excellent company, and a wondrous consolation. No wonder that we miss our tobacco, and invent all manner of schemes to prevent our pipes being extinguished altogether.

For my part I am content to go without coffee-grounds, tea-leaves, bits of rope's end, or any other vile and villainous substitute for the " precious Indian weed," as the poet Hawkins Browne terms it. At the same time I miss my morning pipe, and mourn for it as for a real friend gone and lost. I have put my old clay pipe away upon the shelf with " *Resurgam* " written over it, for, depend upon it, if I am spared to get back to Shetland, my pipe, Phœnix-like, will " rise again " out of its own ashes. Let's trust that joyous day is not far distant.

But a truce to this nonsenical twaddle about jampots and tobacco-pipes! My heart feels very heavy, and I am trying to write myself into a different humour by amusing myself (and probably tormenting you, O reader) with such precious nonsense. So have the goodness to overlook it. Judge not harshly of a poor, shivering, half-starved, weakened, most miserable fellow (" half-fed, half-clothed, half-sarked," as Burns has it), who is thinking about this time last year, when he suddenly left Edinboro', friends, college studies, and home, " and his father's house," and " went into a far country." " And he began to be in want "; " and there arose a mighty famine in that land "; " and he would fain have filled his belly with the husks that the swine did eat "; " but no man gave unto him."

Ah! there it is, that most wonderful and touching Parable of the Prodigal Son. There it is—just *my* case! Have I, too, not done as he did, and am I not, like him, reaping the bitter fruits?

Yes! This time last year I signed this ship's articles in the shipping office at Hull. Now what a change has come over me! Here I am, sitting in the cabin, shivering with cold, my clothes worn out and in rags and tatters, hungry and famished with more than five months' privations, with no near prospect of escaping from the ice, with a horrible and certain death staring us in the face should we lose our ship or our provisions run short, scurvy on board, men sinking and failing daily before my eyes, myself as weak and feeble as a child, perhaps with my turn to die coming next.

But " why art thou cast down, O my soul, and why art thou disquieted within me?" Hope in God, for something at times bids thee trust that thou shalt be spared yet to praise Him who (with all humility and reverence) is the strength of thy countenance and thy God. At times things seem very dark, very dreary; again, they look brighter and more hopeful. Oh, that I could always say and feel with the Psalmist: " In Thee, O God, do I put my trust. Let me never be confounded."

CHAPTER XV

ESCAPE FROM FROBISHER BAY

Saturday, February 16*th.*—The day commenced with thick, foggy weather, and a wind from the South-West. As the morning wore along the wind increased to a stiffish breeze, which drove the loose snow along the pack and across the dimly visible face of the sun. In the opinion of the mate and officers there is a gale blowing outside the pack. It is a curious fact that a heavy gale may be raging outside a pack, yet scarcely a breath of air may be moving over the surface of the ice. In sailors' phraseology, " the frost kills the wind." We do not expect the long-desired westerly and north-westerly winds until the weather moderates.

At 11 a.m the sky cleared up beautifully and the sun broke out with uncommon warmth, the temperature being positively mild and spring-like. This happy change, resulting from the southerly wind prevailing just now, is a wonderful relief and blessing to us, more especially to those of our company who are disabled with scurvy

Twenty bucketfuls of ice were removed to-day from the beams, etc., in the 'tween-decks.

Sunday, February 17*th.*—The air was so mild last night that the ice was thawing off the cabin skylight between 10 and 11 p.m., while the thermometer stood at 42° with only a small fire in the cabin. This morning was thick and foggy, with a strong easterly wind, which was so cold that two or three men had their noses frost-bitten, myself among the number.

We dined and tea'd sumptuously to-day upon a pudding composed of a " whack " of beef, half a whack of pork, a biscuit broken up small, and our $\frac{1}{2}$ pound allowance of flour, all boiled in a basin. The said " whack " of meat and biscuit had been saved up from my miserable pittance during the past week.

We all agreed to perpetrate this dismal joke of starving our stomachs on week-days in order to furnish a good dinner on Sunday—at least, just for once—to see if the plan would answer.

Our steward took a world of pains in the composition of these precious meat-puddings. Flavoured with a little dried mint or rue, or some such herb, I do assure you they furnished us with the best meal we have sat down to since our Christmas dinner.

I don't know why I record such items as the above, but they will serve to show you that we are doing our best aft to make our present misery as tolerable as possible, and that *the thoroughly English sentiment of a good dinner on a Sunday* is not yet extinguished in our breasts. I fancy we shall repeat the experiment if spared for another week.

We are all a little bit dull to-day. We remember that this day last year was our last Sunday in England, it being the day previous to our leaving Hull. I remember that I spent the afternoon in walking about the docks and piers, went to the chapel in the evening with Captain Gravill and his family, and sat up nearly all night writing farewell letters to my friends. What a change of places and circumstances! Here I am sitting in the ship's cabin, whilst a fearful gale is raging fit to blow the masts out of the ship, the night wild and thick with blinding showers of sleet and snow. You can hardly face the strong, fierce, cutting blast. The men doggedly retire from the deck as soon as their spell at the pumps is over. Several who tried to weather it out had their noses and faces frost-bitten in a few minutes.

The gale commenced to blow very heavily at midday, and appears to have increased in violence up to the present time (8.30 p.m.), when it is raging with great fury, coming from due East. It is no good trying to keep on deck for more than half an hour. The air is so thick with driving snow and sleet, you could scarce see 20 yards from the ship.

You may depend upon it, there will be many a wet cheek to-day in Hull. Mothers, wives, and children will be thinking of parents, sons, and brothers who were with them for the last time this day twelve months ago, and are now God only knows where. Whether we are living or dead they cannot tell. May the God of all consolation comfort their hearts.

His all-seeing eye beholds both them and us; He sees our miseries and dangers, He counts all *their* tears. Lord, have mercy upon us, and bring us out of this awful ice.

I have just been entering in the official log a list of eight of our crew who are more or less disabled with scurvy. A number of others show most unmistakable symptoms of this dreaded and altogether hopeless disease. Some of the poor fellows are very bad. Blanchard, Alec Robertson, Mitchell Abernethy, and Haslas Anderson are only just able to crawl about. O God, deliver us! Moderate this terrible weather! 'Tis killing these poor fellows. Bring us out of the ice speedily

If we are beset many weeks longer and experience such cold, cutting weather, we must lose a number of our crew. There is nothing else for it. The men are falling away daily. Johnny Aitcheson, Tom, the blacksmith, and Bonsall Miller, are all in a most critical condition. Magna Nicholson is so thoroughly weakened and exhausted from long deficiency of food that he is hardly able to stand upright. Little Dick and several others are falling off in strength and appearance daily. I can see a change for the worse in them every day. How all this will end I dare not think. I can only hope and trust in the mercy and pity of the Almighty. Spare us, O God, for we are all poor, hardened, miserable sinners. Cut us not off in this awful wilderness, for few, if any, of us are prepared to die.

It is a fearful night. The gale from the eastward is raging with uncommon fury, the air filled with whirling snow and sleet. God grant that nothing may give way; that the ice may keep quiet during the night; that we may not be subjected to nips or heavy pressure, or come foul of that ominous iceberg towards which we must be drifting fast.

It is a wonder at times to me how we in our fearful position can lie down calmly in our berths and sleep soundly when surrounded on all hands by dangers, and a swift and sudden death staring us in the face. If the ship goes to-night, there is no hope of our lives. Four-and-twenty hours on the ice in such weather as this would inevitably finish every man and boy of us. Not one of us could stand it. It would be impossible to rig a tent with such a fearful gale raging. We would have no protection, no shelter, no hope—nothing but sure and certain death.

Monday, February 18*th.*—The gale blew very heavily throughout the night, with thick, blinding showers of snow and sleet.

Upon coming on deck at 8 a.m. I found the gale blowing apparently as hard as ever. The morning was raw and cold, and the snow-showers driving constantly along the deck. The pumps were frozen solid, and required to be thawed. Bread was served out this morning, 3½ pounds per man.

During the afternoon the gale gradually moderated. When I went on deck at 4 p.m. the red globe of the sinking sun was glowering out of a narrow chink in the murky clouds, as though it were scowling at the mist and misery below. In the evening the wind had fallen away completely.

So ends a most miserable day, a day on which I have scarce shown myself on deck, a day rendered none the less tolerable by the mournful reflection that it is the anniversary of our leaving the port of Hull upon this melancholy and disastrous voyage.

Bill Reynolds's dog, Murphy, one of Gyp's pups, went out of its mind yesterday, and was drowned immediately. The officers tell me it is by no means unusual for dogs to become affected in this way in this climate. Whether 'tis the cold or the deficiency of food, or a combination of both, that deranges them I cannot tell. Anyhow, I am glad the animal was despatched before it could do anyone a mischief. Only one dog remains now on board the ship, and we expect to see it similarly attacked, and trust it may be as speedily put out of the way as its late companion.

Tuesday, February 19*th.*—Last night was remarkably mild. At about midnight the thermometer in the cabin stood at 42°.

These sudden variations in temperature are extremely trying, and affect the health of the men a good deal, more especially those who are crippled with scurvy.

This morning the watch was engaged in breaking up the jolly-boat for firewood.

As our oatmeal is almost exhausted, we had a very novel and ingenious substitute for it for to-day's dinner. This was a broth or soup composed of biscuit crumbs boiled with scraps of beef, bits of pork, and other *refuse* which the cook had collected and " rendered down " for his own private perquisite during the earlier part of the voyage. This unheard-of dish, composed of what would have been sold for pig's meat, was really extremely good and palatable.

By the by, we took the trouble to weigh the " whacks " of beef and pork sent aft for the cabin dinner for yesterday and to-day. The piece of beef, which was quite free from bone and which weighed 2½ pounds, did not draw down the scales at ¾ pound when brought to the table. *Twelve ounces of meat to be divided amongst five hungry men,* and the only animal food the said hungry men would have to live upon for the next four-and-twenty hours ! This will show you how our nominal ½ pound of meat apiece shrinks up and wastes away in the boiling. Should the piece of meat selected for the cabin be bony, why, so much the worse for us ! I assure you, when the bones are cut out and the meat fairly divided, sometimes it doesn't average more than *an ounce and a half or two ounces apiece !*

The 2½ pounds piece of pork for to-day's dinner did not draw down the scales at 1½ pounds after being boiled. Sometimes we are favoured with two or three rib bones with the meat, but to-day's pork, being quite free from bone, was a very favourable specimen for weighing and computing the loss in boiling.

Wednesday, February 20th.—During the night the wind worked round to *that long-desired quarter, the North-West.* The ship and the ice in which we are beset have moved a very considerable distance during the night to the South and East, as shown by the altered appearance and bearings of the iceberg to which we were so close yesterday.

The morning is beautifully clear, sunny, and sharp; bright, bracing weather. One really feels 50 per cent. better on such a day. The poor fellows who are disabled by scurvy " hoylt and hobble " about the decks, " waymont like a saumon cobble," as the farmer says of his " auld mare Meg," and pluck up fresh life and hopes, whilst the officers and I cheer them up with the most abundant promises of getting out of the ice speedily if this blessed North-West wind only lasts two or three days.

In fact, this particular wind is the only thing, in conjunction with the spring tides which prevail just now with the full moon, that will ever bring us out of this deep, land-locked bight.

There is no limit to human invention ! Our barley having been finished at last Wednesday's dinner, our cook, Joe Mitchell, furnished all hands to-day with a very excellent substitute— a soup made out of 7 pints of rice and two tins of bouilli. This made a most admirable dinner for eight-and-forty hungry mortals.

I attach considerable importance to this meal, owing to the fact of its being a *fresh* feed. *Nearly all hands are more or less affected now with scurvy* in their mouths and gums, so it is resolved to have a similar fresh meal of bouilli soup and rice every Wednesday in place of the barley broth, lately come to an end after holding out for a marvellously long time. The six worst scurvy cases, who were receiving bouilli soup, are to return to the same fare as the rest of the crew, scurvy being so universal amongst us now that we cannot favour one man more than another in the all-important matter of fresh provisions.

Evening.—Thank God, this favourable North-West wind has increased since sunset.

Retired to bed about nine o'clock. We are all anxious, uneasy, uncertain, dreading lest the wind should fall away or chop round to the eastward, dreading lest we should get foul of the South Island or be brought up by the bergs or have the " nips " on again. We can only lie down, trusting in God's mercy.

Thursday, February 21st.—I did not sleep very well last night, being anxious and uneasy. In fact, most of us lay down in the full expectation of hearing once more that ominous cry, " All hands ahoy !" Fortunately, though, the night passed over our heads without the least disturbance amongst the ice.

Upon going on deck at breakfast-time I found we were very near to the South Island, and further to the southward of it than we have been yet. A vast number of large bergs are aground in the offing, and stretch across what might be termed the outlet from this dreary dead bight at the entrance of Frobisher's Inlet. They extend in a chain from the South

Island to the extreme point of the South Land, termed on the map Queen Elizabeth's Foreland.

Through this network of bergs, which are grounded in groups and clusters, with odd ones forming the connecting-links, we must run the gauntlet before we can consider ourselves fairly out of this wretched gulf and in a fair way of driving down to the Labrador coast with the current. We trust we may be mercifully guided through this thicket of bergs without injury to the ship and, if it be God's will, without breaking out of this sheet of heavy ice in which we are so securely fast. It will form an admirable protection in the event of " nips " and heavy pressure whilst weathering these icebergs. Most of them are of large size, aground, and planted so thickly across our pathway that there seems but slight prospect of passing through them without great risk and danger to the ship. However, we are slowly but surely driving down upon them, and can only put our trust in the mercy and compassion of Almighty God.

The morning is clear, bright, and sunny, the horizon obscured by dense columns and clouds of mist rising from the surface of the numerous holes and lanes of water which form as the ice slacks off or is held up here and there by the opposition of the bergs and islands. There will be a fearful pressure and commotion amongst the heavy pack ice as the solid masses tear and rend and force themselves through these obstacles to their passage outwards. Pray God the old ship may not become involved, as she has been too often already, amongst these whirling, crashing masses as they are borne on by wind and strong spring tides against the immovable stolid faces of the iron-bound rocks and icebergs. If once forced into such a conflict, the ship would be crushed *instanter*, like an egg-shell. So you can understand why we do not like the looks of this chain of bergs towards which we are driving.

In the afternoon, whilst sitting reading in the cabin, the steward came running down in great haste. " Oh, doctor ! doctor ! get your gun !" he exclaimed; " there's a black fox on the ice close against the ship."

Now a black fox is extremely rare—so rare, indeed, that Mr. Clarke assures me the masters of the sealing schooners on the Labrador coast told him that a single black fox skin is worth no less than £40.   Our engineer, too, says that Mr. Taylor, the Governor of the British settlement at Exeter, valued them at the same exorbitant sum.

A black fox is not a distinct species, but a *lusus naturæ*, similar to a white sparrow or a human albino.   One whelp out of a litter of white, blue, or grey foxes occasionally turns out to be a jet black, doubtless to the astonishment of his parents, relatives, and acquaintances.

This accidental variety in the colour of the various species of Arctic foxes is so rare that William Lofley assures me two, or sometimes three, specimens per annum is the average number obtained from their vast territories by the Hudson Bay Company.

So no wonder I loaded my rifle and rushed on deck.   There was the fox, looking black enough as he stood upon the dazzling surface of the snow-covered pack.   He was too far off, though, to shoot at with certainty, and when I descended the ship's side and attempted to approach him he ran away swiftly. I fired a parting shot at him, which added materially to his speed.

When first seen by Joe Mitchell, honest Joe mistook it for poor Spring, the engineer's dog, and commenced whistling and calling it.   Strange to say, the fox continued to approach, and was quite near the ship before its real character was discovered.   So ended the fox hunt.

These animals are reckoned unlucky by sailors.   Captain Gravill hated to see them shot and brought aboard the ship. Lofley tells me that, when with Captain Gravill in the *Polynia*, he shot a fox and brought it aboard.   The old gentleman muttered and talked about it for two or three days afterwards; said he " didn't like it at all—very unlucky."

The sun set at about 4.30 p.m., perhaps the most beautiful sunset I have seen this year.   The tints and flushes of deep purple, crimson, and lake were indescribably brilliant and beautiful.

The night is dark.   God keep us this night in peace and safety.

Friday, February 22nd.—Thank God, the ship was quiet during the night.

During the 'spectioneer's watch (midnight to 4 a.m.) the ship remained stationary, being prevented from drifting northward with the tide by the breeze from the North-West, which continued to blow strong and steady throughout the night. The ship commenced to move to the southward and eastward with the change of tide at about four o'clock this morning.

Upon coming on deck at breakfast-time I found the sun shining brightly and the ship evidently much altered in her position during the previous twelve hours. The South Island was nearly due astern of us, the South point of the land (Queen Elizabeth's Foreland) was well off our starboard bow, whilst we were much nearer the chain of bergs and, in fact, had passed some of them. One monstrous square fellow lies off our port fore-rigging. The wind is strong from the North-West.

The ship continued to move to the South and East until 11 a.m., when the north-going turn of the tide set in and she became stationary, the strong wind holding her and the ice up against the current of the tide. Thank God, the wind is powerful enough to enable us to hold our ground instead of being carried back to the northward in the direction of our late prison-house.

We are all in high spirits, but at the same time uneasy and anxious lest any change should take place in the wind or accident happen to the ship. The mate tells me he trusts that the next change of tide will carry us clear of the large square berg which looms so ominously on our port side. We hope the set of the current will carry us between Scylla and Charybdis. Once safely past these threatening dangers, our ship ought to commence driving very fast to the southward once more. God grant such may be the case with her, and that this longed-for, prayed-for wind from the North-West may continue for some time to come and give us " a good shove off " the land. The further we are off the land, the more rapidly the ice moves southward.

Afternoon.—This North-Wester continues to blow strongly still. It is the very first North-West wind we have had worth mentioning since our first coming into the country in May last. By tea-time the large berg that was abreast of our fore-rigging this morning was well abaft our port quarter.

Evening.—The night is dark and starry. We hope and trust we are on the eve of our deliverance from this wretched, hopeless, despairing, fatal Frobisher's Gulf, where we have been beset so long and suffered so much.

Saturday, February 23rd.—Last night I went to my berth at nine o'clock, and awakened at half-past eleven. I do assure you I never slept a wink afterwards throughout the night. Thoughts, hopes, and fears; the knowledge that we were drifting at last to life and liberty; fears lest any change of wind or accident to the ship should destroy this pleasant prospect; recollections of home, relatives, and friends; anticipations— bright and happy, you may be sure—of seeing them once more before long, etc., chased each other through my excited and anxious brain, and effectually drove away " sleep from mine eyes and slumber from mine eyelids."

I rose and dressed at 7.15. Learnt that the ship had commenced to drive to the southward and eastward at about seven o'clock, and that *she had passed the chain of bergs in safety*.

The morning was clear, sun shining brightly, very hard frost, and the wind blowing uncommonly strong and keen, sending the drift snow whirling along the surface of the pack in driving clouds. From the mast-head a great quantity of slacks, lanes, and holes of water can be seen, all becoming covered with bay ice, though, as rapidly as the surface of the water is exposed to the present low temperature. It is marvellous how rapidly bay ice forms, and how tough and tenacious it is.

There is a very long, low iceberg off our port fore-rigging, and there are numerous other bergs ahead of us grounded on the reefs. Once safely past this second rank of bergs, we think we shall have a clear drift down the country.

By observation we find we are some 25 miles distant from Cape Warwick—at least, so we conclude it to be according to our charts. We likewise comfort ourselves with the belief that we can now, *at last and most unmistakably,* set eyes upon the much-talked-of, thought-of, veritable *Resolution Island.*

For our dinner to-day we had a potful of oatmeal porridge for the last time. So good-bye to " burgoo." I am sorry this article of diet is exhausted—sorry for the sake of the men more than for my own sake, as it formed a nourishing and valuable fresh feed twice a week. Its place is to be taken by rice and scraps boiled down together.

Afternoon.—The barometer continues to rise higher and higher. This may indicate winds from the northward or eastward, or a spell of fine weather. When this instrument falls, look out for winds from the southward or westward, or for wet, snowy, or thick, dirty weather.

Evening.—The ship is continuing to move to the southward. There is a light breeze from the North-West, but nothing like such a breeze as we have been so highly blessed with during the morning.

I am now (8 p.m.) just off to my berth, feeling tired and sleepy from want of sound sleep last night. I trust that we may be preserved during the hours of darkness from all dangers, from the " terror by night," the fearful cry, " All hands ! All hands !" with which we are acquainted so well.

So ends another week, a week of wondrous mercies, the week of our escape from Frobisher's Gulf. May to-morrow's dawn find us safe beyond the last remaining line of bergs. By Jove ! some of them *are* monsters !

Sunday, February 24th.—The wind, which had died away almost entirely last night, sprang up strong from the *southward* early this morning, and when I went on deck at breakfast-time I found the wind blowing violently *dead against the ship*. I could just see the long, flat berg we were close to yesterday afternoon.

The ship is driving very fast inshore to the westward. The morning is thick and foggy, and the wind blowing at times very strong and obscuring everything with the driving snow from the surface of the pack.

The weather is milder with this southerly wind, but this is very poor consolation to us. This sudden change of wind has proved a great damper to our sanguine hopes of getting soon out of the ice. God in His mercy grant that we may not drive once more into that fearful Frobisher's Gulf, and that we may keep clear of the numerous bergs which we could see inshore of us yesterday.

This southerly wind *may* bring in a heavy swell which would smash up the pack for us if the sea-edge is not too far off. In fact, this disappointing adverse wind, which has cast us all down so much, in reality may be working for us a world of good, and even conduce more towards our liberation than we dare hope or think.   At any rate, I am trying to console myself with these thoughts and with the reflection that, from whatever direction the wind may set in when this breeze has blown itself out, the change *must be for the better*.   Humanly speaking, a *worse* wind for our purpose we could not have.

We have just dined sumptuously upon meat puddings, as we did last Sunday.   It was composed of half a " whack " of beef, a half-ditto of pork, with half a biscuit, some biscuit dust, cook's fat, a little suet, and a dash of powdered mint, boiled in a small basin.   I do assure you that I never made a better dinner (to my thinking) in my life than I have made to-day upon half of this poor mess.   The other half is warming now behind the cabin stove, and will be fried over the said stove in a small tin pie-dish and serve me for my tea.

The cook tells me that his coppers were filled with these little meat puddings, the men, poor fellows, having saved up their meat and biscuit during the week to enjoy one good full meal on a Sunday.   I assure you this Sunday's dinner causes quite a sensation on board.   'Twould do your heart good to see these poor miserable fellows, many of them suffering with scurvy, their gums, teeth, and cheeks affected so that they are scarce able to eat the daily hard biscuit and scrap of tough salt meat—I say, 'twould do you good to see these poor, helpless, dying men enjoying their Sunday's dinner just now on board the *Diana*.

Two or three of our company are failing very fast.   Mitchell Abernethy is quite unable to get up and down the companion ladders.   Alec Robertson, George Blanchard, and Haslas Anderson are very stiff in their muscles, and scarce able to get about at all.   Several more men are becoming similarly affected, while nearly the *whole* ship's company shows unmistakable signs of scurvy in their mouths and gums.   I do not think there are a dozen men on board the ship who are not affected more or less—of course, some but slightly at present.

The great and only remedies for this dreaded disease—namely, *fresh meat, fresh vegetables, change of diet*—are not to be had. Medicines are of no use in curing this complaint. You may relieve some of the symptoms, but medicines cannot remove the source of them. You cannot cure the scurvy with drugs or any amount of medical treatment.

There is nothing for us but the compassion and mercy of God. O God! almighty, all-powerful, able to save as well as to destroy, bring us out of this fearful ice, we implore Thee. We are all dying men, slowly but surely drawing nearer daily to our inevitable fate, unless Thou, in Thy great mercy, wilt condescend to hear our cries and deliver us speedily. Have pity upon these poor helpless fellows, some of whom must die soon unless Thou liberate us speedily. They cannot hold out much longer. Have mercy upon us, for Christ's dear sake.

Afternoon.—I took out a bundle of letters and sat and read them over the fire. I read every one of them through from beginning to end, and when I had finished the last one I was quite surprised to find 'twas five o'clock. Thanks to the kind thoughtfulness of my various friends, I received a good supply of letters at Lerwick. These, with a few that I brought away with me from Edinburgh, make quite a respectable bundle. There were letters from father, Ellen, Louie, Harry, Alfred, Fred* . . . ; from my various medical friends, Drs. Thyne,† Davidson, Fothergill,‡ Simpson, Campbell; also the " medical fellows " (as Bob Sawyer termed them when he invited Pickwick to supper at his lodgings in Lant Street), Messrs. McKen, Taylor and Co.; with letters from old Stephen Overdale, Miss Otto at Pathead, little Jane Mitchell, and others.

These letters formed a most delightful medley, and brought back old faces, old times, old thoughts, affections, and feelings in a way that quite moved me. I assure you I rose from their perusal with a softened, saddened, yet happier feeling in my heart. I went forward and talked to the poor scurvy-stricken

* Sisters and brothers.
† The late Dr. Thomas Thyne of the Minories, London.
‡ The late Dr. J. Milner Fothergill.

fellows, and endeavoured to cheer them up, even as the " old news from home " that I had just been reading had cheered me.

By the by, in one of Ellen's letters there were some English wild flowers which had retained their colour and some of their fragrance. They looked strangely pleasant and homely in this fearful wilderness of snow and ice, where no flower ever blooms. It really did me good to look at them.

Evening.—This southerly breeze is blowing as strong as ever. Where we are driving to no one can tell. God grant we may not find ourselves in Frobisher's Gulf once more when the weather clears up. The wind is howling and tearing through the rigging as I sit writing this log.

The weather is uncommonly—nay, unpleasantly mild. The ice upon the cabin skylight and wainscoting is thawing, dripping, and running about in all directions. The cabin feels very hot and close. Of course, this sudden change of temperature is caused by the present southerly wind. We trust that this adverse breeze, warm and mild though it is, may have exhausted itself before to-morrow morning.

Monday, February 25th.—Upon going early on deck I found the temperature extremely mild, with a strong wind from the West.

The day broke clear and pleasant, and showed us our position—a matter of no little anxiety, you may be sure. *The ship has driven close to the South Island at the entrance of Frobisher's Gulf, and is entangled once more amongst the chains of large bergs aground upon the reefs that extend across the entrance !*

Had yesterday's southerly wind continued a little longer, there is no doubt we would have been blown right into our old prison. There is nothing to stop us from driving right up Frobisher's Gulf once more—nothing but water covered with bay ice.

The wind increased during the morning, and was extremely keen and cold. The barometer is rising, which makes us hope that this strong West wind will work round into the North-West. At present 'tis doing us very little good. We want a wind more down the country, as well as off the land, to carry us clear of this dismal gulf with its labyrinth of islands and icebergs. During the morning the ship was moving slowly to the southward and eastward.

I served out stores to the men for the last time—namely, ¾ pound of tea apiece. Our tea, sugar, coffee, and, of course, tobacco, are all served out now. 'Tis a great wonder and a great mercy that our stores have lasted us so long. 'Tis bad enough to be without tobacco, but what we should do without *tea* I cannot tell.

As we anticipated, the wind worked round from due West to West-North-West and blew very heavily, at times almost strong enough to twist the masts out of the ship. *But she moved not !*

The large sheet of ice in which we are frozen is wedged between three bergs aground upon the reefs. These said bergs are holding us up and keeping us at a standstill, whilst (alas ! that I should have it to write) there is nothing to be seen beyond these bergs but holes and lanes of water stretching away to the eastward as far as the eye can range from the mast-head.

Evening.—The night is dark. The ship is rattling and cracking a little, the ice evidently moving or slewing about, or altering its position in some way, though it is too dark to see in what direction.

Tuesday, February 26th.—During the mate's watch last night the wind was North-West. This morning the ship has drifted some distance to the South and East, and, fortunately, has driven clear of the bergs that held us up during last night. The long-backed berg and its companion that brought us up last Saturday are in sight again from the deck to the southward of us.

This morning is beautifully clear and frosty, and the sun shining brilliantly. It is one of the cheeriest, brightest days we have had this year. The wind has moved round and is nearly due North. The ship is driving slowly to the southward, but the large sheet of floe ice in which we are laid is embarrassed again and retarded by several bergs to the southward of us.

The wind was fresh all the morning, but fell away towards midday, much to our regret. We are longing for a strong

North-Easter to sweep the ice down the country, and carry us
along with it clear of this dubious neighbourhood. We are
frozen up in the midst of a floating pack at least 2 miles in
diameter. This pack is so entangled amongst the numerous
grounded bergs that neither winds nor currents seem to have
sufficient power to force this floating mass of ice through.
Were a heavy swell to set in, 'twould very soon break up the
pack. A strong North-Easter would smash and grind it up
against the bergs, and fairly tear it to pieces and force it
through in fragments.

Steward busy scraping the ice off the cabin skylight. Our
skylight has to be scraped three times a week, else we should
sit in a dismal twilight. This ice, which was an inch thick
to-day, is formed from the congealing of the moisture in our
breath, and in the steam from tea, coffee, soups, etc.

For the second time we dined to-day off the new dish—viz.,
soup made of biscuit dust and cook's scraps.

Cook's scraps are odds and ends of meat, scraps of fat,
gristle, and other remnants that the men had rejected during
the early part of the voyage, and which Joe had carefully
collected and headed up in a cask for his own private emolu-
ment, to be sold by him as *pig's meat*. I assure you this
singular compound formed a most admirable soup. It is
admitted by all on board that this day we have enjoyed one
of the best and most nutritious, abundant, and satisfying
dinners that we have had since first we went on short
allowance.

Afternoon.—Went to the mast-head, and saw plenty of
water inshore and to the southward. Certainly we are hard
and fast in the centre of an immense sheet of pack ice, with
bergs all around us holding us up. Resolution Island is in
sight upon the southern horizon.

Wednesday, February 27th.—Last night the wind set in
strong and steady from the North-East. When the day broke,
we found the ship had been driven a long way to the southward
and inshore, the South Island, and even the long-backed berg,
which was to the South-East of us last evening, being upon our
northern horizon.

I was called up to see one of the Shetland men, Haslas

Anderson, who had fallen insensible in the 'tween-decks. The man is one of our bad cases of scurvy—very weak, becoming rapidly exhausted, scarce able to move about, has not kept his watch on deck for some time. . . .

Our men are failing very fast indeed. Many of the younger men and lads complain of great weakness, pains, and inability to exert themselves, or even do the little work there is at the pumps. Besides this, they are beginning to lose heart, more especially the Shetland men. God grant we may be out of the ice soon, or we shall lose a lot of them.

The morning was most beautifully bright, sunny, and very clear. The ship has drifted inshore a good bit, and continued to move steadily southward during the whole morning.

I went on the ice, taking a stool and sketch-board, thinking, as the day was so sunny and there was so little wind, that I might attempt a sketch of the ship. Had to flounder about a good deal in the deeply drifted snow before I could get a suitable distance from the ship to effect my purpose. Then down I sat on my stool and commenced. Bless you! in a few minutes my gloved hands were numbed and deadened, and my feet frozen like lumps of ice, so that I was very glad to beat a hasty retreat to the ship. It must have been freezing very keenly to have affected me in so short a time. In truth, the weather is so keen that the pumps, which were unshipped and melted out between four and five o'clock yesterday afternoon, again required to be unshipped and cleaned out at ten o'clock this morning.

Afternoon.—Occupied in the cabin making an almanac for the months of March and April, to be hung up in the half-deck.

These almanacs show not only the day of the month and week, but also the moon's age and the daily declination of the sun. The men can satisfy themselves as to the sun's progress northward, and console themselves with the cheering fact that he is approaching us just now at the rate of 23 miles daily. Every day that rolls over our heads is increasing in length, whilst at the same time the sun increases in power. Time, patience, and the merciful protection and guidance of the Almighty are what we need. The spring is coming upon us rapidly. Everyone exults to think that the season is advancing, and that the worst and most trying months are over. What a blessed thing Hope is ! Thus does Cowper express it :

> " . . . Hope, sweet hope, where'er my lot be cast,
>   In peace and plenty, *or the pining waste*,
>   Shall be my chosen theme, my glory to the last."

An owl, a seal, a raven and, what's far more interesting to us, as it is a sign that water cannot be far off, a *mallie* were seen to-day.

Thursday, February 28th.—The wind blew strong from the North-West during the whole night. This morning the ship evidently has moved a considerable distance to the southward and eastward.

Whilst walking alone upon the pathway shovelled out in the snow upon the lee side of the ship, wondering in my own mind what would be the probable duration of time ere we were liberated, I was startled suddenly from my profitless conjectures by a loud, rattling, cracking noise. At first I thought the noise proceeded from someone getting over the ship's rail into the quarter-boat suspended above my head, but a moment's glance round convinced me that the ice was in motion. Whilst I paused to ascertain *where*, the ice split across the pathway close to the spot where I was standing, and immediately opened out and parted into a broad crack. I need hardly add that I jumped across the chasm and climbed up the ship's side at the double quick. I found considerable commotion on deck—the watch gazing over the rail, whilst officers and men who had been aroused by the noise whilst sleeping below were rushing on deck to learn the nature of the disturbance.

The large sheet of ice, in the centre of which we have been frozen so long, had caught upon the berg to the southward of us and split completely across. The fracture runs in a pretty straight line diagonally across our ship, leaving a small quantity of ice adhering to our port bow and port side, whilst her counter and stern are barely protected.

In a very short time this crack widened into a lane of water. That portion of the floe which had broken off remained stationary, being hung up by the berg, while the half in which we are fixed continued driving rapidly to the southward.

Our anxiety now was lest our sheet of ice should be brought up by the berg, and be carried, rasping and tearing, along the berg's side by the force of the current. In such case the ship most certainly would be crushed flat. However, our sheet of ice continued to drive South, till it was evident we should clear the berg.

Preparations were made now for blasting the ice that remained upon our port side so as to liberate the ship, that we might get her further to the eastward amongst bay ice and out of this fearfully heavy stuff. During the afternoon we fired seven or eight blasts, but without loosening the ice. The ice is so heavy and, moreover, the ship is " bedded " so completely in the mass, that the small blasts (wine-bottles containing 2 pounds of powder) had little or no effect upon it. After making repeated attempts to destroy the ice and liberate the ship, we gave up the job as hopeless.

To our poor finite judgment this seemed a great misfortune, for there is nothing but loose ice, lanes, slacks, and light ice away to the eastward. With the present favourable breeze from the North-West we could have run a good many miles, probably, towards the sea-edge into younger and lighter ice, where the ship might have been considered safe enough.

As it is, we are laid just at the edge of a large sheet of heavy ice, which is driving down the country amongst bergs and heavy ice. We stand a remarkably good chance of getting " nips " or pressure as the sheet twists and slews about amongst the numerous bergs that obstruct its progress, or with the changes of the currents, winds, and tides. In our poor way of thinking, we would much rather have retained our unwieldy, embarrassing, but at the same time *protecting*, mile or so of pack ice to serve as a shield and bulwark to us whilst driving amongst these bergs. Now, our port side and more especially our quarters are almost completely exposed and defenceless, yet we cannot get the ship out of her berth or improve her position. Let us continue to rely implicitly upon a kind and overruling Providence, nothing doubting but that this tantalising and embarrassing position, close to water,

water close alongside yet unable to get into it, the ship exposed to any and every danger, will turn out ultimately to be for the very best.

Saw a raven and *two mallies*. The sight of the latter is very cheering. We conclude that the outside edge cannot be a great distance off, as these birds seldom leave the neighbourhood of water or range far inside a pack. When sealing in Greenland, you see abundance of " burgies " and snow-birds feeding upon the crangs of the seals that are scattered over the pack, but never a mallie. They remain at the outside edge. Therefore, having seen these birds both yesterday and to-day, we conclude that the open water cannot be far off.

The afternoon was extremely cold—in fact, to-day has been the coldest day we have had for some little time. The pumps required unshipping and thawing out again to-day. The frost is very severe. I may mention that the ink with which I am writing was frozen in a small inkpot which I carry constantly in my waistcoat pocket, over which, moreover, my jacket has been buttoned throughout the day. I never knew this to occur before during the day-time. 'Twill give you some idea of the severity of the climate.

Our careless, blundering steward lost the key of our cabin clock a few days ago. The engineer manufactured a new key out of the key (which, of course, I had contrived to bring away with me) of my late lodgings, Windmill House, Edinburgh. With this we set the cabin clock agoing this morning, but it stopped this evening in consequence of the cold.

COAST SCENERY

CHAPTER XVI

DRIFTING SOUTH

Friday, March 1st.—Last night the breeze from the North-West increased to a brisk gale. The night was as dark as the grave, with driving sleet and snow, while the ship was drifting with the ice we knew not whither.

Last thing yesterday we could not see any bergs to the southward or eastward of us, but, as you may suppose, it is an anxious and perilous position, driving down this country amongst heavy ice, your ship stuck on the extreme edge of a very heavy floe, handy for catching any obstacle, without sufficient ice outside her to protect her in the event of " nips."

The wind was extremely cold, with intense frost. Early this morning the pumps were completely choked up with solid ice, though they were being worked every few minutes.

It is a matter of thankfulness that our pumps are of *iron*, and not of wood, as was the case formerly. We are able to melt out the ice by unshipping the pumps and placing them over fires made in cressets upon the decks. This is a ready method which, of course, we could not have pursued had our pumps been of wood. It is a great mercy also that our pumps are so constructed as to unship at the bottom, where the ice forms—an unusual arrangement with most ship's pumps.

During the forenoon the wind continued to blow a heavy gale from the North-West. The weather is thick, the air being filled with sleet and clouds of driving snow from the surface of the pack. Occasionally the sun sent through the murky atmosphere a fitful gleam which served to enliven the scene, though, to be sure, we had not a very extensive prospect, as the sleet and mist did not permit us to see three ship-lengths ahead or around us.

It is impossible to tell where we are driving, whether there are bergs ahead or in our neighbourhood, whether we are in sight of the land still, etc.

This strong North-West wind will make a great alteration, not only in our position, but also amongst the ice generally. We trust it may continue to blow for some days, for it is the very wind we have been in need of so long and for which we have watched and waited so long. Thank God, it seems to have set in at last in earnest.

Afternoon.—The gale continued as strong as ever, increasing towards and after sunset. The weather cleared up a little between four and five o'clock. We could see no bergs ahead of or, in fact, anywhere near us, which is a great mercy.

I was on deck an hour and a half. Weather very cold. The ink (which I had been using previous to going on deck) was frozen again in my waistcoat pocket.

Evening.—A thick, dark, murky night. The gale continues as steady and as strong as ever. God keep and guard us during the night, and continue this favourable wind to us.

Mitchell Abernethy is becoming rapidly worse; failing daily. Haslas Anderson is confined to his bed. The Shetland men in general are very shaky.

There has been a good deal of stealing lately. Some scoundrel has robbed the little half-deck boy and another lad (Peter Shewen) of their entire stock of tea, which, as you will remember, was served out for the last time on Monday. The cook has been robbed of some of his fat to-day, whilst (you will hardly credit it) some selfish, unfeeling, contemptible fellow has actually stolen three biscuits from the box of poor Mitchell Abernethy, who is stretched helpless and wellnigh hopeless upon what I fear will be his death-bed.

Saturday, March 2nd.—The gale continued last night up to midnight, and blew heavily till 3 a.m., after which it fell away gradually.

Upon coming on deck at eight o'clock I found it had subsided to a moderate wind from the North-West.

I was called a little after half-past seven to see Haslas Anderson, who had fallen again and fainted away. This man has been confined to his berth for the last two or three days.

He is in a very weakened and exhausted state with scurvy. He held out pluckily, knocking about upon his stiffened limbs as long as he could, and only gave in the other day, when he was found prostrate in the 'tween-decks, as before mentioned. This morning he had fainted again. The slightest exertion now is succeeded by more or less syncope.

From the deck we are out of sight of land, but from the mast-head land is in sight and also three bergs. Thank God! we seem to be clear at last of bergs, reefs, rocks, headlands, treacherous bights and other hindrances, and have the pleasing prospect of a clear drift right down the country.

During this twenty-four hours' gale the ship has driven some 12 miles due South and, say, 10 miles out to 'he eastward. Since the last observation was taken (on Wednesday) the ship has driven no less than 40 miles.

The land in sight from the mast-head is Cape Warwick, a headland about half-way along the coast of the much-thought-of, talked-of, Resolution Island, from which we are distant 30 miles. I see by the charts that we are only 80 miles now in a direct line from Cape Chidley, the northern extremity of the Labrador coast.

All these items are very cheering indeed. I do assure you it is a very great relief to have got clear of the land and the innumerable bergs and the perpetual danger of "nips," heavy pressure, injury to or loss of the ship. *Matters are beginning to look at last very bright and cheery.*

The watch are employed on deck cutting up a foretopmast stunsail boom for firewood for the half-deck and galley stoves.

We dined to-day for the second time on a dish composed of some 7 pounds of biscuit dust and 14 pounds of cook's scraps. A most admirable dinner it was, too, pronounced by all on board to be the best dinner by far of the week. In future this singular compound is to take the place of the oatmeal porridge, which is all consumed. It will form our dinners twice a week—viz., on Tuesdays and Saturdays.

I am extremely delighted to think that our poor exhausted fellows will get two such nourishing and satisfying meals in the week. As I have remarked before, many of them have fallen away very fast lately. All they want is *more food, more food*. Such a dinner as they have had to-day is worth half a dozen of the miserable whacks of pork and salt beef.

So, you see, matters are " looking up " a bit on board the *Diana*. The beauty of it is, these two abundant dinners weekly are supplied without touching our ordinary stores of provisions. Biscuit dust is not made use of aboard ship, and generally is sold for pig's food at the end of the voyage. Our cook's scraps are the refuse and waste which has been saved up by Joe to sell for the same object. These scraps usually are thrown overboard as not being worth the trouble of taking care of, their marketable value being only three-halfpence a pound.

Thus, most providentially are we enabled to *feast* in this waste, howling wilderness of snow and ice. At the same time, we have the pleasant reflection that every such meal is so much saved to our scanty remaining stock of salt provisions.

Afternoon.—I went forward and examined our two worst cases of scurvy. Haslas Anderson is extremely prostrated. The poor fellow has not long to live. Mitchell Abernethy is in a bad way also. He tells me he is conscious of becoming weaker and weaker, and knows that his end is not far off. Have been giving him medicine, but 'tis of no use. Alas! I cannot supply the poor fellow with the necessary change of food. I am helpless. He must go. There is nothing else for him but the mercy of God.

The wind commenced to blow from the South-East, with thick, foggy, cold weather.

Evening.—The wind is blowing strong from the *South*, *directly against us*. Lord, give us patience to wait Thy good time, and accept even these disappointing adverse winds as from Thy sovereign hands.

Sunday, March 3rd.—At eight o'clock last night the wind was South-East, at midnight 'twas East, and two o'clock this morning it had worked round to the North-West and commenced to blow very heavily from that quarter.

When I went on deck at 8 a.m. I found a very heavy gale blowing, with very fierce squalls, which were almost strong enough at times to carry the masts clean out of the ship.   The sleet and snow were driving in a dense mist, completely obscuring everything around us.   We could hardly distinguish an object at a yard's distance from the ship, whilst such was the violence of the wind that it was almost impossible to face it upon the decks, the sudden squalls nearly carrying us off our feet at times.   It is a most glorious wind, carrying us right down the country, with a clear drift and no bergs or other obstructions that we are aware of.

I did not attempt to get my usual two hours' exercise on deck.   'Twas impossible to face such a keen, cutting, and irresistible gale.   The air was thick, and blinded one with the whirling sleet.

At noon I was asked to go forward and look at one of our lads, Fred Lockham, the fireman.   I found the unfortunate youth in a state of extreme exhaustion, with extremities cold, mental faculties bewildered, and articulation difficult.   In short, he was suffering from the combined effects of scurvy, exposure to cold, and downright hunger and starvation.

This fellow is one of several of our company who invariably have continued to get through their biscuits by the middle of the week, and consequently have had to go without for three or four days at a stretch, with nothing to eat in the twenty-four hours but their dinners.   Warnings, expostulations, remonstrances, threats, were all in vain.   Eat up their biscuits they must and would, in spite of reason and common sense.   They were so ravenously hungry that I very much doubt whether they were able to control the impulse to eat all their biscuits directly they received them.   The consequence is that three or four of these pitiable wretches have so seriously reduced themselves in strength that they are utterly useless to the ship, and a hindrance to the rest of their watch.

Fred Lockham is in a very dangerous condition.   I am afraid he will slip through my fingers in the same way that Purvis Smith did.

Afternoon.—The wind continued to blow a fearful gale from the North-West—one of the heaviest gales, if not *the* heaviest, we have experienced since coming into the country.   The ship is quivering fore and aft with the weight of the wind, while the men at the pumps can hardly keep upon their feet. The pumps required lifting and burning out at 4 p.m.

Evening.—The gale is raging as strong as ever. Fred, the fireman, is in a critical state.

Monday, March 4th.—The gale continued to blow from the North-West with great violence throughout the night. At 2 a.m. there was a movement amongst the ice and some pressure upon the most exposed and weakest part of the ship—viz., the port quarter. During breakfast-time the ice on our port side was moving about and pressing up, doubtless being disturbed by the currents. The pumps required lifting last night and again this morning, being fairly frozen up solid with ice, though never allowed to stand for more than a few minutes between each spell. There is a very keen frost indeed this morning. Bill Lofley, who has faced the weather hitherto with impunity, had his cheek severely frost-bitten whilst ascending to the mast-head.

Fred, the fireman, is better, but still very weak. I am not a little anxious about him. Poor Mitchell Abernethy is in a very bad way, sinking rapidly.

Biscuits were served out this morning. Our men are becoming so exhausted and the weather continues so severe that Mr. George Clarke has ordered 4 pounds of biscuit per week to be served out during this month—very much to my satisfaction. You can have no idea how our poor fellows have fallen off in strength and appearance during the last few weeks.

At midday a swell set in, though from what direction is uncertain. We suppose it to come from the westward out of Hudson's Straits, the ship being 40 miles to the South-East of Cape Warwick.

Evening.—I had been forward to see poor Abernethy immediately before tea-time (six o'clock), and found him very near his end. At seven o'clock one of the harpooners came running aft and desired me to go forward immediately, as the poor fellow was worse. I found him dying, and at 7.15 he breathed his last.

Tuesday, March 5th.—After breakfast busied with the melancholy task of making an inventory of the clothing and effects of poor Mitchell Abernethy. The body has been laid on the quarter-deck alongside that of Purvis Smith, both being covered over with a boat sail.

A great many of our men are troubled with their digestive organs, and complain of great weakness and exhaustion. The scurvy is making rapid progress with some of them. I assure you it takes me an hour every morning to get through my patients—*i.e.*, to listen to all their woes and troubles, to make up the medicines, gargles, and what not, and in cheering up the downcast and faint-hearted amongst them.

The medicines, more especially the gargles, are of very little use in treating scurvy. I find it best, though, to give the men something or other as a " placebo." It satisfies the poor fellows; they think themselves better, and give me the credit of doing all I possibly can to relieve them. Just now I am treating them to gargles of a weak solution of bichlorate of soda, a lump of which was given me by the cook the other day. My tannic acid and alum are exhausted. I find these astringent solutions harden the gums and cheeks, and give sensible relief to the sore and tender mouths.

I spent the afternoon knocking about the decks. The wind sprang up cold, sharp, and biting from the South-East, increasing towards sunset. The weather was so keen that my nose was frost-bitten again.

The wind increased during the evening, whilst the ice also is in motion, screwing up and pressing upon our port side.

The moon enters her first quarter to-night. We are looking out for spring tides, which, with the usual equinoctial gales that prevail during March, we trust will carry us rapidly down the country.

Wednesday, March 6th.—This morning the wind veered round to the most favourable quarter for our purposes—viz., North-East. The morning was cold and clear, with a severe frost.

The ship has driven no less than 11 miles to the southward since yesterday, and now is well opposite the opening of Hudson's Straits. We are only 24 miles from Button Islands and 45 miles due North of Cape Chidley, the most northern point of the long-desired Labrador coast. We have driven

90 miles to the southward of Queen Elizabeth's Foreland, and at the same time have drifted 40 miles out to the eastward. This is most satisfactory and cheering progress.

Afternoon.—Immediately after dinner a half-grown bear made its appearance directly ahead of the ship. Half-a-dozen rifles were loaded immediately and half the ship's company peered over the forecastle, cautiously watching " John's " approach. The galley funnel vomited forth a most fearful stench of burning whale-oil, which, borne upon the breeze, formed an irresistible attraction.

When within 60 or 70 yards a scattered volley saluted him, and one ball broke a hind-leg. The bear leaped round and snapped angrily at his wounded limb. He then scrambled away, at first very slowly, but gradually increasing his speed.

Bill Reynolds, Harry Smith, Bill Lofley, and I set out after him, but he completely distanced us, and we returned to the ship after an eager and exciting chase.

I am very glad the bear escaped us. Had we shot him and kept his hind-quarters for dog's meat, I am perfectly certain that no fear of illness or disease or even death would have deterred some of our crew from eating the flesh. I am assured that bear's meat is extremely unhealthy. When the s.s. *Eider* was wintered in this country, her crew was reduced to living upon whales' flesh. They shot some bears also, and it is a remarkable fact that the only men that died were those who had eaten bears' meat. The skin of their hands and arms came off in flakes. Neither the Esquimaux nor their dogs will touch the flesh of a bear.

During the afternoon I was engaged in manufacturing a compound chalk powder out of some little packets of aromatic spices (which Captain Gravill was in the habit of bringing with him to flavour puddings) and a lump of chalk supplied me by our cooper. My medicines are exhausted, the men are suffering from a digestive disorder, and look to me to relieve them. I am nearly at my wits' end, but, you see, necessity is the mother of invention. I trust the patent medicine will turn out an infallible cure.

Haslas Anderson is in a very weak state with scurvy. He

is sinking gradually, and made his will to-day. I have no hopes of him.

Thursday, March 7th.—This morning the breeze was from the North-West, and a very cold, keen, cutting breeze too, seeming to search us through and through.

We have driven no less than 9 miles to the southward and are now midway across the entrance of Hudson's Straits.

The last remaining dog on board the ship, belonging to the engineer, was drowned to-day, greatly to my satisfaction. The poor brute was nearly starved to death, being a mere walking skeleton. I was in daily fear lest its accumulating miseries should drive it mad, and I dreaded and avoided the poor wretch as carefully as a Turk avoids a Hebrew, or, as he terms him, "a Christian dog." In truth, all of us in the cabin are glad that Spring at last is out of *his* miseries and out of our way.

We finished our last pot of blackberry jam to-day. At my recommendation, the five of us were accustomed to have a teaspoonful daily after dinner as an antiscorbutic. The three jars have lasted us exactly three weeks. Also our steward brews us every day a jugful of linseed syrup, of which we each drink a cup as a fresh vegetable infusion that *possibly* may assist Nature in warding off the much-dreaded scurvy. So, you see, we are doing our best in our poor way, and in the total absence of lime-juice, pickles, fresh provisions, and other antiscorbutic remedies, to preserve our health. At the same time, we do not neglect the necessary exercise in the open air. Generally I suppose I contrive to spend from four to six hours daily walking up and down the decks.

During the latter part of the afternoon and after tea I was engaged in examining the entire ship's company, being anxious to ascertain to what extent scurvy prevails amongst us. The result, which was copied out into the official log, was as follows:

In a Dying Condition.—Haslas Anderson.
Disabled, More or Less.—Gideon Frazer, John Thomson, Alec Robertson, George Blanchard, David Cobb.

Extensively Affected.—John Robertson, Robert Hewson, Magna Grey (sen.), George Stone, Thomas Stokes, Richard Gibbins, Bonsall Miller, Tom Himsworth, Fred Lockham, Laurie Stewart, Edward Hoodlas, James Williamson, Christopher Tait, Philip Pickard, Basil Smith, Arthur Yell.

Slightly Affected.—Magna Grey (jun.), Peter Acrow, John Hewson, John Aitcheson, Magna Nicholson, Henry Smith, Peter Robison, Robert Robison.

Very Slightly Affected.—Charles Cobb, Peter Shewen, William Shewen, Joseph Mitchell, William Clarke, Emanuel Webster, Laurence Smith, Stephen Winbolt, John Irvine, Charles Edward Smith.

Show no Symptoms.—John Webster, William Lofley, Andrew Donald, Joseph Allen, Richard Byers, William Reynolds, George Clarke.

This list may be tabulated thus:

Out of the ship's company, which consists of forty-seven souls—

   1 is in a dying condition.
   3 are completely disabled and unfit for work.
   2 are disabled more or less.
 16 have mouths extensively ulcerated, some fearfully so.
   8 are slightly affected.
 10 show very slight symptoms.
   7 show no symptoms whatever at present.
   ―
 47

So, you see, out of forty-seven men, only seven are free from scurvy at the present time. This disease has made very rapid progress with some of our poor fellows. With others it seems to have come to a standstill.

But more on this topic at another time. I am sick at heart, and very much cast down at the fearful prospect before us, should we remain beset much longer. O God, in mercy bring us speedily out of this awful ice.

The men are failing and falling away in strength and appearance daily. 'Tis certain death for a number of them, unless we break out very soon. The general complaint is extreme weakness, pains in the back, difficulty of breathing, inability for any exertion, with great depression of spirits.

Thank God, Fred, the fireman, is much better and out of danger, though still extremely weak.

Friday, March 8th.—Soon after midnight a large whale rose in a hole of water close to our port quarter. She lay blowing alongside the ship, so near that you could have pitched a biscuit on to her back. The mate tells me she was an uncommonly fine fish, 11 or 12 feet at least, and probably would yield some 20 tuns of oil. After blowing some fifteen or sixteen times she went off, heading out to the eastward.

We all regard the appearance of this fish with great satisfaction. We consider it a sure sign that the season for the return of the whales northward has set in, and that the South-West pack (in which we are laid), once a favourite fishing ground, ought to begin to break up soon.

During the morning a light wind prevailed from the East; cold, biting weather. The pumps again required lifting and cleaning out. Philip Pickard, whose toes are severely frost-bitten, is in a very depressed and debilitated condition. His berth is wet, bedding, etc., soaked with the moisture that thaws from the top and sides of the bunk with the warmth of their bodies. At 9 a.m. I was sent for to see him. Found him shivering and crying with extreme cold and weakness, chilled through and through. . . . Am very doubtful whether the lad will live to reach home. His system is so exhausted with long privations, while the ulcerations upon his feet show no signs of repairing, but rather grow worse.

Afternoon.—I was sent for to see Alec Robertson, one of our worst scurvy cases. He had attempted to sit up by the stove for a short time, and fainted away several times. I found him in a very low and exhausted condition, with pulse hardly perceptible. He fainted twice whilst we were arranging him. I was afraid at one time that he had gone altogether. I fear both these poor fellows will not survive much longer.

After sunset the horizon to the southward and eastward presented an unusually dark and watery appearance. Judging from this, our officers are certain that the open water cannot be far distant. A great many holes of water appeared in the ice to-day. A seal, believed to be a harp seal, was seen close to the ship—a very cheering sight.

This day last year the *Diana* left Lerwick Harbour for the Greenland sealing voyage.

Watch employed in the afternoon cutting up stunsail yards for firewood.

Saturday, March 9th.—I was on deck nearly all the morning, and could not but notice that this North-East wind, though blowing pretty strong, was very much altered for the better in temperature, being comparatively mild, with little or no frost in it. The ice has slacked off into lanes and holes *which remain open*, no bay ice forming over them.

Afternoon.—The weather is remarkably mild, though the wind is blowing a fresh breeze. 'Tis a most genial and blessed change for the better. The pumps, when being cleaned out, required very little firing to melt the ice which had formed within them, whilst a hole of water astern of the ship remained open and free from bay ice.

Was on deck, occupying myself working at the pumps and in assisting the steward to saw up a stunsail boom for fuel for the cabin stove. Half the watch have been engaged cutting away the ice from our starboard side and quarter, so as to weaken its hold upon the ship as much as possible, and thus facilitate our breaking out. We don't expect to remain in our present quarters much longer.

Evening.—The ship is nearly abreast of Button Islands, which are about 60 miles to the westward. God grant these favourable winds may continue.

Sunday, March 10th.—The north-easterly wind, though strong still, was much altered for the better in temperature, being much milder; very little frost. The pumps worked well, and the fountains in the bird-cages were found unfrozen this morning for the first time for many weeks.

This morning the horizon looked very dark to the South and East, whilst numerous lanes and slacks of water showed themselves.

We are all of us in high spirits, and sanguine of breaking

out of the pack ere long if these northerly winds continue. God in mercy grant they may.

John Aitcheson, Gideon Frazer, old John, Jimmy Williamson, and several others, are failing fast, especially Aitcheson.

Evening.—A nice breeze from the North-East still. The watch engaged in sawing up another stunsail boom for firewood.

WHITEY SEAL

CHAPTER XVII

FIGHTING A WAY THROUGH THE PACK

Monday, March 11th.—At about eleven o'clock last night a swell set in, but from what quarter was uncertain. The heavy ice, in which we have been laid hard and fast for so long, began to break up, but the night was too dark for us to distinguish either the direction of the swell or the extent to which the pack was affected by it.

The motion of the ice against the port bow aroused me soon after 5 a.m. At 5.30 I rose, dressed, and went on deck.

I found the ice had parted completely from the ship's port side, leaving a clear space of 4 feet or more of water. On the starboard side the pack had broken away from the ship, but had left a mass of ice hanging tenaciously over the ship's side, causing her to heel over very considerably, for this mass was remarkably heavy. It had been formed principally by the freezing of some hundreds of tons of the water which we had pumped out of the ship. The intensity of the cold had converted the water into solid ice almost immediately after it had left the pumps.

The watch on deck was occupied in cutting a trench between this ice and the ship's side, so as to weaken the ice's hold upon the ship, and so assist in her liberation as much as lay in our power.

I knocked about the decks till breakfast-time, assisting at the pumps or anxiously watching the long heavy roll of the swell as it curved the masses of ice around us in broad heaving billows. It was very tantalising to see the ship so *nearly* free, at liberty everywhere except along her starboard side.

When I went on deck after breakfast I was surprised to see canvas set—namely, jib and fore and main topsails. We were attempting to wear the ship's head round to meet the swell.

Whilst making up some medicines in the cabin two loud explosions, followed by the cheering of the men on deck, told me that something uncommon had occurred. Running on deck, I found that the ship was *at liberty !* A couple of blasts, fired under the ice on her starboard bow, had first cracked and then detached the enormous mass of ice that was dragging her down and holding her hard and fast.

" All hands ahoy to work the ship out !" rang down the hatchways. Presently up tumbled every man and boy who was able to get on deck (for some of our poor fellows are too much crippled with scurvy to manage to get up the companion ladders), and set to work at hauling the yards about and heaving at the capstan bars.

It was a most delightful feeling to be able to walk the decks " on end," and to feel the old ship sitting upright once more upon the water.

I was on deck during the remainder of the morning. The weather was somewhat dull and hazy, and uncommonly mild and open, certainly the softest day we have had since the mild weather at the beginning of January. The ice in the berths and in the 'tween-decks was thawing and dripping off the beams; ice and snow melting on the decks; the rigging quite slack, supple, free from frost and working easily; the pumps showing no sign of choking, thus rendering the work of the watches much lighter.

Our position, by good observation, is latitude 60° 35′ North longitude, 61° 42′ West. The ship has only driven 11 miles due South since midday on Saturday, but has made no less than 29 miles easting since the last observation of longitude obtained on Friday.

This observation places the ship a little to the southward of Cape Chidley and *at last off the Labrador coast,* which is distant 80 miles in a direct line to the westward of us.

Thank God for such a mercy ! At last we are abreast of the longed-for, prayed-for Labrador—so much thought about and talked about. How often has the desire been expressed: " If we were *only* off the Labrador coast !" and here we are at last ! Once more, thank God for His sparing, guiding, and **protecting mercies**

Afternoon.—I was on deck most of the afternoon. The ice has slackened and the long swinging roll of the swell has increased. The sky is very dark to the southward and eastward, whilst a lane of water is in sight from the mast-head distant 4 or 5 miles. In the opinion of the officers this lane most probably would lead us direct to the outside of the pack. The swell is ranging in from the South-East.

Evening.—The winds were mere light and variable airs flying about during the day from N.N.E. to E.S.E., and finally, about tea-time, settling down into a steady breeze from the South, directly ahead of us.

Before tea we were busy tracking and wearing the ship's head round to the E.S.E., so as to meet the swell *bows on*, as we are expecting a stiff breeze during the night with a heavy swell coming right in before the wind. We have got the fenders up on deck and have set topsails, hoping that the ship will forge out a little so as to get clear of the heavy ice amongst which we are laid, and which is now (8 p.m.) nudging and striking unpleasantly about the ship's sides.

The sky to the South-East is very dark. Our officers believe that the outside edge of the pack cannot be more than 8 or 10 miles away, or this swell would not have " fetched in " so far amongst heavy ice.

So ends an eventful day. God guard and preserve us during the coming night, and keep us in safety.

Tuesday, March 12th.—The wind continued to blow strong all night from the southward—very strong at times. The ship was laid to under three close-reefed topsails, with her bows towards the swell. The heavy ice pounded and ground against her bows as she rose and fell with the long heaving roll of the swell.

My berth being immediately under the fore rigging, you may be sure none of the three of us (carpenter, Reynolds, and self) slept very soundly. What we dreaded was lest the wind should increase to a gale from the southward, and send in such a heavy swell as would imperil the safety of the ship, laid as she was amongst very heavy ice. About midnight the ice closed and the swell was kept down, so I had a little broken sleep during the remainder of the night.

I rose at about 7 a.m., went on deck, and found a wonderful change in the weather. It was mild, open, soft, and sloppy. The decks were running with water, the rigging dripping, masses of ice falling heavily off the yards and rigging, the watch engaged in scraping, sweeping, and shovelling away the snow and ice. Topsails and main staysail were set to wear the ship round if possible. The wind was blowing strong and steady from the southward, whilst the horizon to the South-East was very dark and heavy, with lanes of water visible from the deck.

I was on deck nearly all the morning. The weather was remarkably mild, genial, and sunny, just like an English spring day. The sun was shining brightly, snow and ice melting and falling off the rigging, the decks all in a mess with the sudden thaw. The watch was employed cleaning out the boats and clearing away the snow from the decks, ship's upper works, and from the fore and main hatches, main hold, 'tween-decks, etc. The engineer was engaged in removing bucketfuls of snow and ice from the sides of the engine-room, whilst the men below were scraping ice from the top and sides of their berths. Reynolds and the carpenter removed three arge half-deck tinfuls of ice from the empty bunk above ours. Joe, the cook, was scraping away the ice and frozen moisture which had actually accumulated in so (generally) warm a place as the ship's galley. Everything and everywhere about the ship was wet, sloppy, damp, and dripping. The steward was cleaning out his pantry and mopping and swabbing about in the cabin. The cabin skylight positively is free from ice, the glass once more admitting daylight undiminished in intensity by having to pass through a thick medium of frozen moisture. The clock is ticking cheerfully once more, and the linnet and canary are singing as if their little throats would burst, no doubt delighted, like ourselves, with the genial sunny weather.

By observation we find the ship is in latitude 60° 46′, longitude 61° 19′. This southerly breeze has driven us 11 miles to the northward, but, at the same time, 11 miles to the eastward, which is by far the most important direction for our purpose.

The swell continued to range in from the South-East in long heavy rolls, whilst the wind continued blowing strong and steady all the morning from about due South. All of us are anxiously watching the dog-vanes and compass, and conjecturing as to the probable duration of the unfavourable breeze, trusting that it will blow itself out speedily or work round to the South-West.

Afternoon.—At about two o'clock the wind began to western a little, and was accompanied by showers of snow and thick murky clouds and mist, especially to the South-West and North-West. Gradually the wind got round till, about 4 p.m., it blew from due West, then West by North. Before five o'clock it had actually settled down to a strong breeze from the *North-West,* the very quarter of all the points of the compass from which we most desired a breeze !

Watch engaged working the topsails and heaving away at the fore capstan in an attempt to turn the ship's head from North-West to South-East, so as to get canvas set in order to drive out of the pack immediately. However, the ice closed, either from a change in the currents or tide, or because of the swell lessening, so for a long time we only moved the ship's head round inch by inch, her quarters being jammed by some heavy pieces of ice.

The weather is considerably cooler now the wind has got into a northerly quarter.

Evening.—About seven o'clock (the ice having slackened and opened) the ship wore round. The watch got more canvas upon her immediately, and the second mate came down to the cabin to ask Mr. Clarke *to ship the rudder,* as the ship was driving along through nothing but young ice, and towards what must be the open water.

For the last half-hour the mate's watch and the captain's watch have been making a tremendous noise over my head, they being engaged in the all-important and most eventful operation of shipping the rudder. " Lower !" " Look out !" " Quick there !" " Let go !" " Heave away at the capstan there !" " Go it, my lads !" " Yo heave oh !" " Hold on !" are some of the exclamations. There's the mate saying, " No, it's the rudder rope that holds it. Pull upon the line, lads.

Look out to starboard while we lower. Heave on that capstan," etc.

The fact is there is a confounded piece of heavy ice frozen hard and fast to the stern post, and I fancy 'tis this that is giving them so much trouble.

I am now (8 p.m.) going on deck to lend a hand at the capstan. This is no time for any man that is able to wag one leg before the other to be sitting below. We are going out of the pack! Hurrah! God guard and keep us in safety, and protect the old ship during this last and, frequently, most trying and dangerous battle with the ice. Already she is banging and thumping and battering amongst it.

I go on deck and find them hauling up one of the waist boats, " Yo-heave-oh-ing !" most energetically. The ship is driving across a hole of water, then plunging stem on into a broad, broken-up sheet of young ice, now brought up by a heavy piece of ice, now feeling her way round it or wedging her way amongst the masses of ice like an intelligent sentient being with its eyes blindfolded. The captain's and mate's watches on deck are hauling away at braces, running the jib up and down, swinging the yards about, or working the pumps. All these operations are carried on amidst the greatest clamour and confusion of tongues, and loudly reiterated orders, whilst the officers stand on the forecastle directing the ship's course.

At 8.30 p.m. the captain's watch was sent below to get their suppers, and be in readiness to come on deck at a moment's warning if wanted. The mate goes to the mast-head and reports that the dark line bounding the horizon ahead of us, over which the heavy night clouds hang like a pall, is to the best of his belief none other than *the open sea*, the outside edge of the pack. Bill Lofley next ascends to the crow's-nest and confirms the impression.

Meanwhile the ship continues steadily to force her way amongst the broken-up sheets of ice, sometimes coming to a standstill, again splitting with steady pressure the opposing fragment, now running across a broad hole of water and dashing into the ice on its opposite side with a crash that makes the old lady rattle again, or, rising with her forefoot upon the top of the ice, she forces it down beneath or to one side, or splits it into fragments like a thing of naught.

The night is somewhat gloomy, the moon gleaming at short intervals through the clouds and scud that are driving rapidly across her face. The sky ahead of us is black, black, black as ink—sure sign that the long-wished-for water is directly ahead of us. A strong swell is lifting up the ice in long heaving billows, the swell becoming stronger and stronger as we approach the edge. The wind is blowing a fresh breeze at times from the very quarter we have been anxiously desiring that it might work round into during to-day—to wit, the North-West. Sometimes the breeze falls away a bit, and our hopes and fears and fond anticipations rise and fall with its fluctuations. Pray God that the wind may not cease or shift into some other quarter, but rather continue to blow strong and steadily, slackening the ice off more and more as we approach the much-dreaded outside edge, where the heavy ice and hummocks always hang. May we be mercifully preserved from all danger and damage to our poor old, much tried and much enduring ship, our only hope, our only home.

And thus, O reader, thou seest the crew of this *lost vessel* (over which, I doubt not, there has been many a tear shed and many an aching heart amongst the loved ones at home) are rapidly approaching the crisis of their fate. Alone in this awful ice, 80 miles from the nearest land, and that a barren and inhospitable wilderness, with no human aid or succour at hand in case of accident or damage, this solitary English ship is about to run the gauntlet, to try conclusions once more with her old enemy the ice for the last time. Her crew, once consisting of fifty souls, now reduced by death to forty-seven, worn down by privations, exposure, disease, scurvy, fearfully reduced in physical strength by more than six months' stern endurance of hunger, cold, and nakedness, by the terror by night, living on from day to day fully expecting each day to be their last; men who have long been face to face with a horrible and certain death, who have borne up as they best could against the slow, wearing, reducing influences of deficient food and intense cold, and the heart-sickening effects of hope long deferred; men who have struggled through the severities and privations of an Arctic winter under such circumstances as you are acquainted with already, totally unprovided and unprepared for such a trial of endurance, without sufficient food, without firing, without the necessary clothing—in short, *wanting everything*—these men feel and know that *to-night* will probably decide their fate.

After six months' longing and lingering, *the time has come at last*. We are close to the pack edge. To-morrow's sun will probably see us either at liberty, on our road to homes and friends, returning once more to the world as men plucked from the very grave itself, dead and yet alive again, *or* the rising sunbeams may light upon a water-logged, disabled ship, and a crew dumb with hopeless and helpless despair.

Lord, have mercy and pity upon us. Let us not lose our ship and perish miserably after having seen and suffered so much. O Thou whose compassions fail not, look down upon us with compassion, and guide and guard our ship in her perilous passage through the heavy ice at the edge of the pack. Hear the many cries and prayers that I cannot doubt are ascending up to Thee from the hearts of many a one amongst us. Thou seest and knowest our danger much better than we can. To Thee alone can we look with confidence to bring us out of this ice in safety.

Eleven o'Clock.—The mate comes down from the mast-head and reports that he can see the outside plainly, and that we shall be outside the pack very soon if the breeze continues and all goes well.

Whilst writing this in the cabin (11.30 p.m.) in comes Bill Lofley, who has just descended from the crow's-nest. He assures us he can see the water as plain as possible, and that we may reasonably expect to be *out in an hour*.

Twelve o'Clock.—The mate and Lofley come below, their watch having been relieved at midnight. We eat some biscuit smeared with fat, with some coffee, and for a few minutes converse cheerfully, but soon each man of us becomes absorbed in his own thoughts. We know the fearful risk we are running, the dangers that threaten the ship on every side as, unable to select the best and likeliest leads for her, not able to distinguish where we are going, she drives on headlong in the darkness towards that murky sky which indicates the position of the open water.   I say, thinking of the risks we are now running, each of us becomes absorbed in his own thoughts and eats his biscuit in solemn silence.   What if she should get stove in ?   What if the pack edge is very tight and heavy ?   What if the swell increases ?   What if the wind dies away just now, or, what's worse, chops round to the South-East ?

To most of these questions your heart replies with a single monosyllable—*death !*   Then the inevitable and solemn thought occurs to the mind, " Am I prepared to die ?"

Reader, try and put yourself in our place, imagine yourself in our position as we are just now.   You will find abundant reasons for restlessness, uneasiness, and anxiety.

12.30 *a.m.*—*The wind has fallen away considerably.*   The ship has been brought to a standstill, partly by the want of wind as a motive power, but principally from the *heavy ice closing ahead of her.*

1.30 *a.m.*—The moon has disappeared below the horizon, and the night is dark and gloomy.   Ship moving ahead occasionally, wind alternately light and heavy; nasty ice all round us, rasping and grinding against the ship, especially on her starboard quarter.

Writing this log in the cabin is not very pleasant work; one feels a little agitated and excited.   God grant the ship may not get stove.

2.30 *a.m.*—Bill Clarke, in charge of the watch on deck, has just come down.   He tells us that the wind at times dies completely away, at times blows in strong puffs.   The ship is creeping along slowly, and has just passed through a lot of very ugly heavy ice.

As I write she is receiving a succession of severe blows. The night is dark and gloomy, our hearts troubled and anxious enough, as you may suppose.   The mate is lying in his hammock, but cannot sleep.   Lofley has gone to his berth forward, whilst I am scribbling this poor log for thy amusement with a pen that trembles in my hand and my heart in my mouth. 'Tis now a quarter to three; daylight breaks pretty early now. Would to God it were the morning.

4.15 *a.m.*—Have been walking the decks.   Wind blows

stronger. Ship brought up by a lot of heavy pieces of ice.
Ice packed tighter. We have just passed two or three pieces
of washed ice, a sure indication that we are approaching the
pack edge.

The mate has just come down from the mast-head, and tells
me that there is nothing but light ice as far as he can see,
with no indications of water excepting the heavy black sky
ahead of us. He is going to turn in, and advises me to do ditto,
as there is no chance of the ship getting out of the pack, at
any rate, before breakfast-time.

The day is breaking, and the morning is cold and sharp.
Ship forging ahead under topsails, main topgallant sail, jibs,
main staysail—in short, under all the canvas we can bring to
bear upon her.

Wednesday, March 13th.—I slept heavily for a couple of
hours.

On going on deck at breakfast-time I found the men engaged
in attempting to clear the ship's stern post and starboard
quarter of an immense mass of ice which was adhering to the
ship and seriously interfered with her sailing, but more especially with her steering. A boat was lowered, and three blasts
fired beneath this cumbrous impediment to our progress.
The last blast dislodged it. Slowly and gradually it turned
over and then fell clear of the ship, sinking and then rising
to the surface with a sudden rebound, and floating sullenly
astern in our wake in two huge masses some 10 or 12 feet
thick.

The ship's bilge is still heavily encumbered with ice from
her stern post right away to her main rigging, considerably
impeding her progress, nor shall we get rid of this hindrance
until the ship shakes it off in the open seaway. Anyhow, we
are very glad to have got rid of the mass that was attached
to her stern post and interfered so much with her steering
during last night.

At breakfast-time the ship was running to the South-East
before a stiff breeze from about North-East. We are amongst
light young ice with a great deal of mush and pancakes amongst
this young ice which is well open, reminding me of the appearance of the pack when we first entered the ice in Greenland.

Reynolds tells me that a flock either of loons or rotches flew past the ship this morning, and that several kittiwakes and a burgie or two were seen, sure signs that the sea edge cannot be far distant.

Though still in the pack, such is the favourable appearance of the ice, the swell, the horizon, and of things in general, and so smartly is the old ship walking through this young stuff towards the southward and eastward, that we all of us entertain the most sanguine and pleasing hopes of being speedily in the open seaway. God grant that to-day may prove to be the ever-to-be-remembered day of our deliverance.

Went on deck at 10 a.m. Found the weather thick and foggy, with snow-showers and driving sleet, the horizon obscured, the wind blowing strong, and the ship, with all possible canvas set, brought up by a broad piece of ice at her bows and by the closing of the ice upon her quarters. The pack had tightened, and there was nothing for it but patient waiting until a change of tide, or currents, or a swell, or some other piece of good fortune, should slacken off the ice and permit us to proceed.

A mallie was seen by the watch on deck flying about close to the ship, a sure sign of open water.

Afternoon.—Thick weather, with showers of snow. Wind continuing to blow strong from the North-East, but the ship remained immovable. As for self, I turned into my berth and had three hours' sound and refreshing sleep, which, after the anxieties of last night, you may be sure I stood well in need of.

Joe, the cook, has finished the third cask of "fat," an extra ½ pound having been served out to the men to-day at my request. The shocking state of the gums and mouths of many of our poor fellows prevents them from eating their miserable little " whacks " of hard salt beef.

There is a most extraordinary amount of digestive trouble prevailing amongst the men. I attribute this to the now almost universal custom of soaking their hard biscuit in water before they attempt to eat it, the state of their gums preventing them from biting and breaking up the biscuit in its dry state. I find the newly invented " Compound Chalk Powders " work indifferently well in checking and curing this complaint.

During to-day the water which leaks into the ship has been pumped into the ship's tanks through a hose, instead of overboard. This is to ballast the ship. The engineer turned on the sea-cock in addition, to enable the watch to fill the casks and tanks with water for ballast. He tells me he was obliged to force an iron rod *at least 5 feet through the mass of ice adhering to the ship's side and bottom* before the water would flow into her. This will give you some notion how heavily the ship is encumbered with ice. She was fairly " bedded " in the pack before she broke adrift, and will continue to drag this prodigious quantity of ice adhering to her bottom until the motion of a seaway shakes it off.

Evening.—Thick, foggy, with constant snow-showers. Our decks once more are encumbered with snow. The wind is strong from the North-East.

We expect the pack wiil slacken during the night and, if the present breeze continues, will enable us to work along still further towards the South and eastward.

The sun was obscured, so that no observation was obtained to-day. We expect that the ship and ice are moving rapidly down the country before this North-East wind.

Thursday, March 14th.—Slept very soundly and heavily till 4 a.m., when I was called to look at Haslas Anderson, one of the worst scurvy cases. He had had occasion to rise from his berth and had fainted away. With three of our men the slightest attempt to sit upright or move about is invariably followed by alarming syncope.

Got this poor wretch into his berth again and saw him comfortably settled, then returned to my own bed and was favoured to sleep soundly till 7.30 a.m.—a very unusual thing for me to do.

When I went upon deck this morning at four o'clock I found the weather thick and hazy and uncommonly mild and open. The decks were cumbered with snow which had fallen during the night, while everything was wet and sloppy. Daylight was well advanced even at that early hour. There was very little wind during the night—varying and unsettled, flying round to the North-East, North-West, etc., and at one time blowing strong from that ominous quarter, the South-

East. However, on coming upon deck at breakfast-time it was blowing pretty fresh from that most desirable direction, the North-West, having chopped round to that quarter at about 5 a.m.

This morning has been a busy time with us. About 9.30 the weather cleared up, the sun broke out with great warmth and fervour, and the morning turned out uncommonly mild and genial.

Whilst attending to my patients below ('tis very little I can do for the poor fellows) the cheering cry, " All hands ahoy to bend the mainsail and get in the boats," rang down the hatchways. Soon every man and boy on board that was able to get about swarmed on the decks. The great sail, that had been unbent and sent below when we were going up the East side, was hauled on deck. The blocks and running tackle belonging to it were sent up from the line-room. Presently twenty men were ranged along the foot ropes of the main yard, with twenty others hauling and straining at the ropes, and slowly the great sail travelled up to its old berth and once more was bent on to the yard arm.

Next came some really hard work getting the boats in over the side. Our men are so weak and exhausted that nothing but constant driving and urging on can make many of them exert themselves. I assure you a good many of these poor fellows find it hard work to *walk* along the decks, so much is their strength reduced by the privations and hardships they have undergone during the last six months, more particularly by the rapidly advancing ravages of scurvy.

The ship, which hardly had moved ahead during the previous twenty-two hours, began to go on at eight o'clock this morning when the ice slacked off. The wind was pretty fresh from the North-West throughout the morning. The ice light and uncommonly slack, the swell one long, ever-increasing, heavy roll—a regular Western Ocean swell, rising and falling at least 6 or 7 feet. This was well shown by the wash of the water-line upon a small berg which we passed close to. We went by a considerable number of small bergs adrift amongst the ice and driving down the country along with it.

I cannot describe to you the joyous, exhilarating feeling

that not only myself, but I dare say all on board—even the most apathetic—must have felt more or less during this morning. The ice is light and thoroughly slacked off, becoming slacker and slacker the further we advance; the swell is rolling in heavier and heavier every hour; the sky to the southward and eastward dark and heavy, the wind favourable, the sun shining brightly, the weather warm and genial as an English spring day, our hearts buoyed up with the delightful certainty that we were going out of the pack and might expect soon, if all went well, to be in open water once again.

And so we tugged and positively perspired at the ropes, swung the yards about, and hung on to the tackles and strained every nerve and muscle with a will. We were working with the energy of men who had long wellnigh despaired of life, but who *now*, AT LAST, were escaping from a horrible prison-house to life and liberty, to homes and friends.

I don't know that I exerted myself more than others, but I do know that at midday I was so faint and far spent (being, like the rest of our company, in a very weakly and reduced condition) that I was extremely glad when dinner-time arrived. I sat down to a biscuit, a scrap of salt beef, and a little morsel of cheese, saved from yesterday's allowance, with a relish that an epicure might have envied.

Good observations of the sun were obtained to-day. We are in latitude 59° 57', longitude 60° 33' West, having gone no less than 49 miles to the southward and 20 miles to the eastward since our last observation of Tuesday. The ship is 110 miles due East from Aulizaveek Island off the Labrador coast. We are at the very entrance of Davis Straits, being barely 12 miles North of the parallel of Cape Farewell, the most southerly point of Greenland. The heavy swell, which is now ranging into the ice and increasing every hour as we approach the edge of the pack, is none other than the long regular roll of the *Atlantic Ocean !*

After getting a chain-boat and a waist-boat inboard, the waist-boat was lashed fast to the bulwarks, while the chain-boat, a precious old affair, a regular Noah's Ark originally built for the *Venerable*, was broken up for firewood. This process occupied a very short time, I assure you. Almost before you could turn round, this five-oared boat was smashed into fragments by twenty willing hands and passed below to the 'tween-decks.   The remaining boats were lashed and made secure ready for our getting into the open water.

Afternoon.—The wind has fallen away, the ship rolling in a heavy swell, the ice well slacked off, and rising and falling upon the crests of the long heaving ridges.   We passed some very nasty heavy ice, 10 or 12 feet thick, and very much under-run.*

Two watches on deck engaged in sending below our miserable 3 casks of pork, 1 cask of " fat," 1 of oil, and 1 of coals—the last of what was at one time a goodly phalanx of provision casks.

By the by, Joe, the cook, *burnt the last remaining half of a shake* this morning.   This was the last of sixty odd shakes and twenty odd puncheons that have been consumed for firewood, and a very expensive kind of firewood, too.   Steward engaged in sawing up *oars* for the cabin stove.   Some of the skeads were cut up yesterday for the same purpose.   *Our last cask of coals* was sent below to the cabin coal-hole this morning.

Last, last, last of everything !   Almost daily I am using the last of this, that, and the other medicine.   As the mate has remarked just this moment, " 'Tis a great mercy we are not eating our last biscuit."

The wind has fallen away, at times almost to a calm.   The sails are all aback, every stitch of canvas set.   Officers standing in an anxious group upon the forecastle, and Bill Lofley at the mast-head with the long telescope pointing out to the eastward, where the dark sky tells us the water is.   Swell heavier and heavier, ice slacker and slacker, ship rolling already in such a style as makes me feel somewhat squeamish.   We are very anxious to get a wind, and get the ship out of the pack before nightfall.

2.15 *p.m.*—Bill Lofley has just come down from the crow's-nest with the cheering news that he can see the outside *plainly*, and that a few hours, with a good breeze, would see us out of

---

* Extending more widely under water than the part showing above the surface.

the ice. The ice is slacker and slacker towards the sea edge, where there seems to be *a very heavy ridge of ice.*

God keep us in safety, and preserve us from all harm and injury. We are now on the eve of our last conflict with the ice.

Bill tells us there is a tremendous swell ranging outside.

Four o'Clock.—The ship has been knocking and hammering about, and has just received a heavy blow upon her quarters. The wind has increased, and so has the swell. The afternoon is drawing to a close. Soon night will set in, and we are nearing the edge of the pack. All of us anxious, uneasy, excited, restless, knowing that the *crisis* is approaching, knowing the fearful risk we are about to venture upon. Mr. Clarke has just turned out of his hammock—can't sleep; must go on deck. So must I.

Bill Lofley just come below. Says that the ship is just passing through some very heavy ice, and that the wind has increased into a pleasant breeze from the North-West. And now for the deck once more.

4.15 *p.m.*—Sails all aback; hardly a breath of wind; ship rolling heavily on the swell; won't answer her helm.

4.30 *p.m.*—A light breeze from the South-West; our hopes again in the ascendant.

Harry Smith has just come down from the crow's-nest, and reports that the ice is all slacks and lanes right to the outside edge, where there appears to be a stream of heavy ice which looks to him to be 3 miles wide. A very heavy swell on the outside of this.

Throughout yesterday and to-day the ship has been almost unmanageable from the enormous quantity of ice that encumbers her bottom, and interferes with her sailing and steering qualities most seriously. Her present unmanageable condition—hardly answering to her helm at all—adds not a little to the danger and risk of passing through the heavy ice at the pack edge. If spared to get out of the pack ice in safety, we trust that she will soon shake off this impediment. They tell me that the *Chase* carried some ice still adhering to her bottom *to Shetland,* though she had not been subjected to anything like such heavy and long-continued pressure amongst the ice as this poor old *Diana* has experienced during the past six months.

Five o'Clock.—Watch stowing the mainsail for the night. Wind fallen away entirely; sails all aback; ship rolling helpless on the swell, which comes ranging along in tremendous style. We are all most miserably anxious as to which quarter the next breeze will hail from. Sky looks like wind from the South-West, which would suit our purpose very well.

5.15 *p.m.*—Light winds from the South-East. The swell catches us abeam now; the ship rolling over and at times striking the ice heavily.

God grant in His great mercy that the wind may shift to a more favourable point. Should a heavy breeze or gale spring up from this quarter, I fear we are *all lost men*. Our only chance of life would be to run the ship at all hazards once more into the pack. 'Twould be a second Good Friday! We would be without steam at hand to assist us, with a crew reduced in strength, many of them nearly disabled, a few completely disabled with scurvy, and all of us worn down and weakened by the privations and miseries of the past six months. Further, we have a ship that will not answer her helm, and is almost as unmanageable as a log upon the water. A gale from the South-East, with a heavy swell amongst this heavy ice, I fear would be fatal to the *Diana*. There would be no hope of saving a soul of us if the ship goes from under us.

Let us humbly trust that He who has guarded and preserved us through so many dangers will mercifully spare us now. In Him alone can we put our trust.

GREENLAND'S ICY MOUNTAINS

CHAPTER XVIII

THE GALE AMID THE ICE

Friday, March 15th.—I retired to my berth at about nine o'clock last night, but never slept a wink. Anxiety and the noise of the ice hammering against the ship's sides kept not only myself, but I dare say a great part of the ship's company, awake.

At about 2.30 a.m. the mate came below and called up the captain's watch. The wind was blowing half a gale from the South, the ship was driving through the ice towards water, and so the mate wished to have these additional men in readiness in case of need.

I jumped up immediately, dressed, and was on deck in a few minutes.

I found the wind blowing very strong, night dark and wild, with driving snow and sleet, and there was a most fearful swell running. The ship was laid over on her side by the force of the wind, being under main topgallant sail, topsails, fore-sail, fore-spenser, fore-topmast staysail, and jib, and driving through lightish ice.

We had passed through some streams of very nasty heavy ice during the fore part of the watch—masses of blue washed ice, like little bergs, that made a most ominous roaring and rushing noise as they rose and fell with the heavy swell.

3 a.m.—The wind has worked round to about South-South-West. By compass, the ship is heading East-South-East, but she will not lay up to the wind on account of the ice adhering to her bottom, which circumstance, as remarked before, continues to interfere seriously with her sailing and steering.

We are all of us on the decks; a most intensely anxious time. We know by the tremendous swell that we cannot be far from the edge of the pack, and dread having to run an unmanageable ship in the darkness through the streams of heavy ice which we know we must encounter when we break out of the pack. Every man and boy aboard knows and feels that the ship may be stove in at almost any moment.

3.15 *a.m.*—Whilst sitting in the cabin eating half a biscuit, the inspectioneer in charge of the watch came down to tell the mate that we were close either to a large hole of water or to the outside edge itself. In his opinion it was the veritable outside of the pack, and the ship would be out of the ice in a few minutes.

We rushed on deck, and, leaning over the rail, saw that the ship was close to a large body of open water, the extent of which we could not distinguish for the darkness. In a few minutes the ship glided from amongst the ice, and once more was rising and falling and leaning heavily over upon the rolling swell of the Atlantic.

Most of the officers were persuaded that we were at last clear of the ice, and at liberty to square the yards and bear up for home with the first clear daylight. We reefed the topsails and laid the ship to, to dodge about till daylight appeared. We seem to be in a very large body of water, and all of us are sanguine that it *is the outside*. There is a most fearful swell on, the ice edge rising and falling in tremendous billows. It is a *very* great mercy that we are able to dodge in peace and quietness.

Four o'Clock.—Ship dodging for daylight. I went below with the officers for half an hour. We are awaiting the break of day with the greatest anxiety, that we may determine our whereabouts, and whether we are really outside the pack or not.

4.30 *a.m.*—Called on deck to help work the sails, etc. Ship approaching a small stream of straggling ice, beyond which nothing can be seen but water. We still cling to the idea that we are outside the pack. Would to God it were daylight.

4.45 *a.m.*—'Spectioneer's watch called on deck to put the ship about, as there are streams of ice ahead. A very heavy swell; wind blowing heavily from the South-West; ship dodging for daylight.

5.15 *a.m.*—On deck again to put ship about. The daylight

breaking at last; can see the ice edge and a *most fearful* rolling swell on.

5.30 *a.m.*—Reynolds has come down from the mast-head. He says he can see nothing but streams of ice and light brash outside the pack. Too thick to see far.

5.45 *a.m.*—Much lighter. A small iceberg off our port quarter. Weather thick, with showers of snow and sleet. If it had been clear, the sun would have made his appearance about this hour. Streams of ice ahead. Ship dodging for clear daylight.

6.10 *a.m.*—Upon going on deck, found that the ship had been allowed to run and was some little distance, not in a stream, but in a pack of ice, the extent of which we could not make out. The ice is pretty heavy stuff, mixed with light ice and brash, with some very heavy blue washed pieces and bergs scattered amongst it. The ice tightened on us, and the ship came to a standstill, the wind at times falling away, leaving the ship rolling on the tremendous swell and striking the ice heavily.

At one time the ship was close alongside a frightfully heavy mass of old washed ice, which rose and fell and rushed towards us and then retreated again and again upon the crest of the swell until it approached within a few feet of our starboard quarter. Most providentially a little breeze sprang up and carried us clear of this threatening danger. Had it struck us, nothing could have saved the ship or ourselves. It would have gone clean through us !

Seeing it was impossible to force the ship through this ice, we attempted to wear her. After a long time, and with no small risk from some heavy ice alongside, she worked round and commenced dodging once more in the hole of water which we had quitted.

Noon.—After breakfast and up to 10 a.m. the ship was dodging in the hole of water. This was of large size, but was only a hole of water and *not the outside edge*.

This disappointment was keenly felt, more especially as the pack was rapidly streaming off to leeward and closing upon us. The weather is most unutterably miserable—a raw, damp, thick, foggy, muggy day, with driving snow and sleet. The deck, the ropes, everything, are wet and sloppy and cheerless in the extreme. The atmosphere was so ladened with fogs and obscured by the driving snow that 'twas impossible to see where we were, or to find a road out of the dangerous vicinity of the pack edge. A most tremendous heavy swell on. The wind blowing strong from the *most adverse quarter*, the South and South-East. The ship liable to the greatest dangers, close to the dreaded outside edge, driving and drifting we know not whither. All of us unutterably anxious, wretched, miserable.

About ten o'clock the mate ordered the ship to be allowed to run before the wind. Throughout the morning we were running along this broad lane of water *dead to the northward*, trusting to Providence to preserve us. Ship running none knows where to, or whether towards or away from the pack edge. Weather thicker and thicker and thicker, still more raw, sloppy, and uncomfortable.

I was on deck all the morning assisting in working the ship to the best of my ability.

A great number of kittiwakes and loons seen, also a few dovekies in their beautiful winter plumage.

Afternoon.—Ship driving through a lot of lightish ice, but at times receiving heavy blows about her quarters. As I was feeling very tired and knocked up, I turned into bed.

4 *p.m.*—Awakened by the heavy blows of the ice against the port bow, the ship receiving very heavy blows indeed. Got up hastily, went on deck, and found the officers in great consternation. The wind had fallen away, and *the ice, carried by the current, had closed round the ship like a shot*. The ship, taken all aback, had run astern and SMASHED HER RUDDER!

She was lying helpless amongst heavy ice, broadside on to the fearful swell, which was hammering the masses of ice about her sides with a force which she would never be able to resist for long. Every moment we were expecting to see her stern post carried away or her quarters stove in. There was very little wind, so we could not get the ship round bows on to the swell.

Ship in the greatest peril. All hands called immediately, but what to do to better our position or save the ship from what seemed to everybody certain destruction was the question. Backed all the sails, but she would not go astern towards a large hole of water which she had just quitted when closed in upon by the swirling ice. Next got up a strong warp and fixed an ice anchor upon a heavy piece of ice. Taking the warp to the main capstan, we attempted to drag the ship's head round to the swell. Though the capstan bars were trebly manned, the swell was too much for us, and I was horrified to see the capstan fly round, sweeping half the men over upon the deck. How they escaped being smashed or severely injured by the capstan bars I cannot tell, but can only thank God with a full heart that no limbs were broken or lives lost.

Again we attempted to warp the ship's head round, and again the force of the swell sent the capstan bars whirling round amongst us. (I am told that three men were struck dead at once on board a Hull whaler by the capstan bars flying round and overpowering them.)

The men were very backward in manning the bars for a third time, but as we were engaged in a struggle for life there was no help for it. This time we held our ground, but the thick warp broke. Got up another warp, and attempted several times to wear the ship's head on to the swell, but the ice anchor drew out. So had to give up the attempt as hopeless.

Meanwhile the ship was thundering and battering amongst the heavy ice, and men were gazing at each other's faces in mute despair. The ship was unmanageable. Mortal man could do no more for her. We were expecting to hear every moment the fatal crash of her timbers, as the surging masses of ice dashed against her sides. Hope was fast dying away; apparently there was nothing for us but a miserable death.

And now *mark my words!* At this very moment, when we found ourselves foiled, baffled, helpless, at the mercy of the ice; at this very moment, when our situation seemed utterly hopeless and helpless, and our fate inevitable, mark the finger of God! A strong wind sprang up in an instant, *right aft, from due North*, a wind that in a few minutes blew half a gale from the very quarter which we could have most earnestly desired.

The ice commenced closing tighter and the swell began to

subside. With wondering and astonishment at this most signal interposition of Divine Providence on our behalf, we hauled up the topsails and set more canvas to force her further into the pack.

As the ice tightened and the wind increased, the swell subsided and the numerous blows of the ice upon our poor old ship's sides became lighter and lighter. With a heart overflowing with joy and thankfulness I went below to look after my poor patients, whom I cheered up to the best of my power. Then I returned on deck and assisted in making all snug.

An extra pound of biscuit was served out to all hands, partly on account of the unusual exertions the men have been called upon to make to-day, but principally because many of our poor fellows have eaten their weekly allowance in the expectation of being out of the pack and on full allowance before the end of this week. Nor am I one whit better myself. I find myself reduced to half a biscuit out of 4 pounds of " bread," so this additional pound is very acceptable.

A glass of grog was served out to all hands. So ended the afternoon.

Evening.—A tremendous gale blowing from the North. This will beat down the outside swell and carry us and the ice out to the eastward, provided no accident befalls the ship. She is laid amongst heavy ice with a damaged rudder (thank God, 'tis not so severely injured as was supposed at first!), and a heavy swell still ranges, causing the ice to crash in the most ominous manner against her quarters as I sit writing this log in the cabin. Watch engaged in hauling up foresail, stowing and reefing topsails, and making all snug for the night.

I am now off to my berth to try and snatch a little brief sleep, for I am tired to death with to-day's exertions and intense anxieties.

So ends another most eventful day—one of the most eventful in my life, if I am spared to reach home. It has been a day of the greatest anxieties, the greatest dangers, and the most remarkable deliverance from the jaws of death. Never did I see such an extraordinary instance of Divine mercy, help, and succour in the sorest need as was shown by this remarkable and totally unexpected change of wind. The wind which, but a moment before, had been blowing strong from the southward, in an instant blew a violent *gale* from an exactly opposite quarter.

Nor can I conclude to-day's account without expressing my gratitude to Almighty God for His mercy and compassion upon us poor creatures. May I never forget this day's deliverance.

The gale is blowing very heavily from the northward. Mate just come below, his clothes frozen stiff upon him. Swell has gone down somewhat, and ship is not subjected to such repeated and heavy blows.

Am now off to my berth, trusting solely in Divine Providence to guard and preserve us all during this night, remembering that we are close to the sea edge and in the greatest danger of losing our ship and our lives unless He condescends to watch over us. To Him alone can we look with confidence.

Saturday, March 16th.—The gale blew very heavily from the northward throughout the night. Ship running dead to the eastward all night. A fearful swell on, the ship meeting it bows on.

About 12.30 a.m. or one o'clock we began to fall in with streams of very heavy ice—ugly blue washed masses, more like small icebergs than anything else. Any one of them would have stove in the ship had it struck her broadside on. As it was, the ship received a fearful hammering.

I retired to my berth about 9.30 last night, but not to sleep. The crashing of the heavy ice against the ship's bows kept me —and I dare say all on board—miserable, anxious, and wide awake. As I lay in my bunk I could distinctly hear the roaring and rushing of the backwater formed by the monstrous masses of ice as they rose and fell upon the swell. When the ship struck them bows on, fortunately for us, she reeled and staggered again, though under all possible canvas and running before a gale of wind.

During the mate's watch we ran a long way to the eastward. Weather thick and sleety, with very hard frost. A heavy snowfall rendered it impossible to see where the ship was driving or to avoid the most serious collisions with the terribly heavy ice. During the 'spectioneer's watch the pack tightened and the ship didn't make such progress.

Day broke soon after 4 a.m., and the glimmering light revealed to our eyes the dangerous nature of the ice amongst which the ship was driving. I am told it was frightful to look at.

5 *a.m.*—The wind flew round into that ominous quarter, the South-East, with mild, thick, foggy weather. The swell, no longer meeting the ship end on, hurled the heavy masses of ice upon the ship's broadside, or caught her about her lee quarters as she rolled over with the press of canvas she carried. The poor old ship fairly quivered under the tremendous and incessant blows she was receiving. It seemed impossible for her to stand such severe hammering, especially amidships and about her quarters.

6 *a.m.*—I rose and went on deck. Found a high wind blowing from the South-East; the ship labouring under all possible canvas; the swell tremendously high; weather wild, thick, and gloomy; decks, rigging, everything covered thickly with snow; the officers and men utterly disheartened.

Harry Smith remarked that the prospect before us really made him " feel dead sick at heart." The mate said that it seemed to him as though we were all doomed men. He could not see how the ship could possibly escape much longer being stove in amongst such heavy ice and with such a fearfully heavy swell on.

With the wind blowing half a gale dead on to the face of the pack and the weather so thick and miserable it was impossible to see where we were going or what we were doing, whilst all the time we knew by the swell that we must be close to the pack edge, with heavier and heavier ice to contend with.

I knocked about the decks till breakfast-time, assisting in hauling yards about, shortening sail, pumping, etc. As you may suppose, I felt utterly miserable and dejected at the awful prospect before us. You can have no idea of the dreadful Western Ocean swell that swept round us, lifting the masses of heavy ice in gigantic rolling billows far into the murky sky, reminding me of last Good Friday's experience in Greenland.

Troops of kittiwakes flew twirling and sweeping round the doomed ship, and were gazed at by her miserable crew in silent apathy. I really envied these poor birds their powers of flight, longing as I was to escape from this dreadful pack, dreading to hear any moment the fatal cry, " All hands ahoy ! Ship stove in !"

And yet we were preserved hour after hour.

7.30 *a.m.*—Having come to what appeared to be a pretty soft place in the pack where the ice seemed lighter, we took canvas off the ship and let her lie to under reefed topsails. Ship laid with head to the South, the swell catching her broadside on, the heavy ice hammering her severely. However, the " mush " or " sawdust " (ice ground up by the constant collision of the large fragments) and smaller fragments of ice protected her a good deal.

Eight o'Clock.—Breakfast-time. The mate and engineer (who had been up all night and seemed utterly worn out, especially the former) and Bill Lofley were sound asleep as they sat at the table. None of us could eat much, our prospects of escaping from this awful ice seemed too hopeless. Adverse winds (the very worst wind that possibly could blow at this critical state of affairs), the fearful swell, the heavy character of the ice (old, blue, washed, gigantic masses hovering thickly around us as if awaiting the opportunity of crushing us), and the thick, murky weather (the thickest and most deplorable weather we have experienced since the early part of January)—all these calamities, occurring at this most critical juncture when the ship is close to the sea edge and in the greatest danger of being stove in even under the most favourable circumstances, seemed to point to no other conclusion but disaster, despair, and death.

You can have no idea of the wearying, heart-sickening, utterly desponding state the mind gets into under such trials and disappointments. I am certain that not a few of our crew are utterly indifferent how soon the ship goes down. As for self, I feel dead sick at heart and utterly worn out with fatigue, intense anxiety, and want of sleep. Yesterday was one of the most trying days we have experienced, even during this trying voyage. Last night was one of the most agonising nights of the many nights of dread and danger through which we have been preserved. To-day bids fair to be as gloomy and as pregnant with disaster as any of its predecessors.

One commences such a day as this with the solemn feeling that, in all human probability, it may be your last day on earth. Then comes the awful question, "Am I prepared to die? Can I face death?" Your neglect of all the warnings, providences, preservations of the past, and a thousand other thoughts, pass in rapid succession through the mind and fill your cup of misery, anxiety, dread, and despair to the very brim. Meanwhile you go about your work mechanically, and lay hold of a rope's end or work at the pumps with an energy that astonishes the more apathetic members of the crew.

After breakfast I went forward to see my poor patients. When engaged in this, to me, distressing but necessary duty (for, you see, I can do little or nothing for the poor scurvy-smitten fellows), Bill Lofley came down and reported that he had been to the mast-head and could see the outside edge. At first this news was received with indifference, as we have been deceived so frequently now on this point. However, the mate, cooper, and others, having descended from aloft with the same impression, the good news was circulated speedily through the ship, and hope revived once more in our breasts.

I was on deck throughout the morning. Weather cleared up towards midday. The ship laid to amongst lightish ice and "sawdust," with heavy pieces here and there. Wind blowing very heavy from the South-South-East. The swell fearful to look at. Ship at times receiving heavy blows from the masses of ice. The "sawdust" and small fragments form a regular bed to some extent keeping down the swell and serving as fenders to protect the ship from the full force of the blows.

Afternoon.—Weather clearer and wind moderated. At 2.15 the 'spectioneer came down to the cabin and reported that the sea was visible from the forecastle, and that the ice had slacked off very much.

Four o'Clock.—Have come below to add that, the wind having got more southerly, we have just wore the ship's head round, crowded all possible canvas upon her, and are slowly and painfully *forcing our way through the ice towards the outside edge.*

God grant us His blessing on our efforts for life and liberty, and keep our ship in safety in the conflict between her much-tried timbers and the heavy ice.

The ship's progress is very slow, and we do not expect to arrive at the edge before dark. If she would only lie up a little bit nearer the wind we should soon fetch the outside water, but as it is she falls away so much to leeward.

Seven o'Clock.—The ice, which had kept very slack, began to close, and our troubles commenced once more. The darkness overtook us whilst beset amongst a nest of very heavy washed pieces. The wind has fallen away and the swell increasing. The ship rolling heavily from side to side in the trough of the swell and striking with tremendous force upon the cruel, blue, glistening masses of ice which hem her in closely.

We attempted to wear her head towards the swell, but the pack was so tight and the wind had fallen away so much that it was impossible to do so. There was nothing for it but to square the yards and trust to the ship drawing gradually ahead and away from the imminent dangers that threatened her on all hands.

For more than half an hour an immense mass of ice nearly as long as herself lay alongside her, the ship rolling and falling upon it with a crash that made all her framework rattle again. At the same time, another very heavy mass was pounding away at her opposite bow enough to stove her in.

Dejection and despair again took possession of our minds. It seemed impossible that any ship could resist such rough usage long. Bitterly did we reproach ourselves for having left our comparatively safe quarters amongst the lighter ice, where we ought to have continued dodging and waiting patiently for a change of wind. It seemed as though everything we did for the ship, every purpose, was crossed and thwarted. Everything seemed to miscarry. As the second mate remarked, " We were never out of trouble."

All we could do for the ship was to protect her sides with rope fenders (and we had only three) from the terrible collisions, trust to her creeping away gradually from this collection of heavy pieces to some lighter stuff ahead of us, and trust to the continued mercy, pity, and protection of Almighty God.

Was on deck till 10 p.m., engaged in working the fenders, boxhauling the yards, hauling the head of the mizen in and out, and seconding, to the best of my power, the efforts of the officers and crew to save the ship.

By ten o'clock the ship had made her way from amongst the heaviest of the ice, whilst the wind had got more round to the eastward. By that time I felt utterly done up, worn out with fatigue, great and protracted anxiety, and want of needful sleep. I saw my patients, and then tumbled into my berth, hoping and trusting that God in His infinite mercy would protect the ship during the night and, if it were His will, send us a northerly wind.

CORMORANT

CHAPTER XIX

THE FINAL STRUGGLE

Sunday, March 17th.—Don't remember much about last night. I only know that I slept heavily, undisturbed by the rising of my companions at 2 a.m. to keep their watch, though at times aroused by the tremendous thumping and battering of the ice against the ship's bows.

6 *a.m.*—The cry, " All hands ahoy!" roused me in an instant. Was soon dressed and on deck. Found that the wind was blowing fresh—blessed be God!—from the *North-East*, that the pack was very tight, and the ship laid among heavy ice still.

One gigantic fragment of ice, after punishing her severely, drew astern and, catching her rudder, injured it still further. All hands were called to get up the spare rudder from the 'tween-decks in case it was necessary to unship the injured one.

Ship's head laid bows on to the swell, which was very heavy. We are forging our way along slowly towards the dark sky ahead. The open water visible from the forecastle as the swell lifts it.

We are in the middle of a long point of ice, surrounded by water on three sides. If this favourable breeze continues and the ice slackens off, as we expect it will, and if nothing happens to the ship, *we expect to be out of the ice some time to-day!* That time, though, principally depends upon the slackening of the ice.

Engaged till breakfast-time heaving at the main capstan to get up the rudder, a gigantic mass of wood and iron, from between-decks.

9 *a.m.*—*Ice slackening off!* Ship beginning to move ahead.

10 *a.m.*—The mate reports that we are only some ¾ *mile from the outside.*

Passed through some very heavy, nasty ice. Was busy with the fenders, protecting the ship's quarters.

Eleven o'Clock.—Can see the surf breaking over the heavy ice at the outside edge. *All of us in state of great excitement.* Ice continues well open, being spread by the breeze of wind, which has got round more to the North, acting against the rolling swell. Ship making good progress. Ice just now not so heavy. We fall in with heavy pieces here and there, generally in groups and streams.

11.30 *a.m.*—Ran below to scribble these remarks.

As you may suppose, I am as anxious and excited as possible. A very heavy sea on outside the pack. God grant all may go well with the poor old ship.

We are rapidly approaching either home and friends, life and liberty, or else a swift and sudden destruction. As I have remarked frequently, the very heaviest ice always hangs at the sea edge and forms the greatest danger, especially when there is a heavy sea running, and especially with a ship like ours, with rudder injured and the ship rendered almost unmanageable by the ice adhering to her bottom.

Ten minutes to twelve. Must run on deck again.

12.15 *p.m.*—Worked away at the fenders. Had the pleasure of warding off some heavy blows. Sea edge well in sight.

Mate came down from aloft. We sit down to dinner. Ate our poor ½ pound of dumpling with exceeding satisfaction, the steward producing for the occasion a bottle of raspberry vinegar, the existence of which on board the ship was known to no one save himself. All of us happy, hearty, and hungry.

12.35 *p.m.*—Dinner soon despatched, we run on deck again. Find the ship driving along before a stiff breeze, the outside edge a very short distance off. Watch on deck making boats, etc., all secure.

12.50 *p.m.*—Have run below to scribble these few lines.

Ship forging along at a fine rate through the pack, which is well spread. At times she receives heavy blows from the heavy pieces thickly scattered about. Old *Diana* well laid over on her broadside driving toward the sea edge in style. Streams of young ice, loose masses of ice, and small berg pieces adrift in the open water, having been blown off the face of the pack by this North-East breeze, which is blowing more strongly than ever, for which we are thankful.

Now for the deck again.

1 *p.m.*—Have been standing on the forecastle for the last ten minutes. The old ship is driving along through the pack under every stitch of canvas, laid well over on her broadside by the force of the stiff North-Easter. The outside edge very near at hand.

Would to God my friends in England, who, doubtless, have given me up as lost, dead and gone, could see us now! On the very edge of the pack, *the happy moment so long desired, so oft despaired of, now at hand!*

I trust that no unforeseen misfortune will dash our cup of happiness from our lips, as happened to the fabled Tantalus of old, who, parched and dying of thirst, ever raised the brimming goblet to his lips to find it turned dry on touching them.

I should like a painting of the *Diana* just now, as, staggering under the heavy press of canvas, she forges her way through the swirling ice, the dark, black water heaving and rolling only a few ship's lengths ahead of her; her crew pale, wan, ghastly, emaciated with scurvy, and worn out with long privations, gazing joyously yet anxiously over the bulwarks, eyeihg the blessed water so close at hand and, doubtless, every man and boy of them thanking God with overflowing, grateful heart for His sparing and preserving mercies.

Once more on deck to see her break out!

1.45 *p.m.*—*We are well out of the pack!* Ship bowling along in fine style, the heavy swell crested with scattered fragments of ice blown away from the pack edge.

For the last quarter-mile of pack the ice was remarkably broken up, every piece being worn round and smooth by the action of the waves and the constant trituration.

As I write, the ship, which has great way on her, is striking heavily against the drifting fragments of ice which she encounters on her hurried flight from the dreaded prison house in which she has been beset so long. Mate at the mast-head, two men at the wheel, all hands on deck engaged in sending

the spare rudder below again. The rudder now at the ship's
stern post was not injured so severely as to render it useless.

Glory be to God that we are out of the ice at last. Looking
astern, the long white heaving pack makes one shudder to
contemplate. Looking forward, the rolling ocean and the
dark sky seem to welcome us once more. The officers on the
forecastle are gazing with beaming faces at the pleasing
prospect and saying, " Well done, *Diana!*" " Thank God,
Dick, we've lived to see this day!" " Thirteen months of it,
and now for home again at last!" " Wish my poor wife could
see us now!" " Ah, doctor, now's your chance for getting
that bottle of *East Water* which you've talked about!" (I
reckoned it was the best medicine I could prescribe.)

Three o'Clock.—Have been pulling, tugging, and heaving
away with the rest, getting two boats in over the side, sending
the spare rudder below, taking in main top-gallant sail,
fore-spenser, etc.

George Clarke just down from mast-head. *Says we've got
another body of ice to go through,* but he can see water beyond.
Trust we may get through it safely. Ship flying through the
water at great speed.

3.45 *p.m.*—Ran close up to the ice edge, and then put ship
about to weather the point. 'Tis a long point of ice running
out from the pack. Had the wind been quite fair, we would
have shoved the ship straight through it. As it is, with night
coming on, and the possibility of the wind falling or the ice
closing upon us, we prefer to put the ship about and make
a long board which should bring us clear of the point end.
The ship is heading now towards her old enemy the pack.

So it seems we are not clear of the ice altogether yet, nor
must we congratulate ourselves upon having clean escaped
from it till we leave the last fragment astern.

Am feeling very tired with hauling and pulling at the ropes.
We have got one boat in over the side, and on to its chocks.
It really looks quite strange to see boats once more stowed
away upon the decks in readiness for a sea passage.

* * * * *

As we approached the ice, the question was discussed
earnestly amongst us whether we should lay the ship to,

attempt to run to the northward to find and get round the point end of the ice, or risk the passage through the pack.

George Clarke requested the other officers to go to the mast-head and see for themselves what the ice was like, and give him their opinion as to the best course to be pursued. One after another they ascended to the crow's-nest, from which the long telescope could be seen fixed steadily in the direction of the opposing ice. One after another they descended slowly to the deck, and each gave it as his opinion that it was not sane or prudent to shove the ship once more into a pack with such a heavy swell on. George Clarke went to the mast-head again and, finding that the pack consisted of light and heavy ice intermingled and very much spread, he determined to push the ship through at all hazards whilst the wind was in our favour.

Soon after five o'clock we were running at a great speed through young ice at the edge of the broad stream. By tea-time (six o'clock) we were fairly in the pack.

The swell was tremendous, the ice very much open, and consisting of light ice with streams of very heavy pieces. The ship, under every stitch of canvas, driving at great speed before a stiff breeze, and reeling and staggering under the press of sail she carried.

A little group of us stood on the forecastle, holding on by ropes as the ship lurched heavily to leeward, anxiously eyeing the masses of ice ahead of us; the officer in charge of the watch shouting out to the men at the wheel; the helm in constant motion as we wore the ship's course to avoid coming into collision with the heavy ice; George Clarke in the crow's-nest further directing the ship's course; the men boxing the yards about, others vainly attempting to interpose fenders between the threatening masses and the ship's sides as we tore along through the ice; the poor old ship incessantly coming in contact with the floating blue washed pieces, striking them with a shock that fairly made her reel again, and filling our minds with grave apprehensions lest her bows should be stove in. Happily we were bows on to the swell, but I assure you that, much and sorely as the old ship has been tried during this fearful winter, she never experienced such a severe hammering as she did whilst running through this last opposing barrier of ice.

Meanwhile the night drew on apace. The ship dashed through the innumerable dangers that surrounded her on all sides, sometimes shaving close past some immense mass of ice, hard and dangerous as a rock, whilst we stood looking on with bated breath and trembling, anxious hearts; again driving stem on against some heavy fragment with a shock that made both us and her stagger again. Then, recovering her way, on she went towards the dark, inky horizon ahead of us, where the blessed open water lay in sight from the mast-head.

Terribly exciting work this, gentlemen, running the gauntlet for dear life, with every chance of our ship being stove in, with not the faintest hope of saving your life if accident befell her.

Hour succeeded hour, the night fell cold and dreary, the wind increased to half a gale. There seemed no limit to that interminable ice. I do assure you, such hours as these seem the longest one has ever lived. Such hours of agonising anxiety are never to be forgotten.

However, at about nine o'clock we could see *the veritable and most unmistakable outside edge.* By 9.30 we were past all heavy ice, and running amongst streams of light ice and " pancakes." The long rolling Atlantic swell became heavier and heavier, the ship pitched and rolled more and more.

At ten o'clock the mate came down from the crow's-nest and informed us that there was no more ice ahead, that we were well out of the pack at last, and running with all possible sail set ON OUR PASSAGE HOME !

(Here ends the diary.)

CHAPTER XX

THE RACE WITH DEATH

So ends this remarkable diary.

Why it abruptly came to a termination in this fashion, with the voyage incomplete, must remain unknown. That the keeping of the record was a great toil is stated definitely in two or three places, but that it should have ended at this juncture has been a disappointment to those who have been privileged to read it.

A few reasons may be hazarded as to why the diary was left uncompleted. Its writer may have considered the interesting part of the voyage was over. Perhaps the mental reaction following the ship's escape from the ice was so great that it was impossible to continue with the toil of writing. More likely, the steady increase of the scurvy amongst the crew, and the serious condition of the worst cases, would keep the surgeon busier than ever in the 'tween-decks. Again, the ship being at sea now would throw additional labour on those who were able to get about on deck and work the sails. Of the few still fit for manual labour, the surgeon was one, and he did his full share of it. Possibly all these reasons combined were responsible for the diary being neglected, and for the surgeon's account of this part of the voyage having remained unwritten.

However, there are other sources from which information concerning the further adventures and tribulations of the *Diana's* homeward run can be extracted. The ship's official log records some of the facts in cold and laconic words. The late Captain Allan Young of the *Pandora* wrote in the *Cornhill Magazine* for 1867 an account of this voyage of the *Diana*. It is very obvious that this article was drawn, in the main, from my late father's diary, but the description of the last phases must have been obtained orally, probably partly also

258

from the surgeon. The late Dr. John Milner Fothergill (a close personal friend) wrote a long article, which appeared in *Good Words* in 1880. Miss Mary Gravill, daughter of the *Diana's* captain, published a short account of this voyage in the *Wide World Magazine* for February, 1906. Newspaper cuttings and other fragments complete the tale.

From this material it is possible to draw some sort of an outline of the conditions prevailing aboard the ship during the fortnight's run to Shetland.

During this time the ship's log is filled mostly with such remarks as: " Stiff breezes with thick weather," " Brisk gales with thick, hazy weather," "Heavy cross sea running," " Showers of snow," " People forced to stay at the pumps," " A heavy sea running," " Strong breezes with gloomy weather." This makes a melancholy picture as regards external aspects.

With regard to conditions within the ship, life during this fortnight must have been wretched in the extreme. Captain Allan Young describes this portion of the voyage as follows:

" The broad Atlantic was now before them. They were released, and bore away for home with a cheer, but they were so reduced in strength as to be almost incapable of working the ship.

" The dreadful scurvy increased in violence with the sudden change from the frosts of the ice-pack to the damps and fogs of the open water. The 'tween-deck was in a fearful state on account of the sleeping berths, which had been almost constantly coated with ice, now becoming thawed and dripping wet.

" They had stripped the ship of almost everything inflammable, and so were unable to make any fire below. Many of the crew lay in their berths, unable to help themselves or each other. All who were capable of duty were constantly called to work on deck. That finished, they were so fatigued as to be just able to crawl to their beds. Some of those who had struggled upon deck in the first excitement of their release soon fell down at the pumps. Deaths began to occur among the worst scurvy cases, and the bodies were brought up from below, wrapped in canvas, and laid in rows upon the deck.

"Some of the deaths of these scurvy-stricken men were so sudden as scarcely to give time for the surgeon to be called to the bedside. The slightest exertion on the part of some of these poor men would be followed by a fatal syncope.

"On one occasion the surgeon was assisting on deck, when a sailor came up and said: 'Doctor, you're wanted below.' The doctor arrived between-decks only in time to find a poor fellow who, in struggling out of his berth, had been thrown down by the rolling of the ship, and was lying dead upon the deck.

"On another occasion the slight exertion of crawling out of bed was instantly fatal in the case of Arthur Yell. He was found lying dead upon two of his companions, over whom he had tried to pass, and who were too weak to remove his dead body from off them !

"Most providentially strong winds drove them across the Atlantic, and they flew before the wind in their race with death. At last three only out of the whole ship's company were able to go aloft.

"The surgeon appears to have done everything in his power. Besides attending the sick and performing the sad offices for the dead, he took his turn at the pumps, kept watch, and assisted with the sails and ropes. Messrs. George Clarke, Lofley, Byers, Smith, and Reynolds (mates and harpooners) worked with desperate energy, as, indeed, did all while capable of the least exertion."

The ship's log of March 26th records the death from scurvy of Bonsall Miller of Hull.

On March 27th the surgeon appears to have made another general survey of the crew, for the official log that day contains this entry:

"The following is the state of the ship's company's health:

13 completely disabled and confined to bed.
2 completely disabled with ulceration of feet.
14 severely affected.
6 getting very bad.
3 slightly affected.
5 very slightly affected.
3 show no symptoms of scurvy.
———
46 total."

On March 28th the log records the death of Basil Smith of Shetland, and, on March 29th, of Philip Pickard of Hull.

On March 30th the log remarks, " Strong gales with squalls and showers of sleet." That the ship truly was racing is evidenced from the daily record of distance covered in the twenty-four hours—190 knots, 202 knots, 208 knots—a very fine speed for a strongly built, broad-beamed, bluff-bowed whaling-ship, a considerable proportion of whose topmasts and spars had been burnt for firewood.

The log for March 31st laconically states that " the ship's company is very much exhausted with pumping the ship. At 6.30 p.m. Arthur Yell, Shetlandman, died of scurvy."

On the morning of April 1st they had their first sight of some fellow-creatures, for the log states, " Saw a ship. Got his longitude."

Of this portion of the voyage Dr. Fothergill wrote:

" Certainly it was not for want of paper that the diary was not continued. The surgeon had something else to do. There was the Atlantic to be crossed in a leaky ship, and with a scurvy-stricken crew mumbling their biscuits with their loosening teeth and swollen, bleeding gums. Men were dying, the survivors getting weaker; the surgeon had his sick to attend to, and took his turn at the watch and at the pumps as well.

" ' He was one man in a thousand, and we should have perished without him,' said one of the survivors. He animated them by his example; he cheered them by his undaunted courage; he shared their work as well as their danger.

" Fortunately they had fair winds for their race with death, and starvation—inevitable death—was behind them. Even at the last, when the land was sighted, the ship was nearly lost in a gale because they had not men enough to handle her properly."

Captain Young adds the information that " so completely were they exhausted that, had they been out for another day, they must have been lost; for the night previous to sighting the land three men fell at the pumps and one of the principal sails blew away from their inability to secure it."

The ship's log records that, on the afternoon of April 1st,

the leadsman " struck soundings at 54 fathoms," and at 6 p.m. they " saw the West side of Shetland."

On April 2nd the sorely tried ship crept into the little inlet of Ronas Voe, in Shetland, and the race home was over. The ship's log for that day simply reads as follows:

" At 2.30 a.m. Robert Robinson of Shetland died of scurvy.

" At 11 a.m. brought up in Ronas Voe, the crew being in a very exhausted state and the ship making a deal of water. Engaged six men to pump the ship, the crew not being able to work any more.

" At 1 p.m. Frederick Lockham of Hull died of scurvy and exhaustion.

" At 1.30 p.m. Gideon Frazer of Shetland died of scurvy."

So the race had been run and three poor fellows had been beaten at the very winning-post, two of them actually in sight of home.

Captain Young's account goes on to say:

" On entering Ronas Voe, nine* corpses were lying on the deck, two men only could go aloft, while two other poor fellows died in their berths that afternoon.

" With the aid of help from the shore the ship was brought safely to anchor, and a message despatched to Lerwick for assistance.

" The kind people of the neighbourhood sent off refreshments, and every attention was given to the poor worn-out sailors, who speak with the greatest gratitude of all the kindness they received.

" Now that their anxieties were at an end, the men soon began to improve in health. Help, however, came too late to save three other poor fellows, who died within the next few days."

According to the log-book, Hercules (" Haslas ") Anderson died on the morning of April 4th, and John Thomson died that evening. On April 6th Alexander Robertson died, these three men being Shetlanders. The death of Robertson was the thirteenth and last death to occur aboard the ship.

The *Diana* remained at Ronas Voe for a week, while fresh provisions poured aboard from the surrounding district, sundry

* A mistake. The number was eight.

repairs were made, and some 7 hundredweight of coal obtained locally to enable the cabin and 'tween-deck stoves to be lighted and kept burning once more.

On April 6th the ship's log mentions that thirteen new hands were engaged to help in getting the ship ready to go to sea again, fitting new sails to replace the old worn-out ones, etc.

On April 8th 8 tons of coal arrived from Lerwick for the ship, and were stowed away in the bunkers with the aid of shore labour.

The log states that the pilot came aboard at 5 a.m. on April 9th, the anchor was got up, and the ship steamed out of the harbour. At 9 p.m. the ship entered Toft Voe, where she anchored for the night.

The ship proceeded at eight o'clock the next morning, under steam and sail, through Yell Sound, and anchored in the evening in Dourgie Voe. There was no need for speed now. Fresh provisions and medical stores were aboard, and the chief consideration was the comfort and safety of the crew.

The anchor was dropped in Lerwick Harbour at eight o'clock on the morning of April 11th.

That the *Diana* and her crew must have presented a ghastly sight is evident from the following extract from the Edinburgh *Scotsman* :

" The sight which met the eyes of the people from the shore who first boarded her cannot well be told in prose. Dante might have related it in the ' Inferno.' Coleridge's ' Ancient Mariner ' might have sailed in such a ghastly ship—battered and ice-crushed, sails and cordage blown away, boats and spars cut up for fuel in the awful Arctic winter, the main deck a charnel-house not to be described. The miserable, scurvy-stricken, dysentery-worn men who looked over her bulwarks were a spectacle, once seen, never to be forgotten.

" As the tidings of the ship's arrival went through Shetland, the relatives of her crew journeyed to her to meet their living and to claim their dead. By instalments, as they were fit to be removed, the survivors were brought ashore and removed to their homes in the island. Some, not able to be transported, are still in the ship, but the bulk of the survivors have left her. Most pitiable sights of all were the ship's boys, with their young faces wearing a strange aged look not easily to be described."

The *Scotsman* also printed an account of the voyage by a survivor, who, amongst other things, stated: " The doctor did everything he could, and was all a man should be, taking his watch regularly and working as hard as anyone; but he couldn't save them. . . . We sighted land just two weeks after leaving the ice.

" Unluckily, we took the land we saw to be Orkney, and, wanting to go to Shetland, we stood away to the northward along the West side of Shetland, all the time supposing it to be Orkney. We beat about there till Tuesday morning, when the mate said he would take the first harbour he could find We ran her into Ronas Voe that day at noon, finding to our surprise that we had been off Shetland all the time. Had we been out another night none of us could have stood it. The night before three of my watch dropped down at the pumps, and only four of us were fit for duty, and they not much to speak of.

" On Sunday night, when we were carrying double-reefed topsails, the jib halliards gave way. Out of both watches, three were all who could go out to stow the main topgallant sail when we brought up, and we were just able to crawl. When we came down we were done up.

" The people of Ronas Voe were uncommonly kind; I never met so much attention in all my life. They would have done anything for us. They sent men and boats to help us, and supplied us with all kinds of provisions."

The *Dundee Advertiser* printed a long account of the *Diana's* adventures. The following extracts are interesting:

" The crew had to look forward to passing at least six months in the ice with a supply of food and fuel calculated only to last them for two months. . . .

" The cold was so intense that the very medicine in the bottles which were put in at the heads of the berths by the doctor, so as to be within reach of those who were ill, was actually frozen, and had to be taken to the fire and thawed. . . .

" The prospect from the ship was dreary beyond expression. On every side there was a vast, inhospitable, snowy wilderness which seemed ready to enclose ship and crew in one fearful winding-sheet. Nothing was to be seen but one dazzling expanse of white, while the awful silence was unbroken save at such rare intervals as an owl or a raven approached the vessel. Snow also fell heavily at intervals, and I was informed that the depth which fell during one week alone amounted to about 7 feet. . . .

" Towards the latter end of December Captain Gravill, who had not been in very good health from the commencement of the voyage, began perceptibly to droop. . . . He bore up nobly for the sake of his crew. Three of the men had sailed with him for a period of eighteen years, and gone with him from ship to ship. They state that his attention to his crew was beyond all praise, and that in the discharge of his duties he seemed animated by a higher than an earthly motive. When finally confined to his berth, he was resigned and prepared for whatever fate might befall him. It may be stated that his last moments were those of a true man and humble Christian. In these days of mere pecuniary ties between master and servant it is cheering to find that the brave men who served under Captain Gravill cannot yet speak of him without their voices being choked by emotion and their eyes filled with tears. . . .

" Ronas Voe is a small village consisting only of five families. It is situated in the hollow of a bay, and the villagers did not descry the *Diana* till after she had rounded the headland and was close upon them.

" Immediately upon seeing her, one of the villagers put off in a boat and piloted the ship into a safe part of the bay. The whole of the people in the village—about forty in number —came down to the beach and landed those of the crew who were able to go ashore in boats. They sent on board fresh provisions for the sick, and also relieved the crew by working the pumps. The survivors speak very highly indeed of the kindness with which the villagers and the country people received them. . . .

" I may here mention the heroic conduct of the ship's surgeon, Mr. Charles Edward Smith, to whose unwearying exertions and attendance all concur in ascribing the salvation of the survivors. As a number of the men are still affected with scurvy and frost-bite, and incapable of removal from the vessel—four or five of them not being expected to survive— Dr. Smith has remained at his post, and, I believe, intends to remain till the men are brought to a port where they can have proper accommodation and treatment. . . . ."

The *Diana* remained eight days at Lerwick, awaiting instructions from the owners in Hull. She was prepared further for sea, and another 5 tons of coal were taken on board. The funerals of all those—save Captain Gravill—who had died aboard the ship took place during this time, and an entirely new crew took possession of the vessel, only some of the Hull invalids being left aboard as passengers.

Of those of the old ship's company that were able to get about, only William Reynolds (harpooner) and Richard Gibbins (deck-hand) and the doctor remained aboard, the others being sent home to Hull by train. As Dr. Fothergill put it, " Dr. Smith attended his patients till Hull was reached. They and he had been too long together to part. Neither he nor they could bear the idea that they should be in fresh hands."

The news of the *Diana's* dramatic reappearance at Lerwick was telegraphed to Hull and quickly spread throughout the town. It caused immense excitement there, as well as a feeling of intense relief and joy to those who had relatives in the ship. The receipt in Hull of letters written aboard the *Diana* while in Lerwick by some of the survivors added to the excitement, while the general interest was deepened by the publication of these letters verbatim in the *Eastern Morning News* of April 13th, 1867.

In the same issue of this newspaper the arrival in Hull of some of the survivors was chronicled thus:

" On Thursday morning the relatives and friends of the crew of the *Diana* anxiously awaited the delivery of the letters. However, in four houses husbands came unexpectedly by five o'clock in the morning, and were more gladly received than the letters which came to the same houses four hours afterwards. The names of those who arrived at that hour were Henry Smith (harpooner), Richard Byers (second mate), William Clarke (harpooner), and Stephen Winbolt (steward). . . .

" Last evening the *Edina* (steamship) from Leith brought the following members of the crew of the *Diana* : G. Stone, Hoodlas, C. Cobb, and Stokes, all being seamen.

" Upon the arrival of the steamer, a boat put off from the shore to fetch the men, it being low tide. The meeting between the men and their friends was painful. The seamen, who were in a worse condition than the four who came by train, were much exhausted and bore signs of the hardships they had endured. Cabs were procured, and the men proceeded to their respective residences. One was placed in a cab immediately after he had fallen prostrate in his wife's arms. A very large number of people witnessed the landing of the unfortunate men. . . ."

The same newspaper also published the following statement by a survivor regarding the abandoning of the *Diana* by the *Intrepid* :

" The ship was overtaken by the whaler *Intrepid* of Dundee, Captain Deuchars. The latter captain came aboard the *Diana* and said he had been two days looking for the Hull vessel. It was apparent that strenuous endeavours would have to be made to get away into the ocean.

" After a consultation between the captains, in which the Scottish one stated his willingness to do everything for his companion and remain by the *Diana*, he returned to the vessel (*Intrepid*).

" Both vessels proceeded a short distance South, the *Diana* leading. They soon were hemmed between two large floes of ice, the Hull vessel attempting to strike out one way and the Scottish one the other.

" The *Intrepid* was seen clear, she being twice as powerful as the *Diana*. . . . The *Intrepid* steamed ahead, and in three hours could not be seen from the mast-head.

" The crew of the *Diana* solemnly assert that, had Captain Deuchars allowed his vessel to break the ice from the stem of the *Diana* by going astern a little (which would take a few minutes), the vessel and men would have been home six months ago. The crew attribute Captain Gravill's death in a great measure to his lamenting their position. . . ."

The newspaper quotes six letters from survivors to their

relatives. That of Emanuel Webster, the engineer, is worth quoting, as showing the indomitable cheerfulness of the man:

" . . . Me and my cousin are first-rate, and have been all the voyage. Our only complaint has been the knife and fork not being so brisk. . . . My bird (the linnet) is living, but the dog I had to drown a short time since."

The letter of David Cobb to his mother is curiously like the style, in its opening phrases, of the letters written home from the trenches in Flanders and our ships in the North Sea during the weary years from 1914 to 1918:

" It is with pleasure that I write these few lines to you, hoping to find you in good health, as it does not leave me so at present. I am now laid bedfast with the scurvy, but I hope that I shall soon get better now that we are in safety. . . . The doctor is attending me very carefully, and I am getting a little better, thank God."

The seventh letter quoted in the newspaper is from my father to Mrs. Gravill, announcing the death of her husband, giving a brief outline of his illness, and expressing the deepest sympathy with Mrs. Gravill and the family.

On April 16th Captain Robert Day arrived from Hull, and took charge of the ship as master, with William Reynolds as mate. An examination of the ship on that date showed that she was leaking at the rate of 14 inches an hour (28 feet of water in the twenty-four hours), and the pumps still had to be kept working at regular intervals to prevent the ship from foundering.

On April 22nd the owners' Lerwick agent directed Captain Day to continue the voyage to Hull. At one o'clock that afternoon the pilot came aboard and the ship departed, apparently under sail only, for her home port. The run down the East coast seems to have been a fair and uneventful one.

At 8 a.m. on April 25th Whitby was sighted, while Scarborough Castle came into view two hours later. At noon, Flamborough Head was only some 7 miles to the South of them. At 8 p.m. a pilot came aboard, some sail was taken in, and at ten o'clock the assistance of a steam-tug was accepted. By 11 p.m. the ship was lying at anchor in Grimsby Roads

The last entry in the old *Diana's* log-book was made on April 26th, and reads prosaically thus:

" At 5 a.m. were towed to Hull, and entered the Humber Dock

" *Noon.*—Moored the ship in the Old Dock.

" *P.m.*—Crew employed clearing the decks. SO ENDS THIS VOYAGE."

The announcement that the long-lost whaler had actually arrived in the River Humber flew round Hull with lightning speed. Thousands of people thronged the piers and jetties to see the weather-beaten old hulk come back at last to her own home.

A special edition of the *Eastern Morning News* of April 26th, 1867, contained the following account of the scene:

"ARRIVAL OF THE 'DIANA.'

" This morning, about half-past eight, the *Diana* arrived in the roads. She was sighted about six o'clock off Paull. The previous intimation of her approach had attracted thousands of persons to the South End even last evening, and this morning the throng was much greater. She at once entered the Humber Dock and, as she passed through, the quays and shipping on all sides became crowded.

" Of course, the *Diana* was boarded by many, and the yards were manned and other portions of the vessel crowded. The half-mast flag indicated the presence of a corpse on board, and it was seen that the shell containing the late Captain Gravill was placed upon the bridge, being covered with canvas. The dilapidated state of the ship was at once observable, and the deepest interest was manifested. The vessel is now proceeding to the Queen's Dock."

"FURTHER PARTICULARS.

" From the accounts which we published in our early edition, the *Diana* was expected to arrive by the first tide this morning, it being generally thought that she had arrived in Grimsby Roads on the previous night. This surmise proved to be correct, for the *Albert*, from Rotterdam, which arrived at Hull about five o'clock, reported that she had passed the *Diana* lying at anchor at the above port.

" The news spread with great rapidity, and the townspeople began to assemble on the piers even from that early hour. So much excitement has never been manifested in regard to a Hull vessel, nor a wider-spread interest created, though at the best it is of a painful character. There is no parallel in the records of suffering and misfortune at the Greenland fishery —at least, so far as Hull is concerned.

" The multitudes of expectant people who lined the piers and the quays of the docks this morning, assembling as they did as soon as the approach of the *Diana* became known, must have reminded many elderly people of the golden age of the whale fishery, when Hull sent the magnificent fleet of vessels to prosecute the arduous trade.

" There was, however, this morning an almost entire absence of joyousness on the part of the people, although they occasionally burst out into a ringing cheer as the now far-renowned *Diana* passed through the docks. The larger portion of the spectators wore a subdued expression, and, as the shell containing the body of the late Captain Gravill became visible, all sounds but that of the noisy and unreflecting juveniles who gambolled about the rigging of the ship were hushed, partly in tribute to the excellent qualities which the deceased possessed, and partly to the melancholy and subduing influence which the presence of death exercises over most people."

In Dr. Fothergill's account of the voyage there are a few incidents which may be recorded here :

" At last their voyage was over. It would be impossible by extracts, however numerous, to convey to the reader an idea of the mental condition of Surgeon Smith and his companions during this long, long time that they were face to face with death. They never despaired; at least, he did not. He saw a providential interference in their numerous escapes from what seemed certain death. When he had to shoot his little dog, he fastened its collar round his arm,* so that it might help to identify his corpse when it drifted on to the coast of Labrador —the sole hope and consolation almost that remained to him.

* This incident is not recorded in the diary.

" Once only his fortitude gave way, and he threw himself on the ice and wished to die. Death was near at hand; it would not be long before the cold hand of death would have chilled the little left of life out of him. But there rushed upon him the thought: ' What will these poor fellows do without me ?' He got up and went back to the ship.

" Shortly after this the blacksmith, the finest man in the ship, despaired and would not take his daily walk in a path cut out of the ice. Smith threatened to have him pushed round. It was no use; the blacksmith declared he would never see his wife or children any more. Smith's own recent experience flashed upon him, and he exclaimed: ' I will take you back to your wife yet !' ' Will you, doctor ?' He took his word; the blacksmith's breast was once more inspired with hope. Smith kept his word; the blacksmith at length was restored to his wife and family. No wonder the crew adored the surgeon !

" One more anecdote of the ship's crew. Precious few were the biscuits left in the ship when she reached Shetland. One of the crew kept a biscuit, bored a hole in it, and hung it up in his house. Some time afterwards, when Smith went to see him, the seaman pointed to this biscuit and said: ' Whenever I feel inclined to quarrel with the missis about my grub I just look at that biscuit, and think how precious glad and thankful we were, doctor, for the chance of one of them when in the ice in the old *Diana*.'

" The value of Smith's services and the heroism displayed by him met with ready recognition. The doctors of Hull gave him a public dinner and a silver inkstand ' in recognition of his services to their fellow-townsmen under circumstances of extreme peril, privation, and difficulty.' The Board of Trade presented him with a set of surgical instruments, the most complete I have ever seen, together with a testimonial signed by the President, in which his services to the crew are described as having been ' generous, humane, and unwearied.' The townspeople of Hull and the underwriters of Lloyd's presented him with a testimonial and a sum of over one hundred guineas."

In her article in the *Wide World Magazine* for February,

1906, Miss Mary Gravill gave a few further details of the closing scenes in connection with this voyage:

" And so the good ship *Diana*, which had sailed away so proudly in February, 1866, returned from her perilous voyage, broken but not defeated, fourteen months later, having been frozen in for over six months.

" The captain's funeral was one of the largest ever witnessed in the port of Hull, fifteen thousand being the estimated number of followers. A handsome marble monument, bearing a facsimile of the *Diana* locked in the ice, was erected over his grave in Springbank Cemetery as a token of respect from his fellow-citizens.

" Lerwick, too, is not without its monument. In 1890, after the death of Dr. Charles Edward Smith, his brother, Alderman Frederic Smith, then Mayor of West Ham, erected a marble drinking fountain on the pier-head close to where the crews of the whaling-ships used to land. It stands there as a thank-offering for the providential return of the *Diana*.

" ' They cried unto the Lord in their trouble, and He delivered them out of their distress.' "

THE DAVIS STRAITS WHALING FLEET, SEASON 1866.

Port.	Ship's Name.	Horse-Power of Engines.	Captain.	Surgeon.	Number of Whales Caught.	Amount of Oil in Tuns.
Dundee	*Camperdown*	70	Bruce	—	4	50
,,	*Narwhale*	70	Sturrock	McEwan	3	30
,,	*Esquimaux*	70	Yule	—	1	15
,,	*Alexander*	70	Walker	T. G. Kerr	6	75
,,	*Polynia*	60	Nichol	Van Waters-huit	—	—
,,	*Tay*	60	Birnie	Shiels	1	10
,,	*Intrepid*	60	Deuchars	Galloway	2	25
,,	*Wildfire*	50	Souter	Traill	6	65
,,	*Victor*	50	Walker	—	—	—
Peterhead	*Windward*	60	Sellar	—	—	—
,,	*Mazenthian*	60	Gray	—	—	—
Kirkcaldy	*Ravenscraig*	60	Allen	Souter	5	60
Greenock	*Lion*	—	McLennan	—	2	20
London	*Eric*	70	Jones	—	—	—
Liverpool	*Retriever*	50	Wells	—	—	—
Hull	*Diana*	30	Gravill	Smith	2	24
,,	*Truelove*	—	Wells	—	2	20
Peterhead	*Queen*	—	Brown	Philpots	—	—

PARTICULARS OF "DIANA."

Built at Bremen, Germany, in 1840. 355 tons. Owners, Messrs. Brown and Co., Hull.

Made her first voyage to Davis Straits in 1856. Steam engines put into her in 1857, she being the first Hull whaler to be provided with steam.

She was wrecked and lost in 1868 on the Lincolnshire coast near the mouth of the Humber when homeward bound from that year's whale-fishing.

THE "DIANA'S" OFFICERS AND CREW.

Rank.	Name.	Town.	
Captain	John Gravill	Hull	Died.
First mate	George Clarke	,,	
Second mate	Tom Hornsby	,,	
Engineer	Emanuel Webster	,,	
Carpenter	Andrew Donald	Dundee	
Surgeon	Charles Edward Smith	Kelvedon, Essex	
Inspectioneer	William Clarke	Hull	
Harpooner	William Reynolds	,,	
,,	William Lofley	,,	
,,	Richard Byers	,,	
Cook	Joe Mitchell	,,	
Fireman	Fred Lockham	,,	Died.
,,	Philip Pickard	,,	Died.
Seaman	Richard Gibbins	,,	
,,	George Stone	,,	
,,	Bonsall Miller	,,	Died.
,,	Charles Cobb	,,	
Boat-steerer	David Cobb	,,	
,,	George Blanchard	,,	
Seaman	Thomas Stokes	,,	
Harpooner	Henry Smith	,,	
Steward	Stephen Winbolt	,,	
,,	Josiah Allen	,,	
Fireman	John Webster	,,	
Seaman	Edward Hoodlas	,,	
Harpooner	Laurie Stewart	Shetland	
,,	Mitchell Abernethy	,,	Died.
,,	Purvis Smith	,,	Died.
,,	Basil Smith	,,	Died.
,,	Magna Nicholson	,,	
,,	Magna Grey, Sen.	,,	
,,	Magna Grey, Jun.	,,	
,,	Peter Acrow	,,	
,,	Peter Robison	,,	
,,	Robert Robison	,,	Died.
,,	Alexander Robertson	,,	Died.
,,	John Thomson	,,	Died.
,,	Gideon Frazer	,,	Died.
,,	Hercules Anderson	,,	Died.
,,	John Robertson	,,	
,,	Arthur Yell	,,	Died.
,,	Laurence Smith	,,	
,,	James Williamson	,,	
,,	Peter Shewen	,,	
Half-deck boy	William Shewen	,,	
,, ,,	John Aitcheson	,,	
,, ,,	Robbie Hewson	,,	
,, ,,	John Irvine	,,	
,, ,,	Christopher Tait	,,	
,, ,,	Tom Himsworth	,,	
,, ,,	John Hewson	,,	

GLOSSARY OF WORDS, TERMS, ETC.

Bay ice. Ice freshly formed on the sea.

Blink. Reflection in the sky of a distant large field of ice.

Blubber. The layer of oily fat beneath a whale's skin.

Bottlenose. The Round-Headed Porpoise.

Brash (and Mush). Broken-up ice.

Burgomaster. A species of gull of unusually large size.

Cran or crang. A carcase.

Crow's-nest. A lookout place, often made out of a barrel, fixed near the mast-head.

Dog-vane. Mast-head wind direction indicator.

Dovekie. The Lesser Guillemot.

Fathom. Six feet.

Finny whale. This is the largest and strongest species of the whale family.

Flinching or flensing. Cutting the blubber out of a carcase.

Floe. Large sheet or field of ice.

Galley. The ship's kitchen.

Inspectioneer. Chief harpooner of a whale-ship.

Kittiwake. A species of seagull.

Land-floe. Field of ice attached to the coast line.

Loon. A species of duck.

Loonery. Nesting and breeding ground for ducks.

Making off. Cleaning the blubber off the carcase and stowing it away in the holds.

Mallies. Fulmar Petrels.

Old ice. Ice formed the previous season, generally that formed from shore glaciers.

Pack. Field of floating ice.

Piggin. A wooden dish used in the boats for baling and also for dashing water over the harpoon ropes to prevent them from getting hot.

Pot-heads. Round-Headed Porpoises.

275

Ratching. Frequent alterations of a ship's course.   Dodging.

Red-heads. The Redpole Linnet.

Rotch. The Little Auk.

Sea-floe. Field of ice afloat and subject to ocean currents and changes of wind.

Sea-horse. Walrus.

Shag. Cormorant.

Shake. The staves, head, and bottom of a cask, bound in a bundle and ready for putting together to form a cask when required.

Skead. Wooden framework for holding barrels in position in the holds.

Snickle. To catch with the loop of a rope.   Lasso.

'Spectioneer. Chief harpooner of a whale-ship.

Warp. Stout rope used for mooring or towing a ship.

Yak. Esquimaux.

Young ice. Ice freshly formed on the sea.

APPENDICES

APPENDIX I

KILLING WHALES FOR WHALEBONE ONLY.

To kill a whale for the whalebone only appears to have been considered by the old whalers as a very great crime and an act liable to bring bad luck.

In another diary kept by my father, one Captain Iverson (an old whaling captain) is quoted as saying, " I never met a man who'd done it. If I had, I would have run his ship down for it. 'Twould be a most damnable shame and waste to kill a whale for the sake of her whalebone and turn the carcase adrift, with your ship full and you unable to take any of the blubber. I never knew personally of this having been done, and never expect to.

" It would be unlucky to kill a fish for the sake of her bone only. I have heard of the master of a full ship killing whales in Pond's Bay for their bone and turning their carcases adrift unflinched, *but his ship was lost on the passage home and he never prospered afterwards.* 'Tis a wicked thing to do !"

C. E. S. H.

APPENDIX I (A)

THE EXETER SOUND SETTLEMENT.

THIS settlement was maintained for three and a half years, and was broken up in 1868, when Mr. J. W. Taylor, Dr. M'Kenzie Fergusson, and twenty-nine others, returned to Lerwick in the whaler *Narwhale.*

The settlement was established by Messrs. Anthony Gibbs and Sons, merchants, of London. Its object was the prosecution of the whale-fishing in the early spring and autumn, but the project was a financial failure. During the whole time the settlement was in existence not a single whale was obtained, and but comparatively few walruses and seals. The cost of the whole enterprise was estimated to have been not less than £10,000.—*Cutting from* " *Dundee Advertiser,*" 1868.

APPENDIX II

THE FORMER PLENITUDE OF WHALES.

THAT the whales were very numerous at one time is borne out by the following extract from the log of the Hull whaler *Cumbrian* on a whaling voyage in 1823.

The log states:

" On July 27th we were turning to the southward along the land-floe near Pond's Bay. Here and there along the floe edge lay the dead bodies of hundreds of flenshed whales, and the air for miles around was tainted with the foetor which arose from such masses of putridity. Towards evening the numbers come across were ever increasing, and the effluvia which then assailed our olfactories became almost intolerable."

This voyage was made during the period when the slaughter of whales was at its height—namely, from about 1818 to about 1824. At that time the port of Hull had over fifty whale-ships which, between them, used to bring back over 5,000 tuns of whale-oil each season. In 1823 over 2,000 whales were killed.—*Extracted from " Hull Museum Publication," No.* 31.

In my father's 1869 voyage in the private yacht *Diana* of Glasgow, the mate of the yacht was an old whaler. In the diary for that voyage the following statement made by the mate is recorded:

" I mind in 1846, which was the first year I went to Cumberland Gulf in the old *Alexander*, we was terrified to go out in the boats, the whales was that large and numerous. They raised quite a heavy sea with their fins and tails.

" Them Americans kills a great deal of fish they never gets, even lancing loose fish from the floe edge, which, of course, are lost, so I have been told."

C. E. S. H.

APPENDIX III

THE STRENGTH OF WHALES.

In the *Hull Museum Publication*, No. 31, the following incident is related:

"In 1821 the *Baffin* (Captain Scoresby of Whitby, the most famous of whaling captains), whilst in latitude 77° in the Greenland Sea, struck a whale, which ran out fifteen lines of 240 yards each and dragged two boats and fifteen men for a long time. When the fish was killed, it was found to have been also dragging under water six similar lines and a boat belonging to the *Trafalgar* of Hull. The 5,040 yards of line weighed 1½ tons, and there was also the resistance of the sunken boat and the two floating boats and their crews."

However, the power of Greenland whales appears to be put in the shade completely by the astonishing strength of the Rorqual or "Finner" whales, which used to frequent the neighbourhood of the North Cape of Norway and Spitzbergen Island. In another diary kept by my father in 1869, when surgeon of the private yacht *Diana* of Glasgow (owner, the late Sir James Lamont), the following astounding tale is recorded:

"Captain Fovin, of the Norwegian screw steam whale-ship *Spes et Fides*, fired two harpoons from the ship into a 'Finner' whale. Against a stiff breeze, the whale towed *the ship, with her topsails aback and her engines going full speed astern, for a distance of* 80 *miles in ten hours*."

C. E. S. H.

APPENDIX IV

THE " DIANA " RELICS, ETC., AT HULL.

In the Fisheries Museum, Hull, some actual relics of the *Diana* are on view.

Exhibit No. 777 is a finely mounted specimen of an Iceland Falcon. This was brought home by the *Diana's* mate, Mr. George Clarke, and was presented to the museum by his son, Captain J. E. Clarke. Almost certainly the bird's skin was preserved originally by the ship's surgeon.

Exhibit No. 69 is a sailmaker's smoothing tool, with the name *Diana* carved on it.

Exhibit No. 232 is a picture similar to the frontispiece of this book. The original sketch from which this picture was drawn is said to have been made by my father.

Exhibit No. 680 is a fine oil painting of the above picture.

Exhibit No. 147 is an Esquimaux baby's pair of shoes, brought to Hull by the *Diana*.

Exhibit No. 615 contains sundry whaling pictures, among them being some relating to the *Diana*. Also there is a copy of the *Hull News* of April 13th, 1867, announcing the *Diana's* return to Lerwick, and containing copies of the letters sent from there to Hull by the survivors.

Exhibit No. 667 is the most interesting one of the lot. It is described as " the medicine chest of the *Diana*."

It is a very roughly made small oak box, bound with iron and with hinges that are merely nailed on. Within are five large square bottles and a space for a sixth. In a rough tray are two glass tumblers and a wineglass. Beneath the tray are four small square bottles. Thus the whole box only contains ten medicine bottles.

My opinion is that this box was constructed aboard the ship (possibly not during this 1866-67 voyage, as there is no mention in the diary of any such box being made), and was merely for keeping a reserve stock of certain medicines or else was intended for emergency purposes, such as for boat-work, expeditions, or abandoning ship.

There are no labels on the bottles, while some of the partitions of the box are quite loose and look as though they had been glued in position originally.

The *Diana* was wrecked on the Lincolnshire coast in 1868, and I hazard the opinion that this box was washed ashore or salved from the wreck of the ship, and that the real medicine chest was lost with the ship. Certainly the *Diana's* medicine chest would have been a larger box than the one exhibited, and would have been constructed more after the style of Exhibit No. 668. This is the medicine chest of another Hull whaler called *The Brothers*, and is a fine mahogany cabinet, evidently made ashore by an expert cabinet-maker.

" Wilberforce House " is another museum in Hull. Wilberforce, the famous anti-slavery advocate, was born in this house in 1759. While the museum mainly contains relics of Wilberforce, there is also a small collection of whaling relics which seem rather out of place.

Amongst these relics there is a curious-looking disc-shaped object, so much worm-eaten as to make it almost sponge-like in consistency. This object is one of the few biscuits remaining aboard the *Diana* on the termination of this terrible voyage.

Below this biscuit is a hermetically sealed jar containing a yellow oily liquid. I was informed this was some of the preserved food brought back by the *Diana*. It looks as though it must have come out of Joe Mitchell's cask of " fat," which he had been saving for pig food.

The only other *Diana* exhibit in this museum is a rather quaint old oil painting of the ship. In those days the whaler captains (and sailing-ship captains generally) were very fond of getting some local artist to make a painting of the ships under their command. I expect this painting was done by a Hull artist, but I was unable to make out the signature.

The picture represents the *Diana* in the Arctic, with icebergs and floes on either side. On one floe are two very ghost-like polar bears. On another floe some of the crew are very busy clubbing seals, while there is another party in a boat alongside a dead whale.

C. E. S. H.

APPENDIX V

FUNERAL OF AN ESSEX HERO

" ON Thursday, last week, the remains of Dr. Charles Edward Smith were interred in the Friends' burial-ground at Coggeshall, his native place. . . ."—*Cutting from the " Stratford Express,"* *September 20th,* 1879.

INDEX